A
PROMISE
TO PROTECT

"A taut story of mistakes and betrayal, a mother's fierce love, revenge and danger—and the redeeming wonders of faith and love."

—**Lorena McCourtney**, author of the Cate Kinkaid Files
and the Ivy Malone Mysteries

"Old secrets, second chances at love, and a skillfully crafted small-town suspense. You will fall in love with Ben and Leigh and cheer them on as they fight for their happy ending. I'm making room on my shelf for all of Patricia Bradley's novels!"

—**Susan May Warren**, bestselling and award-winning author
of *When I Fall in Love*

Previous Praise for *Shadows of the Past*

"Readers will love the thrill of trying to solve the crimes surrounding Taylor as they root for her and Nick's relationship to blossom. Bradley infuses the plot with questions of faith too, as her characters learn that at the end of the day, only God knows all, and that faith is what makes life's traumas bearable."

—*Booklist*

"Heavy on action, Bradley's debut inspirational novel . . . is a page-turner in every chapter . . . culminating in a climax readers won't want to miss It will be gratifying to watch Bradley's characters evolve in future installments of this new Logan Point series."

—*Publishers Weekly*

"This is a fantastic first novel of thrilling suspense. The nonstop action and the sympathetically drawn characters' narrow escapes will keep readers mesmerized. The gripping tension also makes Bradley's title a winner with fans of Iris Johansen and Mary Higgins Clark."

—*Library Journal*

"This crime mystery held my attention with plenty of suspense and just the right amount of romance to spice things up."

—*Suspense Magazine*

A
PROMISE
TO PROTECT

A NOVEL

PATRICIA
BRADLEY

Revell

a division of Baker Publishing Group
Grand Rapids, Michigan

Published by Revell
a division of Baker Publishing Group
P.O. Box 6287, Grand Rapids, MI 49516-6287
www.revellbooks.com

Printed in the United States of America

Library of Congress Cataloging-in-Publication Data
Bradley, Patricia
    A promise to protect : a novel / Patricia Bradley.
        p. cm. — (Logan Point ; #2)
    Summary: "In a steamy small town of secrets, danger, and broken promises, a woman reaches out to a former love to save her brother's life—can she prevent her own secret from being revealed?" — Provided by publisher.
    ISBN 978-0-8007-2281-4 (pbk.)
    1. Brothers and sisters—Fiction. 2. Women physicians—Fiction. 3. Sheriffs—Fiction. 4. Family secrets—Fiction. 5. Memphis (Tenn.)—Fiction. I. Title.
    PS3602.R34275P76 2014
    813'.6—dc23   2014012133

14 15 16 17 18 19 20   8 7 6 5 4 3 2

1

Tony Jackson shouldn't be dying in a ritzy hotel room in downtown Memphis on a hot July night.

He shouldn't be dying at all.

"Who shot you?" Sheriff Ben Logan pressed a blood-soaked towel against the victim's chest. The left sleeve of Tony's Armani suit had bullet holes where he'd lifted his arm in defense. Otherwise the bullet would have killed him instantly.

This meeting wasn't supposed to go this way. Tony would show up, deliver his information. Ben would save the day.

The coppery scent that hung heavy in the air turned his stomach as Tony's life drained away, his blood staining the plush white carpet. Ben cradled Tony's head and glanced toward the opened door. Where was that ambulance?

Tony wrapped his fingers around Ben's wrist, and Ben leaned closer to the man he couldn't keep from dying. "Stay with me, man."

"Tell Leigh . . ." Tony's breath grew shallow. "I'm . . . sorry." The grip faltered.

"Hang on, buddy."

Sirens. Ben snapped a look behind him to where a few people had gathered in the hallway. "Tell them to hurry."

"Your dad . . ." Tony closed his eyes and took a shuddering breath then coughed, blood gurgling in his chest.

Ben jerked back to the dying man. "What about my dad?"

"I'm sorry . . . should've told . . ." He coughed again. "Something . . . got to tell . . . Blue . . . dog . . ."

"Don't die on me." What did Tony know about his dad's shooting?

"Both know . . ." Tony's voice faded.

Ben eased the man's head up. "Stay with me. Tell me who did this to you."

Tony closed his eyes, then his lips moved, and Ben strained to hear.

"Protect . . . Leigh."

"Come on, man, you'll—"

Tony's eyes popped open, the light in them fading. "Promise . . ."

Ben couldn't escape the haunting gaze. "I . . ." The words lodged in his throat.

Tony tightened his fingers on Ben's wrist. "Say it."

"I . . ." He swallowed. "I promise." The grip eased as Tony slumped in his arms and slipped into eternity.

A low moan escaped Ben's lips. He dropped his head, sending a prayer heavenward as Tony's death settled in his chest like lead. He'd let him down. *Just like with Tommy Ray.* Ben pushed the thought aside. Revisiting the past wouldn't bring either back.

He pulled his arm free from under the body and stood. What a waste. Tony had been only a few years older than Ben, thirty-five at most. He'd liked what he'd known of Leigh's brother, even though they hadn't run in the same circles. By day, Tony worked at Maxwell Industries as the chief financial officer, and by night he gambled with the high rollers.

Tonight, he'd gambled and lost.

Ben's hands curled into fists. Tony's death was wrong on so many levels, but now the living became his priority. Unclenching his fists, he tugged his cell phone from his pocket and dialed his chief deputy. "Wade, what's your location?"

"I'm at the Thunderbird."

"Get over to Bradford General and shadow Leigh Somerall."

"Come on, Ben, it's my night off. I have a date."

"I don't care if you're in the middle of proposing, get over there. Someone murdered her brother. They may be after Leigh too."

"Tony's dead?" Shock rang in Wade's voice. "How?"

"I'll fill you in later. Just get over there and keep her under surveillance."

"Do you want me to tell her about Tony?"

Ben fingered a small Boy Scout medallion in his pocket. It'd be so easy to let Wade take care of this. He could even plead he needed to stay and aid the Memphis Police. *Coward.* "No. I'll tell her. Just keep your eye on her until I get there."

Ben broke the connection and slapped the phone against his palm. He didn't have a clue how he'd tell Leigh her brother was dead. He knelt one last time by Tony's body.

Protect Leigh. Tony's dying request.

How could he protect someone who hated his guts?

Ben rocked back on his heels. Tony had mentioned a flash drive when he'd called earlier in the day. On the off chance the killer hadn't taken it, he wrapped his hand in a handkerchief and checked Tony's pockets, not only for the USB drive but for his cell phone. Knowing who Tony had talked with today might help in the investigation. His eyes widened when he pulled out an almost-inch-thick wad of folded one-hundred-dollar bills. Maybe Tony was going over to the casinos in Tunica after their meeting.

But there was no flash drive and no cell phone. Just like there'd be no information on what Tony knew about Ben's dad.

Getting that information was why Ben had driven to the Peabody Hotel in Memphis, room 5210, where he'd discovered Tony dying in a pool of his own blood.

Rising, he glanced around the room. From what he could see, Tony hadn't brought luggage or clothing. The black duvet cover appeared untouched, and the gold damask draperies were closed.

An unopened bottle of Scotch sat on a corner table beside the wing-back chair. On the floor, a silver ice bucket lay near the doorway.

In his mind's eye, Ben saw Tony set the Scotch on the table and pick up the ice bucket. The killer must've been waiting for him when he opened the door. Backed him into the room, then "Bang! You're dead." Probably used a silencer. Then all he had to do was close the door and walk down the hall like any other guest.

Ben stepped out into the burgundy-carpeted hall as the elevator dinged and paramedics spilled out. He held up his hand. "You're too late."

Another elevator opened, and Detective Olivia Reynolds emerged, flanked by two uniformed cops. He groaned. A homicide detective with the Memphis Police Department . . . and his cousin. She was not going to be happy he'd brought a murder to her doorstep. "I don't remember saying anything about a homicide when I called 911."

"I was in the neighborhood." Livy's mouth quirked upward. "And hello to you too, Ben. What brings you to Memphis?"

"Checking out a lead." He jerked his head toward the open door and then followed the petite detective inside the room.

His usually unflappable cousin caught her breath. "Tony Jackson? He's the victim?"

"Afraid so."

"Oh, man, this is bad." She stared at the body. "I just saw him at church on Sunday."

Even though Livy lived in Memphis, she still made the thirty-minute drive to church in Logan Point each Sunday.

"Tony was coming to church?"

She eyed him. "Yeah. But you'd have to be there to know."

Heat crawled up his neck. "Hey, by the time I ride herd on those nine- and ten-year-olds in Sunday school, I need a break. Was Leigh with him?"

"You didn't need a break *before* Pastor John started his series

10

on forgiveness. But to answer your question, no, Leigh wasn't with him. Does she know what's happened?"

"Not yet."

"I don't envy you, having to tell her." She gave him a thoughtful stare. "Didn't you and Leigh have a thing for each other in college?"

He shot her the flintiest stare he knew how. Yeah, they'd had a thing, and hearing from her this week had almost blown him away. *"Ben, Tony needs your help."* Even now, his heart thumped a little harder, remembering her voice. That was why he'd kept his distance since she returned to Logan Point six weeks ago, a widow with a young son. He'd stayed just close enough to know she still had that chestnut hair framing her face. His memory supplied the rest. Green eyes. Porcelain skin. A smattering of freckles across her nose.

"What happened?" Livy flicked her hand. "Oh, I forgot, you're Mr. Love 'Em and Leave 'Em."

"She did the leaving." He squared his shoulders. "Let's get my statement over with so I can go. I don't want someone else getting to Leigh first. She may not be safe." Wade should've called by now.

"What are you talking about?"

"Tony's last words . . . he told me to protect her."

"You think whoever did this might go after Leigh?"

"I don't know. Tony didn't live long enough for me to find out. I've sent Wade to shadow her at the hospital, but he hasn't checked in."

Livy took out a notepad and pen. "Let's step out into the hallway, and you can tell me why a Mississippi sheriff is involved in a Memphis murder. But first, are you carrying?"

He pulled out the .38 Smith and Wesson holstered in his front pocket and handed it to her. "Hasn't been fired since I cleaned it two days ago."

She took the gun and sniffed the barrel before handing it back to him. He followed her into the hallway, where the two uniforms stood guard. "Why were you meeting Tony *here*? Why not in Logan Point?"

Ben slipped the gun back in his jeans. "No clue. He called me on my cell phone this afternoon. Said if I'd meet him at the Peabody, he'd give me information on Dad's shooting and a flash drive he said the U.S. Marshals would be interested in."

"What was on it?"

Ben glanced toward the door, the taste of disappointment bitter. "Not a clue—he didn't get a chance to tell me anything, and he doesn't have the flash drive on him. His cell phone is missing too. But he does have a wad of hundreds."

"You went through his pockets?"

"You would have done the same thing." He rubbed the knotted muscles in the back of his neck.

"You know better than to—"

"Look, Tony was from Logan Point. I'm sworn to protect the people there, and I let him down. I thought I might find something to help me catch whoever did this." He pulled himself up to his full six-one height. "I want to work with you, Olivia, but either way, I'll get the person who did this. His murderer will be brought to justice."

She pursed her lips. He felt heat rising in his face, but he held her steady gaze.

Livy gave him a hint of a nod. "We'll work together." She scribbled in the notepad then tapped her pen against the page. "Why would he be carrying so much money?"

"Tony liked to gamble."

"Did he say anything other than the bit about Leigh?"

Ben replayed the scene in his head. "Something about blue and a dog, but I have no idea what that's a reference to."

"Was she aware you were meeting Tony tonight?"

"I don't know. She contacted me a couple of days ago, said Tony wanted to talk to me, but not on the jail line. I gave her my cell phone number."

"Why didn't he want to talk to you on the land line? Did he suspect your phone is bugged? Have you checked it?"

"Do you think I'm totally incompetent?"

"Don't get testy. What did he say when he called?"

"He wanted me to get in touch with the U.S. Marshals Service. Said he had information they would be interested in, and he was bringing it tonight."

"Why did he come to you instead of going straight to them?"

"It's no secret I have friends in the U.S. Marshals Service. Guess he figured I might have pretty good connections."

Livy paused in her note taking and glanced up at him. "Didn't you interview with them about a job?"

"Yeah."

"What happened?"

"They filled it." He avoided her gaze, instead stared at the gold numbers beside the door to the hotel room. His dad would still be sheriff of Bradford County if Ben had been with him instead of in Memphis on that interview. "All I'm interested in now is keeping my town safe and finding out who shot my dad. And Tony."

The corner of Livy's mouth turned down as she put the pen in her purse. "I stopped by the house the other day to see Sheriff Tom. He tried to talk, so I think he knew me. He just couldn't say my name."

The stroke had happened on the operating table while the doctors dug out the bullet. "The speech therapist doesn't give us much hope that he'll get a lot better. Appreciate you stopping by—visitors do him good."

Ben's cell rang, and he jerked it from his pocket. Wade. He didn't bother with preliminaries. "Is Leigh okay?"

Wade cleared his throat. "I can't find her."

■ ■ ■

"Hi, this is Tony. Sorry I missed your call. Leave your num—"

Dr. Leigh Somerall punched End on her phone and then jerked open the door to the stairwell and hurried up the steps from the

Bradford General's cafeteria to the first floor. Why wasn't Tony answering?

He was fine. He was with Ben Logan.

Ben. The name evoked memories better left in the past. But he'd promised to help her brother, and the sheriff better not disappoint this time.

At the nurses' station, the RN on duty handed her a sheet of paper. "Jimmy West's PT and INR as well as his CBC came back while you were downstairs. Looks like it was a nonpoisonous snake-bite after all."

"Thank you, Cathy." Leigh glanced over the report then made a notation on the nine-year-old boy's chart and handed it back to the nurse. Her first snakebite case. "After I talk to the parents, you can unhook him from the IV."

Cathy bent over the keyboard, typing in the discharge orders. She raised up. "Oh, I almost forgot. The ward clerk said Wade Hatcher was looking for you."

Leigh's heart hitched. Maybe it was about Tony. Or not. The last time she saw Wade, she got the distinct impression he intended to ask her out. "Do you know what he wanted?"

Cathy shrugged and shook her head.

Leigh glanced past the RN, searching in vain for Ben's stocky deputy. Evidently it wasn't too important. She tucked the chart under her arm and knocked on the patient's door before pushing it open.

Jimmy's mother leaned against the wall, her arms crossed and eyes closed. His father sat beside the ER bed, holding his son's good hand. Leigh tweaked the boy's toe, and his eyes blinked open. "Good news, Mr. and Mrs. West. It looks like Jimmy's snakebite was nonpoisonous."

The father's shoulders relaxed, but not the heavy brows that pinched together. "You're certain?"

"Yes. His blood count is perfect, as is his clotting time. I do want you to watch the wound, and if it shows signs of infection, take him to his regular physician for antibiotics."

"Oh, thank you, Doctor." The mother moved to the side of the bed and brushed her son's hair back.

Jimmy sat up, wincing as he drew his hand to his chest. "You . . . you're not going to cut my hand off?"

Leigh's lips twitched. She knelt down until they were eye level. "No, Jimmy. You're going to be just fine."

His eyes widened. "You sure?"

The boy made her think of TJ. "I'm sure." She patted his good hand and stood to address the parents. "The nurse will be in to give you instructions and to remove the IV, and then you can go home."

After acknowledging the parents' thanks, Leigh tucked the chart under her arm. Just before she opened the door, she glanced over her shoulder. Jimmy's mom rested her head against her husband's chest as his arms wrapped around her. A Hallmark moment.

It almost made coming home worth it. Almost made her forget it was only the end of July and she had ten months and twenty-nine days left until she could leave Bradford General and Logan Point. That was when her National Health Service contract would end and her student loan would be paid off. Then she would be free to pursue a position at Johns Hopkins. She'd had to turn down one offer because the position didn't fit the qualifications of the payback program, and no way was she going into private practice with debt hanging over her head.

Leigh slipped from the room and pulled her phone from her pocket. Nine-thirty and still nothing from Tony. Back at the nurses' station, she made a few more notes on the chart and then leaned back in the chair and flexed her shoulders.

"You look tired," Cathy said.

In the month Leigh had been at the hospital, she'd come to regard the competent nurse as a friend. "I meant to go to bed earlier last night, but TJ wanted to watch a movie." Spending time with her son was worth losing sleep over.

"I don't know how you did it—going to med school and raising a child by yourself."

"I had help." Her friend Sarah, who had taken them in. "But it wasn't easy then, and it still isn't. It's like everything a mother does is measured. Either it goes in the Good Mom column or the Bad Mom column."

"I know what you mean," Cathy said with a chuckle. "I heard someone say you saw patients at Helping Hands today."

"Four hours." She loved her time at the free clinic, and the hours spent there counted toward her loan.

"Why don't you put your feet up for a second while everything is slow?"

"I think I will." Leigh had learned to catch rest whenever she could during her residency. But even as she leaned back in the chair, her mind returned to her son. Lately it seemed everything she did fell in the Bad Mom column. Like uprooting him from everyone and everything he knew by transferring from the UM Medical Center in Jackson to the hospital in Logan Point. She should have refused to come back home even though Tony kept insisting. That would have been the smart thing to do, but Leigh had never been able to say no to her brother. But at least last night scored one for the Good Mom side.

Now, if she could only rest her eyes for five seconds . . .

"Dr. Somerall, Sheriff Ben Logan asked to see you in the doctors' lounge."

Her eyes flew open, and she stared up at the ward clerk. "Is anyone with him?"

The clerk shrugged apologetically. "I don't know. The night supervisor called. That's all she said, except that Dr. Blakely will cover for you."

Fear, sour and metallic, filled Leigh's mouth. Tony and Ben were supposed to be together. After giving Blakely a quick report on her patients, she hurried to the doctors' lounge.

Tony is with Ben.

The words kept rhythm with her slapping feet. In the lounge, Ben stood alone at the window. The instant he turned, she knew.

Tony was hurt.

"Ben?" Icy prickles stabbed her heart. It wasn't a question of bad. It was a question of how bad. "Where's Tony?"

His Adam's apple bobbed as he stepped toward her. The light from the overhead fluorescent cast dark shadows under his eyes. She'd expected him to be in uniform, not jeans and a polo shirt.

"I'm sorry, Leigh. I don't know any other way to tell you except . . . he's dead."

"Tony's dead?" Coldness seeped into her cheeks. Her stomach roiled and tried to expel the sandwich she'd eaten less than an hour ago. She grabbed the back of a chair to steady herself. "You were supposed to help him."

His shoulders squared. "I know. I'm sorry. I keep thinking . . . if only I could've gotten to the Peabody ten minutes earlier, but there was a wreck on the parkway."

"Peabody? What was he doing at the Peabody?" She sank into the chair and rubbed the hard vinyl of the armrest, her finger finding a jagged tear in the material.

Ben knelt in front of her, sweat beading his face. "He wanted to meet at the hotel. Didn't you know?"

Of course she didn't know. "He said he was having dinner with you." She closed her eyes as Ben's voice droned on.

"He'd left a key at the front desk. When I opened the door, I found him on the floor. The bleeding was bad. I called 911, but I knew it was too late. He . . . he said to tell you he was sorry." Ben patted her arm. "I'm so sorry."

She drew back. Her brother got himself killed, and all he could say was he's sorry? Tears stung her eyes, and she flicked them away. "How did it happen?"

"Shot. In the chest. He . . . he died in my arms."

"Shot?" Not bigger-than-life Tony. Sure, her brother could be a hotshot, and he had swagger, but it matched his smile . . . and no one would love her son better than his uncle Tony. The gray walls closed in, smothering Leigh. No, this could not be happening. "I want to see him."

"That's not a good idea. They've taken his body to the morgue."

"You think I haven't seen a dead body on a slab before?"

"You haven't seen your brother on a slab."

Leigh flinched. Maybe she shouldn't have been so sharp. He was right. That wasn't how she wanted to remember Tony.

"Did . . . he say anything else?"

Ben wiped his face on his sleeve. "Yeah. He told me to protect you. It scared me half to death when Wade couldn't find you."

"Is that why he was looking for me?" She furrowed her brow. "Protect me? From what?"

"I was hoping you'd know." Ben stood and dragged another chair close to her. "Do you know any reason you'd be in danger?"

"No."

"How much do you know about our meeting tonight?"

"Nothing. I never even understood why he asked me to call you." She pressed her fingers to her temple. "I can't believe you're grilling me."

"I'm not grilling you. I just need a little information. He never mentioned a flash drive? Or that he knew something about who shot my dad?"

She jerked her head up. "Your dad? So this is about you now? About who shot your dad? My brother is killed, and all you can think of is your dad's case? I don't *know* who shot your dad. Maybe Tony knew, but I don't. And you know something else? Right now,

I don't care. I want to know why my brother is dead, and if you can't tell me, then just leave."

He held his hand out. "Leigh, I . . . I didn't . . . I'm sorry."

She couldn't take the pity emanating from his face, his eyes. Dark chocolate eyes. How could she even notice them at a time like this? She stood and escaped to the window that faced a small walking park. Pity was the last thing she wanted from Ben Logan. In fact, she didn't want anything from him. He let her down once. He wouldn't get the opportunity to do it again.

"I want to be here for you, Leigh."

You had your chance ten years ago. Leigh clenched her fist. "Just leave."

She didn't think he would, but when she turned around, he was gone. She turned back to stare through the window. Giant oaks stood guard around the small grassy area, their canopy a backdrop for the one flickering security light.

As usual, it was up to Leigh to help herself. She hugged her stomach and leaned against the wall. Tony was dead. How many times had she delivered news of death to a family? She'd always tried to be compassionate, caring. Maybe she hadn't been compassionate enough. Perfect enough. Maybe God wanted to teach her a lesson.

She licked her parched lips and blinked against the stinging in her eyes. Searching for a tissue in her pocket, her fingers closed around the plastic key ring Tony had given her when she finished her residency, and she pulled it out. *How do you keep a doctor busy for hours? Turn over . . .* She turned it over and read the same message.

Leigh's knees buckled, and she slid down the wall.

Her wacky brother would never make her laugh again.

2

Voices from the waiting room blended in the background as Ben found two Styrofoam cups at the refreshment center. His hand hesitated at the decaf carafe. No, he needed real coffee, and Leigh probably did as well. As he filled the cups, he spotted a hazelnut creamer. She liked hazelnut. He peeled the top back, dumped the liquid in, and marked the cup with an *H*.

"Ben!"

He looked up as his burly chief deputy approached the snack area. There was no way to miss Wade in his boxy colorful Hawaiian shirt and khaki shorts. How had he missed that getup earlier when he arrived at the hospital and Wade updated him on Leigh's whereabouts? "If you find a louder shirt, I'll have to buy new sun shades."

"Ha-ha. Ruth likes the way I dress."

Ruth from the library. His deputy's hot date.

Wade poured himself a cup of coffee. "How did Leigh take the news?"

Ben shrugged. "She's mad. She thinks I let her brother down." And he had. He should've set the place and time, not Tony. He should've been there. Period.

"What was this secret meeting you two were having, anyway?"

Ben fastened a lid on Leigh's coffee. "It was Tony who insisted that no one know we were meeting. He claimed he knew something about my dad."

"You're kidding." Wade slipped a tiny Rubik's Cube from his pocket. "What was it?"

"Finding out is going to be your job. Interview all of Tony's friends, acquaintances, even enemies, if he had any. The information had to come from someone he knew, probably one of his gambling associates."

"That'll be a lot of people."

"I know. But Tony is the only lead we have." Ben cocked his head. "You were the last person to see Dad before he went on patrol that day. Have you—"

"I've gone over it in my head a thousand times," Wade snapped. He ran his fingers over the cube. "Sometimes I wake up in the middle of the night thinking about it, trying to figure out what he was doing on the back side of the county."

Ben lived the same nightmare his chief deputy did. Wade believed he should have gone with the sheriff. Ben believed he should have at least answered his dad's phone call that day, but he'd been in the middle of the U.S. Marshals interview. Before he could return the call, he'd received the one telling him about his dad's shooting.

"I offered to go with him." Red crept up Wade's neck. "Wish now I'd insisted."

"I know you did all you could that day."

Wade grunted and leaned his back against the counter. His fingers arranged and rearranged the cube, and in less than a minute, all six sides lined up.

"How do you do that?"

"Do what?"

"Work that stupid cube without looking at it."

"Oh, I don't know. I just do it." Wade glanced down the hall. "Where's Leigh?"

"In the doctors' lounge. She told me to leave."

"What'd you say to her?"

"Doesn't matter what I said, I pushed her too hard." Her out-burst had reminded Ben of the smart-mouthed teen with an attitude he'd first met in junior high. Purple hair one day, streaked the next. She'd come a long way, and it was hard to reconcile the old Leigh with Doctor Somerall now. Until she went off on him. He glanced down at the coffee, which was no longer hot. "This was supposed to be a peace offering." He put the two cups in the microwave and nuked them.

"You need me to stick around?"

"If you don't mind. If she'll let me, I'm going to drive her home, and you can drop her car off. Then I'll bring you back for yours."

"Why not just let her drive herself home?"

"I told you, she may be in danger. Tony knew he was dying. He used his last breath to make me promise to protect her."

"Maybe she knows—"

"She only knew we were meeting."

"Then I don't see the problem. Why would anyone want to hurt her?"

"Because there was more to our meeting . . . Tony was bring-ing information he said the feds would be interested in. It was on a flash drive, and the killer must've taken it, because Tony didn't have it on him."

"And you're sure Leigh doesn't know anything about it?"
Ben shook his head.

"Then I'm telling you, you're worrying for nothing."

"The killer may not know that. I just have this gut feeling."

"If Tony knew he was dying, maybe he wanted you to be there for her in the days after his death."

"Maybe." He took the hot coffee from the microwave. "I'll call you in a few minutes and let you know about the car."

Ben walked back down the hall to the doctors' lounge and pushed the door open with his elbow. "I know you told me you wanted to be alone, but I figured—"

22

Leigh was sitting on the floor with her back against the wall, turning something on her key ring over and over in her hand. He set the coffees on the table and knelt beside her, inhaling the rose petal scent she'd always worn. Even after ten years, she made his heart do funny things. "Are you okay?"

She glanced up at him with red-rimmed eyes and took a shuddering breath. "Tony's really gone, isn't he?"

"I'm afraid so." He sat on the floor beside her, the stained concrete cold and hard.

"Thanks for coming back."

"I didn't leave. Just went after coffee. Hazelnut, the kind you always liked." He reached for the coffees and handed her the cup with the creamer in it.

"You remembered?"

That and so much more. He shrugged away the memories from the summer before their junior year in college and sipped his coffee. For a minute, he said nothing. A wall clock ticked minutes away as they both sat on the floor and drank their coffee. A hundred different apologies ran through his mind, all lame. He sucked in a breath. "I'm sorry."

She leaned her head against the wall. "I know."

"I didn't mean to sound more interested in finding my dad's shooter than about Tony. But I want to find out who killed him, and that seemed a logical place to start." He shifted on the hard floor. "You reminded me of the Leigh I knew back in high school. The one with an attitude and temper to match."

"I wasn't very nice back then."

"You were nice enough. Can we start over?"

"From tonight? Yeah."

So, Leigh wanted to pretend their summer romance so many years ago never happened. He wished he could. Or could understand why she never returned his phone calls.

But if that was the way she wanted it, he could play by her rules.

Which was probably better anyway. She had her brother's death to deal with, and he had a case to solve, one where she could end up being a victim. He certainly didn't need to carry any baggage into the case.

He stood and offered her a hand up. "How about we sit somewhere more comfortable?"

Leigh hesitated only for the briefest moment, then allowed him to pull her up. In spite of his resolve, her touch sent a shiver to his heart. She settled in a brown leather recliner, and he took the chair facing her. "I'd like to drive you home."

"Home." She sighed the word then lowered her gaze and stared at a spot on the floor. "Tony took us in when we moved back, you know. He didn't want us to get another place." Her voice rang hollow in the room. "So he gave us his room until the beds we ordered arrived. He even bought my son a cot." She pressed her lips together and closed her eyes. "The beds are supposed to come this week."

He figured there'd be more than a few times when reality would jolt her. "Is there anyone you can call to come stay with you? Your in-laws, maybe?"

She bit her lip. "Matthew's parents are dead."

"No other family?"

"I never met any of them. We were only married for eight months before he was killed in a car accident. I have a friend in Jackson I'll call tomorrow." Leigh rubbed her temples. "I keep thinking it's all a bad dream. I'll wake up, and Tony will be on the couch, or just coming in. My son will be on the cot across from me, all curled up with the bear Tony won for him at the fair in Jackson a couple of years ago." Leigh winced. "Forget what I said about the bear. He thinks he's too old to sleep with a stuffed animal."

Ben glanced at his watch. Wade was waiting. "Will you let me—"

She grabbed his arm. "The news. Tony's death will be on television. I've got to tell—"

"Leigh, slow down. It's late, and Tony's name won't be released tonight. You can wait until morning to tell your son. Right now what you need is rest. Let me drive you home."

"No . . . I'll drive myself. I might need my car."

"Wade will bring it. You're in no shape to drive."

Words formed on her lips as she seemed to struggle with his offer, but in the end, she nodded. "Let me get my things."

"Good. How about your son? Do we need to pick him up?"

"No, he's asleep by now. I'll get him in the morning."

The sticky July night wrapped around them in sauna-like heat. Ben guided Leigh to his pickup, the overhead security lights casting gloomy shadows over the first few rows of cars. Beyond that, total darkness. The skin on Ben's neck prickled, and he glanced around. A tiny light flared in the darkness near the street, then a red glow. Only a smoker. But if Tony's killer wanted to get Leigh, this would be a perfect place.

At least she didn't have on her white coat, and the green scrubs blended into the night. "Right over here." Ben shielded her as a car entered the parking lot. Somewhere to the left, a motorcycle roared to life, and he tensed. Once he had her in the truck, he relaxed a little. But only a little, as Leigh's fragrance filled the cab, bringing back memories of another truck and another summer evening.

Ten minutes later, he stopped in front of the white frame house that had belonged to her grandmother. "Why are all your lights on?"

"Tony." She pressed her lips together and sniffed. Probably trying not to cry in front of him again. "He didn't like coming into a dark house and insisted the living room lights be left on."

"Okay. Then, house key, please." Ben held out his hand.

"Why? I'm perfectly capable of opening my door."

"Could we just do it my way and save time?" When she huffed, he added, "It's the gentlemanly thing to do."

He didn't think she was going to comply, but finally she found her house key in her purse and held it out.

"Thank you," he said as she put her hand on the truck door.

Evidently she couldn't wait to get away from him. "What time do you want to pick up your son tomorrow?"

Leigh's eyes narrowed. "I don't need your help getting my son."

"You don't have to go through this alone. Tony wanted me to help you."

She turned to him. "Look, Ben, you've done your duty. I'll take it from here and deal with it in my own way." She grabbed the key from his hand and jumped out of the truck.

His duty had not ended. Not until he saw her safely through this. Ben banged his knee as he scrambled out of the truck to catch her, but by the time he reached the porch, she was already inside. He yanked the screen door open as her scream split the night air.

"No!"

Leigh's guttural cry would haunt him the rest of his life.

3

His heart pounded against his ribs. That was close. If he hadn't heard the truck pull up, the sheriff and the doctor would have caught him red-handed. As it was, he'd barely gotten out the back door before they came in the front. He peeled off the latex gloves, stuffing them in his pocket as he crept through the woods behind the Jackson house to the side road where he'd left his car.

Defeat tasted sour in his mouth. He'd been so sure Tony had hidden the flash drive at his house, and with a little more time he might have found it. But it was such a tiny thing, and so easy to overlook.

Maybe if the sister found it, she wouldn't know what it was . . . He licked his dry lips. No, Tony told the sheriff he was bringing it, so Logan would be looking for it. Probably had already questioned the sister about it. *Maybe she has it.* He dismissed that option—if that were the case, Logan would be looking for *him* instead of bringing the doctor home.

He clenched his jaw against the nausea that roiled in his stomach. The look on Tony's face when he fired . . . why couldn't he just go along, instead of forcing his hand? He hadn't wanted to kill Tony, had even liked him, but he wasn't going to jail.

Once he reached the pavement, he slipped Tony's cell phone from his pocket. Loading the software that enabled him to listen to Tony's phone conversations had proven invaluable, but if Logan found the phone, that same software could be traced to him. He dropped the phone to the road and ground it with his foot. On his way home, he'd dispose of it. And the gun . . . He knew exactly where it was going as well. But that still left the problem of the flash drive. If he were Tony, where would he hide it? And how was he going to find it?

■ ■ ■

Leigh stared at the war zone that was her living room—cushions ripped from their coverings and strewn about, books dumped on the floor along with the contents of a few boxes she hadn't unpacked yet. Even photographs had been separated from their frames. She pressed her hands to the side of her face and barely noticed when Ben pushed past her, his gun drawn.

"What the—" He disappeared down the hallway.

"No . . . not Bear!" Leigh stumbled forward and scooped up TJ's stuffed animal. Her fingers shook as she tried to poke the white filling back through the gash in its stomach. TJ would be crushed.

What had she brought her son into?

A minute later, Ben knelt beside her. "They're gone."

"Why?" She pulled the plush material together, overlapping it. If she could find a needle and thread, she could stitch TJ's stuffed bear up good as new. The band circling her chest tightened. She *had* to make Bear whole again. "Why did they do this?"

"They were looking for something," he said. "Probably the flash drive I told you about. Are you sure Tony never mentioned it?"

She shook her head. "With my shift at the hospital, we were barely ever in the same room, and when we were, we didn't spend our time talking about work." Lately her brother had spent most of their time together talking about the little church he and TJ attended.

Car lights flashed across the window, and Leigh froze.

Ben stood and eased to the window. "Wade Hatcher with your car."

Her car? Her breath hitched. She'd forgotten Wade was bringing it. Her hands gripped the stuffed animal as Tony's death slammed her heart again. She was all TJ had now.

"Try not to touch anything," Ben said as he lifted her up and helped her to the one chair that still had a cushion. "We have to process your house as a crime scene."

Leigh swallowed. Crime scene. A lightbulb flashed in her head. Ben was not going away. Looking around the room, she realized she should be glad and welcome his presence, maybe even apologize for being so rude all night. The words stuck in her throat.

What she should do was pack her bags and get out of Logan Point. Tonight. And she would do exactly that if she didn't have a contract with the hospital. She'd just have to stay under his radar, keep TJ away from him until she could finish the contract and escape to Baltimore.

The next few hours passed in a blur as more deputies arrived and scoured her house, dusting for prints, looking for clues. But at least most of the things she'd brought from Jackson were still in storage. Leigh could imagine the mess if all those boxes had been dumped. She helped where she could, checking each room for missing items. Bear was the only casualty, with everything else scattered but intact. Even the sofa cushions had only been stripped. Whoever it was had definitely been looking for something specific.

As the deputies finished a room, Leigh put it back in order. At two in the morning, she finished up the kitchen and put on another pot of coffee. Only the living room remained. And Bear. He lay on the counter, awaiting her needle. As the rich aroma of coffee filled the room, she remembered times spent with her grandmother in the white kitchen with its brick-red countertops. Tony was with Gram now, in heaven. Maybe that was the sole purpose for her to return to Logan Point—for Tony to take TJ to church and get saved. She bit her lip. Her brother couldn't be gone.

Leigh grabbed the brown thread she'd found, her fingers shaking as she tried to thread the needle. She closed one eye and stabbed at the eye of the needle again. Finally. With quick motions, she sutured the bear's stomach, leaving a puckered seam that wouldn't smooth out no matter how hard she rubbed. Leigh jabbed the needle back in the pincushion. How was she ever going to explain to TJ what happened tonight when she couldn't understand it herself?

"Good job," Ben said.

Leigh jerked her head up. She hadn't heard him come into the kitchen. She pointed to the stuffed animal's eyes that didn't match. "Not the first time I've operated on Bear. Would you and your men like a fresh cup of coffee?"

"Sure."

She put the toy aside and poured his coffee, trying to ignore the way his presence filled the room. *Apologize.* She pressed her lips together, chewing on the inside corner of her mouth. "Uh, thanks for . . ." Her voice broke.

Ben took the coffee from her shaking hand. "It's going to get better."

Such simple words to bring a fresh round of tears. Leigh fanned her face as she stared at the ceiling and blinked wetness away. "I'm sorry."

"It's normal to cry in times like this."

"No, I mean, I'm sorry for the way I've acted. I appreciate all you've done tonight."

"Oh." He stood straighter. "Just doin' my job, ma'am."

His mischievous smile clamped a band around her heart. How many times had she seen that same smile on TJ's face? She forced herself to breathe. "The house—are your men finished?"

"Almost." He picked up the coffee and took a sip. "Have you thought about where you'll go?"

"Go? I have nowhere to go. This is my home. Has been since Daddy died."

He held out his hand. "You could stay with my folks. They've always opened their house to those who need a place to stay, even since my dad's stroke."

The Logans? That was the last place she wanted to stay. "I don't want to intrude. I'll change the locks, get a security system. Besides, your dad doesn't even like me."

"New locks take time. And where did you get the idea my dad doesn't like you?"

Tom Logan's words from ten years ago burned in her memory. *"Break up with my son, and I'll drop the marijuana charge against Tony. If you care anything at all about Ben, you'll stay away from him. You'll only drag him down."* But it hadn't been all Tom. If Ben had really loved her, he would not have given up so easily, and he would not have gotten engaged to someone else three months later.

Leigh lifted her chin. She would rather face whoever broke into the house than depend on the Logan family. "I'm staying here. No one is running me out of my home."

"Leigh, that 'no one' killed your brother tonight. Whoever it was came here looking for a flash drive that Tony had."

"And it wasn't here. This is probably the safest place I can be."

"What if we interrupted him? What if he comes back?"

She rubbed her brow. This was not happening. "There has to be another place I can go."

"Leigh, I don't have time to find a safe house tonight."

"Well, how safe would I be at your dad's? You said it yourself—he's had a stroke."

"My house is in their yard. Don't be so—"

From the doorway, Wade cleared his throat.

They turned in unison to stare at the deputy.

Wade looked around, then down at his Hawaiian shirt. "What? This shirt ain't that bad."

Tension dissipated from Leigh's body. She gave him a tired smile. "I don't know about that. Would you like a cup of coffee?"

The deputy hitched his khaki shorts and eased his bulky frame into the kitchen. "Yes, ma'am."

She poured dark brew into a cup and handed it to him. It was hard not to compare the tense and brooding sheriff to his easygoing chief deputy. Ben was by far the more handsome, his body lean and fit, his dark hair in need of a trim, and a five o'clock shadow that'd grown into a day-old beard. Wade, on the other hand, projected a good-ole-boy image, one Leigh suspected he worked on. He carried an extra fifty pounds well on his tall frame. He was yin to Ben's yang.

Wade set a folder and notepad on the counter. "Do I need to take Leigh's statement, or did you already get it?"

"We haven't gotten around to it." Ben gave her a sour look. "Been trying to talk her out of staying here."

"What's wrong with that?" Wade looked puzzled. "Whoever did this took their time, and either they found what they were looking for or gave up. Don't think they'll be back."

"Don't tell her—"

"My thoughts exactly," Leigh said. She hadn't expected an ally in Wade and shot Ben an I-told-you-so look. In answer, Ben folded his arms across his chest, his mouth clamped tight.

"I would put new locks on since there's no sign they broke in." Wade eyed her. "Unless you left the door unlocked."

"I didn't, and I don't see Tony leaving it open."

"She's not staying without protection." Ben scowled at her.

"I don't need a bodyguard, and that statement you mentioned— can it wait until tomorrow?" She glanced at the clock over the sink. "I mean, later this morning. I have to straighten the living room before I pick up my son in five hours, and I could use a little sleep."

"Tell you what," Ben said. "Why don't you let Wade and the other two deputies straighten up in there while you give me your statement."

"Whatever." Anything that would get him out of her house and out of her life.

As soon as Wade left the kitchen, Ben flipped over to a new page in the notebook. "You're not staying here by yourself." Before she could comment, he continued, "Did Tony ever say anything about a flash drive?"

"For the tenth time, no." She cocked her head. "What is this flash drive you keep mentioning?"

"When Tony called this afternoon, he said he was bringing one to our meeting, but I didn't find it in his pockets. Didn't find his cell phone either." He scratched his head. "You've had a little time to think . . . do you have any idea why he wanted to meet with me?"

"Not a clue . . . unless it was about . . ."

"About what?"

"He'd been taking my son to church." She pressed her lips together. "Said he'd found Jesus. I caught him a time or two talking to himself. When I questioned him, he just said he had some things to fix."

Leigh picked up Bear from the counter and hugged the stuffed animal to her chest. "One night he had a nightmare, and he was yelling in his sleep . . . something about dogs. I figured it was just a silly dream."

"A dog?" Ben's head jerked up. "He talked about a blue dog before he died. I don't know if it had to do with my dad or the flash drive. You're sure he didn't tell you anything else? Maybe something that didn't sound relevant?"

"I don't remember him mentioning the color of the dogs." She rolled her neck. "I wish I could help you, but like I said, we haven't had a lot of time to talk. I've been busy, settling in at the hospital, and Tony . . . well, he wasn't home a lot. Talk to Ian Maxwell—he was more than Tony's boss. They were pretty tight."

Ben walked to the coffeemaker and poured himself another cup.

"Do you know if he was friends with anyone else at Maxwell Industries?"

"Ben, I've only been back a month." She shrugged. "Other than Ian and Danny Maxwell, I don't know anyone at the plant, and I certainly don't know any of his gambling buddies. Tony never brought anyone around. He kept his work life separate from our family time."

Ben glanced around the small kitchen. "Do you know why he'd live here instead of a fancier house? I mean, I'm sure Maxwell Industries paid him well, and from what I understand, he usually won at gambling. He had a roll of hundred dollar bills in his pocket."

"He liked it here, and he didn't have many needs. But he'd been talking about building a bigger house." She stared into space. "I warned him that he had no business carrying that much money around."

For the next fifteen minutes, Ben plied her with questions that she had no answers to. Finally she held up her hand. "Stop. I'm done. I can't do this tonight."

Before he could answer, Wade stuck his head in the doorway again. "We're finished here, and I'm going home to bed. Told Andre you might want him to stay."

Two other deputies came into the kitchen with him, and while she didn't recognize the one that Ben introduced as Randy Jenkins, she did recognize the other one. Andre Stone had brought his little brother to the ER last week with a gash on his arm that had taken six stitches. She held up the nearly empty pot. "Either of you want this last cup?"

"I've had my quota for the night," Jenkins said.

"I can sure use a cup, Doc." Andre removed his navy ball cap and ran his hand over his closely cropped hair. "Black, please."

She poured the coffee into a mug and handed it to Andre. "How's your brother?"

The deputy's dark face broke into a grin. "He's good. Says he

34

wants to be a doctor like you. Thanks for asking." Andre sipped the coffee. "His pediatrician okayed him to play ball this weekend. You coming to the game, Ben?"

Ben rubbed the back of his neck. "No, I have other plans."

Andre shot Ben a puzzled glance. "Most of the boys in your Sunday school class are playing. In fact, I was hoping you'd help coach while your brother-in-law is out of town."

"It's Emily's class. I'm only there because Jeremy is in Afghanistan for three months."

Emily ran the Helping Hands clinic, and Leigh hadn't known her husband was in Afghanistan. But then, other than yesterday afternoon, she'd only worked at the clinic one Saturday, and Ben's sister hadn't been there.

"Ben, you were a great ballplayer," Wade spoke up. "You ought to help them out."

"Don't you start." Ben glowered at his chief deputy. "I'm not coaching. Now, can we get back to the problem at hand?"

"There is no problem," Leigh said. "I'm not leaving my home, and you don't have the resources to put a deputy here."

"Andre could drive by here every hour," Wade said.

"There's no need for that. I'm staying until morning." Ben ran his hand through his unruly hair. "I'll sleep on the couch."

"No." Leigh scrubbed a spot on the red countertop. Ben Logan was not sleeping on her sofa. "I'm good with the patrol."

"Well, I'm not."

"What will my neighbors think if they see your truck parked in my drive at five-thirty in the morning?"

"That's another reason for me to stay what's left of the night—your nearest neighbor is a quarter of a mile away. We'll talk about the patrols after you get the locks changed and a security system."

"Look, Ben, I don't think whoever did this will be back."

"Either I sleep on the couch or in my truck. Your call. And I will be taking you to pick up your son in the morning."

Now she knew where TJ got his stubborn streak. Coming home to Logan Point had been such a mistake, but she couldn't unscramble eggs. She'd just have to find a way to keep Ben from discovering he was TJ's father.

■ ■ ■

For a minute Ben thought she was going to make him sleep in the driveway, which he would if he had to. He'd promised Tony that he would keep Leigh safe, and it was a promise he aimed to keep. "The couch would be better—that way if the intruders came back, I'd know it immediately."

A look he couldn't identify crossed her face, and then she waved her hand. "Whatever. See your men out. I'm going to bed."

Suited him fine. He walked with his men to their patrol cars, and after working out a plan for drive-by checks, he sent them on their way. When he returned to the living room, Leigh had put bedding on the couch. Quiet settled in the house as Ben tried to get comfortable. He couldn't believe Tony had slept on this couch for a month.

Ben stared at the ceiling, making plans for the morning. He'd go with Leigh to pick up her son. How old had she said the boy was? He couldn't remember . . . something about him being too old for a stuffed bear . . . Ben did the math. He hadn't seen her in ten years, so the boy couldn't be over eight or nine. Probably about his nephews' age, and they were eight. Which meant she hadn't pined away after that summer. Anyway, the boy might want to play on that Little League team that Andre kept trying to get Ben to help with—which wasn't happening. Not now. Not ever.

He took out the Boy Scout medallion and ran his finger around the edges. It wasn't that he didn't like kids, it was just that since Tommy Ray Gresham had drowned three years ago, Ben didn't trust himself around them. Kids made him uncomfortable, even his own nephews.

Another thing that was just as certain—he needed to keep his relationship with Leigh strictly business. Maybe he should let Wade shadow her. He sighed and slipped the medallion back in his pocket. But he had promised Tony to look after her himself. Being around her would be difficult. He still wanted to know what happened that summer when she wouldn't take his calls, and he didn't believe for one minute she broke up with him because she didn't have time. Maybe he'd ask in the morning. Ben's eyes drooped . . . Needed to stay alert . . .

A light, flowery scent invaded Ben's dreams as he walked a darkened path, searching for something he'd lost. Running water jerked him awake. Someone was in the kitchen. He was halfway off the couch when the aroma of freshly brewed coffee slowed him down. Leigh. She must be up already. He checked his watch. It was after seven.

"Oh, good. You're awake."

He looked around. Leigh stood at the door, dressed to go out.

"Coffee's on the counter. I'm going to pick up my son. You can let yourself out—I fixed the door so that it'll lock behind you."

He scrambled off the couch, tucking his shirt in his pants. "Wait. I'm going with you."

"Why?"

"What do you mean, why? I told you last night I'd go. You don't know who's out there waiting for you."

"This is crazy, Ben. There's no reason for anyone to be after me. I thought about it after I went to bed. Whoever broke in here was looking for a flash drive I know nothing about. It has nothing to do with me. And I can't live my life in fear, and I certainly don't want my son afraid. Houses get broken into every day. You deal with it and get on with your life. That's what I'm trying to do here, and I don't need your help doing it."

"What's with you? What are you afraid of?" He touched his chest. "Me?"

"No!" Her hands balled into fists. "I just want to be left alone. Please don't be here when I get back."

Ben's jaw dropped open as she turned and slipped out of the house. He snapped his mouth shut and raced after her, fumbling with the door and finally getting it open. He blinked in the bright sun. "Wait!"

He'd almost reached her when the crack of a gunshot sliced the air. A bullet plowed the earth between them, then another crack. The next second seemed to last an hour. Silence filled his head except for the pounding of his heart. In slow motion, Leigh turned, her body silhouetted against the morning sun as she fell toward the ground. More dirt and rocks spit from the ground followed by another gun report. Leigh struggled to her knees, and he dove for her. "Get down!"

Another bullet ripped the ground. They seemed to be coming from the hill across the road. Ben pulled his gun, firing three shots in that direction. Another bullet chipped the concrete walk before thudding into a tree beside the car. He shielded Leigh's crouched body with his own and reloaded his gun as he scanned the hillside for the shooter. Nothing moved. Ben felt for his cell phone with his free hand, wishing he'd worn his radio. Something bigger than his .38 would be nice too. "Stay down. What's this address?"

She stared up at him, her eyes wide. "Uh, 406 Ch-Chalmers Drive."

Still scanning the area, he speed-dialed the jail, and his dispatcher answered. "Maggie, I need every deputy at Tony Jackson's house." He repeated the address. "Someone's shooting at us."

"On it, Ben. Andre called his location in a few minutes ago. He's near there."

Over the hill, a motorcycle roared to life. "Tell him to watch for a cycle—probably a sport bike."

Ben slid his phone in his pocket as the whine faded. With a jolt he realized he'd heard that sound at the hospital last night. With a wary eye, he knelt beside Leigh. "Are you hit?"

"I don't think so. The gunfire startled me, and I tripped."

When she went down, he'd been certain she had been shot. "Good. I think whoever it was is gone, but let's get you in the house."

She gripped his arm. "I want to get this . . . this—"

"I'll get him, Leigh. I promise you. Now, come on, let's go." He shielded her from the hillside where the shooter had been, not speaking until they were safely back inside. "You sure you're okay?"

She brushed dirt from her pants. A chestnut strand of hair curled across her cheek, and she hooked it behind her ear. Red splotched her cheeks. "No, I'm not okay. I'm mad. What if TJ had been with me? He might've been killed."

"TJ?" That new kid who had just started coming to Emily's class at church? "You're TJ's mom?"

Leigh's face went from fiery red to almost gray. He figured there'd be an adrenaline dump, just not this quick.

"How do you know TJ?"

"He's one of the boys in the Sunday school class."

4

Sirens cut off whatever else Ben might've said as patrol cars converged on the driveway, and he left her to brief his deputies. Not that it mattered. The roar in her head would've made talk impossible. With wooden legs, she stumbled to the sofa.

TJ and Ben had met.

The one thing she'd wanted to put off. Forever, if possible. Oh, why hadn't she said no to her brother?

Now he was dead, and someone was trying to kill her. With no one else to rely on, she just might have to depend on Ben to keep her and TJ safe. Her whole being cried out against that option. Already she'd done everything humanly possible to avoid Ben Logan. She'd moved into their grandparents' house with Tony in a neighborhood that attracted little of the sheriff's attention. Then, when TJ wanted to go to Sunday school, she'd chosen a small nondenominational church nearby instead of the big church in town that Ben's ancestors had founded. Just in case Tony couldn't take TJ some Sunday.

And somehow picked the church Ben not only attended, but where he evidently helped his sister teach a boys' Sunday school class. That so did not fit her image of the sheriff. She propped a hand under her chin. Could it get any worse?

"Leigh."

She hadn't heard Ben come back and jerked her head up as he knelt beside her. She didn't know how much time had passed, only that he now wore a black vest over his shirt, and he had a microphone attached to his shoulder. Andre and the other deputy that had been here the night before stood at the door.

"I'm going across the road to help comb the area where the shooter was, but Randy's going to be here with you." He nodded toward the other deputy.

"TJ. I need to get him from the sitter."

"Call the sitter, and tell her you'll be late."

"But—"

"Leigh, someone was shooting at you. You don't want to put your son in danger. When I finish here, we'll get him, and I'll take you both to my parents' house. Dad might have had a stroke, but Mom's an expert with firearms."

"I'm not going to your parents' house." Stroke or no stroke, she and Tom Logan wouldn't get along five minutes.

"Then you can stay at my place, and I'll move in with them until this is over. Unless you can think of a safer place."

There had to be another option. "Those bullets were closer to you than me. Maybe the shooter was after you."

"Leigh, be reasonable. Someone killed your brother, trashed your house . . ." He spoke slowly, as though he thought she might be having trouble understanding him. "He wasn't after me."

"You don't know that for sure."

He rubbed his forehead. "I don't have time to argue with you right now. But consider what could've happened if your son had been with you."

She opened her mouth and closed it. As much as she hated to admit it, there was no denying that until this person was caught, she and TJ needed Ben's protection.

But who would protect her from Ben if he discovered TJ was his son?

■ ■ ■

Ben stared at Leigh. She was the most stubborn, strong-willed woman he'd ever met. But what if she was right that the shooter had been aiming at him? His radio crackled to life with Wade's voice.

"I have the cyclist in sight. I'm doing eighty-five, and the crazy fool is pulling away."

Ben stood and spoke into his mic. "What's your location?"

"Highway 310. Coming up on Dead Man's Curve."

"Back off but try to keep him in view."

The radio jumped to life again. "Ben, he didn't make the curve. I'm calling for an ambulance."

"Approach the situation with caution, Wade. I'm on my way." He turned to Leigh. "Stay here, and do not go after your son."

Her brows shot together in protest.

"Just once, do what I ask. We don't know that this guy is the shooter. And give me your cell number so I can keep in touch."

She spit out the numbers, and he tapped them into his phone, then hurried out of the house, taking Andre with him. His deputy caught up with him at his truck.

"The doc has a lot of backbone," Andre said.

"Too much." He climbed into his truck and followed Andre's squad car as he peeled out of the driveway. Once on the highway, Ben checked in with his chief deputy. "Wade, what's the situation?"

"No pulse. Ambulance ETA, five minutes. I'm administering CPR."

"Who is it?"

"Billy Wayne Gresham."

His stomach soured. "You sure?"

"Yeah. I don't think he'll make it."

Ben fingered the small Boy Scout medallion in his pocket. Tommy Ray Gresham's little brother. He'd pulled him over a week ago for speeding on his motorcycle and let him go. Just hadn't been able to write the ticket, not to the brother of the boy Ben had let drown. "Once the paramedics arrive, secure the scene."

He did the math. Dead Man's Curve was seven miles from Leigh's house. If Billy Wayne was their shooter, he'd been laying down some rubber. It was a wonder he hadn't crashed earlier.

When Ben reached the scene, Wade was directing traffic. A green Kawasaki that Ben recognized as the one he'd pulled over lay twisted around a huge oak that had claimed more lives than Ben cared to remember. Paramedics huddled over a body twenty feet from the tree.

"How is he?" Ben asked. Even this early in the day, the July sun beat down with a vengeance, and within seconds, his shirt was plastered to his back.

"Not good." Sweat ran down the side of Wade's face.

Ben jogged over to where the paramedics were working on Billy Wayne. One of them looked up and shook his head. A few minutes later, the medic rocked back on his heels. "He's gone."

Ben pulled the Boy Scout medallion from his pocket and stared at it. Three years ago, he'd planned to give the medallion to Billy Wayne's brother on the last day of camp. He didn't look forward to telling Mrs. Gresham another one of her boys had died.

"Hey, Ben, come get a look at this," Wade yelled from where he stood by the broken Kawasaki. He carefully lifted a small satchel from the saddle bag. A black barrel protruded from it. "I think you have your shooter."

"Let's see it."

Wade pulled on latex gloves and carefully lifted out a folded carbine. He unfolded it, sniffing the barrel. "Hasn't been long since it was fired. Looks like a Sub-2000."

"Got an extra pair of gloves?"

He donned the gloves Wade handed him and riffled through the bag, finding two casings and a magazine loaded with 9 mm rounds.

"Never figured Billy Wayne for anything like this," Ben said. "I want a full report on his activities for the last couple of months. I especially want to know if he had any contact with Tony Jackson."

Wade nodded. "You think he shot Tony?"

"Entirely possible," he said as Andre approached with a wallet and handed it to him.

"Driver's license says he lives over on Washington Street."

"You two check it out but call Judge Morgan first and get a search warrant. If you find any evidence, I don't want it thrown out on a technicality. I'm going to find his mother and tell her what happened." It was the least he could do. "After that, you can find me at Leigh's house. Maybe by the time I get there, the third casing will have been found. Or the bullets."

Wade hitched his gun belt. "Ben, you might want to leave Andre here to wrap up the scene. I don't need any help."

Ben nodded then walked back to his truck. Something niggled in the back of his mind. He turned around. "Andre, didn't you go to school with Billy Wayne?"

"Yeah, that boy was always in trouble—when he showed up." Andre pulled his cap off and wiped his face with his sleeve. "Last time I saw him, I thought he'd straightened up. Said he had his own computer business and was doing some work for the Maxwells."

Tony's employers. "He was working at Maxwell Industries?"

"No, more like consulting. Something to do with their computers. Real cushy job, he said. I think one of his brothers works at the plant, though."

"Okay. Write down anything else you think of." He turned to Wade. "I'll join you at Gresham's house as soon as I can. As Ben pulled away from the scene, he took out his cell phone and called Livy in Memphis. He'd apprised her of the break-in at Leigh's, and now he needed to update her on the morning's activities.

"How's the investigation coming?" he asked when she answered.

Livy gave an exasperated snort. "Dead ends everywhere I turn. Would you believe the hall camera on that floor had been tampered with and nobody even noticed it was out?"

"I may have a lead." He filled her in on the shooting.

"I know the Greshams. My aunt Kate is friends with the mother,"

Livy said. "The old man isn't anyone I'd want to be around, but according to Kate, a couple of the boys took after Ruby."

When Livy paused, Ben knew she was remembering the youngest Gresham. "Tommy Ray was like his mom," Ben said, more to break the silence than anything.

"Yeah," Livy agreed softly. "You're not still blaming yourself, are you, Ben?"

"Nobody else to blame but me. How about the others?"

"I heard the oldest brother is in California somewhere. Not sure about the other one, but Billy was the one most like his dad. Do you think he killed Tony?"

"He looks like a good suspect. Ninety-nine percent sure he's the one who fired on us, and it wouldn't be a stretch to connect the dots from Tony's death and the house ransacking to this morning."

"Unless Billy was shooting at you."

"Except for the timing. I'm an easy target so why wait until I'm with Leigh? No, I think he was shooting at her. I just don't know why unless it had something to do with that flash drive."

"Do you think Billy knew how to disarm the security camera at the hotel?"

"Andre says he's computer savvy. I thought I'd check at Maxwell Industries and see if he worked with their security system as well as their computers. I've been kicking another idea around in my head. What if Tony downloaded confidential information from the company, like the plans for that new rifle I've heard rumors about? Thought I'd go out to Maxwell later today and rattle a few cages, see what shakes out."

"You don't seriously think one of the them is a murderer? I don't see that. Ian is a lover boy, not a killer, and while Danny might skirt the law, I don't think he would do anything outright illegal. And you can definitely rule out Danny's dad, Phillip Maxwell."

Ben hoped Livy was right and they weren't involved in anything illegal. The Maxwells were a fixture in Logan Point. They owned and operated Maxwell Industries and employed over two hundred people. Founder Phillip Maxwell was a friend of his dad's, and as far as Ben knew, squeaky clean. It was well known around town the old man and his brother had started the company with five hundred dollars and a strong work ethic. Ben wasn't too sure of their sons, though.

"How is Leigh holding up?" Livy asked.

"She's okay. Worried about her son. I'm trying to get her to stay with my folks."

"Good idea."

"Did you retrieve a bullet from Tony's body?" Ben turned onto the road the Greshams lived on.

"Yeah, but it was messed up pretty good. I sent the bullet to the crime lab in Nashville, and it'll take a week at least to get the report back, depending on how far they're backed up. But I'm betting it's a .38 or 9 mm. Keep me in the loop on Leigh's location."

"Ten-four."

■ ■ ■

Leigh paced the dark room, wishing the curtains could be opened. She hated to be enclosed in darkness. Why hadn't she heard from Ben? She checked her watch. He'd been gone over two hours.

The babysitter had said TJ was watching cartoons. What if somehow he heard about Tony's death before she could tell him? She bet he was already wondering why she hadn't come after him. Leigh stopped and turned to one of the deputies Ben had left guarding her. Jenkins. She thought that was his name. The other one was stationed at the back door. "Look, I need to get my son."

The deputy hitched his gun belt. "Aw, Doc, I wish you wouldn't do that. Sheriff would skin me alive if I let you leave."

She tapped her foot against the floor. "You can follow me, discreetly, of course."

"No, ma'am, I can't. Ben said to stay here. You don't want to put your son in danger, do you?"

Of course she didn't. Leigh clenched her jaw, sending a spasm down her neck. Deputy Jenkins was entirely too complacent. He could at least sound worried. "But what if whoever did this goes to the babysitter's house? He may even be there now."

"Ben sent a county constable over there. He'll contact the sheriff if anything unusual shows up."

Fear's grip on her heart loosened a little, but she still wanted TJ with her. Then again, she didn't want to scare him. And showing up at Jenny's house with a strange man wearing a gun . . . that would definitely freak TJ out.

She sank into the overstuffed chair and rubbed the bridge of her nose. No need to add that to her Bad Mom column. Along with uprooting him and bringing him to Logan Point. Only last week, she'd overheard him confide in Bear that he missed Miss Sarah and his friends. Sarah. She needed to call her, tell her about Tony.

Leigh turned her head toward the window as tires crunched in the drive. "Maybe that's Ben." Or the shooter returning. Her heart lodged in her throat.

"I got this," Jenkins called to the deputy in the kitchen. He eased to the window and looked out. "Ian and Danny Maxwell."

She took a shaky breath and rose. "Tony's bosses. Let them in."

The other deputy stood guard beside Leigh as Jenkins opened the door before they knocked. "Come in, gentlemen."

Ian stepped through the doorway first, his brows knit into question marks over his light blue eyes. "Leigh, what's going on? Are the deputies here because of what happened to Tony?"

Danny was right behind him, a slightly taller and heavier version of his cousin with high cheekbones and blond hair but with darker blue eyes. "Are you all right?"

Unexpected tears sprang to Leigh's eyes, and she blinked them back. "I'm okay now. How did you find out about Tony?"

Ian was beside her in an instant, clasping her hands in his own. "When Tony didn't show up this morning, I called his cell phone, and it went to voice mail. Then Danny came in and said he'd heard Tony was killed last night. Why didn't you call?"

It had never occurred to her. "I . . . his death was such a shock . . . then the house . . . shooting this morning—"

"Shooting? What are you talking about?"

She pressed her hand against her head. "Someone ransacked the house last night. Ben thinks the person was looking for some flash drive that Tony had." She swallowed, remembering the sound of gunfire. "This morning someone tried to kill me."

"What!" they said in unison.

Leigh caught her breath. The words had tumbled from her mouth, and now tremors started in her shoulders and worked through her body. Tony's death, the shooting this morning—nothing seemed real until this very minute. It was as if suddenly her mind comprehended that Tony was gone and nothing would ever be the same.

Ian wrapped his arm around her and guided her to the couch. His concern set off her tears, and she buried her face in his shoulder, inhaling the faint fragrance of sandalwood cologne. It reminded her of the fragrance Tony wore. She couldn't stop the flow of tears.

"It's going to be okay, Leigh." Ian patted her shoulder. "But you can't stay here. You need to be somewhere safe."

She pulled away from him. Black mascara streaked his white dress shirt, and she pressed her fingers against her lips. "I've ruined your shirt. I'm so sorry."

"Don't worry—it's washable. Let's talk about a place for you to stay. I have a condo and a house sitting empty, and it won't take but a couple of days to get either one ready. Take your pick."

She dabbed her eyes with a tissue he handed her. "I want to stay here. My son's life is going to be disrupted enough when he learns Tony died."

Danny cleared his throat. "You said something about Tony and a flash drive. What was on it?"

A nerve pinched in her neck, and she massaged the knotted

muscles. "I don't know. Ben thinks it's important to find it, though. But why would someone try to kill me because of it? None of this makes sense." More tears flowed. Why couldn't she quit crying? She wiped her eyes with the back of her hand. "Why would anyone want to kill Tony in the first place?"

"That's what I want to know," Ben said.

Leigh turned toward the door as Ben entered the house like a bull elephant. She hadn't heard him drive up.

Ian stood and held out his hand. "Sheriff, I'm so glad you were here this morning."

Danny nodded curtly.

The Golden Boy. Danny's nickname from high school stirred in her memory. The three of them graduated together three years after Ian. Tension mounted in the room as Ben took Ian's outstretched hand and barely acknowledged Danny. So their rivalry had carried beyond high school.

Ben eyed the two men. "Which one of you employed Billy Wayne Gresham?"

Ian straightened the cuff on his dress shirt. "Billy Wayne? He maintains our computer system."

Danny tilted his head. "You said employed, as in past tense."

"He just wrapped his motorcycle around that oak tree in the big curve on Highway 310. Dead at the scene. We found a Sub-2000 and two 9 mm magazines in his saddlebag."

Leigh gasped. "Is he the one who shot at us?"

"Possibly. Unfortunately, he died, so I can't ask him."

She pressed her fist against her mouth. First Tony and now another death. This Gresham man had tried to kill her, but she couldn't help but feel pain for those he left behind. She didn't want anyone to hurt like she hurt over Tony.

"If Billy Wayne fired the shots and he's dead, then the danger is over for Leigh?" Danny asked.

Hope edged its way into her mind. Could her nightmare be over?

And she could stay in her house. She wouldn't have to go to the Logans'. Leigh held her breath, waiting for Ben's answer.

"I won't know until I get the ballistics report back," Ben said. "Until then, I'll operate under the assumption that the person who shot at us this morning is still out there."

That meant Ben wouldn't let her out of his sight. Her shoulders sagged.

Danny rubbed his chin. "But you believe Gresham is that person. Do you think he killed Tony?"

"Look, I'm not discussing this case with you." He turned to Leigh. "Would you like to go pick up your son?"

"Definitely. But you don't have to go now. There's no danger."

He rested his hand on his gun. "I'm afraid it doesn't work that way. I'm ready whenever you are."

She didn't want to argue with him in front of Ian and Danny and turned to the cousins. "Thanks for stopping by. It means a lot."

"Tony was a good guy. He'll be missed." Danny shot Ben a dark look as he walked toward the door.

Ian squeezed her hand. "If you need anything, anything at all, give me a call."

"I will. And thank you for offering me a place to stay."

When the door closed behind the Maxwells, Leigh eyed Ben. "What is it with you and Danny? You're still like oil and water."

"You think? What did you mean about Ian offering a place to stay?"

She lifted her shoulder. "He had a couple of empty rental places and thought one of them would be safer than here. But now I don't need to leave." She cocked her head. "Why don't you like Danny? I mean, this isn't high school anymore."

His lips pressed together in a thin line. "He's never had to work for anything—everything just falls into place for him."

"You sound a little jealous. How about Ian?"

Ben stiffened. "I am not jealous. And Ian's different. He works hard. I've heard he's the first one at the plant and the last one to leave." He stared at her a moment. "I thought you wanted to go get your son."

"I do, but I want to go by myself."

"Ain't happening. Until I know for sure that Gresham is your shooter, either me or one of my deputies will be with you. I can send Jenkins, but are you sure you want to pick TJ up with some deputy he doesn't know tagging along? At least he knows me."

Leigh hated to admit he might be right. But she didn't understand Ben's attitude. What was his problem? "Okay."

"What's your plan? Will you tell him at the babysitter's or bring him back here?"

Leigh winced. She hadn't thought about what she'd tell TJ, much less where she'd tell him. An ache settled in her heart. TJ had loved his Uncle Tony. She pinched the bridge of her nose. "Here, I guess. I just wish Sarah was here."

"Who's Sarah?" Ben's voice had softened.

"Sarah Alexander took me in after Matthew died. She needed someone to take care of her after a minor surgery but ended up taking care of us." Leigh rubbed the back of her neck. Sarah would know what to do. The older woman's words rang in her head. *"Call God. He's always home and you never get a busy signal."*

Maybe God would help her—she was his child, had been since right after Matthew died and Sarah had led her to him. But the way she'd ignored God lately, it'd be more likely that he'd have a hard time remembering who she was.

5

Leigh pulled her white Avenger into the drive of the babysitter's red brick house and parked in the shade of a maple tree.

"Is this okay?" she asked. At least Ben had acquiesced to coming in her car rather than his truck with the Bradford County Sheriff logo on the side.

Ben craned his neck, looking around. "Should be."

She'd talked with Jenny on the drive over, and the babysitter had assured her TJ was fine, albeit a little antsy because she wouldn't let him outside. Leigh waited for Ben to get out and scan the area. She'd noticed he kept glancing in the side mirror, presumably to make sure no one followed them. The thought sent a shiver down her spine.

"It's clear."

She stepped out of her car and led the way around to the back door and pressed the bell.

"TJ, your mom's here!" Jenny yelled over her shoulder as she opened the door. Then she hugged Leigh. "I'm so sorry about Tony."

"Thanks," Leigh whispered. Every condolence got a little harder. She quickly pulled away as TJ bounded into the kitchen, dressed in his favorite ragged jeans.

"Mom! You're late!" He wrinkled his freckled nose.

Lately he'd been talking in nothing but exclamation points,

nearly wearing her out. She knew better than to hug him in front of Jenny; instead she tousled his straight copper hair that stuck out in all directions. A straw hat and corncob pipe and he'd be perfect for the role of Huck Finn.

He skidded to a stop when he saw Ben. "Whoa! What're you doing here, Ben? And you're wearing your gun!"

"I, ah, was at your house and decided to come with your mom."

"Cool." TJ turned to Leigh. "Are you off today? 'Cause if you are, you can come to baseball practice with me this afternoon. You remember, I told you about the team . . . Miss Jenny took me to practice last week, and Uncle Tony's taking me this afternoon, but if you're not working—"

"Slow down, son."

"But I want you to see me play. We got a game this weekend, and you'll probably have to work."

"Oh . . . We'll see." Leigh vaguely remembered something about a ball practice last week. "Are you ready to go home?"

"Can I start the car?"

She held out the keyless remote. He grabbed it and shot for the door. "Wait and walk out with me," she called to him. At the door, Leigh paused. "I'll call you later today," she said to Jenny.

TJ stopped a few feet from the car and pressed the remote, and the car jumped to life. He grinned at Ben. "It's like magic."

When Ben grinned back, Leigh's breath caught in her chest. For the barest second, the resemblance between TJ and Ben flashed like a neon sign. She blinked, and it was gone. What if someone else saw it? No, she was just looking for it. TJ looked just like her. Everyone said so—her coloring, her hair, the shape of her nose. He didn't have her eye color, but neither were they dark brown like Ben's. More of a hazel. But what if someone did notice the little ways he was like Ben? That grin, for one thing, and he had Ben's lanky frame and broad shoulders. But it'd be years before that would be noticeable.

Tony was gone, no need to stick around Logan Point now. She would call her advisor, see if she could get a transfer to another rural hospital until she finished her contract.

Ben touched her arm, sending a shiver straight to her heart. "Leigh, are you okay?"

She shook her head, clearing it. "I'm fine. TJ, hop in the back and fasten your seat belt."

On the short drive back to her house, Leigh rehearsed what she'd say to her son. Everything that came to mind sounded so stilted, cold. Her stomach churned at the thought of telling him. She glanced in the rearview mirror and caught TJ's eye. "When we get home, come inside with me."

"Aw, Mom, I want to practice my swing."

She gripped the steering wheel and stared straight ahead. "After we talk," she choked out.

When they pulled into the driveway, Leigh realized she should've taken TJ to the park to tell him about Tony—she'd forgotten Ben's deputies were still combing the area for evidence. She flicked Ben a glance. "Why didn't you remind me they were still here?"

He shrugged. "You were so bent on doing things your way, I thought I'd let you."

Leigh ground her molars. She needed someone to save her from herself.

"Mom, what are those guys doing here?"

"They're looking for something," Ben said before she could answer.

"Can I help?"

"Not right now. Let's go in the house. Your mom wants to talk to you."

TJ jumped out of the car and raced to the door. "Mom!" He pulled it out to two syllables. "The door is locked! Hurry. I want to get my bat!"

Leigh dragged her feet. She didn't want to do this. Tony was the closest thing TJ had ever known for a dad. And this last month after they'd moved in, her brother had really stepped up to the plate.

"Do you think Uncle Tony will take off from work early?" TJ's eyes widened in little-boy eagerness.

"There's something I have to tell you about Uncle Tony . . ." Leigh sucked in a deep breath.

■ ■ ■

Leigh listened from the hallway outside the living room as Ben and TJ talked. Ben had given her a startled glance when she asked if he would stay with TJ while she found something, but he'd stayed. It had taken her a few minutes to remember where she'd put TJ's stuffed animal, but after finding it, she'd hurried back to the living room with every intention of making her presence known. But a glimpse of Ben in the living room mirror, sitting stiffly beside TJ, stopped her.

"It's okay for boys to cry, you know."

Ben was trying, at least. In the reflection, TJ's chin quivered, and he looked down. "Big boys don't cry."

She swallowed down the lump in her throat. She waited for Ben's reply, wanting to stop this interaction, but could not get her legs to move.

"Sometimes they do, TJ. When a hurt is this big, it's okay."

She covered her mouth with her hand as TJ threw his arms around Ben, burying his head in Ben's shoulder. His small frame shook as the tears came.

"Why did God take Tony?" TJ's muffled words echoed in her own heart.

Ben's hand finally came up to pat TJ on the back. "I don't know, TJ. Bad things happen sometimes, and we don't know why. But God is here with you. He'll get you through this."

She leaned against the wall. This didn't sound like the Ben of ten years ago. Maybe he'd changed.

55

"It's going to be okay. You've got your mom."

"But what if someone hurts her?"

There was silence, and she could imagine Ben patting her son's back again. "I won't let anyone hurt her."

"Will you come to ball practice with me?"

The want in TJ's voice curled around her heart, squeezing it. As much as she didn't want Ben around her son, it would mean so much to TJ for him to be there, especially right now. She held her breath, waiting for Ben's answer.

"Ah, uh . . . I'm sorry, TJ, I just don't have time."

Relief mingled with disappointment. Relief that she didn't have to worry about Ben spending time with TJ, but disappointment for her son as he heaved a sigh.

She rounded the corner into the living room. "Hey, look what I found." She held the stuffed animal out to her son. His look said "Aw, Mom, not now," and she pulled the bear back, hugging it to her chest. "Maybe I'll hold on to him for a bit."

She gave Ben a sidelong glance and caught her breath. Sweat beaded his bloodless face. "Are you okay?"

"Yeah." He clipped the word off and stood. "I need to help my deputies finish up."

She laid the toy bear on the sofa and followed him to the door. "The deputies won't be staying, will they? I mean, if this Gresham is the shooter, I won't need protection any longer," she said, keeping her voice low.

Ben seemed to be fighting for control. He took a deep breath. "They will be staying." He wiped his hands on his jeans. "Gresham may not have acted alone."

"You don't know that." She wanted to get her life back to normal.

"No, I don't, and that's why Jenkins and Ford will be hanging around." He opened the door, and his gaze slid past Leigh to her son sitting on the couch. "You have a good kid there."

"Yeah, I know."

"Look, uh, if TJ needs someone to talk to . . ." He licked his lips. "You can, uh, call me."

Ben puzzled her. One minute he didn't have time, the next, he wanted her to call him. "Thanks. Now if you'll excuse me, I have a funeral to plan."

He paused before going out the door, and she looked away from his intense stare.

"I'll be around if you need me," he said.

Where was he ten years ago when she came home to tell him she was pregnant? She shook the thought off. That wasn't all his fault. She hadn't exactly given him an option. "Thanks."

With one last glance, he turned and walked toward his deputies. She shut the door firmly behind him and leaned her head against it with her eyes closed.

"You okay, Mom?"

TJ's subdued voice snapped her eyes open. Her son hugged Bear to his chest. She mustered a smile. "I'm okay." She crossed the room and sat beside him. "How about you? Are you okay?"

He shrugged. His chin dimpled as he pressed his lips together. "Will the bad guy come back?"

Her stomach sank to her feet. She and Ben had tried to downplay what happened this morning, but evidently it hadn't worked. "I don't think so, honey. Ben was pretty sure the man that wrecked is the bad guy. He won't be coming back. Okay?"

He stared at Bear's belly, picking at the seam she'd stitched. "Why did Uncle Tony have to die?"

Leigh pulled him close, smelling the fruity scent of his shampoo. She kissed the top of his head. "I don't know."

After a few minutes, TJ pulled away. "Can I go outside?"

"Hmm, maybe not just yet. Why don't you play a game on your iPod?"

His eyes grew round. "Really?"

"Just today." She limited the time TJ spent playing video games to an hour after dinner, but she had calls to make, calls she didn't want him to overhear. And the first one was to see how fast they could get out of Logan Point.

■ ■ ■

After Ben left instructions with his deputies to hang around, he climbed into the cab of his truck. For five minutes he didn't move, just breathed slow, deep breaths and pictured a big stop sign. What kind of man had a panic attack when a kid asked him to come to ball practice? He was the sheriff, for goodness' sake, a man's man. Not some weak-kneed sissy who couldn't handle being around kids. Except he was, and no matter how hard he tried, he couldn't stop the panic attacks. Maybe it was time to see that counselor again.

When his heart finally returned to normal, Ben called his chief deputy and learned Wade was at Gresham's house. "Did you get a search warrant?"

"Yep," Wade replied. "How did Mrs. Gresham take the news?"

Ruby hadn't cried. Just thanked him for coming to tell her, then turned and walked back into the house. "Stoic. Almost like she was expecting me." Ben sighed. "See you in about ten minutes."

Since Billy Wayne lived alone, a search warrant probably wasn't necessary. But Ben had learned a long time ago, it was better to have the warrant than to wish down the road he'd obtained one. Now, if there was only something at Gresham's house to settle his mind, something that would tell him whether the kid acted alone or with someone else. Leigh seemed determined to stay in that little house, and he'd like to be comfortable in agreeing with her.

He'd like to be comfortable around her period—without getting too close. Leigh was getting to be a bit like a barnacle, attaching herself to his heart. For a nanosecond this morning, the wall between them hadn't seemed so thick, and it'd been like old times. Then in a heartbeat, she couldn't get rid of him fast enough. Which suited him fine.

Turning onto the highway, Ben flipped his sun visor down, and TJ's earnest face popped into his mind. *Will you come to ball practice with me?* Why couldn't the kid stick with easy questions? Like the one Sunday. *How did Jonah get spit up by the whale? Did he go through the blowhole?*

No, he had to ask the impossible. If Ben showed up at ball practice with Leigh's son, his deputy, Andre, would hound him about coaching, and no matter how much he'd like to coach, he truly didn't want everyone to see him in full-blown panic mode. Kids, little ones or teenagers, came with a high price tag, and the plain fact was, he couldn't take the responsibility.

He slowed for the intersection ahead as a car and boat shot across the highway. One of the most popular boat landings on Logan Lake was Caney Point, two miles from the intersection. A cloud crossed the sun, dimming its brightness. Tommy Ray Gresham had been fifteen with his whole future ahead of him when he drowned at the Point. Ben blew out a deep breath and white-knuckled the steering wheel down the road.

His radio crackled to life. "Ben, found something interesting at Billy Wayne's."

"Be there in five." Ben pressed his foot to the gas. Minutes later he rolled to a stop in front of a brick bungalow and parked behind Wade's truck. Weeds brushed his legs as he cut a swath to the front door. He opened the screen door and stepped into a tiny living room. "Where are you, Wade?"

"In the bedroom. Down the hall on the right."

Ben's footsteps echoed on the hardwood floors. "What did you find?"

Wade sat at a desk in front of a laptop. "For starters, that," he said, jerking his head toward the dresser. A .38 Smith and Wesson lay on the dresser, with a numbered card beside it. "It was under his mattress. Has Olivia Reynolds mentioned what caliber gun was used on Tony Jackson?"

"She won't know until she gets a report back from the crime lab in Nashville, but she thought it might be a .38 or 9 mm. Anything on the laptop?"

Wade scooted his chair where Ben could see the monitor. "See for yourself. He was a big-time gamer."

Ghoulish images against a blood-red background filled the computer screen. Hooded or masked cartoon images depicting death and murder. Ben read over Wade's shoulder as his deputy scrolled the page.

"Looks like he's a game programmer," Wade said.

"Apparently for some pretty violent games." Ben shook his head.

"Look at this." Wade moved the cursor to another link. "He played them as well. And evidently he was pretty good—this one has twenty levels and four bonus ones." The deputy glanced up at Ben. "He'd made it to the bonus rounds."

"You sound like that's something good. Real or not, all that killing can mess with the mind."

"Not saying that people don't get the game world and the real world mixed up, just pointing out he thinks like a killer. It could be a motive if he killed Tony and then went after Leigh." He popped another screen up. "Read this. It's a teaser for one of his games."

Ben read the first lines and sucked in a breath. *The Assassin* read like a script for stalking and murdering a victim. He scanned to the bottom of the page. "What does that link to?"

"His fan page on Facebook." Wade clicked on the link and another page opened.

"He chose the Reaper as his name?" Ben muttered. "Really classy."

Wade nodded toward the gun. "If that matches the slugs found in Tony's body, I'd say you have your killer. And Leigh's shooter."

"Which begs the question of why," Ben said as he slipped his cell from his pocket and surveyed the blacked-out windows, the clothes littering the floor. He could imagine the oily-haired gamer hunched over the computer, plotting death. He shuddered. It was impossible to understand the depravity that existed in the world. He turned back to the computer screen as he punched in Livy's number. She answered without any preliminaries. "Did you find anything at the house, Ben?"

"Maybe. We found a .38 Smith and Wesson at Gresham's." He filled her in on the rest. "I'll send two deputies over with the gun."

"A .38, huh? I've seen a lot of fired bullets, and what the coroner dug out of Tony could have been fired from a .38."

"I'll email you his websites," Ben said. "You might want to check them out." He hung up and emailed the sites from his phone.

"Check this out, Ben. A couple of comments you might be interested in. One from Billy Wayne grousing about losing money to Tony and a reply from his brother."

Ben leaned over the computer again. Wade had found Billy Wayne's personal Facebook page, and Junior Gresham had left a rather rude comment. "He doesn't think much of his brother's gambling abilities."

Wade chuckled. "No, he doesn't. Junior works at Maxwell Industries."

"Wrap up the investigation here while I pay a visit to the plant." Ben checked his watch. "It's eleven now. We'll meet back at the jail around one to discuss getting the gun to Livy in Memphis."

Maxwell Industries was located in the industrial park on the western side of Logan Point, near the bypass, and fifteen minutes later, Ben pulled into the visitor's parking area. He stepped from his pickup into the hot, humid air and surveyed the factory that sat on twenty acres of ground. A far cry from its beginnings.

Brothers Phillip and Anderson Maxwell started a porcelain factory in 1980 when a vein of kaolin was discovered in Bradford County. Since then, two things had happened. Manufacturing costs had risen to the point that Maxwell Industries now shipped the raw product to Mexico, where it was processed into fine china and then shipped back to Logan Point for distribution.

Then, in the late nineties after Anderson died, Phillip Maxwell turned a desire to build a quality rifle into a reality. Built with precision and quality craftsmanship, the Maxwell .270 soon became a hot item with deer hunters, and the porcelain side of Maxwell Industries took a backseat to the rifle division. Ben even owned one of the firearms.

But the .270 wasn't the only rifle manufactured at the plant. Five years ago, Phillip Maxwell took the factory in a different direction when he developed a variation of the AR-15 for the law enforcement community. Again, because of the quality, the new rifle was a success. Ben's department had five of the assault rifles. He sincerely hoped none of the Maxwells were involved in this case. If the plant shut down, more than two hundred people would lose their jobs.

He stopped at the receptionist desk and asked to see Phillip Maxwell, noting the name on the brass plate. Tiffany Davis. After a brief phone conversation, the tawny-eyed brunette nodded. "Mr. Maxwell will see you."

"Thank you, Tiffany." Ben climbed the stairs to Maxwell's office.

Maxwell opened the door before he knocked. "Come on in."

Ben's feet sank into plush gold carpet as he stepped into the room. Like everything else Phillip Maxwell touched, the office reeked of class—walnut paneling, rich tan leather, and an ornate desk designed to intimidate. But then, even in his late fifties, the man himself intimidated. Standing at six-four, the former quarterback for the New Orleans Saints shook Ben's hand with the same confidence he'd handled the pigskin more than thirty years ago.

"I stopped by to see Tom last week," Maxwell said as he released Ben's hand. "His speech doesn't seem to be improving that much."

"I know. For some reason, he won't work with the speech therapist."

"I told him what a great job you were doing, and he seemed to understand that. And, if there's ever a time you need something from me, just say the word."

"I appreciate that." He waited until Maxwell had seated himself behind the massive desk before he chose a leather chair that didn't put him lower than the older man.

Maxwell leaned forward, his blue eyes intense. "Do you know who killed Tony yet?"

"His case falls under the Memphis Police Department jurisdiction."

"I didn't ask whose jurisdiction it fell under."

Ben crossed his ankle over his knee. Maxwell was used to getting what he wanted, when he wanted it. "Nothing concrete. Just a person of interest."

"Billy Wayne Gresham? Leigh's shooter?"

Danny and Ian had wasted no time reporting back to Maxwell. "Billy Wayne hasn't been identified as her shooter. Or Tony's murderer."

The ice-blue eyes bored into him. "Come on, Ben. Your dad couldn't bluff me, and neither can you. Are you looking for anyone else?"

His dad and Maxwell had been friends for years, coffee buddies at Molly's Diner, and they played golf together before his dad's stroke. Maxwell had his finger on the pulse of Logan Point, and more than likely, Tom Logan wouldn't have hesitated to confide in him. But Ben wasn't his dad. "What can you tell me about Billy Wayne? Do you know who he hung out with?"

Amusement flickered in Maxwell's face as he leaned back in his chair and tented his fingers. "Billy Wayne and I ran in different circles. He was a strange boy. Wild, and I feared he'd end up dead too young. Feel sorry for his poor mama. She works here, you know. In packing. As does one of his brothers. I've told her to take as much time off as she needs."

"She didn't say much when I told her he'd been killed." Ben took out a pen and pad. "I understand Billy Wayne did some work for Maxwell Industries. Did he answer to your son and nephew or to you?"

"Ian hired him. He answered to him."

Ben nodded. "Did Ian or Danny pal around with Billy Wayne?"

"I hope you're not insinuating either of them are involved with Billy Wayne's illegal activities or Tony's death."

Ben paused with the pen raised. Odd that Maxwell would jump to that conclusion. Maybe there was fire in the smoke. "Ian? No. Your son, maybe."

"You're barking up the wrong tree with Danny." Maxwell leaned forward. "And I wouldn't be too quick to put Ian in a box labeled squeaky clean."

Ben hid a smile. Irritate people a little, and unusual things popped out sometimes. "Really? Anything you'd care to share?"

"No. Just be careful about prejudging. Danny is a good boy. Perhaps a little reckless sometimes. I'd hoped he would marry Bailey Adams and settle down, but . . ." He shrugged. "I know you two have been rivals in the past, but he respects you."

That was news to Ben. He didn't realize Danny respected anyone or anything, except maybe Bailey. But she'd chosen to teach school at a mission in Mexico instead of marrying Danny Maxwell.

Maxwell leaned forward. "Where Danny's focus might be on seeing how close he can get to the fire without getting singed, Ian is more preoccupied with the ladies."

The image of Ian with his arm around Leigh pricked Ben. "I heard he's getting married."

Maxwell stood and walked to the expanse of glass across his office. "Girls have been chasing him since he was sixteen, and he's avoided matrimony for twenty years. Not sure if this latest girlfriend will rope him in." He put his hands behind his back. "You didn't mention me. Am I under suspicion as well?"

"Hardly. And I never said Ian and Danny were. Just trying to find some answers." Ben joined him at the window that looked out over the plant. "So from here you can tell who's shirking and who's not?"

"That's not a problem around here. We treat our employees well. Good pay, great benefits, and stock in the company equal good morale. No, I just like to look down at the line and know one of the best rifles in America is being made here."

"Do you know where Billy Wayne could've bought a Sub-2000?"

"Is that what he used to shoot at Leigh?"

"Maybe." A question answered with a question. Phillip was crafty. "Do you have a connection with Billy Wayne?"

Maxwell slapped him on the back. "I like you, Ben. If you're looking for an accomplice, you can stop. From what I know about him, he was a loner and definitely smart enough to pull this off without any help. Okay? As for the Sub-2000, he could've picked one up at a gun show, a private dealer, the Internet, even. They're not expensive, and from what I hear, a fairly decent gun."

Ben cocked his head slightly, studying the older man. Maxwell held his gaze, not flinching. "Do you mind if I ask a few questions about Billy Wayne around the plant?" He didn't have to ask permission, but it cost him nothing to defer to Maxwell's position.

Maxwell gave a faint nod. "Help yourself."

Ben extended his hand. "Thanks. Do you suppose someone could let me into Tony's office?"

"I'll instruct the receptionist to show you the way." Maxwell grasped his hand in a firm grip. "One more thing. You and Danny go way back, so you know he's hotheaded. Your dad always cut Danny a little slack. I'd appreciate it if you carried on the tradition."

Ben released Maxwell's hand and crossed his arms over his chest. He'd observed Danny breezing through town in his SUV or a little red Lexus convertible, just barely over the speed limit—not enough to pull him over and have to argue with him about. "I hope you're not asking me to break the law."

He palmed his hand up. "Of course not. I never asked your dad to break the law. I'm just asking for a little grace now and then. I don't want him to lose his license."

"Then I suggest you tell him to slow down." He started toward the door and stopped. "I know Ian manages the plant, but I've never understood Danny's job here."

"He oversees the international aspect of our operation. The shipment of raw supplies to Mexico, the points of distribution all over the world, that sort of thing."

Which probably fed his roving nature. "He doesn't handle the rifle sales and distribution?"

"I still handle that aspect of the business."

Ben opened the door. "Don't forget to tell him to slow down."

He felt Maxwell's eyes on him as he walked down the steps and across to Tiffany's desk.

She hung up the phone and stood as he approached. "Mr. Maxwell said you wanted to see Tony's office?"

"Please." As he followed the petite brunette, he couldn't help but notice that she kept herself distanced from him. Rigid back and shoulders, cool demeanor. "Were you and Tony dating, Tiffany?" he asked as they stopped for her to enter a code before going into the office complex.

Her fingers missed a button, and she had to start over. "What makes you think that?" She pushed the door open and allowed him to go through first.

"Am I right?"

She lifted her shoulder in a half shrug. "A few times."

"Is that allowed here?"

"Tony did pretty much what Tony wanted to do, but he never, you know, abused it. He just had that kind of personality. I don't know why anyone would want to kill him." Unshed tears brightened her golden eyes.

Ben studied the receptionist. "How was your relationship lately?"

"It was fine."

The tremor in her voice indicated their relationship was definitely not fine. "When did you last see him? As in a date?"

66

"About six weeks ago." The corners of her mouth turned down. "Tony had been acting a little strange lately, but he'd been busy getting his sister and her son settled in, so he didn't have much personal time."

"Did that bother you?"

"Of course it bothered me, but I didn't kill him over it. I knew sooner or later, he'd be back. Of course, now . . ." She heaved a sigh.

"Who do you think will get Tony's job?"

Her eyes narrowed. "Geoffrey Franks. He's been eying Tony's job ever since he worked his way into management. Not that he would've ever gotten it as long as Tony was around."

"This Franks, has he worked at Maxwell Industries long?"

"He was here before I came, and I've been here eight years."

Ben nodded. "That's a long time to work as a receptionist. I imagine you see a lot that goes on."

She sniffed. "Well, you know, I do more than just sit at that desk and greet people. I coordinated Tony's flights, and not just Tony's. I book everyone's commercial flights and hotels. It's kind of my specialty, you know."

"Did you book Tony's room at the Peabody last night?"

She shook her head. "Is that where it, uh, happened?"

Ben nodded.

"It wasn't company business, so I wouldn't have booked it." She walked past him. "His office is down here on the right."

Tiffany unlocked the wooden door. "Like all the offices, it's—oh!" She stopped, and Ben almost bumped into her. "Geoffrey, I didn't know you were in here."

Franks looked as startled as Tiffany. His fingers flew over a keyboard and his computer screen darkened, then he swiveled his chair around to face them. "Can I help you with something?"

"Geoffrey Franks, I presume?" Franks imitated the dress code of his boss Ian, differing only with a bow tie rather than a necktie. Ben reached his hand out. "I'm Ben Logan."

"The sheriff," Tiffany added.

"I know who the sheriff is." Franks unfolded from the chair and stood. He was a couple of inches shorter than Ben, but compact. The accountant adjusted his black-rimmed glasses then clasped Ben's hand with a firm grip. "Yes, I'm Geoffrey Franks."

Tiffany's nostrils flared. "Well, no one told me you had already taken over Tony's office."

Ben didn't know if Tiffany's indignation stemmed from not being told or from Franks already commandeering Tony's office.

"I wasn't aware that upper management informed the receptionist of every change in job description."

Ouch. The man's pleasant appearance belied a sharp tongue. Ben turned to Tiffany. "Thanks for showing me the way. I'll stop by your desk on my way out."

"You're quite welcome, Sheriff." She leveled a frosty glare at the interloper as she walked out the door.

Geoffrey huffed a breath and shook his head. "Sometimes I think I should have accepted the accounting job with the school district. When one starts out on the line in a factory and moves into management, one never receives the proper respect."

"So you started with Maxwell Industries out in the plant?"

"Yes, in the shipping department, loading trucks. Then I moved to drilling the barrels on the rifles, the receiver building, you name it, I've done it here. Put me through college, though."

"And now you have Tony's job."

He nodded. "Not that I wanted it this way. Tony was a good guy."

"What exactly was Tony's job?"

"He kept up with inventory—every piece made each day, every Maxwell .270 and AR-15 assembled—it's all tracked. And he kept all the books, like payroll, federal deposits, insurance."

"Do you know of any enemies Tony may have had?"

"Other than Billy Wayne? I heard he's the one who killed Tony."

As always, news traveled fast in Logan Point. "Maybe. I'm just checking out a few other leads." He glanced around the paneled office. Smaller than Phillip's. A painting with bold red strokes drew his eye. Someone had good taste. "Did Tony download a lot of his work?"

"Oh no, sir. Any type of portable storage disk is totally forbidden here. Industrial espionage is a very real problem in the rifle industry. And there are very strict guidelines we follow. There was no reason Tony would download anything, especially since the new Maxwell .280 is in develop—" Geoffrey swallowed hard. "I should not have mentioned the .280."

"Don't worry, I won't pass it on." Ben jotted a note on his pad. "Did Billy Wayne have access to information on the computers?"

"No, he mostly worked on the networking end, or if one of the computers crashed, he'd get it going again." He scratched his jaw. "Although anyone that good with computers could probably access anything he wanted to."

"One more thing. Did you ever play cards with Tony?"

"I'm not a fool, Sheriff. Tony had a photographic memory—knew every card in play. It wasn't a fact that everyone knew, but if you were around him for any period of time, it became obvious. Of course, Billy Wayne didn't have a clue. I never understood how anyone could be almost a genius when it came to computers and be such an easy prey for Tony. Do you think that's the motive for his murder?"

"Could be." Ben glanced around the room. Nothing indicated Tony had ever inhabited the room. His gaze rested on a gray plastic tub in the corner. On the side someone had written "Tony's Personal Effects." Geoffrey, no doubt. "Were Ms. Davis and Tony an item?"

Amusement glinted in his eyes. "Tiffany would have you believe they were, but Tony was too married to his work and his hobbies to get serious about anyone. And then his sister and nephew took his time of late. I don't think Tiffany was too happy about that."

Ben didn't think the woman-spurned angle was worth pursuing. Unless Tiffany was psychotic, and she didn't seem to be, there didn't appear to be that much of a relationship between them. He put away his pad and pen. "Well, thanks for your time, Geoffrey. If you think of anything that might shed light on his death, I'd appreciate a call."

After exiting Geoffrey's office, he stopped at Tiffany's desk to thank her for her help.

She leaned forward in her chair. "I don't know if you picked up on it," she said, keeping her voice low, "but Geoffrey really wanted Tony's job."

"Do you think he would have killed him to get it?"

The corner of her mouth twitched, and her eagerness deflated. "No, I suppose not."

"I don't, either. But if you come up with anything else, run it by me. It could be important."

Her eyes widened. "I'll definitely do that."

"Is Junior Gresham here today?"

"He was, but he went home with his mother. That poor woman. I feel so sorry for her."

"Yeah," Ben said, thinking about her other son who had died. "So do I."

Ben took his time walking back to his truck. This trip had netted little information, and his thoughts went back to the flash drive. What could have been on it? Tony had indicated he had something the feds would be interested in, but so far Ben hadn't found a single clue as to what it was.

Maybe he wasn't killed over the flash drive. According to Geoffrey, Tony had a photographic memory, something he needed to check with Leigh about. Could that be why he was killed? Because someone lost a lot of money to him in a poker game?

But where did Billy Wayne Gresham fit? All the evidence pointed to him. Ben just didn't buy that he killed Tony over gambling debts. But if it wasn't gambling debts, what was it?

■ ■ ■

"Okay," Ben said. "If you were calling the shots, would you go with Billy Wayne acting alone in Leigh's shooting and killing Tony?"

They were in Wade's office, and Ben sat on the edge of the chief deputy's oak desk as the late afternoon sun filtered through the window. Photos of the chief deputy with his hunting dogs adorned the gray wall behind his chair.

Wade leaned back in his chair and juggled a Rubik's Cube. "You're not putting that monkey on my back. You're the sheriff, you make the call."

It was well known around the county that as Sheriff Tom Logan's chief deputy, Wade had expected the board of supervisors to appoint him as acting sheriff after Tom's stroke on the operating table. To Wade's credit, Ben hadn't detected any animosity from him in the intervening six months.

Ben snagged the cube. Wade had just worked the thing in under a minute. Again. He scrambled the squares before he looked up. "Not asking you to make the call, just a little input. Livy said the ballistics fingerprinting wouldn't be available until at least Thursday, and Leigh wants an answer today."

The deputy shrugged. "Don't see that you need it to confirm what you already know. You have two shootings, and we found two guns that could possibly match the types used in both crimes in Billy Wayne's bedroom. How many people do you know with a Sub-2000? Add to that his online journal where he vented about losing a substantial amount of money to Tony, and his stalker script for a new video game that paralleled the two shootings." He shot an imaginary basketball. "Slam dunk."

That was what bothered Ben. It was too easy. Except no one could've known Billy Wayne would slam into that oak tree this morning. A lucky break in the case. Maybe he should just be thankful. "Okay, pull the deputies off Leigh's detail, but have someone on each shift do random drive-bys."

"Will do."

Ben stared at the Rubik's Cube in his hands. He twisted the top row of squares to the right, then flipped the middle row and succeeded in totally messing up the pattern. Wade took the cube from him and soon had all six sides lined up. "How do you do that?" Ben asked.

He tossed the cube back to Ben. "If I told you, I'd have to kill you." Wade's cell phone dinged, and he checked his watch. "Oops, got to get to the park."

"For?"

Wade grinned. "Since you wouldn't help, Andre roped me into helping him coach." The chief deputy raised his eyebrows. "You know, I don't get it. You were a really good ballplayer, and the kids would learn a lot from you. So why aren't you helping?"

Ben's mouth went dry. Why did everyone keep harping on what he should do? "They don't need me when they have you."

Wade cocked his head. "Someday, Ben, you have to put Tommy Ray's death behind you. It wasn't your fault."

"That has nothing to do with it. I don't have time." He glanced away from Wade's still-raised eyebrows. "Look, here at the office, I have three of Dad's file cabinets to try to make sense out of, and since his stroke, I've taken on a lot of the things he used to do at home. And I have the Sunday school gig until Jeremy returns."

"You can lie to everyone else," Wade said, "but you can't lie to me."

"You're crazy." Ben waved him off. "I have to get started on those files—you've seen them and the crazy way he filed things."

"Yeah, yeah, I hear you."

6

Leigh shifted her weight as yet another person enveloped her in
an embrace and murmured words of comfort. "Thank you for
coming," she said, glancing at the receiving line that stretched
around the wall, out the door, and down the Stafford Funeral Home
hallway. She had no idea so many people loved Tony or that he'd
helped so many.

"Doc, I'm going to miss your brother." The wizened farmer
clasped her hand in his gnarled fingers. "He kept me from losing
my farm last year to back taxes."

At least now she had an idea of what he'd done with his money.
It made her feel bad that she hadn't really known her brother at all,
and that she'd thought Tony stayed in their grandparents' house
because he gambled his money away. "Thank you," she murmured
again as the farmer shuffled on to TJ.

She'd been surprised when her son wanted to stand in the receiving line and thank people for coming. Tony would be amused
to see his nephew dressed in a long-sleeved white shirt and tie, his
straight hair tamed under her hair spray. Leigh turned to meet the
next person and flinched when she spied Ben's mom near the door.
And behind her was Ian. It surprised her that Danny wasn't with
him. The two seemed to be joined at the hip.

"TJ, would you get me a bottle of water?"

A thin arm slipped around her waist. "Honey, why don't you sit down?" Sarah Alexander whispered.

Leigh patted her friend's hand. Sarah had come all the way from Jackson to be with her. "Not just yet."

The people of Logan Point had come out to pay their last respects to her brother. The least she could do was receive them. Thankfully, the funeral director cut off the receiving line before Marisa reached her, moving everyone to the chapel. Her frozen smile cracked a little as the service began with "In the Garden," Tony's favorite hymn. Then the pastor talked about how he'd come to know Tony, and what a fine man he was. Leigh hadn't known who the pastor was when he called and offered to conduct the service. She needed to remedy that—someone had to take TJ to church. Would Sarah consider . . . What was she thinking? Asking a seventy-three-year-old woman to move away from friends and the home where she'd lived for fifty years would be unconscionable. Almost as though she'd read her mind, Sarah squeezed her hand.

Numb. It was as though someone had injected her with a huge dose of novocaine. There was a clinical name for what her emotions were going through—acute stress reaction. She closed her eyes. Tony's death was so senseless. A gambling dispute. So, what part did the flash drive play in the whole thing? Their house had been ransacked—by Billy Wayne Gresham? Ben had said no flash drive had been found at Gresham's house. What if Billy Wayne hadn't acted alone? Only time would tell if the nightmare would end with the funeral today.

Leigh forced her mind back to what the pastor was saying. Something about Tony being the apple of God's eye, that he sees the hidden compartments of our hearts. *Hidden compartments.* A memory tugged . . . she and Tony, playing in the attic . . . a false wall . . . all those little cubicles. Could the flash drive be there?

Finally, the service ended and Tony's body was whisked away to the cemetery. She and TJ and Sarah would go later. TJ walked with the funeral director as he led Leigh and Sarah to the front reception area where more people waited to give their condolences. Leigh didn't know if she could do this one more time. Her father's funeral replayed in her head, and her mother's voice spoke from the past. *"You are a Jackson. These people loved your father, and they want to pay their respects."* She and Tony had stood in the receiving line together that day. Tears blurred her eyes. Today she stood without him.

Ian stepped toward her and took her hands in his. "I want you to know, if you need anything at all, I'm here. I want to help you and TJ."

Ian had caught her off guard. She had not yet fixed a smile on her face, and her bottom lip quivered. "Thank you. But we'll be fine."

Danny materialized on the other side of Ian. "If you want to live in someplace besides your grandmother's house, I have a couple of places. Or you can pick one of Ian's."

Danny's kindness almost undid her. "Thank you." She blotted her eyes with a tissue. "But we'll stay where we are."

She caught a whiff of Ben's outdoorsy cologne before he touched her arm. She hadn't seen him enter the room. Her heart thumped against her ribs.

"I wish I could change your mind about staying in your grand-mother's house. My folks would be glad for you to move in with them," Ben said.

Evidently voices carried in the cavernous room. Leigh clenched her jaw. "Why would I want to do that? You said a couple of days ago that Billy Wayne Gresham was the shooter." She'd caught a glimpse of Ben's truck a few times when he drove through her neighborhood, but he hadn't bothered to stop. And now he wanted her to move in with his parents?

"He may not have acted alone. I'd feel better knowing you were with someone."

"I am with someone. TJ is with me."

"All the more reason." Exasperation tinged his voice.

Leigh looked him up and down. Ben wore no gun today, but the authority of the sheriff's office rested in his stance, feet slightly apart, shoulders squared, and eyes seeming to take in every detail. She lifted her chin and used the voice she'd cultivated to deal with her male classmates in med school. "I see no reason for leaving my house."

He took a step back and held his hands up. "O-kay."

Next to Ben, Wade Hatcher nodded his condolences. More people moved forward, and one by one, Leigh thanked them for coming. Each person spoke first to TJ, then Sarah, and finally Leigh. Then Ben was at her side again, his cologne making her think of a meadow far away from this funeral home. "I had no idea Tony had so many friends," she murmured to him as the next person moved toward her.

"A lot of these people are here for you too."

That hadn't occurred to her, and the thought warmed her heart. "Oh, and thanks for driving by and checking on me."

"Have you noticed anything out of the ordinary?" Ben asked.

"No. Everything is calm. Oh, wait. Are you still looking for that flash drive?"

"Why? Did you find it?"

"No. It's just that during the service I remembered these hidden compartments in the corner of the attic. That would've been a logical place for Tony to hide something. I'll look tonight after it gets cooler. Right now it's 120 degrees in that attic, and there's no telling what's piled on top."

"You want me to come by and help you?"

"I'll wait until Sarah leaves, and I don't know when that will be." From the corner of her eye, she saw TJ squirm as an older lady hugged him. Her stomach flipped when she recognized Marisa Logan.

Leigh touched her son's arm. "TJ, would you like to go outside for a while?"

"Yes, ma'am!" Two black-haired boys, evidently twins, had joined him, and together they scooted out of the room.

"You have a mighty handsome young man there." Marisa's soft drawl chilled Leigh to the bone.

"Thank you." She licked her lips. "Have you met Sarah Alexander? She's TJ's adopted grandmother. Came up from Jackson to be with us."

Soft pressure from Sarah's hand stopped her babbling.

"And you have to be Sheriff Logan's mother," Sarah said. "The resemblance is very strong—the black hair, the dark eyes, he even has your beautiful olive complexion."

Anxiety ebbed away. TJ had none of those characteristics.

"Well, thank you, Sarah. Have you known Leigh and her son for very long?"

Sarah edged Marisa away from Leigh. "Since before he was born. Would you like to sit over by the window? I'd like to ask you a few questions about Logan Point."

Bless her heart and her little gray head. Leigh felt Ben's gaze on her and turned back to him.

"How did you meet Sarah? If you've told me, I've forgotten. Did you hire her as a nanny for TJ?"

"There was no money for a nanny. She was a friend of my husband's, and after Matthew died, I had to find a cheap place to live. Sarah needed surgery and someone to stay with her until she recovered. She had an older house with an apartment upstairs, so I offered, and it worked out very well. Sarah became a part of our lives. She really loves TJ." Leigh caught her breath. Ben hadn't asked for their whole history.

"Too bad she doesn't live here."

"I know. But he seems to like staying with Jenny while I'm at work. Of course, now that Tony's . . ." She simply couldn't say *dead*. "Anyway, he'll be staying there more."

"I'm sure my mom would be glad to keep him sometimes. He'd be good company for Josh and Jacob."

Now Leigh remembered where she'd seen the boys TJ left with.

They were the twin sons of Emily, her boss at the free clinic. And Ben's sister.

Everywhere she turned, TJ was wrapped up with one of the Logan family members. Coming back to Logan Point was such a mistake. A mistake she couldn't undo. She'd tried earlier this week, but the director had turned down her request to move, saying there were no openings anywhere in the state of Mississippi where she could transfer her service hours. She would be stuck in Logan Point for the remainder of her service contract unless someone opted out of the program.

■ ■ ■

TJ turned off the television. "Mom, can I go out and catch lightn' bugs?"

Thunder rumbled overhead, rattling the windows of the little house. "You know it's raining. There won't be any lightning bugs."

"Then can I play Pac-Man?" TJ grinned.

The little sneak. Leigh checked the time. "For thirty minutes."

"Give me a hug before you go," Sarah said. "I'm going back to the motel shortly, and I know you and that game."

"I still don't understand why you can't stay here," Leigh said.

"Girl, I'm not sleeping on a lumpy couch. I need my beauty sleep before I make that long trip back to Jackson."

Mentally, Leigh added the bedroom suite to her list of things to check on tomorrow. "Can't believe you drove two hundred miles from Jackson by yourself. But I'm glad you did."

"You think I'm too old?" She pushed her glasses up closer to her eyes. "I'll have you know, I'm scheduled to go to the Philippines this fall on a mission trip."

Leigh laughed out loud. It didn't take much to get Sarah's dander up. She hoped she had that much sass when she was seventy-three. "Ex-cuse me." She squeezed her thin hand. "I wish you lived up here. I could use a friend."

78

The chocolate eyes watered. She took Leigh's hands in her own strong hands. "I could spare you a couple of months . . ."

"I can't ask you to do that, and I'm leaving here as soon as I can find another hospital. Maybe I'll get one near Jackson." Leigh picked up Bear and traced her finger down the seam. She jumped as thunder boomed again and something hit the side of the house. All she needed was for that old post oak to fall.

"Why did you come back to Logan Point, feeling the way you do?"

"Tony asked me to."

"You could've said no."

"I tried, believe me. But he pulled the family card—said we only had each other, and he didn't want his nephew growing up not knowing who he was."

"He was right." Sarah spoke softly. "TJ still needs a family, especially now that Tony is gone. One you've been running from most of his life."

Leigh's heart caught in her throat, and she gaped at her friend. "I . . . I don't know what you—"

Sarah peered at Leigh over the top of her glasses. "I'm old, not blind."

"Matthew is—"

"No, he's not. Matthew was a good and kind man, but he's not TJ's father. Today I met the one who is. You should tell Ben—it's obvious he doesn't know."

Leigh's insides melted. If Sarah saw the resemblance between TJ and Ben, it wouldn't take long for someone else to make the connection. "How did you know?"

"Didn't have to. I knew Matthew before I knew you, child. That boy was in love with you. He talked to me before he asked you to marry him. He didn't know who TJ's father was, but that didn't matter to him. He loved you, and he would love your baby."

Leigh tried to lift her arms in protest, but her muscles refused to move. Matthew had literally saved her life. They'd worked at the same restaurant, and he'd discovered her in the alley one night, throwing up. He guessed her problem, and a month later when she caught pneumonia, he'd taken care of her. When he asked her to marry him, she'd said yes, partly because her child needed a father. "I did love Matthew. Maybe not like I loved Ben, but he was so kind."

"You made him happy," Sarah said. "Tell me about Ben."

Leigh closed her eyes, thinking back to those years. "We went to high school together, then went off to different colleges. The summer after my junior year, I came home during summer break and worked at a youth camp. Ben worked there too. For the first time, he really saw me. I wasn't just his chemistry partner or someone he teased in high school.

"Besides, I had changed." Leigh pulled on her bottom lip, remembering. "From the time I moved to Logan Point when I was twelve until my first year at college, I wasn't . . . let's just say most parents wouldn't want their kids around me."

"I don't believe you were that bad," Sarah said.

"Picture purple hair one day and jet-black spikes the next. Rings in my eyebrow. Ran with the wrong crowd. Straight A student though and never did drugs. That was Tony's deal.

"No, I just flouted the rules. Even went to work at the local 'dance' club." She held her hand up. "I just worked the cash register. Some of the ladies in town complained, and Sheriff Tom Logan hauled all the girls in one day. Me included. Told us we needed to find a different job. My smart mouth almost got us all put in jail."

"I just can't see you being that way. Why? And what changed you?"

"Why? I had a lot of built-up anger. My dad died, and my mom moved us to Logan Point and then committed suicide two years later. Before she did, she told me I would never amount to anything." Leigh pressed her lips together and looked toward the ceiling. "I set out to prove her right."

80

"I never knew." Sarah patted her hand. "I'm so sorry. How did you go from that to becoming a doctor?"

"I went away to college in Jackson, and a professor took me under her wing. Pointed me in the right direction."

Sarah smiled. "Good for her. But if you were in Jackson, how did you and Ben get together?"

"My grandmother still lived here, and I always came home at Christmas and a few weekends. But the summer before my senior year, I didn't take any classes. She wanted me to come home and talk to Tony. He'd dropped out of college and still ran with the wrong crowd.

"I did, but it didn't do any good. Anyway, that summer, Ben and I ended up working at the same camp. We started dating and kept dating when we returned home. It wasn't long before we realized we were in love.

"His dad didn't like it one bit. He wanted Ben to follow in his footsteps someday and be sheriff. And even though I no longer had the spiked hair and the piercings, he still saw me as that person. But we didn't care. We were in love, and one night . . ." Leigh looked down. "We knew we shouldn't, but we got caught up in the moment." She took a deep breath. "Right after that, Sheriff Logan came to me. He'd picked up Tony and a bunch of his friends on marijuana charges. Said if I'd back away from Ben, he'd drop the charges against Tony. But I couldn't tell Ben why. Tom said it was only a summer fling, anyway."

Leigh lifted her shoulders in a shrug. "I wanted to let Tony go to jail—he needed to learn a lesson. But, before I gave Sheriff Logan an answer, I went to see my brother. He didn't know about the deal.

"Tony begged me to get a lawyer. He swore to me on our dead father's grave it wasn't his marijuana, that one of the guys he was with planted it on him, and if I would help him, he would change. No more drugs, no more hanging out with potheads." Leigh shook her head. "I never could say no to him, and I really didn't want him to go to jail."

Sarah pressed her hand to her chest. "What did you tell Ben?"

"I called him and told him I didn't want to see him again. That I didn't have time to be distracted by a long-distance relationship. That was the last time I talked to him until the night Tony was murdered."

"He never tried to see you again?"

"He called, and my grandmother told him I wasn't there. Once I think she even told him I was on a date. It wasn't long before I went back to college, not knowing I was pregnant."

"Why didn't you tell him when you found out?"

Leigh glanced toward the hallway, listening for the annoying *wawawa* of TJ's game. Satisfied the game still had his attention captured, she turned to Sarah. "Ben gave up too easily. I didn't think he'd want to know."

Sarah took a deep breath and frowned. "Do you smell something strange?"

Leigh sniffed the air and shook her head. "Just the pizza we had for supper."

"It doesn't quite smell like pizza. But back to Ben. Did you expect him to pursue you?"

"I don't know what I expected." She massaged the tight muscles in her neck. "I probably did. My grandmother died right after I found out I was pregnant. Tony had straightened up, gone back to college. As I drove home to make the arrangements, I debated whether to tell Ben. I decided he had a right to know and planned to tell him after the funeral.

"The night before the service, I went to a restaurant, and Ben was there with some girl. It was obvious they were in love . . . he even kissed her right there in the restaurant. I heard the next day he was engaged. Guessed that was why he didn't come to the funeral or to see me. His dad had been right—I was just a summer fling. I was on my own. So I went back to Jackson, and you know the rest."

"Evidently he didn't get married."

"No, he didn't. Sometimes I wish . . . it doesn't matter what I wish. It's hard to undo decisions made ten years ago." She rubbed the back of her thumb, thinking of TJ asking Ben to take him to ball practice. "But, I made the right choice, Sarah. Ben wasn't ready to be a father back then, and he still isn't."

Sarah lifted her head and wrinkled her nose, sniffing the air. "What is that odor?"

Leigh inhaled, and this time acrid fumes burned her nose. "Something's on fire."

She jumped up and ran into the kitchen. Nothing wrong there.

Sarah halted near the door that led to the attic. "I think it's coming from upstairs."

Leigh jerked open the door, and smoke rolled into the room.

■ ■ ■

Rain poured from the night sky, blending with water from fire hoses. Ben stood beside the ladder truck and wiped his brow, thankful the fire that had blazed from the roof of Leigh's house seemed to be contained. Lieutenant Carson James came to stand beside him.

"Thanks for the help. If we'd had another truck, we probably could have saved more of the house," James said. "But this is the third lightning fire tonight."

"You think this one was lightning?"

"Know for sure after the fire marshal takes a look. Any reason you think it's not?"

"I just want to make sure it isn't another attempt on Leigh's life."

"Gotcha. We'll stand by for another couple of hours, in case it flares up again."

Ben turned and scanned the crowd for Leigh and found her near the edge of the driveway, hugging her stomach. The shower had tapered off to a fine mist, and as he approached, she looked up with those luminous green eyes. With her chestnut hair plastered to her head, she reminded him of a waif.

"Do you think they saved it?" she asked.

"I don't know." Ben blew out a hard breath. She didn't look like she could handle his suspicions right now. "We'll know more tomorrow." He looked around. "Where's your friend?"

"Gone to pull TJ away from the fire truck."

Ben frowned. "I was just there, and I didn't see TJ."

"Leigh!" Sarah hurried toward them, her voice frantic. "I can't find TJ!"

Ben scanned the area. "Did anyone see which way he went?"

"The fireman"—Sarah stopped to catch her breath—"said he asked about a bear. He told him there weren't any bears—"

"Bear!" Leigh started for the smoldering house. "He went after the bear Tony gave him!"

Ben caught her. "You can't go in there."

She tried to break away from him. "I have to!"

"I'll go." As he ran to the back of the house, he spied the lieutenant. "There's a boy inside. Going after him."

"Wait, Ben!"

He ignored the lieutenant and sprinted for the front door that stood open. No, someone would have seen the boy if he'd gone in through the front. He turned and ran for the back. The door gaped open. "TJ!"

No answer. Ben stepped through the door and hit total darkness, the house reeking of burnt wood and smoke. He fumbled in his pocket and pulled out a handkerchief to cover his nose and mouth. Overhead, the ceiling hissed and cracked. Even though he didn't see any flames, wood smoldered, waiting for a draft of air to rekindle the fire. A light shone behind him.

"Where are you, Ben?"

Carson. With a flashlight.

"Shine it toward the right over here." The light only made the smoke and haze worse. "TJ! Where are you?"

"Ben?"

TJ's faint voice quivered somewhere to Ben's right, and he stumbled toward it. A smoking board dropped in front of him, and he veered away from it. His head rammed a wall. "Ow!"

He inched along the side. "TJ, talk to me, boy."

"I can't see. My eyes burn."

"Where are you?"

TJ coughed. He was close.

"TJ?"

"Ben!" The boy almost bowled him over as he latched onto him.

"You're going to be okay." He hoisted him on his shoulder. "I've got him," he yelled. "Shine the light on the floor so I can see my way out of here."

"I'm sorry. I thought the fire was out." TJ buried his head in Ben's shoulder. "I just wanted to get Bear."

"It's okay. We're getting out of here now." Staying low, Ben carried TJ toward the kitchen and the light.

■ ■ ■

Leigh paced in front of the fire truck, never taking her eyes off the path that Ben, then the fire chief, took. What was TJ thinking? What if the fire rekindled, trapping them all in the house? Her heart thundered in her chest as Ben rounded the corner with TJ in his arms, and she raced to meet them. Ben set TJ down, and Leigh knelt, wrapping her arms around him.

"Thank you." She mouthed the words over TJ's head then hugged her son closer. Ben had risked his own life to save TJ.

Ben grinned, his teeth white against the soot covering his face. He tousled TJ's hair. "You have a brave boy here. Scared us, though."

She nodded, unable to speak. Leigh wanted to throttle her son and dance and embrace him all at the same time. "Why did you go back into the house?"

TJ looked at her, his eyes wide in childlike earnestness. "I couldn't let Bear burn up. Uncle Tony—" He hiccupped.

"I understand, but don't *ever* do anything like that again!" Leigh brushed his hair back with her hand. Soot streaked his face. The vise that had cut off her breath earlier tightened again. If Ben hadn't gone after him . . . She couldn't bear the thought of what might have happened.

"I won't, Mommy."

He hadn't called her mommy since he was six. The tears she'd dammed back threatened to break and spill down her face. He wiggled out of her arms, and she choked down the knot in her throat. She got to her feet and nodded to the paramedic waiting beside Ben. "I'll check him out."

Ben scooped TJ up and carried him to the ambulance, where Leigh borrowed a stethoscope. After going over him from head to toe, she decided all he needed was a good bath. And maybe a seat warming. At the very least, a good talking-to for the scare he'd given them all. But not tonight—she was too happy to have him safe and sound. She handed the stethoscope back to the paramedic. "Thanks."

"Anytime, Doc." The medic turned to TJ. "Want to see what it looks like inside an ambulance?"

"Sure!" TJ looked down at the stuffed animal in his hand then held it out to her. "Mom, would you keep Bear?"

She wanted to laugh and cry at the same time. He'd risked his life for the teddy bear, but now he didn't want anyone to see him with it. "Sure."

As TJ walked to the front of the ambulance with the medic, tears stung her eyes again. What she wouldn't give to get her normal life back. It seemed an eon since she'd treated Jimmy West in the ER for a snakebite or laughed with Tony over one of his stupid jokes. Her shoulders sank. Tony was gone, and she had nowhere to live—her life as she knew it was over.

Ben cleared his throat. "Tell me what happened tonight."

Leigh reeled in her thoughts and sucked in a shaky breath as she replayed the events from earlier. "Sarah and I were talking . . . it was storming, lots of thunder and lightning. I heard something hit the house, like a limb, and then the next thing I knew, the house was on fire."

"Did you hear a pop?"

She closed her eyes and tried to remember. Did lightning always pop? "I don't think so."

"Well, I can tell you, I don't think it was lightning."

Leigh and Ben both turned to stare at Sarah.

"How do you know?" Ben asked.

She put her hand on her hip. "'Cause I smelled something funny before I ever smelled smoke." She nodded at Leigh. "Don't you remember me asking about that strange odor? And you said it was pizza."

"Are you sure?" Ben asked.

Sarah nodded. "I've been thinking it was gasoline, but the smell wasn't quite right. Now I think it was coal oil."

Ben frowned. "Coal oil?"

"I think younger folks call it kerosene."

Blood drained from Leigh's face and an icy chill shook her body. No. Sarah had to be wrong. Lightning had struck the house. She clenched her hands. It had to be lightning.

Because if it wasn't, her insistence on staying in the house, on handling things on her own, could have cost TJ his life.

7

The muscles in Ben's shoulders tensed. "Are you certain you smelled kerosene?"

"Not 100 percent . . ." Sarah's voice trailed off. "But I smelled something."

If Sarah was right, it meant Billy Wayne Gresham had not acted alone. It meant Ben had made a mistake. It meant three people could've died tonight.

Headlights swung into the drive, and Ben recognized his mother's old Cadillac. How had she found out about the fire so quick?

Marisa Logan slammed the Cadillac door and marched toward them with the look of a drill sergeant. When she was within ten feet of him, she nodded. "You can wipe that surprised look off your face. I heard about the fire over the scanner. The reverend and his wife are with your dad." Then she took Leigh by the hands. "You and TJ are staying with us. Sarah too."

He shouldn't be surprised to see his mom. But, he was glad she was here because he'd already decided the safest place for Leigh and TJ tonight was at his parents' house.

"No." Leigh hugged the stuffed bear to her chest. "I can't impose."

"Dear, you don't have a choice. You don't have a place to stay, and we have plenty of room. You'll need some things, of course, but we can stop at Walmart."

His mother's voice was gentle but firm. There'd be no opposing her. He ought to know. He'd butted his head against her iron will more than once and lost.

"I'll pick up whatever they need," Ben said.

"Wait a minute. I'm not staying with your family. I'll stay at Sarah's hotel."

"I can't protect you in a hotel." He shifted his weight, digging in. "If I have to make it official and put you in protective custody, I will."

"But you don't know if the fire was set. I—"

Sarah laid her hand on Leigh's arm. "Honey, you don't know it wasn't. Do you want to risk TJ's life? I don't see that you have much choice."

Leigh opened her mouth. And closed it. She took a few steps toward the ambulance, and he followed her gaze. TJ, with a Braves baseball cap on his head, had stripped off his T-shirt and had the medic's stethoscope pressed to his thin chest, listening to his heartbeat. He shifted back to Leigh. Worry lines pulled her brows together, and something akin to panic rode in her eyes.

Ben wanted to take her in his arms and hold her until she could smile again. "It's going to be all right."

At first he thought she hadn't heard him, but then she turned and stared at him, her green eyes dark. He knew what she was thinking—that he had let her down.

"Nothing will ever be all right again," she replied just as softly.

■ ■ ■

Leigh couldn't think with Sarah and Marisa pressuring her. She walked toward her car, the teddy bear hugged to her chest. Sarah meant well, she acknowledged that, but there had to be another way besides going to the Logan house.

"Leigh, what's so bad about accepting help?"

Ben had followed her.

She whirled around. "I've taken care of TJ for nine years by myself."

Yeah, and look at the mess she'd made. She was certain that was what Ben was thinking. Stupid, stupid mistake, thinking she could handle this on her own. That she could keep TJ safe after Tony was killed. That she didn't need anyone's help, especially Ben's.

"You and TJ aren't the first my parents have taken in, and you probably won't be the last."

"Your dad doesn't like me. With the stroke, he doesn't need someone in his house that will agitate him."

"I don't know why you keep saying that. But, if it'd make you feel better, tomorrow you can move into my house, and I'll stay with them. Leigh, I just want to keep you and your son safe. Why is it so hard to accept the offer?"

If only she could tell him.

"I've been handling things on my own since Mom died." She rubbed her finger down the seam in Bear's chest. "Even before that really, because Mom was so busy grieving for Dad . . ."

Ben stuck his hands in his back pockets. "You had your grand-mother."

"Yeah, and she only had one grandchild. Tony. Not that I cared. I loved my big brother." Thinking back, she realized her dad was the only person who ever treated Leigh like she was special, but even he hadn't given up time in his clinic to be with her, had instead brought her there to help him. His little nurse, he'd always called her. Did he ever in his heart think she might become a doctor? She doubted it somehow.

She shrugged. "It's hard to relinquish control, and that's what you do when you accept help. Good example—I accepted a loan from the Rural Physicians' fund and ended up back in Logan Point for a year."

"What's so bad about that?"

Leigh stood a little straighter. "Do you know where I *could* be practicing? Johns Hopkins."

Ben whistled. "Wow."

"Yeah, wow. And as soon as I repay my scholarship, I'll apply again." It'd always been her dad's dream to work in a teaching hospital like Johns Hopkins. And now it was hers.

"Look, I'm sorry all this has happened." He nodded toward the house.

"It's not your fault. You tried to warn me. I just thought with Billy Wayne dead . . . But why would someone want to kill me in the first place?" She took in a deep breath. "Is it because they don't want me in town?"

"What?" Ben caught her arm. "What did you say?"

She blinked. "What do you mean?"

"Maybe Tony's death isn't linked to these attempts on your life." He took out a pad. "You've been here a month. Has anything happened at the hospital that could cause someone to have a grudge against you? Maybe someone died and a friend or a family member blames you?"

People died all the time in the ER, but Leigh could see Ben's point. She racked her brain, trying to remember a specific case where someone could point the finger of blame on her. She'd lost six patients since coming to the hospital. She knew each case by heart and ticked them off in her mind . . . the ATV accident, a ruptured appendix, three car accidents, and a drug overdose. In each case, she'd done everything humanly possible, but in the end, it hadn't been enough.

"Maybe," Ben said, "it wasn't even a death."

Another case popped into her mind. "Wait a minute. There was an abuse case I reported to the state. A two-year-old boy had cigarette burns on his arms and legs. The mother's boyfriend was arrested." She pressed her fingertips to her forehead. "I can't remember the boyfriend's name. The little boy's name was Derek . . . Wilson."

"I'll check with Logan Point PD. They would have made the arrest at the hospital."

"Mom!" TJ raced toward her. "I listened to my heart!"

Leigh looked past him at the medic also approaching. "Thanks for keeping him occupied, Mike."

"No problem, Doc. He's a good kid."

She'd check his lungs again when she got home. Leigh caught herself. They didn't have a home, and she had a decision to make. Which was more important? Keeping TJ safe or doing it her way? She turned to Ben, but he had joined his mom and Sarah over by the Cadillac while she'd talked to the medic. She walked toward them, feeling like a convict walking the last mile. TJ ran ahead of her, gliding to a stop on the retractable wheels in his tennis shoes in front of Ben. Yeah, he definitely was okay.

"Whoa, boy! What do you have in your shoes?"

"Wheelies. Mom wouldn't buy them, so Tony did." Pain winced across TJ's face, and his shoulders drooped.

Ben tapped the brim of the cap. "They're cool."

Marisa turned to her. "You'll come, won't you?"

Leigh licked her dry lips. "Just until Ben can find us a safe house."

"Oh, good!" Marisa turned to her son. "Why don't you take TJ to the house in your official sheriff truck?"

Wide-eyed pleasure lit up the boy's face. "Really? Can I ride with you? Can I do the siren?"

Leigh's insides squirmed.

"Sure, kid." Ben didn't sound any happier than she was with his mother's suggestion. He eyed Leigh. "Is that okay with you?"

Leigh swallowed hard and nodded. As TJ ran ahead of Ben, her heart thudded in her chest. What if the freight train of her lie derailed, and Ben found out the truth? But that would be impossible. Now that Tony was dead, only two people in the world knew the truth. Leigh wasn't telling, and there was no way Sarah would betray her.

She had nothing to worry about.

■ ■ ■

Staying with the Logans will not be permanent. Leigh kept repeating the words to herself. If only she could have gone with Sarah to the hotel, but she understood why Ben hadn't wanted her to do that. Finding a safe place that he would approve might be difficult, but she would do it. The longer they stayed with Ben's parents, the greater the chance someone would notice that TJ had a few of Ben's mannerisms. Like the tendency to plant his feet when challenged and dig in.

A groan almost escaped her lips. This was not a good idea, but what other choice did she have? Their smoldering house was proof she couldn't protect herself, much less TJ. *It will not be permanent.*

Leigh held on to the thought as the old Cadillac cocooned her in its stout body. She'd let Ben talk her into riding with his mother after he promised to take her back to the house for her car early in the morning. Gradually, she let herself relax into the soft leather. Beside her in the driver's seat, Marisa Logan softly hummed. She seemed to have a knack for knowing when to talk. And when not to.

Marisa embodied other Southern women Leigh had known, women who wove gentleness and grit together, forming a steel core that endured anything. She longed to be that strong. But if anyone looked inside her right now, they'd find a quivering marshmallow center and very little else. If only her mind could quit playing what-if.

She cast a sidelong glance at Marisa. Sarah was right. Ben did favor his mom with the same olive skin and black hair of her Italian ancestors. And the almost black eyes. But not her size. Marisa looked to be a perfect six petite. His height had come from his father. Leigh swung slightly as the car turned into the Logan drive behind Ben and stopped long enough for him to key in a code at the gated entrance. He hadn't been joking that it was like a fortress.

Marisa pulled the Cadillac to a stop in front of the white two-story frame house. "We're home."

Leigh gathered her courage and got out of the car. She helped

Marisa with the Walmart purchases piled in the backseat as TJ spilled from Ben's truck and ran up the walk to the front door. At least he was embracing the adventure. "Timothy Jackson! Come back here and grab a few of these bags."

"So that's what TJ stands for," Ben said.

"After my daddy."

"I'll get the bags." He scooped up the remaining bags as TJ dragged himself back to the car.

She'd spent a small fortune at Walmart. "I hope Tony kept the insurance up to date on the house," Leigh said. If he hadn't, her bank account would soon be in the red.

"I'm sure he did. Do you know who your agent is?"

Leigh almost stumbled. She hadn't thought beyond getting through the next minute. "Not a clue."

"Do you know where Tony kept that type of information?"

"I think so." Leigh remembered a file cabinet in the smaller bedroom. "Do you think the fire reached the bedrooms?"

"Probably only smoke damage," Ben said.

"Good." She handed her son two packages to carry. "TJ, when we go in, you need to be quiet. No running, yelling, anything like that. Ben's dad, Sheriff Logan, doesn't feel well."

"But I thought Ben was the sheriff."

He tapped TJ's cap again. "I am now, but my dad was sheriff first."

Leigh cringed at how stiffly Ben interacted with TJ. *This is not a good idea.* For the hundredth time, the thought flew through her mind.

■ ■ ■

The first order of business had been TJ's bath, and now Leigh climbed the stairs behind Marisa with the rest of their Walmart purchases. There'd been no gracious way not to leave him with Ben in the kitchen, the two of them eating peanut butter and jelly sandwiches. Tom Logan had already gone to bed before they arrived, so that was one meeting that would wait until morning.

Marisa led her down the hallway. "You can stay here as long as you need. With Tom in the wheelchair and not able to talk, this big old house gets mighty quiet sometimes when the grandkids aren't here."

That would be Emily's twins, Josh and Jacob. The two boys at the funeral with Marisa. She'd heard a lot about them from TJ and imagined when they left it'd be like the quiet after a storm.

Marisa placed her hand on Leigh's arm. "I know you're hurting, and it'll get a lot worse before it gets better, but it will get better. Just remember, over and over the Bible says 'and it came to pass.'" She squeezed Leigh's arm.

If only God didn't seem so far away right now. Sometimes when she saw TJ's excitement for all things God, she missed the closeness she'd had when she first came to know him. But after TJ came, she'd had to fit raising a baby alone and finishing college and then med school into her schedule, and there were only twenty-four hours in a day.

Leigh's conscience pinched her heart. If she was honest with herself, she'd admit she quit reading her Bible after she discovered the verse in the New Testament about lying: "Do not lie to one another, since you laid aside the old self with its evil practices." It'd been a memory verse for a Bible study, one she quit not long afterwards to bury herself in med school. As the distance between her and God grew, it became easier to tell herself she was doing the right thing by letting everyone believe Matthew had been TJ's father. She looked up and caught Marisa studying her.

"You've lost so much for one so young. Your parents, your husband in that terrible accident, now Tony, but God has given you the precious gift of your son."

Leigh blinked back the tears that stung her eyelids. TJ was all that mattered now.

Marisa pushed open the first door they came to. "This is where TJ will stay. It's Ben's old room, and I'm afraid it's still decorated in 'Early Ben.' We'll put TJ's things in the chest, and then I'll show you to your room."

Marisa crossed to the bed and turned back the khaki and brown striped sheets. As Leigh's gaze traveled around the room, she understood the comment about the decor. Ben's plaques lined one wall and trophies sat on every available surface. One trophy towered above the others, a baseball perched on a pedestal. She tilted it so she could read the plate. MVP University of Mississippi.

In high school Ben had always excelled at anything he tried, and TJ had gotten his athletic genes. Evidently, Ben's winning streak had carried over into college. Was there anything he didn't do well?

Leigh placed Bear on the bed, then emptied the Walmart bags into the chest, neatly arranging them—one drawer underwear, one drawer shorts and T-shirts, another one socks. Even though they weren't staying long, she wanted things neat. Not that they'd remain that way.

"When you and Ben were dating, I thought . . ." Marisa sighed and straightened one of the plaques. "I don't think he's ever gotten over you."

Marisa's admission stunned her. "He recovered pretty quickly. When I came back for my grandmother's funeral that fall, I heard he was engaged."

"That was rebound." Marisa shook her head. "And that girl was all wrong for him. She did some pretty conniving things to land that engagement ring. When Ben discovered she'd lied about something, that was it for him. One thing he can't abide is dishonesty."

Leigh's breath caught in her chest.

Marisa beamed at her. "But you've done so well, Dr. Leigh Somerall. We're all so proud of you." She bit her lip. "Even Tom."

Leigh jerked and widened her eyes.

"When he told me how he'd broken you and Ben up, I wanted to strangle him."

"You've known all these years?"

Marisa shook her head. "If I'd known when it happened, I would have done something about it. No, he only told me a couple of years ago—right after the article came out in the paper about our homegrown girl graduating from med school—too late to do anything about it. I'm not defending what he did, but he's always been consumed with Ben following in his footsteps and becoming sheriff of Bradford County."

"And a person with my reputation back then would have hurt his chances."

Marisa's lips quirked in a sad smile. "Tom was wrong, and I wish he could tell you how sorry he is for what he did. I just wished you had told him no."

"I couldn't. Tony . . ." Leigh blinked back tears.

"You must have loved your brother very much."

"I did."

Marisa patted her arm. "Come and let me show you where you'll sleep."

Leigh turned and followed the older woman down the hall.

"This was Emily's room. I think you'll enjoy being in here."

Indeed she would. Moss-green walls, ivory window coverings, and a poster bed with a coverlet that matched the curtains. Such a restful room.

"Put your things in the drawers, and then come downstairs for a cup of hot cocoa. Might help you sleep."

"Thank you, I will. I need to collect TJ, anyway." Leigh hesitated. "I don't know how to thank—"

"Shush. I'm just glad you decided to come." Marisa gave her a smile that would melt glass.

After the older woman left, Leigh placed her lingerie in the top drawer, then found the bathroom and put their toothbrushes in the holder. She rolled her shoulders, and pain shot up her neck. A cup of cocoa did sound good.

Voices came from the kitchen as she descended the stairs. When she rounded the corner, her heart skipped a beat. Tom Logan was supposed to be in bed. Instead he sat in his wheelchair, his gaze intent on TJ as her son held his hand out.

"Hi, Mr. Sheriff. I'm TJ Somerall. I'm gonna be stayin' here. Did you know somebody set fire to our house?"

Tom's hazel eyes burned bright, sending an icy shiver down her back. Now she knew where TJ's eye coloring came from. Would anyone else notice?

"He can't use his right hand, TJ." Ben's soft words bridged the deathly quiet of the room. "And I'm afraid he can't talk, either."

TJ shifted to the left hand. "That's okay. He can use the other one."

Leigh held her breath as Tom lifted his left hand, and her son grasped it. "We're gonna be friends. I can tell." TJ cocked his head. "Can you play checkers?"

Turtle-like, Tom nodded.

"Good! Maybe we can play in the morning, but I'm warning you, I'm good, Mr. Sheriff."

"TJ," Marisa said. "why don't you call the sheriff Pops, like Josh and Jacob do?"

Leigh's heart hung in her throat, her mouth so dry she couldn't swallow. She couldn't do this. She had to get TJ and get out of this house, but one look at the glow in her son's face rooted her to the floor.

TJ's eyes widened. "Can I?"

Marisa hugged him. "I think Pops would like that. And you can call me Granna. All the kids at church do."

Leigh shrank back as Tom lifted his gaze over TJ's head and pinned her with his intense stare. She thought her heart would stop when he flicked a glance at Ben then TJ.

He knows.

8

rmero, cuándo enviará los rifles?"

"Dos semanas." Armero drummed his fingers on the desk as the comprador ranted. No amount of cursing could change the date. The comprador wanted 150 AR-15 rifles, and he only had 130. He switched to English. "I'm sorry, compradre. Perhaps you would like to find another source."

"No. If two weeks, two weeks."

"Bien." They talked briefly, and then he hung up. *Armero. Gunsmith.* He'd liked the name so much, he'd come to think of himself by it. Except he didn't actually make the guns. He just knew where to steal the parts.

Armero turned to his computer and tapped into the inventory for today. It had been a good day on the line. Then he checked the shipping schedule. There were several deliveries of raw ceramic material going to Mexico in the next two weeks. Next, he checked the list of drivers then typed in Gordon Roberts's name for the last shipment—he'd see that the guns were ready. Then he'd let Roberts know to drop the shipment at the Blue Dog Company. Roberts never asked questions, simply dropped cargo where he was told.

He leaned back in his leather chair and tented his fingers, tapping the forefingers against his lips. His thoughts traveled to other problems. Like the location of Tony's flash drive. He'd slipped back into the house the day of the funeral and still hadn't found it, but there were so many places to look in the small house. And now most of the house was gone, and he'd never know if it had been destroyed in the attic.

He hated working with a partner. Especially one with an agenda. It took some of the fun out of the game. But he'd needed help assembling the guns. Armero shook his head. His partner was a problem he could do nothing about tonight. What he could do was walk out to the building where the lower receivers were milled and pick up a couple. It was the only part he lacked for the remaining twenty rifles. If there were no problems on the line, he'd get them in the next two weeks. The problem was getting them before they were stamped with the Maxwell logo and serial number.

He opened the daily inventory sheet for the receivers. Good. Today's pieces had not made it to the stamping line. He reduced the daily productivity count by three. Perhaps tomorrow he could pick up a couple more, and by the middle of next week, he'd have enough for his order.

Even this reminded him of Tony's flash drive. Why in the world Tony had to get religion was beyond his imagination. The old Tony would have looked the other way. After all, who cared if the drug cartels in Mexico wiped each other out as long as they paid good money for his rifles to do it? A grim smile stretched across his lips. The price he set had never been a problem, and a tidy sum was drawing interest in an account in Switzerland.

It had to be that border agent who was killed that did it. But the agent wasn't killed with one of *his* guns. He just hadn't been able to make Tony see that.

His watch chimed an alarm, and he checked the time. The guard should have just left the receiver building. If he hurried, he'd get in and out before he made the rounds in the building beside it.

Fifteen minutes later, Armero's fingers shook as he opened his briefcase and placed three of the dark gray aluminum rifle pieces in it. Then with adrenaline still thrumming through his veins, he hurried to the door, unbolted the lock, and after exiting, relocked it. This is what he lived for. The rush of not getting caught. He understood how a gambler felt as he waited for the dice to land or a card to come up. It wasn't about winning. It was about those seconds of anticipation.

A shout halted him at the end of the building.

"You, there! Stop!"

His blood roared in his ears as he turned around, rehearsing the story he'd devised. The guard approached. Black? No . . . Names raced through his mind. Jett. Richard Jett. "Good evening, Richard. How's the family?"

"Oh, I'm sorry, I didn't know it was you. Working late again, I see. My family is fine. Thank you for the tickets to see the Redbirds play."

"Well, it was really the company. It appreciates the job you're doing here."

"Thank you, sir. I try."

With a nod, Armero turned and strode toward the parking lot. He had won again.

■ ■ ■

Ben set the empty cup of cocoa on the kitchen counter and ruffled TJ's copper hair before he thought. He'd set boundaries on just how close he'd get with the boys in Emily's Sunday school class, and he didn't want to cross that line. It was the only way to avoid a panic attack. But somehow, TJ seemed different. Different even from his nephews. For a second when TJ looked up, he reminded him of someone, but then, most boys his age looked alike. "It's been fun hanging out together, but I have to go."

"Are you going to catch the bad guys that burned our house?"

"I'm not sure that's what happened, but if someone did, I'm going to try." So far he hadn't done too good of a job. Ben hugged his mom. "See you tomorrow morning."

He turned to Leigh, and her gaze was on TJ. Ben wished he could erase the worry lines from her face. She raised her head and caught him watching her. Her face flushed, and his heart betrayed him, beating erratically as her emerald-colored eyes made him think of a particular warm summer afternoon by the lake.

"What's the game plan?" she asked. "I'm not scheduled to work, but I have a ton of paperwork I need to catch up on."

Ben glanced at TJ. The boy's face knit in a frown as his gaze bounced back and forth between them. Evidently Ben's mom saw it too.

His mother turned to TJ. "Would you like to help me?"

TJ's gaze lingered on his mom, and Leigh squeezed his shoulders. "It's going to be fine."

"And afterward, I'll take you up to your room," Marisa said. "It was Ben's when he lived here, and you can see all his trophies."

"Mom, I thought you stored those things out in the barn." He hoped Leigh didn't think displaying the awards was his idea.

"Why would I do that? One day you'll have a son, and I'd just have to go dig them out," Marisa said.

Before she wheeled his dad out the door, Ben hugged him. "See you tomorrow, Dad."

Tom Logan moved his left hand, touching Ben's revolver. "Rila."

Ben suppressed a groan. He'd forgotten to take off his service revolver. About a month after his dad's stroke, he'd gotten upset whenever Ben wore it.

"Rila!" Tom gripped Ben's arm.

He winced at the strength in his fingers. "Yeah, Dad, I have my gun. It's okay."

His dad's eyebrows pinched together, and his shoulders sagged. "Rila."

He was almost in tears. TJ patted his dad on the leg. "What's he trying to say?"

"I don't know," Ben said.

"Maybe I can help him." TJ looked into Tom's eyes. "Tomorrow, we're going to play a game, Pops. I'll show you how to talk."

"TJ, go brush your teeth and leave the sheriff alone," Leigh said. "Your toothbrush is in the holder in the bathroom. I'll be up to tuck you in."

"Aw, Mom!" TJ ducked his head. "Okay, Pops, looks like I gotta go to bed."

Ben noticed he didn't say for her not to come. Leigh swayed slightly, and he steadied her. She'd gone about as far as she could for one day. "Why don't you sit down while I get you a cup of cocoa?"

"I thought you had to leave," she said, sinking into the kitchen chair Marisa had vacated.

"I can spare a few more minutes." He put marshmallows in a cup and poured cocoa from the carafe. Winter or summer, cocoa was a staple in the Logan house.

When he turned around, Leigh had crossed her arms on the table and was resting her head. She looked up and laughed. It was a soft laugh.

"I didn't know I was so tired," she said, stretching. "About to-morrow . . . is it necessary for a deputy to accompany me to the hospital?"

"Can you do the paperwork here?"

"Here? I don't want to pack it all up and bring it to your parents' house. Can't I just go to the hospital by myself?"

"But Leigh, I don't—"

"You don't know for sure the fire was set—it could've been light-ning, Sarah could've been mistaken. *I* didn't smell any kerosene."

He tried to stare her down. "I don't remember you being this stubborn when we were in high school."

"You don't remember a lot of things." Her eyes darkened. "You're not in charge of me, and I have a job to do. No one, not even some lunatic, is going to make me a prisoner."

When she stopped to catch her breath, he said, "Having someone escort you is not treating you like a prisoner."

"I know that, and it's not that I don't appreciate your folks taking us in and what you've done. But I'm going to live my life as normally as I can. Besides, we have armed security in the ER."

"I'd still feel better if you go along with me on this."

She closed her eyes, and when she opened them, she gave him the barest of nods. "I give up. If you think it's absolutely necessary, one of your deputies can escort me to and from the hospital."

"I'll take you myself."

She rolled her eyes.

"We need to explore who and why someone is after you. If you want to look for your insurance papers, I'll take you to the house and then drop you off at the hospital."

"I don't want to go to the hospital smelling like a chimney. Pick me up at nine. Then I'll have time to come back here and shower and change. And when I do go to the hospital, if you insist on escorting me, you can follow me so I'll have my car."

At least she'd agreed to something. "Yes, ma'am."

"Mom!" TJ's voice drifted down the stairs. "Where's my tooth-brush?"

"Coming," she yelled back. She heaved a sigh. "He's like all men, couldn't find something if it was about to bite him."

Fatigue etched its lines in the slump of her shoulders, the planes of her face. "You finish your cocoa. I'll go find it for him." Too late, a warning pierced Ben's brain. This was no way to keep his distance from the boy.

"No, I'll go."

He should let her, but he hated for her to climb the stairs again. And did she have to fight him on everything? "What, you think I can't find it?"

Leigh's mouth opened in protest, and he cut her off. "Sit there and rest a minute. I won't hurt him."

She held herself very still, almost rigid, and then her body sagged against the chair. "Thanks."

Ben climbed the stairs, taking his time. This was one argument he should have let her win, but he was only finding TJ's toothbrush . . . just like he would his nephews'. He was fine around them, for the most part, but they had their dad. He took a deep breath. This was doable. Except . . . with TJ's father dead, the boy only had Leigh. He topped the stairs. Tommy Ray Gresham flashed in his mind, and a cold sweat broke out on his face. He swallowed down the familiar tightness in his throat. *Not now.*

"Mom—" TJ stopped short when he saw him. "Hey, Ben. Do you see my toothbrush?"

Ben took a deep breath, and calmness spread through his chest. "Your mom said it would be close enough to bite you, so let's see . . ." He looked in the toothbrush holder by the sink and picked up a small brush. "Is this it, maybe?"

"Thanks! Can you tell me about that stuff in my room?"

Ben ended up not only helping TJ find his toothbrush but also telling him about each trophy. He even helped him into his pajamas. Once TJ was in bed, Ben asked, "Do you want Bear?"

The boy darted his eyes toward the stuffed toy Ben held out. "Nah, that's for kids," TJ said. His eyes said otherwise.

Ben pulled Bear's flopped ear up straight. "You know, I had a blanket that I slept with every night until I was twelve. Sometimes I kind of wish I still had it."

TJ's eyes widened. "Really?"

Ben nodded. This wasn't so hard.

"I'm just nine."

The boy was already nine? He didn't think the twins were but eight. "Then I expect it'd be all right, don't you?"

The boy reached for the bear. "Wouldn't want Bear to get lonesome."

Ben thought he detected a tear in the corner of his eye. TJ took a shivering breath. "Is my mom going to be okay?"

His stomach lurched. He should've left while he was ahead. "She's going to be fine."

"But what if someone hurts her, I mean, *really* hurts her."

He patted TJ's leg. "I told you before. I won't let anyone hurt her."

"You promise?"

Ben faltered. What if he couldn't keep Leigh safe? He hadn't kept Tony safe, and so far, he hadn't done too good a job with Leigh. He swallowed. "I promise I'll do my best."

TJ's gaze locked into Ben's. Finally he nodded. "Okay," he whispered and hugged the bear to his chest. "I like it here. I wish we could stay forever, and y'all could be my family."

A board creaked behind Ben, and he turned. Leigh stood in the doorway, her face ashen.

■ ■ ■

Leigh had never sensed the depth to which TJ desired a real home before, and his words pierced her heart like a poisoned arrow. She hadn't taken time to listen to TJ's heart. But why did he have to pick *this* home of all homes to want to be a part of? She glued a smile on her wooden lips. "I see you two found the toothbrush and pj's."

"Ben helped me." TJ pointed to the trophies. "Did you know he won all those?"

Her smile turned into a true smile. "I do. I was there when he won most of them."

TJ's eyes popped wide. "You knew Ben before?"

Leigh glanced at Ben, and memories she'd blocked for years ran amok in her mind. The way he held her so gently in his arms, his lips on hers, soft and demanding at the same time. She shook away the memories. She'd been only one of many for Ben. "We went to high school together."

"Yeah," Ben said. "If it hadn't been for your mom, I never would've passed chemistry."

"Did you two ever kiss?"

"TJ!" Heat fanned her face.

Ben recovered first. "Not in high school," he said.

"I think it's time for you to go to sleep, young man." Leigh tucked the sheet under TJ's chin, and he squirmed when she planted a kiss on his cheek.

He scrubbed his face. "Aw, Mom, I'm too big for that."

Leigh's heart hitched, and she glimpsed his future—graduation, college . . . turn around twice and her time with him would be over. She'd better make the most of it now. "You will never get that big," she said, tousling his hair. Then, a cloud of what-ifs engulfed her. What if she'd told Ben the truth all those years ago? Maybe Ben would've been there when TJ was born, or took his first step, or lost his first tooth, or when he started school. Times neither Ben nor TJ could get back. Her fingers curled into tight balls. Keeping the truth hidden ate at her conscience, but if Ben found out the truth now, he'd never forgive her.

■ ■ ■

Sunlight spilled through what was left of the roof on her grandmother's house, all but erasing any hope for restoration. Leigh picked her way around where the kitchen had been, stepping across the smoked-over meter box that lay in a puddle of water. Water soaked everything. Most likely a total loss, the insurance adjuster had just informed her. At least there was insurance.

She hadn't even had to call the agent. He'd called her an hour ago at the Logans' and arranged to meet her at the house. A benefit to living in a small town, she supposed. She would have to wait for the adjuster's final verdict, but he predicted the house would have to be bulldozed.

"I'm sorry, Leigh." Ben picked up a broken mug and placed it on the water-soaked coffee table.

She fisted her hands on her hips and surveyed the mess. The agent was right. It would be easier to build from the ground up, if she were so inclined. But she didn't plan to be in Logan Point that long. "Any idea where I can find a place to live?"

Ben's back stiffened as he planted his feet. "I'd prefer that you stay where you are until the fire investigator rules whether it was arson."

"Oh, come on. Look at the damage. Anyone can see lightning struck the meter box. We need our own place. I don't want to root you out of your house."

"You don't get it, do you?" he asked. "You and TJ are in protective custody and will be until I know for sure this wasn't arson and that Billy Wayne Gresham was shooting at me, not you. I don't even know if he acted alone yet."

Air whooshed from her lungs. She hated it when he was right. Until she knew those same things for sure, she couldn't put TJ in danger. "How long will the investigation take?"

"A couple of weeks, probably." He hesitated. "I know that I said you could move into my place, but would you consider staying where you are? It'd be easier on TJ when you're at the hospital, and it would be easier on me. Even with Dad out of commission, it'd still be like twenty-four-hour protection with the fence, and like I've said before, Mom's a crack shot if it came down to it."

Leigh had already reconciled herself to the fact that Marisa would be watching TJ—it wasn't fair to involve her babysitter in their problems. And now she saw no way of leaving at all. "I guess your parents' place would be the best."

"Good." His cell phone beeped. "I need to take this," he said and walked out the front door as he answered.

Two weeks. That was all the time she was giving him. Her cell rang, and she glanced at her phone. The ER doctor on duty. Leigh punched the answer button. "Dr. Somerall."

"We have four victims en route from a wreck on Highway 7. How soon can you get here?"

"On my way." Leigh pocketed her phone. Thank goodness she'd followed Ben in her own car. She met him at the door. "I have to get to the hospital."

108

"I figured as much. There's been a bad wreck, and I need to get out to the highway. I'll follow you to the hospital, though."

"Ben, go. I'll be all right. The hospital is only ten minutes away, and the wreck is in the opposite direction."

He hesitated. "I'll keep you on the phone until you get inside the hospital."

"Whatever."

Four hours later, Leigh checked on the only patient from the wreck still in the ER and was pleased the teenager's vitals had stabilized. He'd been the lucky one, only a broken leg. The other three had been assessed and helicoptered to the Med in Memphis for treatment. The trauma center offered them a better chance at survival than Bradford General. She stepped back into the hall and walked to the nurses' station, glad to see Cathy had come on duty.

The RN shook her head. "What were those kids thinking? Beer for breakfast?"

"I know. Alcohol plus speed equals bad news. Kids think they're invincible." Leigh checked with OR and was told it'd be another hour before the kid's leg could be set. She rolled her shoulders. "The mother is in the room with her son. Would you let her know it'll be awhile before he goes to surgery? The hospital blood bank doesn't have his type, so they're waiting for units from Memphis."

"Has anyone asked Ben Logan or his sister to donate?"

"What are you talking about?"

"Both of them are universal donors. They have O negative blood and have given before when we have a shortage."

Leigh tensed. TJ had inherited his O negative blood from Ben? O negative tended to run in families, but she'd never considered . . . She took a breath and slowly released it. Nothing to worry about. No reason for Ben to find out. "Call Emily and Ben and let them know the situation. I'm going to get something to drink and sit in the sun for a minute."

It worried her that the hospital blood bank was so low this early in the summer. What would they do a month from now? Leigh took a bottle of tea from the refrigerator and walked through the waiting room, stopping to give an update to the boy's father. She nodded to the guard on duty and tried to remember his name. Gary, she thought and told him she was getting a little fresh air. Outside the benches were empty, and she chose an unshaded one.

Since the hospital had become tobacco free, the benches were usually vacant. She leaned back and closed her eyes, soaking up the midday sun. July heat did not bother her and felt good after a morning in the cold ER. A shadow blocked the sun, sending a shiver through her body. She opened her eyes, but in the bright light, could only make out a man's outline.

"Leigh?"

She relaxed, recognizing Ian Maxwell's well-modulated voice. "You startled me."

He sat beside her and adjusted the cuffs on his long-sleeved white shirt. "I'm sorry. I just heard about your house when someone told me you were staying at the Logans'. I—"

The guard materialized from the entrance shadows. "Dr. Somerall, everything okay?" he asked. "Oh, I'm sorry, I didn't recognize you, Mr. Maxwell."

Leigh waved him off. "Everything's fine, Gary."

Ian took a handkerchief from his pocket and blotted his face. "What was that all about?"

"Ben thinks someone is out to get me."

"And you don't?"

She turned to look at the handsome Chief Operations Officer of Maxwell Industries. His ice-blue eyes were the only cool thing about him. Sweat glistened on his forehead and dotted his upper lip. "Would you like to go inside?" she asked. "We can talk in the break room."

He pressed the handkerchief to his face again. "Thank you."

110

As they walked through the automatic doors, Leigh chuckled. "You know, short sleeves would be much cooler."

"But not nearly as professional."

Inside the ER, she pointed toward the break room. "I'll be there in a second."

She checked on her patient and then joined Ian, puzzled as to why he'd stopped to see her. He stood in front of the television monitor where hospital announcements scrolled at regular intervals. When he heard her enter, he turned.

"This employee of the month . . ." He nodded toward the screen. "His son works at the plant. I wish the boy had some of his work ethic."

"You didn't come all the way out to the hospital to talk about your employees." Leigh pulled a chair away from the table and sat down. The break room was empty, but probably not for long. He smiled at her, flashing ultra white teeth—no Walmart whitening strips for him, she'd bet.

"Very astute, Doctor," he said as he sat in a chair across from her. "No, I came to offer you a house to live in until yours is repaired, or rebuilt, whichever the case may be . . . and to see if you will have dinner with me tonight."

Her breath hitched. "What?"

Ian's lips curved up. "Which *what* are you asking about, the date or the house?"

She gave her head a small shake and took a deep breath. "Let's start with the house."

"Okay. Like I said before when we came to your house after Tony died, Danny and I own rental property, and I have a couple of vacant units. A house on Webster and a condo in Hillcrest."

Leigh blinked and held up her hand. Both were surely way above her means. "I don't think so. Ben probably wouldn't allow it, anyway."

"The sheriff isn't your boss or your husband, and it wouldn't cost you a red cent. It's the least we can do for Tony's family."

Tears stung her eyelids, and she blinked them back. "Thank you. I'm touched. Can I give you an answer in a day or two, after the fire investigator's report comes back? TJ is safe with the Logans, and as much as I'd like to be out on my own, he comes first. If it is arson, we'll have to stay put."

Ian rubbed his hands together. "I'll get the house on Webster ready—he'll need a yard to play in."

"What part of wait did you not hear?"

The gleam in his eye indicated Ian Maxwell was used to getting his way. "Would you give me your cell phone number? That way I can call you to come and look at the house when it's ready. Even if the report should indicate arson, and I don't believe it will, the Webster house is in a gated community with a guard 24/7."

Gated, and with a guard. Ben might actually give his approval. She rattled off her number, and he entered it in his phone.

"Got it," he said and slipped his phone in the pocket of his navy slacks. "If Ben thinks someone set the fire, does he have any clues as to who it could be?"

"He hasn't said. I thought when Billy Wayne Gresham died, my nightmare was over."

"First of all, I can almost guarantee it wasn't *you* Billy Wayne was aiming at."

She eyed him.

"Think about it. Tommy Ray Gresham? The Boy Scout retreat?"

"What are you talking about?"

"The Boy Scout retreat that Tommy Ray drowned at three years ago—oh, wait that's right, you wouldn't know anything about that. Ben was in charge of the troop, and they were camping at the lake when Tommy Ray drowned. Ben tried to save him, almost drowned himself. It wasn't anyone's fault, but the father, Jonas Gresham, doesn't see it that way. He thinks Ben should've gone into the water sooner, and he's been quite vocal about it." Ian adjusted his cuffs.

"And Billy Wayne felt the same way, and he was just crazy enough to try and get revenge. They both are actually."

He held up his hand. "I'm sorry. You don't need to hear all of this. The offer of the house stands. Anytime you want either place, it's yours. And now for the other question. Will you have dinner with me?"

She swallowed, hoping to calm the storm that erupted in her chest. "I thought you were engaged."

"Not anymore." His face gave no clue to his emotions on the subject. "We decided we weren't right for each other."

Leigh doubted it was his ex-fiancée's decision. She'd heard the nurses talking, taking bets as to whether this fiancée would get him to the altar. Wait until they heard the engagement was off—Ian would top any list of Logan Point's most eligible bachelors, higher even than Ben. She crossed her arms over her chest. "You never gave me a second look in high school. Why now?"

He laughed out loud. "I was a senior, and you were a freshman. That would've been robbing the cradle. Besides, you were so in love with Ben Logan, I wouldn't have stood a chance."

"He didn't know I existed." Not in high school. That didn't come until college. A text beeped on her cell phone. Leigh read it and said, "I have to check on my patient."

"Think about that dinner," Ian called after her.

9

Would you put that stupid cube down?" Wade said. "Or learn how to work it."

Ben looked up from the Rubik's Cube he'd bought at lunch. His deputy stood in the doorway with a drink and a Styrofoam box that reeked of fried food. "It helps me to think."

He set the cube on his desk and nodded toward a file cabinet. "I took a break from sorting through Dad's files, if you can call them that. A slip of paper with numbers stuck in an unnamed folder filed under the B's, another one with Lester jotted on it. That one was filed under *D*. No clue what any of it means."

"He definitely had a unique way of filing that made sense only to him."

"And no way to ask him about it. It's a good thing Maggie kept the reports typed and printed out. I wonder if she found anything else." He picked up his phone and dialed Maggie's extension. "Come across any more of Dad's files?"

"A small box with his desk calendar, some letters, and a few emails he printed out. Looks like this stuff might've been on his desk. I was just fixing to bring it to you."

Wade set the white box on Ben's desk and knelt beside the small cabinet, flipping through the files. He pulled one out. "Here's a handwritten report from 1991 that says Jonas Gresham stole five hens from Lucinda Mays."

114

Maggie entered the room carrying a cardboard box. "Gresham hasn't changed, except for the worst. I feel so sorry for Ruby. Don't know what she ever saw in that man." She set the box on Ben's desk. "I think this is the last of it. I don't know how it got up front."

If the sheriff's department had an office manager, it'd be the slightly bow-legged senior with the sensible shoes. The day-dispatcher-slash-secretary had been a fixture at the department ever since Ben could remember. "Thanks, Maggie. I don't know how we'd run this office without you. Hope you're not planning on retiring anytime soon."

"And do what?" She put her hand on her hip. "Besides, this place can't run without me."

"You got that right." Wade opened the Styrofoam box and held it out to her. "Want a hamburger from Molly's Diner? I have three."

Maggie eyed the food. "You sure?"

"Yeah. Ben can have the other one, if he wants it."

"I'll take it to my office," she said as Wade settled in a chair beside Ben's desk and handed him a burger.

Ben checked to make sure it had mustard before he chomped into it. "Why can't I get the squares lined up?"

Wade grabbed the cube and twisted it, his fingers moving too fast for Ben to see the turns. In a little over a minute, all six sides were solid colors. "You mean like that?"

"Yeah." Ben rocked back in his leather chair.

The chief deputy set the cube back on the desk. "I look at it, and my brain sees how it fits together. That's all I can tell you." He took a sip of drink.

A lot of people thought Wade was just a good ole country boy, long on friendliness but short on intelligence. Ben knew better. "Why do you let people think you're dumb?" he asked as he crumpled the hamburger wrapper and tossed it into the empty container.

Wade lifted his shoulder in a half shrug. "Gives me an advantage. Besides, I learned when I was a kid in foster homes that people are going to believe what they want to. Truth doesn't matter—they'll go with what they think they see every time."

Ben turned back to his computer. "If you'd tried to change some minds, you'd probably be sheriff instead of me."

A harsh snort erupted from deep in Wade's throat. "Now *you're* playing me for dumb. You're the sheriff's son. No way for it to go down other than the way it played out. And when you take that job with the U.S. Marshals, the county supervisors will pick somebody besides me to take your place until the election."

"I'm not going with the Marshals. I've decided to run for sheriff. Filed the paperwork last week."

Wade's feet hit the floor as he sat up straight. "You're kidding. What changed your mind?"

Ben glanced around the office, still his dad's office in his mind. Would always be Dad's office, even if Ben painted the gray walls and took down the pictures and plaques with Tom Logan's name on them. "Being sheriff is a lot different from being a deputy under my dad's eye. I still second-guess myself, but at least he's not here to say 'I told you so.'"

"Your dad never in his life said those words."

"Yeah? Well, he was thinking them."

"Come on, Ben, your dad might like to keep everything and everyone under his thumb, but he isn't vindictive. How is he, anyway?"

"I think not being able to communicate is getting to him. He tries to talk, but it comes out garbled. And he won't work with the speech therapist."

"It's only been six months, and he had a lot of healing to do. At least he's not a paranoid schizophrenic, like my mom."

"He goes absolutely nuts if I forget and wear my gun around him."

"It's not the same thing."

"I know. I'm sorry." Wade had been seeing after his mother ever since Ben could remember. First when she was in the state hospital, and now at an expensive care facility just outside of town. He figured all of Wade's money went to keep her there.

Wade eyed him. "I know the real reason you're passing up the U.S. Marshals' job. It's Leigh Somerall and her kid."

Heat flushed him. "I don't know what you're talking about."

"Yeah, you do. You were sweet on her once before, and now that she's back in Logan Point, you want to hang around here."

"How do you even remember we dated? That was ten years ago."

"Yeah, but you were working here that summer and mooning over her like a love-struck puppy." Wade doodled on the desk calendar on Ben's desk. "You let her get away that time. And if you're not interested, I am."

"You've got to be kidding. You're too old for her. Besides, you'd never take on the responsibility of someone else's kid."

"And you would, Mr. Date-them-three-times-and-drop-them? For the record, I'm forty-one, only ten years older than the doc. Hardly ready for the grave." Wade eyed him. "I don't think I've seen you with anyone lately. Is it because of the doctor?"

"Of course not."

"Well, if it is, you better make your move. I'm not the only one I've seen eying the good-looking doctor. I'm pretty sure I've seen her with Ian a time or two."

A band tightened around Ben's chest. This wasn't ten years ago. Leigh wasn't a shy college sophomore. Like a butterfly, she'd emerged from her awkward early college years into a beautiful and confident woman. Bottom line—she'd grown up.

He couldn't say the same for himself. The more he thought about getting married, the more it scared him. Commitment. Responsibility. Sure, he could commit to the responsibility of running the sheriff's department. He didn't shoulder it alone. He had Wade and Andre, and a half dozen other deputies.

"You okay, Ben? I just meant you should either cut bait or fish."

"I'm fine. And for your information, she'll only be here for another ten months. Then she's off to Baltimore." He stood. He was not interested in a future with Leigh Somerall. "I'm going to get a candy bar. See if you can find out when Billy Wayne started that website, and I understand Mrs. Gresham has taken a couple of weeks off from work. We'll take a ride out and talk to her." And hope Jonas Gresham wasn't there.

And that Wade wouldn't bring Leigh up again.

■ ■ ■

Ben climbed the Greshams' block steps and rapped on the screen door. The solid wood door stood open, and from somewhere in the house, a twangy country singer crooned about love gone bad. A thin layer of red dust from the gravel road in front of the frame house covered the glass-topped table on the porch. When no one appeared, he rapped again.

"Maybe she's out back," Wade said. "But I'm telling you, she's not going to know anything about Billy Wayne's activities."

They retraced their steps and went around to the back of the house. Ancient oaks shaded the dirt yard. "Mrs. Gresham, you back here?" Ben called.

"Over here."

They both looked in the direction of the voice. A petite brunette walked toward them, a pail in her hand. Blackberries, Ben saw when she reached them.

"Morning, Sheriff," she said, putting the pail on a homemade round picnic table. A strand of hair had worked its way out of the ponytail that hung down her back, and she tucked it behind her ear. "Been expecting you. You want to talk out here or in the house?"

A light breeze stirred the air. He could imagine how stuffy the house would be. "Here will be fine."

Ruby Gresham sat on a bench and fanned. "Sure is hot."

"Yes, ma'am," Ben replied. He cleared his throat. "I'm really sorry about Billy Wayne."

She looked off into the distance. "Wish I could say I was surprised. He just never was the same after Tommy Ray—" Her hands fluttered to her mouth. "I'm so sorry, Sheriff . . . I didn't mean . . ."

Ben flinched and struggled for something to say.

"It's all right, Mrs. Gresham," Wade said. "Tommy Ray's death affected us all."

She hunched her thin shoulders. "He was a good boy."

Ben found his voice. "Did you know anything about Billy Wayne's gambling debts or his website?"

Leaning forward, she shook her head. "He thought he was growed up. Learned how to play poker from his daddy. Weren't no better at it than him, either."

"How about the website?" Wade prodded.

"Jonas Junior showed it to me after he got kilt. Wished I'd a looked at it before. Might could've helped him if I'd knowed he was that angry."

It didn't look like Ruby Gresham would confirm Ben's suspicion that someone other than Billy Wayne had built the website. "So you think he put it up?" he asked.

"He liked fooling with that kind of stuff. Made up them computer games when he was still home. I told him he ought to get a job doing that instead of fooling with gambling. I was so proud when he got the job working on the computers at—"

"Hey! What are you doing on my property?"

Ben hadn't heard Jonas Gresham come up, and he turned as Jonas charged toward him like a bull rushing a matador.

"Hold it, Jonas." Wade stepped between them, resting his hand on his gun.

"You takin' up his fight?" The burly farmer poked Wade in the chest, his six-two frame a match for the deputy.

"We don't have a fight." Ben stepped forward, flexing his fingers. Just in case he couldn't convince Gresham.

"The devil we don't. You killed two of my boys."

"Jonas." Mrs. Gresham's warning cut through the tension. "The sheriff here didn't kill nobody. Billy Wayne just plain kilt hisself. And what happened to Tommy Ray was an accident. Ben did all he could to save him."

"He could've done more." Jonas's eyes bulged from their sockets. "He was in charge of them boys. He should've seen to it that they didn't horse around in the water like that."

Ben swallowed the bile that rose up in his throat. Jonas was right. He should've stopped the boys from swinging on the grapevines and dropping into the river-fed lake below.

"He's told you how sorry he is about what happened that day," Ruby said.

"Sorry don't cut it. Now git off my property."

Ben held up his hand. He would get no more information from Ruby Gresham today. "We're going." He turned and walked slowly back to his truck, Wade right behind him.

"You want to drive?" Ben asked.

"Sure." As they backed out of the drive, his chief deputy shook his head. "He's a crazy old coot."

Crazy or not, his words had picked the scab off the festering wound in Ben's heart.

Suddenly, Wade slammed the brakes on the truck. "You see that dog?"

"Where?"

"There in the weeds."

Ben scanned the roadside, finally catching sight of a broad-chested mongrel cowering in the tall weeds beside the road. They climbed out of the truck. What he saw turned his stomach. Blood oozed from a wound on the dog's haunches, and scars indicated past wounds. They cautiously approached the shivering dog.

"Okay, buddy, we're not going to hurt you," Wade crooned. The dog offered a halfhearted growl. The deputy motioned Ben back. "Let me handle this."

When he was a couple of feet from the dog, Wade squatted and held out his hand. "Good boy."

The dog whimpered and dragged himself toward the chief deputy until he was close enough for Wade to stroke its head. His tail thumped as Wade whispered soothing words. "You're going to be okay."

"How bad is he hurt?" Ben asked. The dog looked like a mixture of pit bull and Doberman. Wade was always picking up stray dogs and taking care of them. Sometimes, Ben thought he liked dogs better than people.

Gently, Wade ran his hands over the dog, bringing a yelp when he touched the back leg. "Don't think it's broken. Can I put him in the back of your truck?"

"Sure. Want me to help?"

"Naw, I got him."

Ben let the tailgate down as Wade scooped the dog up and placed him on a tarp in the bed of the truck.

"Somebody's been fighting this dog," Wade said through gritted teeth. "Looks like your daddy was right. We got a dogfighting ring going on in Bradford County."

Before he had been shot, his dad had told Ben his suspicions, but Tom Logan had never been able to track down anything other than rumors.

"You have your hands full with Leigh's case," Wade said. "I want this one, Ben."

10

Even though her replacement had come on duty to the ER at three, Leigh had stayed until four, waiting for a lab report on a patient. She checked her lab coat to make sure the pockets were empty before she tossed the coat into the laundry basket in the doctors' lounge. She couldn't believe it was the first of August and a week since the fire. A week living with the Logans. Ian's offer of a house tempted her each day as TJ grew closer to the family, and even though she tried to avoid Tom, when she managed not to, his eyes bored into her with certainty. If he could communicate, she would have already been out of there.

There'd been no word from the fire marshal yet, and there'd been no more attempts on her life. Tomorrow night, she was having dinner with Ian. She'd tell him then that she was accepting his offer of the house on Webster Street. The sooner she got TJ away from the Logans, the better. Now to figure out how to tell Ben.

He still escorted her to and from the hospital and had arrived ten minutes ago to escort her home. Home. She wished. Instead of wishing, she should be grateful the Logans took them in. She should be grateful, period. No one had been hurt in the fire, and everything destroyed could be replaced. She'd even discovered TJ's baby album intact under her bed.

It's me, God. Leigh Somerall, in case you've forgotten my voice.

It'd been so long since she'd prayed that shame wormed its way into her heart. It'd been so hard to get to church all these years, and it had been easier to relinquish TJ's spiritual growth to Sarah. Leigh winced. Sarah. She'd meant to call her last night.

Anyway, God, thank you for keeping us safe.

What about Tony? Why hadn't God protected him? She shoved the thought from her mind. She didn't want to make God mad. Besides, it didn't seem right to question God. She grabbed her purse and headed for the door. Ben was leaning against the front desk, talking to the guard.

"I'm ready."

He fell in beside her. "Those teenagers from the wreck last week—do you have an update on their condition?"

She'd called the Med earlier in the day to inquire about them. "The doctor I talked with said all three were improving and should be released soon. The kid who broke his leg went home the first of the week. Did you learn anything from the fire marshal?"

"He's still sifting through the evidence."

Leigh clicked the remote on her key ring, and her car motor jumped to life. "Did he give any clue to what he's thinking?"

Ben shook his head. "Clancy plays his cards close to his vest. He won't give out anything until he has a complete picture."

She eyed him. "Do you play poker?"

He rubbed the bridge of his nose. "Used to, right after college, but not anymore. Wasn't too good at it, anyway. Besides, I don't think the people of Bradford County would appreciate their sheriff doing anything illegal."

Yeah, the Logan family always had the voters in mind, but she laughed anyway. In the past week, they'd become more comfortable with each other. "Mr. Straight and Narrow."

He held up his hand. "Hey—you do what you gotta do."

She opened her car door. "Wouldn't want anything to tarnish that badge, Sheriff."

Ben put his hand on the door. "Speaking of gambling, someone mentioned that Tony had a photographic memory, and I've meant to ask if he did."

"Only if it had anything to do with numbers. His memory wasn't as good with words. As a kid, I learned early not to play cards with him. Do you think someone realized that and thought he was cheating?"

"It's possible," he said and shut her door.

When she pulled through the gate behind Ben, a white Honda sat in front of the garage. Sarah? She was supposed to be in Jackson. Ben hurried ahead of her to open the back door. As with most homes in Logan Point, the back entrance was the one most people used.

"Thank you," she murmured as she stepped into the den. Ben's nephews, Josh and Jacob, sprawled in front of the TV, their fingers constantly moving on the controller in their hands.

Her breath caught in her chest when she saw TJ with her iPad, sounding out words to Tom.

"Ta . . . ta," TJ said, forming the sound with his tongue as he pointed at an image on the tablet. "Ta-ma-toe." When he saw her, his eyes widened. "Mom, I think I can show Pops how to do it."

Pops. Every time TJ spoke that word, her heart stopped. Tom's gaze went from TJ to Leigh, piercing her. There was a keen mind locked inside his body. He knew who TJ was. What if he learned to speak? "I don't think you should be worrying Sheriff Logan with your games."

Tom shook his head. "Uhh."

"See, he doesn't want to be bothered."

TJ dropped his head. "I'm sorry, Pops. I didn't mean to bother you."

His dejection almost crushed her, but before she could remedy the problem, laughter from the hallway floated into the room, and she turned as Marisa came into the den followed by Sarah.

"Leigh, I didn't hear you come in. Did you have a quiet day in the emergency room?"

"Very quiet. Mostly respiratory distress problems in children because we have a nasty virus going around." Leigh hugged Sarah. "I was surprised to see your car in the driveway."

"Me too." Sarah laughed. "But I got to thinking about you two, and Marisa called and one thing led to another, and here I am."

Leigh's heart warmed. Sarah had been more of a mother to her than her own. "I'm so glad you did. Are you staying at the motel?"

"No, she's not," Marisa said. "Her things are already in the guest bedroom."

"I'm only staying for the weekend," Sarah said. "Maybe long enough to see TJ play a little ball. He tells me he plays in his first ball game Saturday night."

Leigh turned to her son. Why had she not heard about this? "Is that right, TJ?"

TJ's head bobbed up and down. "I can play, can't I? We have practice tonight."

"I'll think about it."

"Mom—"

Marisa clapped her hands. "Everybody get washed up. Dinner's ready."

"Aw, Granna! Can we finish our game?" Jacob wailed.

Marisa crossed her arms. "March, young man."

■ ■ ■

The Logans ate in their kitchen, where Marisa ladled fresh peas and squash and new red potatoes onto plates from stainless steel pots on the stove and topped them off with a square of crusty corn bread. Then they gathered around an oversized table where, after Marisa said a blessing, warmth and laughter flowed. Everyone took part in the conversation except Tom, and where she saw in TJ's eye a hunger that had nothing to do with food.

A shadow crossed her heart, searing her conscience. TJ belonged here. Her fingers curled into the palms of her hands as the cornbread turned to sawdust in her mouth. Why, oh why, had she come to this place where her decision of ten years ago haunted her? Where Marisa treated TJ like he *was* one of her grandsons. Leigh swallowed down the lump choking her. Maybe on some level, Marisa already knew, sensed it somehow, and that drew her to TJ. Even Tom seemed drawn to him.

If Marisa ever found out TJ was her grandson, she'd begin an all-out campaign to get her and Ben together. And Leigh didn't want that. Did she? Her heart betrayed her with a flutter, and she reined it in. Ben Logan wasn't husband or father material. She'd noticed that even though Ben tolerated being around the twins, there was an invisible line he never crossed. It was like his mind was there, but not his heart. And that was the last kind of father she wanted for her son.

"This is great, Mom," Ben said from the other side of the table. "And you boys eat that squash. It's good for you."

In the chair beside her, one of the twins—Leigh couldn't remember which—pushed his yellow vegetable to the side with his fork. At the end of the table, Tom struggled with his left hand to scoop peas into his mouth, only to have them spill. His face flushed, and he banged his fist on the table.

Marisa put her fork down. "Tom, would you like me to help you?"

A growl erupted from Tom's lips.

"I take it that's a no." Marisa sighed, turning to Leigh. "The therapist is trying to get him to move his arm from left to right, but I'm afraid the connection in his brain isn't very good."

"What exercises is she doing with him?"

"Not as many as she'd like." She turned to her husband. "You aren't cooperating with her, are you, hon?"

Tom scowled at his wife.

Marisa patted his hand. "She tries to get him to play games. I'm pretty sure he thinks they are for children."

Leigh couldn't keep from evaluating Ben's dad. Even though his coordination and speech weren't good, Tom had a lot going for him. He could move from his bed to the wheelchair, usually with minimal help, and hadn't had any problem swallowing, a plus in a stroke victim. He just couldn't get the food to his mouth. "Sheriff Logan, the exercises will help you to get better."

His hazel eyes drew a bead on her. "Ummph."

He had great comprehension.

"Tomorrow I'll help you," TJ said. "We'll make it fun."

Not a good idea. The more her son interacted with this family, the harder it would be when they left. "TJ—"

"Let him help, Leigh," Sarah said, her voice soft but firm.

She clamped her lips together. Leigh knew Sarah's motive. "I just don't want TJ tiring him out."

The twin sitting beside her chimed in. "Pops, we'll help too."

She glanced at the boy. "You're Josh, right?"

He grinned, wrinkling his nose. "Nope, Jacob."

"No, you're not!" the other twin yelled. "I'm Jacob."

Leigh flicked her gaze from one twin to the other, their identical faces posturing a fake innocence.

"Boys." Ben's voice carried a warning. "Play nice. And you know better than to yell at the table."

"Pops does."

Ben eyed the offending twin with a warning. "Josh."

He squirmed. "Yes sir." Then the boy turned to her. "I'm sorry. I'm not Jacob."

She pressed her lips against the smile trying to show itself. "How in the world do you tell them apart?" she asked Marisa.

"That's easy, Mom," TJ said before the boys' grandmother could answer. "Jacob doesn't talk much, but Josh is like me. He likes to run."

Marisa laughed. "TJ's right, and if you're around them enough, you'll see their differences. I'm glad Emily doesn't dress them alike."

"Can we be 'scused?" Jacob asked.

Marisa looked over their plates and sighed, and again Leigh struggled not to grin. The boy had hidden his squash with a napkin.

"No dessert, boys?" Marisa asked with raised eyebrows.

The three boys looked at each other.

"Can we have it later? We want to finish our game before baseball practice," Josh said.

"Mom, can I go? Huh? Please?" TJ flashed his most winsome smile.

"It's at the ballpark," Marisa said. "I understand TJ's practiced at least once before, and the twins said he was a good pitcher. From what else they've said, they need one if they're going to make the playoffs. It'd also be a good way for TJ to make a few friends before school starts in two weeks."

With practice canceled for the past week because of rain, she hadn't had to deal with this problem, but now hope burned in TJ's face, and dread once again closed around her heart. Leigh couldn't come up with a single reason for him not to go, other than she didn't want him out in public without her. But going into a new school was hard, and a few friends would help. She swallowed down the no in her throat. "Sure. Maybe I'll even come."

Ben pinched his brows together. "Might be better to wait until next week. Uh, the boys will be much better by then."

For a scant second she'd forgotten why they were at the Logans'. She hated being held prisoner by this unknown crazy person. Surely . . .

Her thoughts were interrupted by the back door scraping open.

"Sorry I'm late." Emily, the twins' mother, set her briefcase on the kitchen counter. The boys hugged her on their way out of the kitchen with TJ in tow. "Good to see you too, boys!" she called after them. "And your dad says hello."

"Jeremy's a geologist," Marisa said to Leigh. "He's in Afghanistan, working on a big government project."

Leigh had met Emily Matthews at a hospital board meeting not long after she returned to Logan Point. Right away, Emily recruited her for whatever hours she could give the free medical clinic and crisis pregnancy center in the downtown area. Leigh was glad for the opportunity to meet some of her volunteer hours. She hadn't talked with Ben's sister since coming to their parents' house—either Emily had been out of town or Leigh had been at the hospital.

"I'll be so glad when this job Jeremy's doing is finished." Emily hugged her dad and nodded at Ben, then emitted a small gasp as her gaze connected with Leigh's then shifted to Sarah. "Oh, I'm sorry, I didn't know we had guests."

"I wondered when you'd notice." Marisa gave her daughter a wry grin. "You remember Leigh, don't you? And this is her friend from Jackson, Sarah."

"I know Leigh, and I'm glad we're finally getting together. I want to talk to you about the clinic." She nodded to Sarah. "And I'm so happy to meet you, Sarah. Mother told me all about how you've helped Leigh with TJ. He's such a sweet boy." She picked up a plate. "Can we talk about the clinic while I eat?"

From what Leigh had observed of Ben's sister, she lived and talked at Mach-1 speed. "Sure."

Marisa rose and pulled Tom away from the table. "Be back as soon as I settle your father in the den."

"I'm going to start on these dishes," Sarah said.

"And I'm going back to the jail," Ben added.

"Wait," Emily said. "I need you to drop the boys off at ball practice. I have a ton of paperwork to complete."

"Em—"

Emily huffed. "If you have time to come by here and eat, you have time to drop them off on your way back to the jail." She turned to Leigh as if the matter were settled. "I'm so sorry about Tony," she said as she filled her plate. "I was out of town and couldn't come to the memorial service."

Leigh suppressed a chuckle as Ben lifted his hands in defeat. She turned her attention to Emily. "I appreciate your thoughts."

Ice crackled as Emily poured tea into a glass then squeezed lemon in it. Marisa came back into the kitchen, and she and Sarah tackled the mound of dirty dishes. Leigh started to get up and help, but Emily motioned her to stay put.

"I have a proposition for you," Emily said. "Dr. Hazelit is leaving Monday for a month-long mission trip, and I don't have a physician for the Helping Hands clinic. Would you like to fill in for him?"

Wow. For a half second, Leigh couldn't breathe. Her own practice. Actually establishing a relationship with her patients long term. Or at least for a month.

Emily buttered a slice of corn bread. "I've already talked to the hospital administrator, and Doug's willing to release you to me. The clinic is under the hospital umbrella so working there will count toward your service contract, along with any hours you work after Dr. Hazelit returns."

Exactly the kind of experience she needed before applying to Johns Hopkins. "Why me? I mean, I'm inexperienced."

"But more than qualified. I looked at your resume again today. I mean, a grade point average of 3.9 and all the time raising a son by yourself. Give yourself credit, girl. You can start Monday morning." Emily paused long enough to take a sip of tea. "I know you're supposed to work the weekend, but Doug said he'd get someone to cover—I want you fresh—but this late he couldn't get anyone for tomorrow's seven-to-three shift."

"Thank you." Tears burned against Leigh's eyes, and the back of her throat tightened. Sometimes it was harder to accept kindness than criticism. A nagging thought speared her. Would the offer hold if Emily found out about TJ? The room blurred as the clink of dishes and Marisa and Sarah's soft voices filled her ears. The weight of her deception threatened to crack the dam around her heart. She was so tired of living a lie. Would it be so terrible if she told the truth? Told this family that TJ was Ben's son?

Are you crazy? You've kept the truth secret for ten years. Denied your son a daddy. What do you think these people would say about that? How would TJ react?

Feet clattering down the stairway snatched her back to reality. No one would understand. Not even TJ.

■ ■ ■

After Ben left with the twins and TJ, the house seemed way too quiet with Marisa getting her husband ready for bed and Emily off to check on the clinic. Sarah disappeared into her room to read, and Leigh wandered outside to the swing in the side yard. She did not like being a prisoner. She glanced toward Ben's house, a ranch-style brick almost hidden by the wooded lot. After they'd settled in with his parents, he hadn't suggested that they swap houses again. She sat in the swing and pushed against the ground, rocking the swing back and forth. Ben had told her the six-foot fence surrounding the property had been constructed about eight years ago, after his dad had been threatened by a drug-trafficking leader he'd put behind bars. She had to admit she did feel safe here, but at what price? Her cell phone rang, and she pulled it from her pocket, expecting it to be the hospital. It was Ian Maxwell. "Hello?"

"Good evening. Do you think you could get someone to let me through the gate?"

"The gate?" She turned her head toward the road. A dark SUV had pulled into the drive. "Is that you in the driveway?"

"Yep. Do you mind?"

"Of course not." Leigh knew the code but didn't feel comfortable letting Ian in without talking to someone first. She hopped out of the swing and walked toward the back door. "Were you coming to see Ben? Because he's not here."

"No, I'm coming to see you."

She almost stumbled. "But it's only Thursday. We're not going out to dinner until tomorrow night."

"I have something to show you."

"Oh. Well, wait a sec until I can find Marisa. I'll call you back." Leigh glanced down at the green scrubs she still wore, wishing she'd changed. She went in search of Ben's mom, finding her in the den, knitting. "Uh, Ian Maxwell is asking if you'll let him inside the gate."

Marisa looked up from her needles. "Ian?"

Leigh shrugged. "Said he wanted to talk to me."

"Oh, go ahead and let him in, and you don't have to ask permission to let someone you know through the gate." She smiled at her before returning to her knitting. "Enjoy your visit."

At the door, Leigh glanced back at Marisa and caught her watching with a thoughtful expression on her face. Marisa wasn't the only one puzzled by Ian's visit. Outside, a black Escalade rolled to a stop near the front door. Ian stepped out, looking like he'd come from a fashion shoot for Ralph Lauren. She had to admit the short-sleeve V-neck tee showed off his chiseled pecs and biceps. And wonder of wonders, he wore a pair of jeans. Designer, for sure, and pressed with a sharp crease, but still . . .

Ian's glance swept over her. "You're looking lovely tonight," he said.

She almost laughed. Green scrubs were probably the least flattering apparel ever designed. "I could say the same about you and be telling the truth. But what happened to the white long-sleeve shirt?"

Ian's slow smile softened his square jaw. "Even I dress down sometimes."

"Yeah, like that's dressing down." She tilted her head. "You said you had something to show me?"

"Grab your purse, or whatever you think you need. My crew finished with the house on Webster, and I want you to take a look at it."

She caught her breath. She hadn't mentioned moving to Ben . . . or anyone else. "I, ah, don't think Ben wants me out alone."

He straightened his shoulders. "What am I, chopped meat?"

Her face burned. "No, but you know what I mean. Somebody with a gun, maybe?"

"I am very proficient in firearms, and have a permit to carry. And the Glock in my console is registered. So that takes care of that problem."

Her jaw dropped. Why did anything about Ian Maxwell surprise her? A cool breeze flitted through the trees, and Leigh rubbed her bare arms. Even though it was only the first of August, the wind carried the barest hint of fall. She tapped her fingers against her arm. What would it hurt to go see the Webster house? She would be with Ian, who could protect her if the need arose. Not that she thought it would.

Besides, Ben couldn't keep her a prisoner here. She had a life to live . . . and tomorrow night a date with Ian. Did Ben expect to come along on that? "Let me tell someone I'm leaving and who with." She would change while she was at it. "Wouldn't want them to worry."

Ten minutes later, the Escalade pulled up to the gate, and Leigh keyed in the code. Ben's mom had given her a long, questioning look when Leigh had told her she was going out. But, bless her heart, she hadn't said a word. Marisa seemed to have a high opinion of Ian and evidently thought Leigh would be safe with him.

When they arrived at the entrance to the subdivision, it was just as Ian had promised. The house was in a gated community, with a guard on duty. TJ would be safe here, and even Ben couldn't complain about this arrangement.

She corrected herself. He'd probably find something wrong with it. "Ian, this is beautiful. It looks brand new. How much is the rent?"

"Don't worry about money. This is something I want to do," he replied as he opened the door and ushered her inside.

A marble entryway led into a great room with a fireplace. With slow steps, she moved throughout the fully furnished house, stopping when she came to the kitchen. Walnut cabinets, granite countertops . . . she'd never lived in anything so grand. "If I can't pay, then I won't even consider it." The Logans had refused all offers of payment, and she wasn't going to be in debt to Ian as well.

A frown pinched his face. "Leigh—"

She held up her hands. "No. How much do you generally receive for your rental property? And I can't believe you rent out a place like this."

His face reddened. "This one is actually staged to sell. That's why it has furniture."

She drew air into her lungs to put an end to this idea. "Ian—"

"Hear me out. Real estate isn't moving right now. I'd rather have you in it than for it to sit here empty. You'd be doing me a favor if you moved into it."

She ran her fingers over the dark gray countertop. It was so tempting. This neighborhood wasn't far from Jenny, the babysitter. It'd been over a week since anything bad had happened. Maybe Ben would even think it was okay to let TJ go back to Jenny. Probably wouldn't make her son happy, though. He liked staying at the Logans. Playing with the twins. Being around Pops and Granna. She sighed. "Let me think about it a day or two."

"Sure, no hurry." He dazzled her with a toothy smile. "How about a cup of coffee at the coffee shop in town? It's not far—another plus for this house—and it's close to town and all the stores."

"You can quit selling. I told you I'd think about it." Leigh really didn't want to make a commitment until she spoke to Ben. She tilted her head. "Instead of coffee, could we stop by the ballpark? TJ's practicing and I'd really like to watch."

"Your wish is my command."

Now why couldn't Ben say something like that?

11

en, stay with us. Help Coach Andre." TJ's earnest face looked up into Ben's with hope in his eyes as they pulled into the park entrance.

Ben rubbed the back of his neck as the familiar tightening of his stomach churned the supper he'd just eaten. "I don't know, TJ."

"Come on, Ben," Josh chimed in. "Coach Andre needs some help with Dad gone, and since Jimmy got snake bit, him and his daddy don't come anymore. I've heard Dad say you're the best ballplayer Logan Point ever had."

"I'm sorry, I have work to finish." Wasn't it enough that he helped with the Sunday school class? He slowed to let a family cross the road that looped through the park, noting that the forty-acre park was full tonight. He drove past three other fields filled with teams practicing and parked next to the ball field where a group of boys stood around his deputy.

Ben stepped out of the pickup and glanced around as the twins and TJ bolted toward the field. Andre was the only adult in sight. Where were the other dads?

Andre's brown face broke into a grin when he spied Ben. "Have you come to help?"

Ben shook his head. "No. Just dropping the twins and TJ off. Where are your other coaches?"

Andre adjusted the ball cap on his head. "I'm it. Usually, Billy's dad hangs around, but he had a meeting to attend. And I don't know where Wade is. He said he'd be here, but . . ." Andre shrugged.

Ben snorted. Wade probably had a hot date with Ruth the librarian.

"Can you help me out, man? I'm dying here. Not enough me and too many boys."

Ben pressed his lips together. He did the Sunday school thing partly to condition himself to being around kids, and it was helping, but coaching was different. What if one of the boys missed his pitch and the ball hit him in the mouth and broke a tooth? Or something worse.

"Just this once," Andre pleaded. "I need at least one base coach, and maybe you could give TJ some pointers on the mound. He has a good arm, makes me think of you, the way he pitches."

"TJ's your pitcher?"

"Yeah, he's the oldest kid I have, barely made the cutoff date."

Ben rubbed his hand on his pants. He didn't have anything pressing, and he could hardly go off and leave Andre with thirteen boys to coach alone. And how bad could it be? It was only baseball . . . it wasn't swimming. But wait until he found Wade. He'd kill him. "All right," he muttered. "I'll stay."

"Thanks, man!" Andre's grin stretched across his face.

For the next hour, Ben worked with the boys, showing them how to tag up for a sacrifice fly, where their feet should be when they rounded the bag, and how important it was to keep their eye on the ball. He explained to TJ why he shouldn't attempt a curve ball just yet. He could do this. He was actually glad he'd stayed.

Finally Andre waved the boys in. "Okay, let's get in a little batting practice. Ben here will pitch. I'll catch."

Ben took his place on the mound. He kicked the dirt, remembering the times before when he'd stood there, settling his cleats in the ground, facing the next batter. His glance slid past home plate to the parking area. Was that Leigh getting out with Ian Maxwell?

What was she thinking? They walked toward the ball field as Andre pounded his catcher's mitt.

"Right here, man. Put it right here."

Ben turned and scanned the area. It *was* the park, very open, very public with a good-sized crowd tonight. Nothing suspicious showed up on his radar. Leigh should be okay. He kicked the dirt again and lobbed a soft pitch to TJ. The boy swung a fraction of a second too late, tipping the ball. Andre stood and pitched it back to him.

"Keep your eye on the ball, TJ," Ben called. "And relax." The kid had a good swing. He threw the ball again.

Thwack! The ball sailed over the center field fence and into the woods that butted against the ballpark. A couple of the people walking behind the fence stopped and applauded.

"Way to go, TJ! I knew you could do it." Andre tipped his cap as TJ crossed home plate, and the other boys came out to pound his back.

Ben left the mound, his glove tucked under his arm. "Good job, TJ!" The boy had a natural swing.

TJ's grin lit up his whole face, then he turned and ran toward Leigh. "Mom! Did you see? I hit a home run!"

"I did." Leigh laughed and hugged her son. Briefly, her gaze sought Ben before she hugged her son again. "You're amazing. I'm glad I was here to see it."

TJ squirmed from her embrace and cocked his head toward Ian. A slight frown formed on his face.

"You remember Tony's boss? Ian Maxwell."

The lines in TJ's face deepened, and Ben agreed with his distrust.

"Your uncle was my friend," Ian said. "I'd like us to be friends. That was a super home run."

TJ stared a second longer, and when his expression softened, a pang stabbed Ben. He brushed it away. He was not jealous of Ian Maxwell.

"You really think it was good?" TJ's eyes widened, almost begging for affirmation.

"Clear out of the park." Ian glanced toward Andre. "I think you have a home-run batter here."

Andre grinned and shook Ian's hand. "Glad to see you here, Ian. You'll have to come back and watch them play next week."

Ian glanced toward Leigh with a proprietary air, and once again jealousy stung Ben. "I might just do that. How's your dad? I miss seeing him at the plant since his surgery."

"He's good." Andre cradled his glove in his arm. "He's about ready to return to work."

Ben turned to Leigh, his eyebrows raised. "I thought we agreed—"

"No, you made the decision. After I thought about it, I decided an impromptu ride to the ballpark wouldn't hurt anything. Who would know I'd be here? Besides, I'm not staying long."

Ian slipped his arm through Leigh's. "Come on, Ben, she's safe—she's with me."

That was what worried him. He hadn't forgotten Phillip Maxwell's remark about Ian being a lady's man. He turned as Andre lifted his whistle to his lips and blew hard.

"Okay," Andre yelled. "Let's give the other boys a turn at batting, and then I'll hit you some fielders."

Ben took his place on the mound as daylight slipped into the dusky part of the day and one boy after another took his turn at bat. Leigh yelled encouragement to each of them. The night-lights flickered on as the last boy finished his stint at bat. Andre gathered the boys around him. "Okay," he said. "First game, Saturday night, here on this diamond. Be here at 6:00 p.m., and we'll practice for half an hour and then let the other team have the field for their warm-up. Maybe Ben will help us out again."

Andre held up his hands for high fives then sent them out to practice fielding under the lights while Ben walked toward the bleachers. Wade better show up next time since there was no way he'd fill in for his chief deputy again. At least one of his pitches hadn't broken an arm or tooth. But the evening was young, and he couldn't shake the dark clouds hovering in his head.

"Think they'll win?" Leigh asked when he got within earshot.

"Maybe, but probably not. Andre said the other team's coach has the state championship in his sights."

"You don't think Andre does?" Ian sounded skeptical.

"I don't think he wants to put that kind of pressure on the kids. He wants baseball to be fun for them. . . besides, it's not whether you win—"

"Or lose, it's the way you play the game." Ian snorted. "You don't really believe that, do you?"

"Doesn't matter what I think—I'm not the coach."

"Andre seems like a really good coach, but it looks like he needs help," Leigh said. "Anyway, TJ had fun tonight. I need to thank your deputy for letting him play."

Ian tapped Leigh with his elbow. "Quick, a fly ball to TJ."

Ben turned as TJ got under the ball and snagged it. Then he hurled it back to Andre.

"Way to go, TJ!" Leigh pumped her fist into the air.

"Where'd he get all that talent? Pitching and fielding," Ian said. "From his dad?"

"Yeah?" Ben said. "TJ has a good arm, and I don't remember you being too good at sports."

Even under the lights, Ben could see the two red circles that appeared on Leigh's cheeks as she pressed her lips together. "I played tennis, but if you remember, Tony was a great pitcher, and TJ *is* his nephew."

On the field, Andre blew his whistle and called an end to practice. Within minutes, thirteen boys surrounded him, clamoring for ice cream. "Not this time. But I do want you boys to police the area."

Leigh waved to her son then turned to Ian. "If they're finished, maybe TJ can ride back with us."

Ben stuck his hands in his pockets. "Or you could ride back with us. I doubt TJ will want to leave the twins." He didn't say it, but he doubted Ian would want three sweaty boys in his Escalade.

Evidently the idea occurred to Leigh as well because she shot an uncertain glance toward the SUV. "That might be a good idea."

Ian squared his shoulders. "I brought you, I'll take you home, the boys too, if they want to ride. But are they ready to leave? I think I just heard the coach tell them the area needs policing."

Ben had heard that as well. "We'll probably be here another half hour."

Frowning, Leigh glanced toward the field. "I really do need to get back."

Ben shrugged. "I'll bring the boys home."

He walked toward the team, stopping to look over his shoulder as Ian and Leigh picked their way through the grass to Maxwell's fancy SUV. Ian's hand rested on the small of Leigh's back.

TJ tugged on Ben's arm, and he turned to see what the boy wanted. He stood with Andre's little brother. "Martin and his family are going to the lake this weekend for a picnic. Could we have a picnic sometime? Go to the lake? We could swim."

Ben's whole body stiffened.

Martin elbowed TJ. "Sheriff don't swim, doofus. Everybody knows that, on account of that boy that drowned. Ain't that—"

"Hey, Martin." Andre's loud voice overrode his brother's words. "Go round up the bats and start picking up the trash."

Martin looked up and ducked his head under the scowl on his big brother's face. He grabbed TJ's arm. "Come on, you gotta help me."

The two boys sauntered to the fence where bats lay scattered like pick-up sticks, Martin's mouth moving like a magpie's. Once TJ looked back at Ben, his eyes wide. No explanation needed for what Martin had shared with TJ. Ben's stomach churned, the meal he'd eaten earlier souring. How did Martin know unless . . . He glanced at Andre.

His deputy averted his gaze. "Who needs rides?" he yelled. "And who has parents picking them up?"

Only two hands went up for rides. "Okay," Andre said. "I'll text your parents that we're done. And while we're waiting, the rest of you help Martin and TJ."

The boys scattered over the field, picking up wrappers and anything else that'd been dropped. Ben slipped the bat carrier on his shoulder, and he and Andre walked toward the fence where the two boys had stacked the bats in a semi-neat order.

Andre held the bag while Ben slid the aluminum clubs into it. "Sorry about what Martin said."

"He only repeated what he'd heard."

"My parents asked why you didn't help coach . . . I guess he heard us talking, but Ben, nobody blames you for Tommy Ray's death."

"Billy Wayne did. His old man still does."

"Well, I was there. Everybody thought Tommy Ray was horsing around. You couldn't tell he was in trouble."

"Thanks, Andre, but you're my friend, and you might be a little prejudiced. I should've gone in after him right away instead of throwing him the inner tube."

His deputy palmed his hands. "But that's what a lifeguard is supposed to do. We took the same training. It was a terrible accident, and it's been three years. It's time to let it go."

If only he could. "I was in charge, and I let Tommy Ray and his family down. I keep thinking if I'd just—"

"Ben, turn it over to God. It wasn't your fault. But if you're convinced it was, just remember God has already forgiven you—forgave you the day it happened. Let. It. Go."

Not one day in the three years since the Gresham boy died had Ben felt God's forgiveness. "Look, let's talk about—"

"Coach!" Yells rent the air.

"Come here quick!"

"There's a snake!"

"Martin got bit!"

Ben jerked in the direction of the screams. Martin sat on the ground near the center field fence, holding his leg. Ben sprinted toward him with Andre right behind him. "Don't move!"

Martin rocked on the ground, holding his leg to his chest with the other boys huddled around him. Andre knelt beside his brother while Ben yanked out his cell phone and speed-dialed Leigh. "Can you get back here? We have a boy with a snakebite."

Ben knelt at the boy's feet. He'd known something bad was going to happen.

Andre pocketed his phone. "An ambulance is on the way. They said to keep him still and for him to lie down."

"It . . . hurts. My leg h-hurts."

Ben used his glove as a pillow for Martin, then he turned to his deputy. "Get the boys to the bleachers, then see if the snake is still around here. All of you, watch where you step." He turned back to Martin. "I'm going to look at your foot, okay? You just lay there and be still."

Martin's small body jerked as Ben gently turned the swollen ankle. "I'll try not to hurt you." He unbuckled the cleated shoe and slipped his shoe and sock off, dread filling him at the sight of two puncture wounds above his ankle, usually a sign of a poisonous snake. Maybe it was a dry bite, one where the snake hadn't injected much venom. "Do you remember what the snake looked like?"

Martin shook his head and squeezed his eyes shut. "I didn't see it. It just jumped and bit my leg."

"I did," TJ said.

Ben snapped his head around. "What are you doing here? You were supposed to go with Andre."

TJ blinked. "I'm sorry. I didn't want to leave my friend."

"Well, what did it look like?"

"It was reddish brown and had some kind of round pattern on it."

Ben's stomach tightened. Copperhead. He examined the boy's

leg. The swelling extended up the leg. "Martin, I need you to be really still until the ambulance gets here, okay?"

He looked over his shoulder as Ian's SUV screeched to a halt, and Leigh jumped out. In seconds she knelt beside the boy while Ian leaned over her shoulder.

"Has anyone called 911?" she asked.

"They're on the way."

Leigh examined Martin's leg. "What happened?"

"Snake bit him. What TJ described sounded like a copperhead." The look she gave him didn't make him feel better.

"Those bites can be nasty," Ian muttered.

Martin wailed, and Leigh's eyes narrowed as she shot Ian a warning glare over her shoulder before she turned to Martin. "How are you feeling?"

"It hurts. Am I gonna die?"

"Look at me, Martin." Leigh lifted the boy's chin. "You're going to be okay. Ben, do you have a first aid kit?"

He tossed Ian his keys. "Would you mind getting it? It's in my truck, under the seat."

"Passenger side?"

Ben nodded as his cell phone buzzed.

"Ben!" Andre's voice sounded panicky. "You gotta get over here!"

Ben turned and scanned the field for his deputy. Andre stood with his back against the center field fence.

Leigh glanced up. "I don't need you. Go."

"Ben!" His deputy's voice quivered. "I really need you, but keep the boys away."

Ben glanced toward his truck. Ian had found the kit and hurried back toward them. "The ambulance should be here any second."

He grabbed TJ's hand and led him to the bleachers before jogging toward center field, where his deputy waited. "This better be—" Ben's heart stilled. He tried to breathe, but icy fingers wrapped around his lungs, locking them down.

"Don't come any closer," Andre warned. "But I'd appreciate it if you'd get rid of these things."

Five copperheads slithered on the ground between Ben and his deputy. "Don't move," Ben said.

"Don't you worry."

With the fence at Andre's back, there was no way for the deputy to walk around the snakes. Ben was going to have to shoot them.

■■■

Two snakebites in three weeks? Leigh hoped it didn't become a pattern. If only she'd stuck her medical bag in Ian's SUV. She smoothed her hand over Martin's forehead. His dark skin had a chalky tone to it. Sweat beaded his face. Signs of low blood pressure. Mentally, she hurried the ambulance.

A tear squeezed from Martin's eye, and he brushed it away. "I don't feel so good."

"You're going to be fine." Leigh had found that if a patient knew what was going on, it kept them calmer. "You're going to the hospital to get some medicine that will fix you up. Now, take a deep breath, and let it out slowly."

Ian squatted beside her and opened the first aid kit. A man she didn't recognize hovered behind Ian. "Shouldn't you suction the venom out?" the stranger asked. "I use to drive an ambulance, and that's what those guys did."

"Must've been years ago," she muttered, shooting him a quick glance before turning to Ian. "Do you see any alcohol wipes?"

Ian handed her a small, sealed packet, and the other man butted in again. "Look, there's a surgical steel blade in this here kit if you need it."

She'd gone through eight years of medical school, and this guy knew more than she did? "I think I know what I'm doing."

His face turned red. "Just trying to help. Sorry, lady."

He probably was, but she'd battled mentality like his her whole way through med school.

Ian turned to him with a frown. "Look, she's a doctor, so if you don't mind . . ."

"Oh." He stepped back. "Guess you don't need my help, then."

"I think she has it under control."

Leigh tore open the wipe packet and gave Martin a reassuring smile. "This will burn, but not for long."

She gently cleaned the wound, noting the bruising and small puncture wounds that were turning dark. "Got another wipe?" she asked as the sharp *wawa* of the ambulance reached her ears. A minute later, two paramedics raced toward them. David, she recognized from the ER. His partner was new to her.

David set his bag on the ground. "Dr. Somerall? What do we have here?"

"We have Martin. And he's been bitten by a snake."

"And it hurts." Martin's voice cracked. "Real bad."

"You're being mighty brave." The medic glanced over the boy's head at Leigh. "Poisonous?" he mouthed.

"Probably. Let's get his vitals and then get him to the hospital where we can do blood work." She turned to Ian. "Could you find out if anyone has called his parents?"

"Andre is his brother. He should be able to give permission for any procedure you need to do."

"Ian, please. I'd rather have it from the parents. You seemed to know them. Would you please call for me?" She stepped out of the boy's hearing range and dialed the hospital. "I have a nine-year-old black male with a witnessed copperhead snakebike to his right lower leg who will soon be en route to the ER. Prepare to draw a CBC and a PT and INR and have antivenom ready to administer. One more thing. He was a patient in the ER around the middle of June. Martin Stone. Would you pull his records?"

Ian stepped toward her. "Martin's dad, Samuel Stone," he said, holding out his phone.

"Thanks," she said. "Mr. Stone, this is Dr. Leigh Somerall. I'm not sure if Ian informed you, but Martin has incurred a possible poisonous snakebite, and I need your permission to treat."

"Doc, you do whatever you need to do. My wife and I will meet you at the hospital."

"I know Martin's tetanus shot is up-to-date from when I saw him in the ER a couple of weeks ago. I have to ask again if he's allergic to anything."

"Let me ask Adrian."

Leigh waited as she heard Stone relay the question.

"My wife says he's not. Is Andre there?"

"I think he's trying to find the snake to ascertain what type we're dealing with."

"Thanks, Doc, glad you were there."

She handed the phone to Ian and then turned to the paramedic who was helping to load the gurney. "How are his vitals?"

"BP is 85/40. Pulse is 120."

Possible mild shock. "Let's transport. I'll ride in the back with the boy." *TJ.* She jerked her head around, searching for her son. "Where's TJ?"

"Ben took him to the bleachers where the other boys are," Ian said. "I think he called in more deputies to help with them until their parents get here. Do you want me to take TJ and the twins to the Logans'?"

Leigh hesitated. If she took TJ with her, he'd have to hang around the ER waiting room until she was finished. Finally, she nodded. "Tell him . . . tell him Martin is going to be okay." She started to climb into the ambulance but turned back to Ian. "Thanks."

"Don't worry about TJ. I'll keep him safe. After I drop the boys off at the Logans', I'll pick you up at the hospital."

Five shots rang out, and Leigh jumped. Frantically, she searched for TJ, but the boys had deserted the bleachers. Finally she found them crowded near the dugout fence, staring in the direction of the shots. She followed their line of sight to Ben and Andre, and she grabbed the side of the ambulance to keep from falling. Ben held out a snake that reached from his waist to the ground.

Martin moaned, and Leigh motioned to the medic for them to leave. "Take care of TJ," she called to Ian as the ambulance door closed.

Fifteen minutes after arriving at the hospital, Leigh studied the first lab report on Martin's blood panel. A slightly elevated white count, but everything else looked normal. Antivenom or not? She had yet to decide. After speaking with Ben about the snakes that had been killed, she'd learned all five had been copperheads, females about to birth. Of all the poisonous snakes in their area, perhaps the copperhead was the least lethal. She turned to her RN, thankful that Cathy was on duty. "Would you accompany me to Martin's room?"

When they stepped inside the room, Adrian Stone looked around. "I'm tired of meeting you this way, Dr. Somerall. But this boy can't seem to keep out of trouble. Is he going to be okay?"

Leigh had met Martin's mother the first time she saw the boy in the ER with the cut on his arm. She patted her shoulder, hoping to erase the worry lines around her mouth. "I think he's going to be fine."

Mr. Stone stood. "Did Andre and the sheriff find the snake and identify it?"

"They killed five female copperheads. Of course—"

"Five?" He rubbed his jaw. "I've never seen that many snakes in one place. Do they know why there were so many?"

Leigh shook her head. "Ben did say they were all full of baby snakes. However, we don't know which one bit Martin, but all appear to be mature snakes." She examined Martin's leg. It had swollen only slightly more, but still, any additional swelling needed to be considered. "Does it still hurt?"

With round eyes he nodded.

Leigh tilted her head. "Let's say that on a scale of one to ten, where one only hurts a little and ten hurts so bad you want to yell, which number is the pain closest to?"

Martin bit his lip. "If I don't move it, maybe five, but if I move it—ten for sure."

"That helps me a lot." She turned to his parents. "I want to give him antivenom—Crofab. Again, is he allergic to anything? "

Adrian laughed softly. "Doctor, that boy isn't allergic to anything, especially food."

"Good." Leigh turned to Cathy. "Get his weight, then prepare four vials of Crofab."

"You sure he's going to be all right?" Mr. Stone asked.

"As sure as I can be about anything, Mr. Stone. We'll admit him to ICU so we can monitor any reaction to the antivenom, but you can stay with him."

"Thank you, and call me Sam. The way Andre talks about you, I feel I already know you."

An hour later, Leigh paused from writing her report on Martin and worked the muscles in her neck. So far, there'd been no reaction to the Crofab, meaning he could be moved to a room in ICU where he would be closely monitored overnight. She'd called Marisa to see if TJ had made it home okay, but no one answered. She'd call back in a few minutes.

Her cell phone rang, and she glanced at it. Dr. Robert Meriwether? Her heart kicked into high gear. He was her contact at Johns Hopkins. Her finger shook as she slid the lock off and answered. "Hello?"

"Leigh. How are you?"

"Fine," she answered cautiously.

"Are you still interested in getting your foot in the door at Johns Hopkins?"

"Yes sir!"

"Then I have a proposition for you. I have an opening at our free clinic beginning October 1st. Interested?"

She swallowed a gasp. The room seemed to stand still. The sounds of the ER faded into the background as she pressed the phone tightly against her ear. She thought about pinching herself to make sure she wasn't dreaming.

"Leigh, are you there?" Dr. Meriwether's voice boomed in her ear.

"Yes, Doctor. I'm . . . yes, I'm definitely interested." She tried not to sound breathless. "When do I need to be in Baltimore?"

"You'll probably want to get settled in an apartment by the middle of September."

She couldn't believe her dream was coming true. Dad's dream too. And she'd be able to fulfill the promise she'd just made to Emily to work at the clinic the four weeks in August. *The scholarship repayment.* "Uh, what about the service contract I signed?"

"The clinic is in the program. I've talked with your adviser, and he'll take care of the paperwork. You and I can work out the other details, like signing the contract, next month."

She stared at the phone long after she'd hung up. She was going to Johns Hopkins. The words danced inside her head. *I can't wait to tell Tony.*

Suddenly, the loss of her brother slammed her, and she blinked back the tears that seemed to come from nowhere.

"Leigh? Are you okay?"

She looked up into Ben's concerned face. "How long have you been standing there?"

"Just got here, why? I brought TJ."

"I didn't hear you come up." She looked past him for her son. TJ's words of their first night at the Logans' echoed in her head. *"I like it here. I wish we could stay forever."* How was she going to tell him they were moving again? "Where's TJ? Is he all right?"

"He's fine. Out in the waiting room with four other boys who want to know how Martin is. Emily is riding herd on them."

Her shoulders relaxed, and she smiled. Visits from Martin's friends would probably be better than medicine. "I think that can be arranged before he goes to ICU. But just two at a time."

"ICU?"

"Mostly for observation. From the looks of the wound, Martin didn't receive a full envenomation, but I'm not taking any chances with the snakebite or the antivenom."

He turned to leave, and she stopped him. "Do you have any idea why there were five snakes on the ball field?"

Ben's face hardened. "I think they were turned loose. On purpose."

■ ■ ■

"You're kidding." Leigh's brow furrowed. "Why? Do you know who did it?"

"I don't know why, and I don't know who. What I do know is a ball field isn't a natural habitat for copperheads. Not five, anyway." Ben had seen female copperheads congregate when about to give birth, but never in a populated area like the park. They preferred a quieter, more rural setting. "I think someone captured them and turned them loose. Maybe someone who handles snakes on a regular basis. Have you treated anyone else for a snakebite?"

"A garter bite a couple of weeks ago, but that was a young boy. You may want to check with the makers of antivenom. I know if I were handling poisonous snakes, I'd keep some on hand."

"Good idea. Do you mind if I ask Martin a couple of questions before the boys see him?"

"Sure. He's in room 6. His parents are with him."

Ben walked down the corridor and rapped lightly on the door to the room. When he heard a muffled "Come in," he pushed the door open.

"Howdy, folks," he said, nodding at the Stones. "Andre will be here soon to check on Martin. Right now, he's taking the dead snakes to a local vet for examination." He turned to Martin. "How are you feeling, buddy?"

"My foot hurts, and I want to go home. Do you think Andre will let me play Saturday?"

Ben glanced at Martin's dad. "Maybe you can cheer them on."

"But I want to play!"

Sam rubbed the top of his son's head. "You want your team to win, don't you?" After Martin nodded, he continued, "Then you want to feel 100 percent so you can play well."

The boy sighed. "First I can't play because I cut my arm and now this. Andre won't ever let me play again."

"Martin," Ben said. "Did you see anyone out by the center field fence? Maybe with a bag?"

Sam startled. "You don't think—"

"I don't know. Just asking questions." He turned back to the boy. "Did you see anyone?"

"There were lots of people walking by, going to the other ball fields."

"Did anyone stop?"

Martin wrinkled his nose as he considered Ben's question, then he hunched his shoulders in a shrug. "I don't remember. What about TJ? Did you ask him?"

"Yeah, but he doesn't remember, either. Tell me exactly what happened. TJ said you two were picking up trash. What did you pick up?"

"A bag. A big one—you know, like a garbage bag."

Ben paused. Was it possible the bag had blown against the fence and the snakes congregated under it? His gut said no, but it was a possibility. "Did you see any other snakes?"

Martin shook his head. "That one was enough."

Ben chuckled. "I imagine it was. Think about it, and if you remember something, tell your brother." Ben stopped at the door. "Oh, and you have a few friends out in the waiting room who want to see you."

"Really? Cool." The grin that spread across Martin's face lit up the room.

Sam Stone followed Ben into the hallway. "Are you thinking someone put those snakes there deliberately?"

"Like I said before, I don't know. But if someone did, I'll find them and bring them to justice."

"Not if I find them first."

Ben grabbed his arm. "Don't do anything rash, Sam. Let me and Andre handle it."

"Then you two better do something pretty quick, because I know where to start looking."

"What are you talking about?"

"There are only a few people in this county crazy enough to fool with snakes."

Ben knew Sam was referring to Jonas Gresham and a few of his cronies. "Let it be. At least until we know for sure someone collected them and turned them loose on the ball field."

Sam slid his hands in his pockets, jingling change. "Takes a sick person to do something like that."

"Well, let's just hope it was a freak occurrence."

"Yeah, right."

Ben left Sam at the door and walked back to the nurses' station, where Leigh stood talking to her son and one of the twins. The light shone down on her hair, reminding him of rich mahogany. There was something different about Leigh tonight. A sparkle in her eye he hadn't seen before, and her cheeks were full of color—she emitted excitement.

She smiled as he approached. "Would you show TJ and Josh which room is Martin's?"

"Sure." Dutifully, Ben turned around and escorted the boys to the room he'd just left and ushered them inside. "Here are your friends. We can only stay a minute, but the boys wanted to see for themselves you're okay."

TJ and Josh crowded around the bed, wanting to see where the snake bit Martin. "Wow. Your foot's big."

"Hurts too. But your mom fixed me up."

TJ grinned. "She's good."

Josh cocked his head. "How come you got bit and we didn't?"

"Good question," Ben said. "Did either of you see the snakes?"

Josh shook his head, but TJ said, "I just saw the one that bit Martin. Where'd they come from, anyway?"

After a few minutes of talk, the blood pressure cuff on Martin's arm activated and the boy became still. He looked a little peaked. "I think it's time to go," Ben said and herded the two boys toward the door. "They'll come see you once you get home."

Outside in the hallway, TJ looked up at him. "Is Martin going to be okay?"

"Yeah," Ben said. "Your mom says it'll just take some time to heal. You two go to the waiting room, and I'll be out in a minute. Tell the other boys that he's okay, and they can see him later, after he gets home."

Ben stopped at the nurses' station, where Leigh was putting away a chart. "Thanks for letting them in to visit Martin."

"I'm sure it did him a world of good." She looked past Ben. "Is Ian here? At the ball field, he said he'd take care of getting TJ to your folks, and then he'd drop by the hospital and take me home."

Ben squared his shoulders. "I informed him I'd take care of getting you home."

Leigh blinked and took a step back. "Okay. That'll work too. After transport moves Martin to ICU."

"I'll have Emily take the boys home, and I'll wait for you."

A few minutes later, an orderly approached the desk.

"Got an order to move a patient." He glanced at his clipboard. "Martin Stone."

"Room 6," Leigh said. She cocked her head toward Ben. "Be right back."

Ben leaned against the counter. Even in their high school biology lab, Leigh had been compassionate. When he'd learned she wanted to be a doctor, he'd known she'd make a good one. Seeing her in action confirmed it. A few minutes later, the door opened and Leigh exited, followed by Martin in his bed.

"I'll check on you in the morning," Leigh said as she bent over and hugged the boy. Then she shook hands with the Stones. "He's going to be fine. And let's quit meeting this way."

"I'll gladly do that, Doctor," Adrian replied.

Ben waited while Leigh walked to the elevator with them, then when she returned to him, he held out his arm to escort her. She hesitated briefly and then took his arm. "Thank you, gallant sir."

"You seem awfully chipper tonight," he said.

She stopped, and when he turned around, she beamed at him. "I have to tell someone. Dr. Meriwether at Johns Hopkins called tonight and offered me a position, starting the first of October. We'll be leaving the middle of September so we can get settled in."

Words escaped him as he stared at her. She was leaving in six weeks? Just like that, she was leaving?

12

When are you going to tell TJ he's moving and leaving his friends behind?"

Leigh jerked her head toward Ben. His disapproval had ridden with them for the last five miles, and now he wanted to lay a guilt trip on her.

"He'll make new friends. Baltimore will be a great experience for him. Museums, the Orioles. There'll be so much more for him to do there. And at least there, no one will be trying to kill his mother. Have you heard from the fire marshal?"

"No. If I don't hear anything today, it'll be Monday before he'll be back in his office. If I don't hear by the afternoon, I'll give him a call to see what the holdup is." Ben rubbed his finger around the steering wheel. "Why don't you want to stay in Logan Point? TJ is happy here."

"How about my dreams? My dad always wanted to practice at Johns Hopkins, and it's all I've ever wanted too. He would be proud of me."

"But is it what you really want, Leigh? I've seen the way you love the people here, and the way they love you. This town needs you. Take Martin—"

"Any doctor at Bradford General could have done what I did."

"But he trusts you. You fixed his arm. And how about my sister. She needs you at the clinic when Dr. Hazelit leaves."

"I'm not leaving until the middle of September, so I can easily fill in for him."

"But Hazelit is retiring next year. You could be her full-time physician at the clinic."

Leigh tried to shut out his words. She had nothing and no one in Logan Point to stay for. *What about TJ? He has family here who would love him . . . if they knew.* She swayed as Ben made the turn onto Logan Road.

Why did he have to bring up these things now? Sure, she was beginning to love her work at Bradford General, and she was sure she'd love working at Emily's clinic, but Johns Hopkins . . . it'd always been her dream, her goal. The way to prove her value. "I don't want my dream to end up like yours."

Ben turned into the Logan drive and keyed in the code on the gate. "What are you talking about?"

"The dream you had ten years ago of becoming a U.S. Marshal. Didn't you tell me that's why you changed from law to criminal justice? Seems to me like you've settled for acting sheriff."

"I'm not settling." Ben pulled through the gate, and it closed behind his truck. Without a word, he drove the short distance to the back of his parents' house and put the gear in park. Finally he spoke. "I have a different dream now. I want to protect the people of Bradford County. That's why I've qualified for the election."

"That sounds like a canned answer. At least I'm being honest."

"Are you? Why is Johns Hopkins so important?"

"It was a mistake having another child." Her mother's words rang in her ears. If she could work at a hospital like Johns Hopkins, it would prove she wasn't the mistake her mother talked about. "You wouldn't understand. Just like I don't understand why you're content to stay in Logan Point."

In the moonlight filtering into the cab of the truck, she could see he was formulating a reply. He took a deep breath.

"I've finally realized it's where I belong. I love Logan Point, and

I do want to protect it. We both know something crazy is going on. First Tony is killed, and then you're shot at. Your house is burned down, and now snakes at the ball field. These are not coincidences. Someone is taunting me, saying I can't protect the people of this town. After tonight, I need you to be really careful."

"Why? The snakes had nothing to do with me." She put her hand on his arm. "You're doing a good job, Ben. Protecting me and this county. And this evening you were where you were supposed to be. I thought you were only dropping the twins and TJ off on the way back to your office."

He turned to her, and she caught the desperation in his eyes. "I didn't want to stay, but it didn't seem right to leave Andre high and dry after Wade didn't show up."

She remembered how he'd turned TJ down when he'd asked him to come watch him play ball. Maybe there was more to his reluctance than she knew. "Why don't you like to be around kids? You're uncomfortable even around your nephews."

His Adam's apple bobbed as he swallowed and shifted his gaze away from her. "It's a nice night out. Want to take a walk to the lake?"

Leigh caught her breath. She hadn't been to the lake since . . .

He opened his truck door, the interior light scattering her thoughts. "Maybe a short walk, just past the barn," she heard herself saying.

In the dim light, his eyes appeared almost black, unreadable. Was he remembering their last time at the lake? He shut the door and came around to the other side and helped her out of the truck. She willed her legs to carry her away from the magnetic pull Ben seemed to have on her.

The August full moon lit their path as they walked in comfortable silence, soon passing the barn. Her steps slowed as they rounded the curve in the grassy road and moonlight spilled onto the water.

"Want to walk out on the pier?" Ben's husky voice broke the silence.

She followed his lead to the end of the dock and sat beside him, their feet dangling over the water. In the distance, a whip-poor-will called to its mate, the sound haunting and lonely. Beside her, Ben sighed.

"What happened to us?" he asked.

She froze. "You had your dreams, I had mine," she said when she finally found her voice.

"That could've been worked out. I thought we had something special."

Leigh had thought that as well. Especially after . . . But it'd been the next day that Tom Logan had offered her the deal. *"I'll drop all charges against Tony. All you have to do is end this summer romance."* Leigh hadn't considered it a summer romance. It'd been for keeps with her. Not that it would have ever worked out—Sheriff Tom had big plans for his son, and Leigh Jackson—the girl with the spiked hair who worked at a questionable dance club—was not a suitable wife for a future sheriff. Between love for her brother and Tom Logan's pressure, she made her choice, and after she discovered she was pregnant, it was too late to undo it. Ben had moved on to someone else, not that she really blamed him. His voice, hesitant and unsure, broke into her thoughts.

"I, ah, I'm sorry for pressuring you that night. I've always thought what happened is why you broke up with me and then didn't take my calls."

Even now her cheeks flamed in the darkness as she remembered waking the next morning, the shame and regret that washed over her. She'd always planned to save herself for the man she married, for her wedding night, and with one rash decision, she'd altered her life forever. But it hadn't been all Ben's fault. "I was as responsible for what happened as you were."

"Was it the reason?"

If only she could tell him what really happened, but then he'd be angry at his father, and Tom Logan needed his son. "You never said what makes you so uncomfortable around kids," she said. Beside her, he shifted, and Leigh felt his gaze on her.

"I didn't, did I," he said. A few small rocks lay scattered on the pier, and he picked up one and skipped it across the inlet. Neither spoke as the water rippled in circles. "The way bad things happen when I'm around, it's probably a good thing. Like Tommy Ray Gresham. Like tonight. First time I ever hang around, and Martin gets snake bit."

"That wasn't your fault. And from what I've heard, neither was Tommy Ray's death."

"If I hadn't let go of Tom—"

"You both could've died."

■ ■ ■

"I saved myself instead of him." Ben had never shared the depth of his guilt with another living soul, and usually didn't even let himself acknowledge it. But somehow tonight, here at the lake with Leigh, the words just came out. "I should have kept holding on to him, but I couldn't breathe, and Tommy Ray was a big kid, a tackle for the junior football team. He pulled me deeper."

The memory of the water closing in on him, his lungs bursting, Tommy Ray fighting him, grabbing him and pulling him down . . . Sweat beaded his upper lip, and he curled his fingers into balls.

"Do you think it would've been better if you'd drowned with him? Ben, it was an accident."

"Then why can't I let it go? Why do I feel so guilty?"

"Ian said Jonas Gresham keeps throwing it up to you. Maybe that's why. Does anyone else in town blame you?"

Electricity shot up his arm as she grabbed it and pulled him around until he was looking into her jade eyes. The moonlight bathed her in a soft glow. Why did he ever let Leigh get away?

"Ben Logan, look at how you saved TJ. You are the strongest, bravest man I know. If you don't believe me, you're just plain stupid, and I can't help you."

He licked his lips, wishing he could accept what she said. But all he could think of was how beautiful she was, how close her lips were to his. Her breath halted as he caught her gaze and held it. He leaned toward her.

His cell rang, and he groaned. Maybe he should just let it ring. But the spell was broken, and he slipped the phone from his shirt pocket. "Logan."

"Ben!" Wade sounded breathless. "Somebody set fire to the jail."

He scrambled to his feet. "What? Never mind, I heard you. Did you get the prisoners out?"

"They're out. Logan Point PD is on the way to relocate them to the city jail. I hear the fire department sirens now."

"How bad is it?"

"Just the roof right now, but as old as this building is, we might have a problem if the fire truck doesn't hurry up and get here."

"I'll be there in ten." He pulled Leigh up. "The jail is on fire."

"You're kidding."

"I wish. Can you jog? I have to get back to my truck, but I don't want to leave you here alone."

"Let's go."

Ben saw Leigh safely into the house before jumping into his truck and speeding to town. At least there hadn't been any dangerous criminals in the cells. But who would want to set fire to the county jail?

The same person who put snakes on the ball field, and burned Leigh's house down, and shot at them, and maybe killed Tony. The same person who wanted to make him look incompetent. And he seemed to be doing a pretty good job of it.

He gripped the steering wheel. But whoever it was would make a mistake, or someone would see him. Ben was going to catch him if he had to put every deputy he had on overtime and pay the cost out of his own pocket.

When he pulled into the jail parking lot, two fire engines and a host of other vehicles filled it. Firemen appeared to have the blaze under control. "What do we have?" he asked as he neared his chief deputy.

"Looks like it's only the roof and the two offices in the front part of the building," Wade said. "Just lucky Andre pulled into the parking lot when he did and saw the fire when it first started. He radioed me, then moved the prisoners, and when I got here, I used a water hose to wet down the back side where the cells and our offices are."

"Anybody see anything?"

Wade shook his head. "Jenkins was manning the dispatch and thought he heard something, then five or six 911 calls came in at once. All of them hang-ups."

"Did he get numbers?"

"Said two were from a pay phone, the others were probably from throwaway phones."

"Ben!"

He turned. Andre was walking toward him with old Mr. Gordon. The eighty-something store owner still opened and closed his hardware store every day.

"Been canvassing the buildings," Andre said. "Mr. Gordon here saw something."

"Yeah." Gordon's voice rasped the word out. "I was locking up and saw this flaming torch fly through the air, so I looked to see where it came from, and about that time another one flew over." He lifted his arm and pointed. "It was right there—between the drugstore and that new lawyer's office. And there was somebody standing there. I yelled, and they disappeared."

"Can you identify the person?"

161

Mr. Gordon took out a handkerchief and mopped his face. "Naw." He stuck the handkerchief in his back pocket. "It was too dark. Couldn't even tell if it was a man or woman."

Ben turned to Wade. "Secure that area. We'll see what we can find tonight, then in the morning when there's light we'll go over it again. Maybe the person left something behind."

Wade pulled him aside. "Ben, mind if I pass on this? I have a hunch, and I want to play it out."

"You want to share this hunch? And where were you earlier? I thought you were going to help Andre with that ball team."

Wade rested his hand on his Glock. "I got a tip that I wanted to follow up on."

Ben stared at his chief deputy. Wade liked to work alone, but right now, Ben needed his help. "Did you hear we killed five copperheads on the ball field tonight? After one bit Andre's brother?"

Wade's head jerked up. "What? Is Martin okay?"

"He will be, but thank goodness Leigh was there. She rode with him in the ambulance to the hospital."

"Why would anyone turn poisonous snakes loose on a ball field?"

"So, your first reaction is someone deliberately did it?"

"Copperheads wouldn't go to an open place like that."

"Not even females about to give birth? All five snakes had babies ready to be born. And evidently they were under a black garbage bag. Martin just happened to be the one who picked up the bag and disturbed them."

Wade slid a square box from his pocket, took out a toothpick, and stuck it in his mouth. He chewed on it for a minute. "Copperheads go away from people, not toward them. They wouldn't congregate where there was a crowd."

Ben nodded. "That's what I was thinking. That's why I think someone put them there. This place is busy from daylight to past dark with mowing, runners, kids playing."

Wade worked the toothpick back and forth in his mouth. "Maybe . . ."

"Maybe what?"

Wade flicked the toothpick to the ground. "The fire and the snakes were a diversion."

"From what?" Sometimes his chief deputy drove him batty with his Lone Ranger mentality. "All right, Wade, spill it. What are you working on? And start at the beginning."

"Remember the dog we found?"

"The one out by the Gresham place."

"Yeah. When I looked him over, I found at least twenty scars from where he'd been bitten before. And since that pup didn't bite himself, I figure he was used as bait by dogfighters. And Jonas is callous enough to just discard an animal."

Ben's jaw tightened. "You think Gresham is involved in the ring?"

Wade nodded. "I was at Molly's Diner this afternoon, heard him talking to Lester Cummings in the booth behind me. At first I thought they were talking about a dice game going down tonight, but as I listened, I figured out pretty quick it wasn't. It sounded like something pretty big, though."

His chief deputy glanced toward the smoldering jail. "If you wanted to direct attention away from one part of the county, what would you do?"

Ben followed his gaze. "Create a diversion. The snakes could even be part of the diversion. Did you hear the location?"

"Not exactly. About that time Ginny Peters came in with that wild bunch of hers and drowned out everything else. That's why I was patrolling up around the Tennessee line. If I was going to do something illegal, it'd be in that part of the county. Saw some traffic around the Edwards farm, but then Andre called, and I hightailed it back to town."

Ben tried to place the Edwards property, and a vague memory surfaced. "Didn't someone from up north buy his land?"

"Yeah. And stopped everyone from hunting on it. Made a lot of folks mad."

"I'll check at the courthouse tomorrow and see who owns it," Ben said.

"Good idea. It'd be the perfect location for dogfighting. The Tennessee line splits it, and you can access it from either state. It's remote, and it's rugged—I've hunted that land and helped cut the timber on it back before I went into the army. Last time I hunted there, the logging roads were passable, so we could walk in easily enough."

"Tonight?"

Wade eyed him. "Why not?"

"Sounds good, but first, let's get Andre and Randy scouring that alley."

Wade glanced down at Ben's feet. "You better get some shoes you can hike in, and make sure they're tall enough to keep you from getting snake bit."

■ ■ ■

Moonlight guided their path through a break in the canopy of trees overhead. So far Ben hadn't seen anything or heard anything except buzzing around his head. He used the back of his hand to wipe his forehead as sweat stung his eyes. Another mosquito bit his neck, and he slapped it as quietly as he could.

He shifted the lightweight backpack that carried binoculars, water, and extra ammo. They had hiked at least two miles after they parked Wade's pickup in a wooded area near the farm. Now they were following Caney River, walking the bank upriver toward Tennessee. Should they get lost, they could follow the river to where it intersected the highway. If Wade didn't argue with the compass, they shouldn't get lost, though. His chief deputy seemed comfortable enough, taking the lead as they slipped quietly through the woods. Maybe Ben ought to get into the woods more often. Faint barking reached his ears, and he almost bumped into Wade when his deputy abruptly stopped.

"I think I know where they are. When I was hunting here, I came up on a basin. It's ringed with bluffs, but there's a road into it. 'Bout as good a place to do something illegal as any place I know."

Ben had never hunted these woods, and he deferred to Wade's judgment, but when his chief deputy veered away from the river to the right, he questioned him. "The barking sounds like it's straight up the river."

Wade grunted. "The river winds and twists, fooling you. That road ought to be nearby—those dogfighters aren't hiking in here."

"When we get back under the trees, how will we see where we're going?"

"We'll have to depend on what moonlight we get. Can't risk a flashlight."

As they picked their way through the dense grove of sycamore saplings, Ben tried to put the memory of the five copperheads slithering on the ballpark field out of his mind. Fifteen minutes later they broke through the underbrush onto a road. One that was well-traveled.

Wade checked his compass. "We've probably crossed over into Tennessee."

"How do you know?"

"When I was hunting here, the only road this good came out on the Tennessee side over on Highway 312. I had forgotten that was the way we took the logs out."

Ben pulled his sweat-soaked T-shirt away from his body. "Why didn't we just go in on the Tennessee side, instead of hiking through the woods? Never mind," he muttered. Like they could just drive right up to the dogfight. "You know a way to get to that basin besides this road? Sure wouldn't want to run into any of their guards."

Wade's teeth gleamed in the moonlight. "Yeah. We'll skirt to the south, climb the ridge, and follow it to the bluff overlooking the basin."

Ben figured there'd be more hiking. He followed Wade, branches slapping his face, and mosquitoes buzzing his ears, and no telling what beneath his feet. When they came to the base of the ridge, the terrain went from flat to straight up.

"Dig your toe into the dirt and grab a hold of the saplings and pull yourself up," Wade said. "Unless you want to feel around on the ground for vines."

"I'll use the trees." Ten minutes later, he caught his breath at the top of the ridge. The barking had become louder and frenzied. "That's not coon dogs," Ben said.

"Nope. From here on out, no talking. I doubt they'll have a guard on the ridge, but you never can tell."

As Ben followed Wade toward the river, curses and whooping blended with the barking. They crawled on their hands and knees to the edge of the bluff and stared down at the scene. Portable spotlights ringed a small enclosure. A man stood in the middle of a circle with a dog on either side of him. One lunged toward him, but his handler jerked him back.

The dogfighters sent a hot rage through Ben. He fumbled in his backpack for the binoculars and raised them to his eyes, scanning the crowd. Where did these people come from? "You recognize anybody?" he whispered.

"Chester Eaton. Over to your right," Wade whispered back. "There with Lester Cummings and Rafe Carter."

Ben shifted his binoculars. The burly logger had his thumbs hooked in his overalls and a wad of snuff in his lip. Seeing Eaton didn't surprise Ben. He never figured all those blue barrels at Eaton's housed anything as innocuous as breeding roosters, but he'd never been able to pin cockfighting on him. Maybe he'd moved on to dogfighting.

He was surprised about Lester and Rafe. Lester was a family man with boys the age of his nephews. Ben shifted the binoculars to the left to the man standing next to Eaton. Jonas Gresham. From the soured expression on his face, he was losing. He trained the glasses on the father of Tommy Ray and Billy Wayne as Gresham counted out something to Eaton. Money, he was sure, and lots of it. No wonder Jonas didn't look happy.

He crawled back out of the line of sight and checked his cell phone. Just as he'd expected. No service. A logistical nightmare. Not to mention they were badly outnumbered.

Wade joined him. "I only made out Mississippi and Tennessee license plates—I don't think this is a big fight. I did recognize a few more men that I know. Coon hunted with some of them in the past, even bought a coon dog from one of them. I might even be able to infiltrate the ring. Make them think I want to buy another dog—a pit bull this time."

"I don't know. Won't it bother them that you're my chief deputy?"

"Nah." Wade chuckled. "Those boys I coon hunted with think all cops are on the take, anyway."

Ben eyed him. "And you did nothing to discourage their thinking. Let's get back to town, and first thing in the morning I'll contact the FBI and Highway Patrol."

"I just wish we could do something tonight."

Ben gritted his teeth. "Me too."

■ ■ ■

TJ slipped his pajama top over his head and hopped into bed. "Mom, can we stay here forever?"

"You mean Logan Point?" Leigh's heart rate slowed. She didn't have the energy to tell her son that they would be leaving town in six weeks.

"No, here at Pops and Granna's house."

Pops and Granna. If Ian had just given her a price for the house

167

on Webster Street, she'd move into it tomorrow. Might anyway. Then in a week or so, she could break the news to TJ that they were moving to Baltimore. "No. We'll be moving out as soon as we find a place to stay. And that might be pretty soon."

"Aw, I like it here. I can play with the twins."

"Even if we move, you can still hang out with them. How would you feel about going back to Miss Jenny's?"

His shoulder drooped. "I like it here with Granna."

"Well, just think about it." She turned at a rustling in the doorway. "Oh, look, it's Miss Sarah."

"How was your practice today, TJ?" the older woman asked.

"I hit a home run, but then my friend got bit by a snake. Mom, why were those snakes on the field? Are you sure Martin is going to be okay?"

She didn't know which question to answer first. "I don't know about the snakes, TJ, but I'm pretty sure your friend is going to be fine. I expect he'll be there Saturday night to cheer you on. Maybe even Miss Sarah will come."

"Since I'm not leaving until Sunday afternoon, I'll be there. So, you hit a home run?" Sarah high-fived him. "Who was pitching?"

"Ben. And Mom got to see it, didn't you, Mom? Why didn't you come with us? Why did Mr. Ian bring you?"

TJ was full of questions tonight. Questions she didn't know how to answer.

"TJ," Sarah said, "have you said your prayers?"

He caught his breath. "Not yet! Will you stay and hear them? You too, Mom."

Saved by Sarah. "Sure."

A few minutes later both women kissed him on his forehead, and Leigh turned out the light before they left TJ's room.

"Mom!"

Leigh stuck her head back inside the room. "Yes?"

"Can I have a drink of water?"

Patricia Bradley

"I'll get it," Sarah said. "You go on and put your feet up."

"Don't be silly . . . there's a paper cup in the bathroom. I can get it."

"I insist." Sarah paused. "Did you hear about the fire at the jail?"

"I did. I wonder how bad it was?"

"Just before I came up, Marisa said the firemen had it under control. Not much damage."

"Good." Leigh hadn't heard Ben's truck return, but she could've missed it while she was in the shower. She moved to get TJ's water, and Sarah stopped her.

"I said I'd get it. You look beat."

So much had happened today, and she was beyond tired. "Just this once," she said with a sigh. "After you tell him good night again, could you join me in my room?"

Leigh padded down the hall to her bedroom and sank into one of the two glider rockers in the room. She put her feet on the bed and massaged the muscles in her neck and shoulders. She might ask around at the hospital tomorrow to see if there was a good masseuse in town.

Thoughts of Ben returned. Would he have kissed her if his phone hadn't rung? *Stop it.* There was no future with Ben Logan.

She put her feet down when Sarah came in and plopped in the other rocker. "Get him settled?"

"Maybe. I think ball practice then his little friend getting bitten has him wound pretty tight. Or he could have picked up on the tenseness radiating from you. You're wound tighter than he is. What's going on?"

Leigh didn't know it was that obvious. She pressed her hands to the side of her face and massaged the sore muscles in her jaw. She'd been clenching her teeth again. Finally, she leaned back and sighed. "I don't know where to begin."

"You could start with the young man who came to pick you up," Sarah said.

"Ian Maxwell—you met him at the funeral. He's offered us a

169

house in town. White picket fence, gated community, guard . . . Ben should approve it, but who knows. He seems to want us to stay right here under his thumb."

"What do *you* want to do?"

She ran her hand over the rough fabric covering the arm of the rocker. "Go back ten years and make some different choices."

"You don't have to do that. You can tell them now. The Logans would understand."

A tremor shivered through Leigh's body, flipping her stomach. Marisa might and Emily, but not Ben. "I can't do it." Her voice quivered in her throat from her too-fast heartbeat.

"Leigh—"

"No. Can you imagine how TJ would feel if he discovered his mother has kept the truth from him for the past nine years . . . I just can't do it. We're moving to Baltimore, anyway."

"What?"

"I received a call from my mentor, and there's an opening at their free clinic—"

"But you've promised Emily to work in Dr. Hazelit's place."

"I don't go until the middle of September. Emily's clinic is just for a month, and this is *Johns Hopkins*. It's been my dream to practice there since I decided to become a doctor."

"Is this your dream, or someone else's?"

She splayed her hand across her chest. "Mine."

"Are you sure?"

"You don't understand. If I can practice at Johns Hopkins, it's proof I'm good enough. I'll make a difference there."

"You don't have to prove anything, Leigh. And you're already making a difference here. Marisa told me how lucky Logan Point is to have you. What if you hadn't been there for that little friend of TJ's tonight?"

"There would have been another doctor on duty."

"You belong here, in Logan Point." Sarah's lips pressed into a thin line. "No need in wasting any more of my breath, 'cause I might need it someday. Would you at least pray about it?"

It was too late to pray. She'd already taken the job. But Leigh nodded. "It's a really good opportunity."

After Sarah left, Leigh sat quietly gliding back and forth. She had to leave Logan Point. And she wanted to. She really did.

■ ■ ■

Ben wiped sweat from his face. Even though the temperature had dropped into what felt like the low eighties, the walk back had been as arduous as the trek in. It was almost 4:00 a.m. when they finally reached Wade's truck. "What time do you think the dogfight will break up?"

Wade slapped at a mosquito on his neck. "Hard to tell. Probably go until just before daylight."

"Sure would like to get some of those license plate numbers. You know the lay of the land. Is there anywhere we can set up?"

"Some may go out on the Tennessee side—nothing we can do about those cars, and on the Mississippi side, the field road is too exposed. I think I know a place where we can park and catch what we can."

Half an hour later, by the time Ben had positioned himself behind a gum tree near where the road exited from the woods, faint wisps of fog curled through the trees. Within twenty minutes, a dense August fog covered the area. There'd be no seeing any license plates today. He cocked his head as a vehicle rumbled his way, then signaled Wade with a whistle, and his chief deputy signaled back.

Maybe he could at least see the driver. The truck crept by, a shadowy ghost in the heavy mist with its lights barely cutting a swath down the lane. As more vehicles passed, Ben could barely tell a truck from an SUV.

He counted ten vehicles in all. Wade was right. This wasn't

a big-time fight. "How many did you count?" he asked when he rejoined Wade.

"Ten. Some of them probably took the Tennessee road. Couldn't make out any of the plates."

"That's what I counted too. Let's talk about a plan on the way back to town." Once in the pickup, they crept along the two-lane highway.

"Okay," Wade said, his eyes glued to the road. "I say I try to get in with those boys I know."

Ben shook his head. "Too dangerous. These people play for keeps. If they discovered—"

"Not going to find out." He slowed for a curve. "Well, what do we have here?"

Ben peered through the fog. The bulky form of a truck materialized on the side of the road.

"Duck down, in case it's somebody from the dogfight. Might be an opportunity here." Wade pulled behind the vehicle and cracked the windows. He slipped his gun from its holster as he stepped out of the truck. "Having problems?" he called.

Ben drew his gun as he slumped in the front seat and kept his ear tuned to what was said.

"Jest a flat," came the reply. "That you, Wade?"

"Yeah. What're you doing out this time of the morning, Lester?"

Lester Cummings, from the dogfight.

"Oh, my coon dog got to chasing something and didn't come back, been looking for her. What're you doing out here?"

"Doing my job, patrolling the county."

"Ain't never knowed you to be that conscientious."

"Let me help you get that tire changed," Wade said.

Ben listened as Wade worked and the conversation turned to dogs.

"You know about dogs, don't you, Lester?"

"Some dogs."

"How about pit bulls. Been thinking about gettin' myself one. Maybe training it a little."

Ben tightened the grip on his gun. Wade was pushing it.

"'Training' it for what?" Suspicion crept into the man's voice.

"Be a guard dog. Saw a video once of one attacking a man. Got ahold of his arm and wouldn't let go. It'd be nice to have a dog like that to protect my house."

"You got something in that trailer of yours worth stealing?"

"You never know, Lester. Just be thinking about it." Wade grunted then asked, "You got the other lug nut?"

A few minutes later, Ben heard what sounded like Wade throwing the tire in the bed of the truck.

"Thanks, deputy. I always thought they should've appointed you sheriff until the election."

Ben cringed. Lester probably wasn't the only one who thought that.

"Yeah, well, Lester, them's the breaks."

"You run, and I'll vote for you."

"I appreciate that. I'll just stand here until you pull out. Hope you find your dog."

Cummings's motor revved to life, and Ben raised his head as gravel crunched and the truck pulled out onto the highway. Seconds later, Wade hopped into the truck. "Put the bait out," he said with a grin.

Ben hoped Wade didn't end up being caught in the trap.

As the truck pulled out onto the road, Wade glanced at Ben. "You mind if we stop at Rest Haven?"

Ben gave him a sidelong glance. "It's just 5:45. Can you get in this early?"

"Sure, the nurses all know me, and Ma will be awake. She gets up every morning at five. You can come in with me if you want."

He didn't have the heart to say no. He hadn't seen Wade's mother in years. From past conversations with his own mother, he knew

173

Mrs. Hatcher had floated in and out of Wade's life, wrecking whatever stability he found in the foster homes he'd been placed in, until finally she'd been committed to the state mental institution in Whitfield.

Somehow, a few years ago, Wade had brought her back to Logan Point and to Rest Haven, but Ben knew it took more money than he made as a chief deputy to keep her there. Had to be eating up whatever retirement he had. "Yeah, I'll go in with you. But first let me call someone to escort Leigh to work."

A mile or two down the road they left the bottomland, and the fog lifted. Too bad they hadn't set up on the hill. When they turned into the parking lot of the nursing home, a comment that Lester made popped into Ben's mind. "Why does Cummings think you're not conscientious?"

Wade parked the truck and killed the engine before he answered. "It's that good-ole-boy image I cultivate. You'd be surprised at the stuff I learn."

"I bet." Ben nodded toward the building. "Nice place."

"Yeah." His deputy tapped his fingers on the steering wheel and stared at the nursing home. "Costs a fortune, though."

"I heard the state facility has improved a lot," Ben said.

"Too far away, and Ma would get lost in the shuffle, like the last time." He opened his door and stepped out, not waiting to see if Ben was coming. He strode toward the door and pressed the buzzer. After a brief wait, an orderly appeared and let them in.

"She's in the solarium," the orderly said.

Wade hesitated inside the door. "Look, Ben, you don't have to come."

"No, I'd like to see your mom. I always liked her."

"Yeah, when she wasn't off her meds."

At the solarium door, Ben waited while Wade approached his mother as she sat facing east. Dorsey Hatcher didn't look at all like Ben imagined she would. Thin, she sat ramrod straight, her ash-blonde hair framing her face. Wade spoke to her for a few minutes, and then she looked toward him, smiling while Wade motioned him in.

"Mrs. Hatcher, Ben Logan." He walked closer.

"I know who you are, Ben." Her smile was soft, gentle. "Wade talks about you often. Now what are you two boys doing out this time of the morning?"

This woman didn't sound at all unbalanced. He masked his confusion and smiled back at her. "Just doing our job."

"Well, you two sit here beside me and watch that window. The sun will be peeking through in about five minutes. I love to start my day off with the sunrise."

"That gives me time to get you a cup of coffee," Wade said. "French vanilla creamer, like always?"

"You're a good boy, Wade. Yes, but hurry so you can see the sunrise."

"Ma, I've seen plenty of sunrises."

"Wade . . ."

"I'll hurry."

While Wade went for coffee, Ben studied Mrs. Hatcher. She seemed perfectly able to function in the real world. Almost as though she read his mind, she chuckled.

"I'm here at Rest Haven because I forget to take my medicine, and the doctors and Wade want me to stay."

"Ah, I didn't—"

"Questions are written all over your face. Don't play cards with my son. He will beat you."

Ben could keep a poker face when necessary. He just hadn't thought he needed to. Wade returned with coffee for them all. "Yours is black and unflavored." He handed his mother the one swirling with cream. "And I think this is the way you like it."

Ben sipped his coffee, enjoying the rush of caffeine as the sun peaked over the horizon through the pink and blue clouds streaking the sky. He wished he had a camera, or that he could paint something as grand as what he beheld. God's handiwork, his mom would say. Mrs. Hatcher had the right idea about starting the day off with the sunrise.

Wade was quiet as they walked back to his truck. As they fastened their seat belts, he cleared his throat. "Thanks. It meant a lot to my mom that you came in with me. Not many people go see her. They all remember the way she was."

Ben was certain his mom didn't know about Mrs. Hatcher. He'd have to tell her. "Does she have to stay at Rest Haven?"

"The last time she lived on her own, she didn't take her medicine right and ended up back in the hospital. I don't want to take that chance again, not as long as I can afford for her to stay here."

"I don't think you should pursue the dog thing with Lester."

"What? I have to. That fight last night was peanuts. I've heard rumors there's an all-star fight coming up. If I can find out when and where, we can raid it and maybe get the organizer."

"Where are you getting your information?"

"I have sources."

Dogs attacking one another while men cheered and cursed replayed in his mind, sickening him. "Then use those sources to find out when the next fight is. I'll contact the U.S. Marshal Service, FBI, and Mississippi Highway Patrol. But you . . ." Ben pointed at Wade. "Don't go through with this scheme to infiltrate the ring."

"Whatever you say, boss."

His gut told him Wade wouldn't listen. Ben rode silently in the passenger seat. Wade was a complex man. If anything happened to him . . . "Think about your mother and what would happen to her if you were hurt or killed."

In the driver's seat, Wade grunted.

The sun had risen over the tree line by the time they reached the jail. Andre and another deputy had pulled water-soaked furniture into the parking lot. Ben walked through the lobby and down the hall to his office. Everything seemed intact. Andre stuck his head in the door.

"Electrician will be here by eight. Then we can get the power turned back on."

Ben turned around. "How's Martin?"

"Going to be okay." Andre stepped inside the office. "You think the snakes happened naturally? Or did someone set them loose?"

Ben ran his hand through his hair. "I think they were set loose to send a message. Just like this fire."

"But who would do something like that? Don't they know those snakes could've killed one of the boys?"

"Whoever turned them loose doesn't care." He chewed his bottom lip. "Is Taylor Martin still in town?"

"I saw her yesterday with her mama at the grocery."

Good. Taylor was one of the top victim profilers in the country. If someone was committing these crimes to show him that he couldn't protect his county, she could figure out who it was.

■ ■ ■

The smell of frying bacon woke Leigh, and she threw back the covers and rubbed her eyes. Six o'clock. She had to be at the hospital at six-forty-five. Her last day for a month. Monday she started working at the clinic. Decent hours, patients she could get to know without it being an emergency situation. She threw on a pair of scrubs and ran a brush through her straight hair before hurrying down the stairs for coffee.

The sight of TJ and Tom Logan in the living room stopped her in midstride. What was TJ doing up at this hour? And with her iPad. Except Tom wasn't concentrating on the iPad. He'd used his good hand to push TJ's hair back and was staring at his face. Leigh's heart almost failed her.

"Try once more, Pops. Point to the glass of water."

"TJ, don't bother the sheriff this early in the morning." She hadn't meant her voice to sound so sharp, and she tried to soften it even as she avoided Tom's eyes. "Why are you up so early?"

"But, Mom, I'm not bothering him. He's getting better, he really is. We've been doing this every morning."

That did it. They were moving. She would call Ian as soon as it was a decent hour, and they would be in the house on Webster tonight. She didn't care whether Ben Logan approved or not. Still avoiding the former sheriff's gaze, Leigh pushed her lips into a halfway decent smile. "He's probably tired now. Have you eaten?"

"Cereal."

Standard fare for him. "I'll be home by four, and I have a surprise for you."

His eyes brightened. "What is—"

"It wouldn't be a surprise if I told you, now would it." Maybe Sarah would consider staying a few days longer while Leigh adjusted to working at the clinic and could get TJ set up with Jenny again. She felt Tom Logan's eyes boring into her and finally glanced his way. His gaze shifted from her to TJ.

"Tee . . . juh . . ." he half-growled.

"Mom! He almost said my name!" TJ's eyes danced. He knelt beside the older man. "You can do it."

"TJ!" Panic tightened her vocal cords. "Come away and let him rest. He's upset."

"Mom, I can help, I know I can." Her son's eyes pleaded with her.

In the quietness that followed TJ's plea, Tom spoke again. "W . . . why . . ."

Cold chills ran over her body. The alarm on her phone she'd set for six-twenty beeped. She couldn't leave TJ here with Tom. And she couldn't be late to the hospital. "TJ, let's go see if Miss Sarah is up. Maybe she can take you shopping to get school clothes."

"Now? I want to stay—"

"I don't have time to stand here and argue with you." She nudged him up the stairs.

"But she's in the kitchen."

Pain shot through her jaw as she ground her teeth. "Then that's where we'll go." She pushed through the kitchen door with TJ in tow.

Sarah sat at the table, drinking coffee with Marisa. "Wondered if you'd overslept," she said and poured Leigh a cup of coffee.

"I didn't hear my alarm." Leigh gulped a sip of the strong brew, burning her tongue. She rummaged through her purse for money. "Sarah, would you mind taking TJ shopping today? Get him something new for school? Since the fire, I've only bought summer clothes. I'd meant to do it tomorrow, but he has that ball game tomorrow afternoon and I have paperwork in the morning." She was rattling on, but she couldn't help herself.

"That's a good idea," Marisa said. She turned to Sarah. "Emily's dropping the twins off shortly. Maybe we'll tag along. She's been so busy, I'm sure she hasn't bought their clothes, either."

Leigh hadn't anticipated Marisa tagging along, but she couldn't very well object. She handed Sarah four crisp twenty dollar bills. "If that isn't enough, let me know." She knelt over and hugged TJ. "I'll see you around four."

He shrugged out of her embrace. "Does Miss Sarah know what your surprise is?"

Leigh glanced at Sarah, who had raised her eyebrows. Her throat tightened and she swallowed. "Nope, she doesn't know." She tousled his copper hair then grabbed a Styrofoam cup and poured fresh coffee into it. "Thanks," she said as she walked to the back door. "I really appreciate you taking him shopping."

"Wait!" Marisa stood. "Ben's not here. You can't go without an escort."

In her haste, she'd totally forgotten her escort. Where was Ben, anyway? "I can't wait. I'm already late as it is."

Marisa grabbed the phone on the wall. "Let me find out what's going on with Ben."

A text beeped on Leigh's phone, and she glanced at it. "That's okay. Deputy Ford is at the gate." Ben could've at least let her know himself.

"Mom, can I start your car?"

She tossed him her keys. "See if you can beat me to it."

He shot out the door ahead of her and, ten yards away, stopped and pressed the start button. The Avenger hummed to life.

"That's so cool," TJ said as he handed her the keys.

"Yeah." TJ loved technology, even if it was packaged in a five-year-old car. She slid in the seat and lowered the window. "See you this afternoon."

■ ■ ■

A little after nine, Leigh took out her cell and dialed Ian. He answered practically on the first ring. "Good morning," she said.

"I hope you're not calling to cancel our date."

Oops. She had completely forgotten their date. Another thing she needed to mention to Ben, along with the news she was moving out. But first things first. "How about if we amend it?"

"As in?"

"I want to accept your generous offer to let us use your house on Webster. I'd like to move in today."

There was a brief silence on the other end. "So, Ben approved the house?"

"Ben . . . I'll make it all right with him. Can you meet me at the house, say around four or four-thirty?"

"What if I drop the key off at the hospital, and then bring dinner around seven?"

"Perfect. And, Ian, thank you."

"My pleasure."

After hanging up, Leigh didn't immediately slide her cell back in her pocket. It was done. Now to tell Ben. She dialed his number and was relieved when it went to voice mail. She left a message asking him to call her. Fifteen minutes later as she was looking over a chart, he called back. "Thanks for getting back to me," she said after she answered.

"I'm sorry I wasn't there to escort you to the hospital, but I've been dealing with the aftermath of the fire here at the jail."

"Your deputy did an excellent job, and for the record, I don't think I need an escort any longer."

"I don't agree. Did you need anything in particular?"

She took a deep breath. "I've found a house and want to move in this afternoon."

"Whoa, slow down. Did you say you wanted to move today?"

"You heard correctly."

"Leigh—"

"Ben, we can't stay with your parents indefinitely. The house Ian is offering is in a gated community with a guard, in the middle of the block with houses all around. It will be perfectly safe."

"I don't want to discuss this on the phone. Would you please wait to make a decision until I pick you up at three?"

He wasn't changing her mind, even if he did sound hurt. Neither did she want him to show up at the hospital and argue with her in the middle of the ER. "I'll see you at three."

Six hours to dread the dragon.

■ ■ ■

Armero smoothed his hand over the soft leather seat. He never tired of the smell of a new car, and the week-old SUV was no exception. Where was Jonas? He should have been here already. The outside heat seeped into the car, and he adjusted the temperature lower. Behind the driver's seat, a box of receivers awaited transfer to Jonas's truck.

The passenger door opened behind him, and he startled as Jonas slid in the backseat. "I didn't see you come up," he snapped.

"Grouchy today," Jonas said. "What's got your goat?"

"You're late, and I have meetings." His lip curled at the odor of sweat and some other foul scent.

"Well, I'm here now. You got the receivers?"

"Beside you in the floorboard." He drew in a steadying breath and almost gagged. The man evidently had come straight from feeding hogs. He'd never get the scent out of his car. He coughed and left his hand over his nose. "Where were you after the fire at the jail? And what did you mean by setting it? What if you'd been caught? Or Logan figures out what you're doing?"

"I wasn't caught. And he won't. At least not until I'm ready. But Logan is going to pay for my two boys."

Armero lowered his hand. "Billy Wayne died because he joined your vendetta against Ben Logan."

"All Billy Wayne wanted was justice for Tommy Ray's death."

"Like shooting at the sheriff would give you justice. If you kill an officer of the law and get caught, it's automatically the death penalty."

"I ain't stupid."

"I don't know about that. You almost killed his father."

"My mistake that I didn't. He was getting too close to my dogs. I came up on him nosing around my pits, then hightailing it back to town. Figured he was going after a search warrant. So I intercepted him and—"

"Just shut up. I don't want to know anything about what you're doing with those dogs, or anything else illegal."

Jonas snorted. "You think there's a difference between the two of us?" He nudged him on the shoulder. "We're cut from the same cloth. I knew that when I came to you about selling rifles to the Mexicans. And you knew I had fighting dogs when you agreed."

Armero clenched his jaw tight. Jonas was a loose cannon. And he knew too much. The idea of selling guns to Mexico had been his idea. Four years ago, the old man worked at Maxwell Industries, and it'd been easy for him to slip a couple of unstamped receivers out when he took a smoke break. Jonas hid them and Armero picked them up. But it was Armero's connections that made the operation a success. He never told Jonas what kind of money he received for the rifles, but Jonas seemed content with what he gave him, which was plenty.

Maybe it was time to get rid of the old man. From the rearview mirror, Armero flicked his gaze over Jonas. Stains of no telling what dotted his khaki shirt. Wet dog. That's what Jonas smelled like. "And I wish you would take a bath and change clothes before we meet."

Armero tried shallow breathing. He remembered something else he'd heard. "Did you put those snakes on the ball field last night?"

The older man cackled. "You ought to have seen Logan and that deputy's face."

"A child was bitten!"

"He survived."

"What was the purpose?" He had to find a way to get rid of Gresham, but another body right now? No, he'd bide his time and make sure there were no trails leading to him when Jonas was caught.

A sly look slid over Jonas's face. "He thinks he can protect this county. Every time I do something, he finds out he can't." He opened the car door and spat on the pavement before exiting Armero's car with the receivers. "I heard he was running for sheriff in the special election. Won't take but a few people talking about the snakes and fires to beat him. He won't want to be sheriff by the time I get through. Won't have the heart for it, anyway. Especially when I get finished with his girlfriend and her boy."

As soon as Gresham pulled away in his beat-up truck, Armero lowered his windows. Maybe a fast drive around the bypass would get the stink out of his car. Fifteen minutes later, he pulled into the company parking lot.

He reached under his seat and pulled out a black box. From it he removed a disposable cell phone and synthesizer. After punching in the code required to block the number of the cell phone, he dialed her number and waited for it to ring. When it went to her voice mail, he hung up. He'd try again later.

13

Leigh was going to drive him crazy. Ben didn't want her to move out of his parents' house. He hooked his phone on his belt and opened his office window to let out the acrid scent of burnt roofing. Maybe he could change her mind when he saw her at the hospital.

What he wouldn't give right now for a thirty-minute nap. He was way past the days of staying up all night and functioning the next day. Even with his door shut, the whine of the cleaning service's shop vac made a nap impossible. At least the electrician had rerouted wiring and restored power. He massaged the muscles in his neck, and his gaze settled on his dad's box of papers. He set it on his desk and removed the top. Might as well go through it now.

There wasn't much. A couple of advertisement letters and an email joke his dad liked enough to print. He picked up another email from some sheriff in Texas. There was a long list of people it had been sent to, and his dad had scribbled a note in the margin. MI with a question mark.

At the bottom of the page was a photo of an assault rifle. He backtracked and read the email. Seems the gun in the photo had been found in a drug raid and had no serial number stamped on it. The sheriff who had sent the email was trying to track down the maker of the gun.

A knock startled him and he laid the email on his desk. "Come in."

The door opened, and Taylor Martin walked in, waving her hand in front of her nose. "This smells as bad as when I burned my biscuits."

"Taylor! You got my message." Dressed in green shorts and a white T-shirt with "Walls of Jericho" printed across it, the psychology professor looked more like a student and certainly not like a crime scene profiler.

"Yep. What's going on around here?" she asked.

He motioned for her to shut the door. "Someone set fire to the jail last night. Used a bow and arrow. Sit down." He pointed toward a leather chair. "How's Nick? And your mom?"

"Busy. Nick is working on edits and finalizing the plans for the boys' camp. Walls of Jericho should be accepting boys by next summer. And Mom's okay. We're all grieving Jonathan."

Ben nodded. Earlier this summer her uncle had died from wounds received when a madman tried to kill Taylor. It'd been a complex case covering three jurisdictions, Tennessee, Mississippi, and Washington State. The Tennessee state judge appointee who attempted to kill both Taylor and her mother had been killed by the man he hired. That man, now awaiting trial, was obsessed with the professor. "I hear the University of Memphis has hired you. Congratulations."

"It was time to come home. I won't start teaching until the winter session."

"Why not the fall?"

She held her left hand up. An emerald-cut diamond glittered on her third finger. "I have a December wedding to plan."

"Nick popped the question!"

Color rose in her cheeks as she nodded. "Last week."

"Congrat—oops, I think that's supposed to be 'best wishes' for you. I'll congratulate Nick when I see him. He made a good choice."

She blushed again and glanced around the office. "Enjoy working this?" She picked up the Rubik's Cube on the corner of his desk.

"About as much as going to the dentist. I just can't grasp the concept."

She tilted her head and studied the cube, then began twisting. When she turned the face to him, she said, "Always remember the center color defines the color for the side you're looking at. And I always start with this."

The face of the cube had a white cross.

"From there it's just a matter of memorizing a few logarithms."

"Logarithms? No wonder I can't learn how to do it. I almost failed trig."

She laughed and set the Rubik's Cube back on his desk. "You didn't call me down here to teach you how to do that. What's up?"

Ben handed her a folder he'd compiled as soon as the electricity had been restored. "That's a file on three crimes. The fire at Leigh Somerall's house—she's probably more familiar to you as Leigh Jackson, Tony Jackson's sister—that one just came back from the fire marshal today. He discovered a broadhead arrow point in the rubble."

It'd been pure diligence on the fire marshal's part that the arrow tip had been found. Ben had driven by once when he was literally sifting rubble through a sieve. "Then we have the five snakes let loose on one of the ball fields at the park last night, and now, the fire here at the jail."

"I remember the Jackson family. Terrible about Tony." Taylor took a pen from her purse then opened the folder and scanned the documents. "Three victims?"

He pressed his lips in a thin line. "Three victims, but I'm beginning to wonder if there's just one target—me." He leaned forward. "I thought maybe you could tell me if someone is out to make me look incompetent, or am I crazy?"

"Why do *you* think someone would do that?"

"I filed to run in the special sheriff's election last week. There are a couple of other candidates, but no one who'd resort to what you see there. Still, they may have friends who would."

"Leigh Jackson." She looked up from the file. "Don't you have a history with her?"

Everyone knowing your business—one of the benefits of living in a small town. If Taylor remembered their relationship, who else did? Ben licked his lips. "That was ten years ago."

"Some people have long memories."

That was what he was afraid of. What if the shooting the morning after Tony's murder was connected to the other three crimes? He turned to a stack of files behind him and took the top one and made a copy. "Add this one to your files."

Taylor scanned it. "Billy Wayne Gresham? I read about this in the paper. Didn't he die in an accident leaving the scene?"

"Yeah. And we found a .38 Smith and Wesson at his house, but Livy hasn't gotten the ballistics report back, so right now he's only a person of interest in Tony's murder." Ben fingered the original file. "Do you ever get a gut feeling about a case? That everything isn't what it seems?"

She chuckled. "All the time. What's your gut telling you?"

Ben sighed. "It's hard to put my finger on. No denying Billy Wayne was the one who pulled the trigger that morning at Leigh's. Bullets matched the Sub-2000 found in the saddlebag on his cycle."

Taylor traced the pen along her jawline. "Is there a connection between you and Billy Wayne?"

"Yeah. I let his brother drown three years ago."

The words dropped into the room, creating a ripple of silence. She stilled her pen. "I remember now. Mom mailed me the newspaper clippings—every month she sent an envelope filled with newspaper articles she thought I'd be interested in. But what I remember is an accident, not you letting someone drown."

"He died all the same." He hoped she didn't try to psychoanalyze him. He waited as she scribbled in her notepad. Ben looked over his notes. "There's one more angle. Leigh has only been working in the ER for six weeks, and she suspected abuse in one of the cases she treated. A two-year-old boy with cigarette burns on his arms and legs put there by the mother's live-in. She reported it to Social Services, and when the mother's boyfriend was arrested, he threatened Leigh."

"Have you questioned him?" Taylor asked as she made notes.

"Unfortunately, he disappeared after he made bail."

"I don't think he's—" She stopped writing and winced. "Forget I said that. I make it a practice to wait until I've studied a case before I offer any opinion. What seems obvious on the surface isn't always what it seems once I get into the case, and I might send you investigating in the wrong direction. I'll work on this and get back to you."

"Can we afford you? The county only pays standard rates."

A twinkle gleamed in her eyes. "And I only charge standard rates."

"Yeah, right. I appreciate any help you can give me." As Taylor stood, Ben did likewise. "Any idea, time wise?"

"Give me a day or two."

He'd have to make do with that. His cell rang as he extended his hand.

"You better get that," she said. "I'll see my way out the back."

"Thanks again." Ben glanced at his phone. U.S. Marshal Luke Donovan.

"Luke, glad you could get back to me so quickly," he said as Taylor shut the door behind her.

"Figured it was important," replied the marshal. "What's going on?"

"I've discovered a dogfighting ring in Bradford County." It made him sick to think anything that repulsive was happening in his county.

"Proof?"

"Saw it with my own eyes last night. Just didn't have enough man power with me to do anything about it—it was only my chief deputy and me. Wade recognized a couple of the men involved, and I'm having to rein him in—he wants to go undercover, try and buy a dog from one of them. Can we get together today and discuss a strategy?"

"How about my office around five? I should be able to pull in an FBI agent as well."

Forty minutes to get to Luke's downtown office. That wouldn't leave him enough time to reason with Leigh about moving out of his parents' house. But these men were busy. "I'll be there. And my chief deputy will be with me."

"Good deal."

Ben broke the connection and called Wade to fill him in on the plan. They made arrangements to meet at Ben's house at four, and then he checked his watch. Almost twelve-thirty. Maybe he could get in a couple hours of sleep before he picked Leigh up at three.

■ ■ ■

Leigh glanced at the oversized clock on the wall at the nurses' station in the ER as the minute hand crept to three o'clock. She'd completed the report to the night shift doctor and had made rounds with him.

Ian had dropped by around noon with the key to the house on Webster and a promise of dinner delivered personally to the house. No sight of Ben, though. Maybe she'd go ahead and leave. She didn't look forward to arguing with him about moving. One thing for sure, he couldn't stop her.

As she strode through the steel ER doors, her heart caught when she saw Ben entering from outside, dressed in his uniform white short-sleeved shirt and jeans and looking none too happy. *Gird your loins.* Leigh couldn't keep from chuckling at the expression her grandmother always used when Granddad came looking for an argument. But her grandmother had been equal to the task, outtalking her grandfather in almost every skirmish. And they'd had plenty.

"We'll talk when we get to your parents' house," she said, breezing by him. No way was she having this discussion in the hospital parking lot. Leigh rehearsed her argument all the way to the Logan house and lobbed the first volley as she stepped out of her car.

"Ben, there is no reason we can't move into the house on Webster. The Oaks is a gated community with a guard on duty twenty-four hours a day."

"Whoa." He held up his hands. "For most people it would be, but you're not most people. A subdivision just isn't as safe for you and TJ."

She glanced around. "There's no difference. Both are gated, and truly, the Webster house might just be safer because it has a guard."

When he didn't respond immediately, she took a second look at him. He looked really tired as he rubbed his forehead. "Are you all right?" she asked.

"Nothing a little sleep won't cure." He rolled his shoulders. "I have a meeting I have to get to, and I don't have time to argue with you about this. We'll talk tonight."

Leigh crossed her arms, and Ben walked to his truck and opened the driver's door. He hesitated, and for a second, she thought he was going to say something. Instead he climbed inside the truck and drove away. She hadn't promised not to move, and she would still talk to him about it . . . after the fact. Leigh hurried inside, looking for Sarah . . . and Marisa. She found Marisa in the kitchen.

"How was work today?" Ben's mom patted a mound of dough then covered it with plastic wrap.

The smell of yeast filled the sunny room. She'd miss the homemade bread. "Busy. But everyone was fixable." She took a deep breath and shoved the words out. "Ian Maxwell has offered a house on Webster for us to stay in, and I've accepted."

Doubt filled Marisa's face. "But Leigh, I thought Ben—"

Leigh planted her feet. "I can't keep imposing on your hospitality. TJ is quite the handful 24/7. I'm going to ask Sarah if she'll stay on for a couple of days until I settle in at the clinic."

Marisa rinsed her hands and wiped them with a paper towel.

"It's in the Oaks, and it's a gated community with a guard." Leigh chewed her bottom lip. This was harder than she'd thought it would be. And she still had to tell TJ.

"Leigh, you're a grown woman, and I can't tell you what to do . . . but I do wish you'd stay here. At least until Ben catches whoever is setting these fires."

"My house fire was caused by lightning, or the fire marshal would have told me." She squared her shoulders. "It's very important for me to stand on my own two feet. I've been doing it all my life."

"You're resilient, I'll grant you that. But there's not just you to think about. How about TJ? He's happy here. He has the twins, and he's actually making a difference with Tom. Why take him away from all of this?"

Tom was what Leigh was afraid of. Maybe now was the time to tell Marisa she was moving to Baltimore. A cough from Sarah stopped her.

"I'm not interrupting anything, am I?" Her friend came into the kitchen.

"No," Leigh said quickly. "I was just telling Marisa about the house Ian Maxwell has offered. I'm moving in tonight and would love it if you'd stay with us." She pleaded with her eyes.

Sarah looked from Leigh to Marisa and back to Leigh. "Are you determined to do this?"

"Yes, it's what I want to do." Leigh turned to Marisa. "You've been wonderful, but I'm used to living alone with TJ . . . even at Sarah's house, we had our own quarters. He makes so much noise, and I come and go at such odd hours sometimes. We're too much trouble. Besides, Tom needs peace and quiet."

"Pshaw. Tom loves having you and TJ here."

TJ maybe, but Leigh had seen the way he looked at her . . . like he'd discovered her secret and couldn't wait until he could tell it. "No, I'm sure it's much harder on Tom to have strangers in his house." Leigh turned to Sarah. "And if it's too much for you, I'll understand."

"If you've set your mind, I'll come and stay a few days." Sarah smiled apologetically at Marisa. "I don't want her to be alone, but you've been so gracious, offering your hospitality to me. I won't forget it."

Marisa raised her hands. "I know when I've been overruled." She hesitated. "Is Ben aware you're moving out?"

"I told him Ian offered a house and that I wanted to take him up on it. Have either of you seen TJ lately?"

Marisa nodded toward the door. "He's in the backyard, playing with the twins."

Leigh strode to the back door. Two down, TJ to go.

■ ■ ■

An hour later, Leigh nodded to the guard on duty in the Oaks. "The Honda is with me as well." When he waved her through, she glanced in her rearview mirror at Sarah as if to say, *See*. Two turns later she pulled her Avenger into the drive of their new home. Not exactly the right type of car for the neighborhood. But she wouldn't be here long.

"I don't like this house. Why couldn't we just stay with Granna and Pops?"

Leigh sighed. TJ had not taken the news they were moving well. She bit back the phrase she'd heard all her childhood. *Because I said so*. TJ didn't understand, and that was okay. There'd be more decisions he wouldn't understand. Like the move to Baltimore. But that news would be saved for another night. "Just give it a chance, son."

She got out of the car and popped the trunk. Sarah approached, rolling her suitcase behind her. "You never said it was this nice."

Leigh followed her gaze to the Cape Cod house with a wrap-around porch. "Totally furnished too. But I don't think TJ likes it."

"Give him time. You want me to help you lift your suitcase out?"

"I got it." Just as she tugged her luggage from the trunk, another car pulled in. An Acura. Much more suitable for this subdivision. Her jaw dropped as Emily stepped out of the car followed by the twins. Leigh had forgotten what kind of car Emily drove.

"Howdy, neighbor."

"You live around here?"

"Next street over. The boys are excited TJ will be even closer."

Marisa had never said a word about Emily living nearby. She glanced at her son. His dark and overcast expression had turned sunny.

"Can we go in the back?" TJ's eyes implored her.

She nodded. "Be sure you stay inside the fence," she called as he and the twins raced around the house. "You may have just saved my life. He was not happy about leaving your parents' house."

Emily chuckled. "Yeah, that's what Mom said. But I can understand why you'd want to move out. This is a nice place. Three-car garage. Mine only has two."

"Yeah. Like my car is used to even one garage. Come on in and see the rest of it."

■ ■ ■

"I don't like it." Ben tossed his pencil on the table. He was 100 percent against his deputy infiltrating the dog ring.

Wade folded his arms across his chest. "Well, I do."

Ben stood and paced the small conference room U.S. Marshal Luke Donovan had ushered them into when they arrived at his Memphis office. FBI agent Eric Raines sat next to the chair Ben had vacated, and Wade sat across the table. A map of Bradford County with the Edwards farm circled was spread across the top.

194

"We need an inside guy," Eric said. "My sources indicate their annual fight is coming up, and it's huge. The top names in the dogfighting world will be there, but no one knows when or where it'll be held."

Luke leaned forward. "And Wade already has an in with one of the players."

"Look, we're talking about Wade interacting with scum here," Ben said. "People who have no conscience. The wrong people figure out what he's doing, and I'll have a dead deputy on my hands."

"I can handle myself," Wade insisted. "All I have to do is gain the trust of a few people on the fringe, and Lester Cummings already trusts me. Then I can get the place and date of the fight."

"You don't think they're going to tell you that right off the bat, do you?"

"It's not like I'm a stranger to the ones there last night. Coon hunted with some of them, and those men already trust me."

Ben had a bad feeling about this, but he also knew his deputy. He was as bad as the pit bulls they were trying to save, clamping on to something and refusing to let go. Maybe if he kept a tight rein on him . . . "Will you wear a wire?"

A no formed on his deputy's face.

Eric Raines spoke up. "We can download software onto your phone, and it'll act like a listening device. We'll use Ben's phone as the monitor, and the software will allow him to silently connect to your phone and listen to conversations around you. And when you make or receive calls, it'll transmit conversation, your location, everything."

Wade held up his hand. "Uh-uh. I don't want anyone listening to every conversation I have."

Eric scratched his head. "We have a pen that will act as a microphone, but it only has a short range. A receiver would have to be close for it to be any good."

"How close?" Ben asked as he took his seat again.

A crooked smile graced Eric's face. "Close enough if anything went wrong we could get to him."

"I'm good with that." Wade shifted his gaze to Ben.

"I'm not. I want the pen, but I also want the software downloaded on our phones. You know I won't listen in unless it's about this case. It'll be that way, or this whole deal is off."

The muscle in Wade's jaw pulsed in and out.

Ben didn't blink. "Think about your mom and what she'd do if anything happened to you."

The muscle stilled. "If I let you download the software, will you be on board?"

Not really. The whole thing was dangerous. Ben would be a lot more comfortable if he were the one making the contact, but he didn't have the relationship with these men that Wade had. "As long as you don't go all Lone Ranger on us. You have to agree that anytime you're making contact with these men, we'll be in the loop."

"I'm not stupid, Ben."

"I hope not." He directed his gaze to Eric. "How soon can you get him the pen?"

Eric hoisted his briefcase onto the table. "Now too soon?"

He opened the case and selected a narrow black box. Inside was an ordinary-looking ballpoint pen that he handed to Wade. "Keep it in your shirt pocket like you would any pen, and always remember to activate it *before* you go into any meeting with these people. They're going to be watching every move you make, and you might not have a logical reason to touch that pen."

He picked up a small box. "This is a GPS chip—it goes in your keyless remote, and it's a backup. Most people carry their keys on them, so if worst-case scenario happens and the pen is discovered, we can still track you."

Worst-case scenario. The words haunted Ben as Wade handed Eric his key chain.

196

The agent inserted a flat screwdriver in the notch on the side and popped the back off. Then he peeled the back off the GPS chip and stuck it on the inside of the cover. He snapped the shell back on and handed Wade the key ring. "It's already activated and can't be turned off. It'll tell us where you are at all times. Now let me have your phone."

"Who will be monitoring all this equipment?" Wade asked as he handed over his cell.

"Ben, primarily, but I can patch into the equipment as well." The FBI agent turned to Ben. "I need your phone as well."

Ben handed over his cell then tapped the map where he'd circled the Edwards place. "The area we were in last night had no cell reception. What do you do about that?"

"All three use satellites, although the pen and phone work better off the wireless towers." Eric connected Ben's phone to the internet and made several keystrokes. "You'll receive a text whenever the pen is activated or when he receives a phone call. In the case of the phone, you'll decide call by call which ones you want to listen to."

The agent tapped a blue icon on the cell phone screen. "Click on this app, and you can find your deputy anywhere he is."

"Better watch where you take Ruth now," Ben said. He nodded toward the map. "I checked the records on the Edwards place. It's owned by some company I never heard of, and neither has Google."

"GrandTeCO," Luke said. "I have an agent working on the paper trail, but so far, it looks legit."

"Let me know what you discover." Ben stood. "And, if that covers everything for tonight, I need to get back to Logan Point."

"A word of advice, Wade," Luke said. The U.S. Marshal ran his hand over his short-cropped gray hair. "Don't push these guys. You've made the initial contact—you let them know you're interested in a dog. Now let them come to you."

"Listen to the man," Ben said. From the expression on his chief deputy's face, keeping him in check would be a full-time job.

■ ■ ■

"It'll work, Ben." An undertow of excitement carried in Wade's voice. "I want to get whoever used that pup for bait and put them under the jail."

For the last fifteen minutes, Ben had listened to Wade dismiss every argument he came up with. His jaw ached from clenching it. That his deputy was a risk taker had never been more evident, and Ben didn't like sitting on the sidelines. He hated that Wade was the one risking everything. "I agreed to it back in Memphis, so shut up already."

"I think I'll drop by Lester Cummings's house after you drop me off."

"No! Luke said to let them make the next move."

"But, Ben—"

"If you can't do this the way we planned it, I'll call it off."

"Come on, don't pull rank on me."

"And don't you go rogue. I'd like to keep you alive, because I don't have the money to keep your mom at Rest Haven."

"I wouldn't expect you to do that."

At least that seemed to sober him up a little. "No? Well, you get killed doing this, and I'd feel obligated."

"I know how to handle myself."

"Then let's do it like we planned. Let them come to you. It probably won't be long until they do, anyway. Dogfighting is fueled by greed, and they'll be looking to turn a quick buck. Besides, I imagine they'd like to think they have a deputy sheriff in their back pocket. Be sure and play that angle up when they contact you."

"I'll give 'em a week. If they haven't contacted me by—"

"You will do nothing. Have some patience, Wade."

For an answer, his chief deputy slouched in the passenger seat and remained quiet until they pulled in front of the jail. In the dusky twilight, yellow tape across the front access fluttered in the breeze.

Wade jerked his head toward the jail. "You know whoever promoted that fight last night did this. And probably put the snakes out at the ball field. I'd think you'd want to catch them."

Ben blew a breath through his lips. "I don't want to lose a deputy doing it."

Finally Wade shrugged. "Okay, we'll do it your way."

"Thanks."

"Do I still get Sunday off? Told Ruth we'd go out to the lake."

"Sure. Until Cummings contacts you, we're pretty much in a holding pattern." The weekend stretched empty before Ben. Maybe Taylor Martin would get that profile completed. "I plan to work."

After Wade climbed into his truck and pulled away from the jail, Ben went inside. "Evening, Mark," he said to the dispatcher. "Everything quiet?"

"For Friday night. But wait until the juke joints crank up."

"Call me if you need me." Ben fingered his keys. For a couple of hours, he'd put the problem of Leigh and her stubbornness out of his mind. But now it was time to deal with it. He walked to his office, unhooking his cell phone along the way, and dialed her number. It went straight to voice mail. Immediately he dialed his mother.

"Is Leigh there?" he asked when she answered. He glanced at the fire marshal's report on his desk.

"Sorry, Ben, but she and Sarah and TJ moved into that house Ian offered."

"You're kidding." He couldn't believe she'd actually gone through with it.

"You have to realize she's a grown woman, making her own choices. She's not under arrest."

Too bad she wasn't. "Where is this house?"

His mother gave him the address, and he jotted it down. "It's a couple of blocks from your sister's house."

Was that news supposed to make him feel better? Although, it was a pretty secure area. "Thanks, Mom."

"Ben," she said before he could hang up. "I, ah . . ."

"Yes?"

On the other end of the phone, his mother sighed. "If she wants to do this, you can't stop her. Don't burn all your bridges trying to."

"Thanks, Mom." He picked up the fire marshal's report and read through it again. He might not be able to keep her from staying in Ian's house, but he could at least try.

14

Chains holding the swing creaked as Leigh pushed against the porch deck. A couple of yards over, a neighbor had just finished mowing his grass in the last light of the day. Ian's light musky cologne vied with the fresh-cut clippings.

TJ had gone home with the twins for a while, and Sarah was unpacking, something Leigh had been in the middle of when Ian had interrupted them an hour ago with a fantastic sourdough pizza. Now she was too full. A light from the living room window illuminated the porch in a soft glow, and she leaned against the back of the swing as it rocked slowly back and forth. She could get used to being taken care of.

"A dollar for your thoughts."

"A dollar? I'm not sure they're worth that much," she said and rubbed her hand over the smooth finish on the swing. "I was in that place men like to go—you know, thinking of absolutely nothing."

"I didn't think women did that."

"This woman does."

He tilted his head to the side. "This has been a hard summer for you. Tony's death, the fire . . ."

She shifted her gaze to the yard, where lightning bugs flickered their mating signals. Hard didn't begin to describe this summer. She missed Tony so much. His crazy practical jokes, his brotherly advice that she rarely took. His presence. She blinked back the tears that stung her eyes. It didn't take much to bring them on. A memory, a question from TJ . . . She'd found out very quickly that she didn't always get a choice of when the tears came, and they sometimes ambushed her in odd places, like the grocery when she picked up a box of cereal for TJ and remembered it was the same brand she and Tony liked growing up. And argued over who had dibs on the last bowl.

"Did you ever get the fire marshal's report?"

Ian's question brought her back to the present. "No. But Ben was expecting to get it today. He still thinks it will show someone set fire to the house."

"Why does he believe someone would want to burn you out?"

"He keeps talking about that flash drive Tony told him about. That whoever wants it thought it might be in the house."

"So, you evidently haven't run across it."

"I'm not sure I would recognize it if I did. Some of those drives are tiny." She turned to him. "Do you have any idea what could've been on it?"

Ian shook his head. "Probably something to do with his gambling endeavors."

"So you think it had nothing to do with his job at Maxwell Industries?"

"That's one thing I can be certain of." He pushed with his foot to keep the swing going.

"You're probably right that it had to do with his gambling. When he started taking TJ to church, Tony changed. Maybe some of the things he was involved in got to him." She sighed. "I don't want to think about it tonight."

They sat in silence as dusk faded into night. The scent of Ian's cologne teased her nose again. She tried to identify the fragrance. Definitely a little musk, a hint of cedar, maybe a little vanilla. She sensed rather than saw his arm slide behind her on the swing. He was so close to her, their legs almost touched. She shifted over slightly and turned to look at him. "Thank you again for this place."

His blue eyes held amusement in them. "That's about the fifth time you've thanked me since I arrived. Enough already. And you're welcome to stay as long as you want."

Heat rose in her cheeks. "Thanks—I mean, well, we probably will only be in Logan Point another six weeks, so I may take you up on that."

"Six weeks? What are you talking about?"

"I've taken a position at Johns Hopkins." She still couldn't believe her dream was coming true.

"I thought you had a service contract to fulfill at Bradford General."

"It'll transfer. I'll be working at a free clinic in one of Baltimore's low-income districts."

"I think congratulations are in order. If I'd known, I would've brought a bottle of champagne instead of pizza."

How refreshing to not have to defend her every decision. Why couldn't Ben be more like Ian?

He leaned closer. "I like Baltimore, and it isn't that far."

Her heart sank as he held her captive with his blue eyes. She should have seen this coming. "Umm—"

Lights flashed across the front porch, and Leigh jumped back. Beside her, Ian muttered something under his breath as she shaded her eyes against the lights.

A car door opened. "Sorry, folks. Didn't mean to interrupt anything." Ben's voice carried in the still night air.

He didn't sound sorry. And he'd probably be just as difficult about the move. "Would you mind dousing those lights?"

"Yeah, sure."

The lights died as Ben slammed his truck door and ambled toward them. Ian stood and held out his hand. "Evening, Sheriff."

"Ian." Ben shifted the papers he held to his left hand. "Nice night," he said, shaking Ian's hand.

Leigh lifted her chin. "Did you need something, Ben?"

He propped his foot on the bottom step. "Thought we might finish our conversation from earlier today."

"I believe the subject we were discussing is no longer relevant."

"I don't know. I have the fire marshal's report and would like to go over it with you."

Ian cleared his throat. "I have paperwork at the office that needs attention." He squeezed her hand. "Why don't I call you tomorrow?"

She smiled at him. "Thanks, Ian. For everything."

Ben waited until Ian drove away before climbing the steps and sitting beside her in the swing. "Nice place. Did you tell him you won't be staying long?"

"What do you mean?"

"The job in Baltimore."

"Oh. Yes, we discussed it." Ben sat as close as Ian had, but the effect was so different. Electricity charged the space between them. Ian and Ben didn't wear the same type of cologne, either. Ben smelled more like Dial soap, maybe like he'd just taken a shower. "You said something about the fire marshal's report?"

He handed her the papers. "That's your copy. It basically says it wasn't lightning. Your house showed none of the usual characteristics of a lightning strike. No path that it took, your wiring wasn't wiped out, no wallpaper peeled around light switches."

"What *does* it say?" She could take the papers inside and read them, but it would be quicker for Ben to just tell her.

"Someone shot an arrow wrapped in a kerosene-soaked rag onto the roof of your house. Even though the shingles were wet, the combination of kerosene and asphalt was enough to start the blaze. Your rafters were old and dry . . . excellent kindling."

Ben's matter-of-fact voice made his words even scarier. "Are you sure?"

"The chemical analysis of one of the samples came back today. It showed traces of kerosene, and yesterday the fire marshal found a single broadhead arrow tip in the rubble he was sifting. A tip exactly like the ones used to set the fire at the jail. Someone tried to burn your house down with you and your son in it."

Leigh bolted from the swing with her hand over her mouth. She barely made it to the bathroom before losing the pizza. Ben followed, and she soon felt a cool washcloth pressed to her forehead as she sank to the floor and waited to see if she would throw up again. When she was certain it was over, she scooted to the wall and leaned her back to it.

Ben re-wet the cloth and sat beside her, gently wiping her face. "I'm sorry, Leigh."

TJ could've died. Sarah. Her. *Why?* She pressed the cloth against her eyes as hot tears filled them and splashed down her cheeks. Ben's arms went around her, and she leaned into his chest. She couldn't do this. Not alone. *Tell him the truth. Tell him TJ is his son. He has a right to know.*

Leigh wanted to, she really did. But how? Maybe if she just opened her mouth and let the words out. "We need to talk."

"No." He stood and pulled her up. "We're packing your things, and you're moving back to my parents' house. Where's TJ?"

Did Ben have a one-way brain? And where did he get off thinking he could order her around? She'd been crazy to think she could tell this bullheaded man the truth. "I'm staying here."

"Leigh, did you not hear one word I said?"

"I heard everything you said. Someone set fire to my house. They used a bow and arrow. Look around, Ben. Do you think anyone will get past that guard at the entrance with a bow and arrow? Your sister lives here, for goodness' sake. TJ is with her now. Your nephews play in their backyard without fear. That's why I moved here."

He stepped back and held his hands out. "Okay. You don't have to take my head off."

"Then quit trying to boss me around. You are not my husband, so quit trying to tell me what to do. And get out of my bathroom so I can brush my teeth."

■ ■ ■

Husband. Is that what he wanted to be to her? Ben paced the living room as he waited for Leigh to appear. No. He was never getting married.

Then why did it make him so mad when he saw Ian sitting in the swing with her?

He glanced around the room. Expensive furniture, real paintings, the house itself. He couldn't give Leigh anything so fancy. He fought the jealousy that filled his heart. It stabbed him again when he remembered how his lights had illuminated Leigh and Ian practically kissing. He turned as she walked into the room. "What's going on with you and Ian, anyway?"

She gaped at him. "Did you just ask me—" Her mouth opened and closed like a fish. "I think you need to go. This conversation is getting absolutely out of hand."

Could he get his size twelve foot out of his mouth? This woman was absolutely driving him crazy. And at a time he needed his focus elsewhere, like the dogfighting ring and figuring out who was going around setting fires with a bow and arrow.

"And forget about us moving. This place is safe."

Ben swallowed the retort on his lips. She was right. The house was located in the middle of the subdivision. It would be pretty well impossible for anyone to shoot an arrow to this roof from outside the neighborhood. With the exception of his parents' home, the house was probably the safest place in Logan Point.

He tried again. "Wait, I didn't mean that the way it sounded."

She stepped closer to him and poked him in the chest. "No. You wait. Who I see and where I live is none of your business. I'm tired of imposing on your folks. I want a place of my own. And—"

"Okay." He stood his ground because if he took another step

back, he'd be out the door. Besides, all he wanted to do was grab that finger jabbing him. Pull her into his arms and kiss her. Hard.

Leigh's pupils filled her green eyes. She dropped her hand and took a deep breath. "Okay. I'm glad that's settled."

Only it wasn't. He still wanted to pull Leigh close and kiss her. He leaned in, and loved the wonder in her face as he traced his finger down her cheek, lingering on her lips. Then he cupped her face in his hands and lowered his lips to hers. They were soft, yielding, and he slid his hands to her shoulders, deepening the kiss. Leigh tasted minty, like toothpaste. Her arms circled his neck as she returned his kiss.

What was he thinking? He broke away. "I'm sorry. I . . . I have to leave."

Color drained from her face except for two red circles on her cheeks. Leigh stepped back. Without another word, she wheeled and ran up the stairs.

Ben's shoulders sagged. Kissing her had been wrong on so many levels, and now he'd hurt her deeply. He picked up the fire marshal's report and put it on the table. Maybe he could straighten this out tomorrow. A door slammed upstairs.

If she would talk to him.

■ ■ ■

With her face burning almost as much as her heart hurt, Leigh stood at her bedroom window as Ben backed out of the drive. Why had she let herself be drawn into that kiss? Because she wanted him to do it. Even earlier, when she believed Ian was going to kiss her, it had been Ben she wanted. Then he had to go and make it plain kissing her was a mistake. And to think she almost told him about TJ. What a mistake that would have been. He didn't want a wife, much less a child.

She turned from the window at a soft tap on her door and pasted on a smile. "Come in."

Sarah opened the door and slipped inside. "You okay?"

"I guess you heard."

"Only the raised voices."

Heat rose to her face once again, and she walked to the side of her bed and sat down, leaning against the headboard. "I almost told him about TJ."

"What stopped you?" Sarah sat in the tapestry-covered chair.

"We got into a stupid argument about what I could and could not do. But even as I was yelling at him, I knew it was because he's worried about us."

"Oh, Leigh, you have it bad."

She passed her hand over her eyes. "Ben doesn't want me. He as much as said so."

"Are you sure you didn't misunderstand him?"

"*I'm sorry. I have to leave.*" Leigh shook her head. "I understood exactly what he meant."

She smoothed the satin pillow that matched the satin bedspread. Her gaze flitted around the room that was decorated with designer bedspreads and expensive rugs and original art. "I don't belong here. Not in this house and not in Logan Point. I don't belong anywhere."

"What are you afraid of, child?"

She stilled her hand, and the words slipped out. "That no one will ever want me. They'll all be like my mother. She never wanted me."

"I'm sure you're wrong about that."

Leigh shook her head. "I heard her tell my dad once I was a mistake, and he didn't correct her." She stared at a spot on the expensive rug. "And the mistakes I've made have proven it."

"You listen to me, young lady." Sarah's firm voice filled the room. "God doesn't make mistakes. He knew you before he formed you. That means he's loved you always. Do you think he was surprised when you were born? Or when TJ was born? No!"

She gave the older woman a thin smile. "Too bad my mother

wasn't more like you. Sometimes I think she took that overdose just to get away from me."

Footsteps clattered up the stairs. "Mom! Where are you! I gotta tell you what we did!" Her door burst open and with it TJ, his face flushed and his eyes wide. "We made a clubhouse!"

Leigh's heart warmed, and she pushed aside thoughts of her mother. Her son was back to talking in exclamation points. She hugged him, and over his head, her gaze caught Sarah's. She wished she could believe her friend's words.

■ ■ ■

"Mom?" TJ's voice worked its way into her consciousness. "Mom, it's church day."

Leigh groaned and rolled over in bed, peeking at the clock on her dresser. Eight in the morning? She sat up. Her son stood at the foot of her bed, dressed in a pair of navy pants and a white shirt. She didn't remember buying those. "Good morning. You look nice."

"Granna bought these that day we went shopping." He pulled at her hand. "Come on. We'll be late."

Granna. She would be at church. Tom too, if he was up to it. Could she talk TJ out of going? Or at least maybe she could stay home. One look at his excited face gave her the answer. "Do I hafta?" she asked, mimicking TJ when he didn't want to get up.

"Mom!"

"Oh, okay. Let me get a shower." She threw back her blanket and climbed out of bed. "Are you okay with losing the ball game last night?"

He shrugged. "Win some, lose some."

Her heart caught. TJ sounded just like Tony. The back of her eyes burned as she swallowed down the ache in her chest.

"Hurry, Mom. Miss Sarah says we have to call Ben to come get us."

Leigh blinked away the sting of unshed tears. She would not be calling Ben. It was hard enough trying to erase the memory of his

209

kiss Friday night without being around him. At least she hadn't had to deal with him yesterday. Andre had escorted them to and from TJ's ball game. Maybe Ben would send his deputy again today. "Doesn't Andre or Wade go to . . ." *What was the name of the church TJ's been attending? Crossroads? No.* "Center Hill. Maybe one of them will come and get us."

"I want Ben to come get us. I miss him. I wish we still lived with Granna and Pops, and I could see him every day."

Leigh stood frozen to the floor. "I thought you liked it here. You can play with the twins whenever you want."

He shrugged his thin shoulders. "It's not the same. Granna's house smells . . . it smells like somebody lives there."

Yeast bread. Cakes and cookies. Yeah, the Logan house did indeed smell like someone lived there. She mentally promised to stop by the grocery on the way home from church and pick up a few items. Not that she was great at cooking, but anyone could open a cake box and follow the directions.

Four hours later, Leigh reflected on the morning as the closing hymn ended. Ben had escorted her and Sarah despite her desire otherwise, while TJ had ridden in the truck with him. It might be the last time for her son, though. She was pretty sure TJ was responsible for the short siren blast that pierced the quiet Sunday morning.

Sarah preferred to sit in the sanctuary during Sunday school, but when Leigh ran into Cathy from the hospital, she ended up in her class. Leigh mostly kept quiet while the other women engaged in lively discussion.

She enjoyed being around the women who were her age and promised to return. She liked the young pastor and found herself agreeing that parents should not neglect teaching biblical principles to their children. It was time for her to step up to the plate and not rely on someone else—and that reminded her of Tony. Would there ever be a time she could think about him and tears not be ready to spring from her eyes?

After the benediction, she stood and motioned for TJ to leave the twins and join her. There had been no gracious way out of sitting anywhere other than with the Logan clan.

"Mom! Granna wants us to come eat dinner with them. Can we?"

Church, then Sunday dinner. A Logan ritual, and she should have been expecting the invitation. "I thought we'd pick up a bucket of chicken and eat in the gazebo in the backyard. You and Miss Sarah and me, and then we'll go down to the pool at the rec center and swim. Doesn't that sound like fun?"

"Mom, please." His eyes pleaded with her.

"You're more than welcome," Marisa said. Emily nodded her agreement.

"Thank you, but I think the three of us need a little family time."

Marisa patted her arm. "I understand. Maybe next week."

"Yes, that sounds nice." Leigh would think of an excuse before Sunday. She glanced around, wondering who would escort them home.

Emily spoke up. "If you're looking for Ben, he went back to his office after Sunday school but said to tell you he'd be in the parking lot when church let out."

So the sheriff didn't stay for church.

Outside, true to his word, Ben's truck sat blocking her Avenger. "Can I start the car, Mom? And see if Ben wants to have a picnic with us?"

She handed over her keys. "I imagine Ben will want to eat with his family." At least that's what she hoped.

■ ■ ■

Two hours later, Leigh shooed Sarah in out of the heat while she cleaned up the remains of their picnic. As soon as TJ gobbled down his food, he'd left them to sulk about not having the twins to play with. So much for family time. But at least Ben had declined, saying he had paperwork at his office to finish. He'd probably realized what a bad idea the gazebo was with the heat and humidity wrapping around them like a sauna. She fanned herself with one of the disposable plates. Time to have a heart-to-heart talk with TJ. Tell him they were moving to Baltimore.

Leigh climbed the stairs to her son's room, rehearsing her words. At his door, she hesitated, then knocked and entered. TJ lay on the bed, his eyes glued to her iPad. Ignoring the fact he'd taken it without permission, she took it from him and sat on the side of the bed. "I realize you wanted to go to the Logans' after church—"

"The twins were going to be there, and I wanted to show Pops a new game I found that will help him talk."

"You need to quit bothering him." Next week she'd see about sending TJ to his babysitter again.

"But—"

"No, listen to me. He has trained therapists helping him. Let them do their job. I have something else I want to discuss."

He crossed his arms across his chest. "When you talk like that, it's always bad."

"What do you mean?"

"You sound just like you did when you told me we were moving to Logan Point."

She felt a headache coming on. "Has this been so bad?"

He cocked his head and pursed his lips. "It was at first. I didn't have any friends."

"But now you do. You're friends with the boys on your baseball team, and you have the twins, and the ones in your Sunday school class. Making new friends wasn't so hard, now was it?"

He shook his head.

So far, so good. She took a quick breath. "I've been offered a new job."

TJ's eyes widened. "You mean at Ms. Emily's clinic? I know about that."

"No, this is a really important job in Baltimore, and—"

"No! I don't want to move again." He flopped back against the headboard.

If he poked his lip out any farther, he'd trip over it. "You'll like Baltimore. There's lots of interesting things to do. We can go to the ocean, and there are lots of museums."

"I don't want to go to no old museum. I want to stay here with my friends."

"I'm afraid that's not an option. I've accepted the job."

"You didn't even ask me what I wanted to do! It's always about your job. What's wrong with staying here?"

"Timothy Jackson Somerall, I am not discussing this with you if you take that tone." While she understood his feelings, she would not allow him to talk with disrespect. His lip quivered, and she softened her tone. "I have to do what I think is best for us. I promise, you'll make new friends, just like you did here."

"But I don't want new friends. I want the ones I have."

His wail pierced her heart. She should not have brought the move up today when he was already upset, but she wanted to prepare him. From the sound of it, she was going to need every day between now and September fifteenth.

Leigh sighed and walked to the door. "We'll discuss this again later." Before she left his room, she looked back. "TJ, it's going to be all right. You'll make new friends."

He turned his head and stared out the window.

Leigh closed the door and leaned her head against it. Maybe things would look better after a nap.

■ ■ ■

Her cell phone rang, waking Leigh from a dead sleep. She grabbed it from her nightstand and glanced at the number. Private. Frowning, she answered. "Dr. Somerall."

An organ played what sounded like funeral music. She hovered her thumb over the disconnect button.

"You have something that belongs to me."

The deep, slow words sent chills racing over her body. Leigh lifted her hand to her throat. "Who is this?"

"I want—" The crescendo of the organ drowned out the eerie voice.

"I can't hear you! What are you talking about?"

"Mind your own business, or your son will pay."

Then, dead silence filled the airspace.

■ ■ ■

Ben picked up the Rubik's Cube on his desk and made a couple of turns. Logarithms. No wonder the thing made absolutely no sense. He set it back down and wandered out into the commons area. The weekend dispatcher waved. "I see you skipped church again."

"Yep. Had some paperwork to catch up on." Not that it couldn't have waited. But seeing Leigh walk out her front door, her chestnut hair silky in the morning sun, the smattering of freckles that makeup couldn't hide . . . the memory of Friday night's kiss had come roaring back. No way could he sit in the same room with her and concentrate on a sermon.

She refused to meet his eye, anyway. He hated that she'd taken his apology as rejection. But until he caught whoever was after her, he couldn't afford to let his heart get involved. Protecting her was hard enough.

Wade stuck his head out of his office. "Ben, can I see you a minute? Outside."

He followed his chief deputy to the parking lot. "What's up?"

Wade rubbed his hands together. "I heard from Lester. He's going to take me to see a dog Wednesday—he knows that's my day off."

"How does he know that?"

"Maybe because I told him last night when I helped Andre at the ballpark. Lester's grandson was on the other team. By the way, we sure could've used your help. Might've kept us from losing five to one."

Ben shifted his gaze down the street. Being on the field with the boys had been good the other night. Until the snakes appeared. "What if Lester is setting you up?"

"He doesn't have any reason to suspect me."

"You're a deputy, Wade. That should be enough."

"But I know how to play Lester. He doesn't see me as a deputy. He sees me as this good-ole-boy he coon hunts with. Do you know how hard it was for me to be nice to him at the ball game, after seeing him at that dogfight? But you know me, I can sell milk to a dairy farm, and by the time we left the ball field, he believed I was his best friend. Besides, I don't see any other way to infiltrate this ring."

"I'd watch my back all the same. Be sure you have that pen in your shirt pocket, and let me know when you're meeting with him to go see this dog."

Wade saluted with two fingers. "Aye, aye, Cap'n."

"I'm serious, Wade."

"I'll be careful, and I'll call before we meet."

"You better." Ben cocked his head. "How is that pup we found?"

A satisfied grin crossed Wade's face. "Rocky is healing, and he's not nearly as cowered down. He's going to be okay."

"Rocky, huh?"

"Yeah. He's not a quitter."

"Good name." Ben took his truck keys out. "Think I'll do a little patrolling."

"Tell Leigh I said hello."

"Just doing a little patrolling, Wade. Not stopping anywhere."

Ben pulled out of the justice center parking lot and headed toward the Oaks. He hadn't driven far when he spied a familiar figure walking down the sidewalk. What was TJ doing three blocks from the jail? He pulled over and rolled down his window. "Where're you headed?"

Sweat dribbled down the boy's face. "Granna's house."

215

"Want a ride?"

"You're not going to take me back home, are you?"

They both knew Ben would. He leaned over and opened the door. "Not until you cool off. Hop in."

TJ fastened his seat belt and then leaned forward, trying to catch the air from the vent as Ben cranked the air conditioner to high. "What's going on?"

"Nothin'."

"You running away from home?"

TJ concentrated on the vent.

"If you are, you forgot your clothes." Ben turned the truck toward the park.

"I just needed to take a walk," TJ said and leaned back against the seat. His fingers inched toward the siren button.

"Don't touch it," Ben said. "Unless you want to go straight home."

TJ slid his hand under his leg. "Did you know my mom is moving us again?"

Uh-oh. Leigh must have told him about the job in Baltimore. It didn't appear TJ was too happy about it, either. He didn't blame the kid. "Is that what this is about?"

A bare hint of a nod. "I thought Granna could talk to Mom. Make her change her mind."

TJ grew quiet, and Ben glanced at him. The boy was studying him with an odd look on his face. Ben shook his head. "Uh, no. I'm not talking to her. Wouldn't do any good, anyway. I'm kind of in the doghouse with your mom."

TJ's shoulders drooped. "Will you take me to Granna's house?"

"I'm afraid I have to take you home."

"Why?"

"It wouldn't be right if I didn't."

"You don't always do what's right. Sometimes you let the twins get away with stuff."

The kid was observant. "How about your mom? Don't you think she'll be worried if she discovers you're gone? In fact, don't you think you should call her now, so she won't worry?" How Ben had hated it as a kid when adults put a guilt trip on him. But TJ needed to be the one to call Leigh.

"I guess. I just don't see why she can't stay here and work at the hospital in Logan Point or for Ms. Emily. Can't you marry her so she'll stay here? She likes you. I know she does."

Ben almost swallowed his tongue. "Uh, I think we better give your mom a call."

"You talk to her."

He dialed Leigh's cell, and she answered almost immediately, panic sounding in her voice.

"Ben, I received this awful call threatening TJ, and now I can't find him. I've looked everywhere in the house, and he's just not here."

"It's okay. He's with me. I found him a couple of blocks from the jail. What call are you talking about?"

"What was he doing near the jail?"

"Said he was on his way to my mom's house."

"I see." She sighed. "He's kind of upset with me right now."

"I'll bring him home, but tell me about this call." Even talking to Leigh over the phone made his heart ratchet up.

"Let's wait until you get here."

"Okay." He hung up and turned to TJ. "Are you ready?"

"You sure you can't take me to your mom's?"

"Afraid not. Tell you what . . . I'll get Mom to call your mom. Maybe all of you can go over and have supper with my folks tonight. How would you like that?"

"She won't do it."

The boy was probably right.

Leigh stood waiting on the front porch when Ben pulled into her drive. Actually seeing her was harder on his heart than talking to her. For a second he thought about what it'd be like if he quit his job and went to work with the U.S. Marshal Service. He could be based anywhere, even Baltimore.

No. When he qualified for the sheriff's race, he made a commitment to his town, something Leigh didn't seem to be capable of doing. Otherwise, she'd stay in Logan Point.

Beside him, TJ fumbled with his seat belt. The boy wasn't anxious to get out, and a wave of emotion swelled in Ben's heart. TJ was a good kid who had somehow burrowed under the stone wall he'd erected.

Suddenly his heart knocked against his ribs while his face grew cold in spite of the sweat that beaded it. A band squeezed his lungs just like the day Tommy Ray had dragged him to the bottom of the lake. If he didn't do something, his chest would explode.

The panic attack blindsided him. *Relax*. Ben focused on taking slow, complete breaths as he imagined the thoughts about Tommy Ray colliding with a huge stop sign. In his peripheral vision, he saw Leigh walking toward him. In the seat, TJ tried to wiggle out of the seat belt. He shook his head to clear it and reached toward the seat belt. "Let me get that for you," he said.

His fingers shook as he unsnapped the metal. Without looking at his mom, TJ scrambled out of the truck and darted into the house. Ben took another breath then lowered the window.

"Are you okay?" Leigh wrinkled her forehead. "You look like you've seen a ghost. Do you want to come in the house?"

He wiped his mouth with the back of his hand then licked his lip, tasting the salt. "I'm fine, but I'll come in so we can talk about this call you received."

"How about if we stay on the porch? I don't want TJ to overhear us."

He nodded and fumbled for a notepad from his dashboard before following her to the house, trying not to remember the last time he had been here. Leigh settled in the swing, and he took the rocking chair. Avoiding her emerald eyes, he stared at the delicate lines of her neck. This was not working. *Focus.* Ben cleared his throat. "This caller, was it a man or woman?"

"I don't know. The number was blocked . . . then there was this awful music, and then a voice like out of a horror movie—"

"Did it sound like he used a synthesizer? Remember the one we used in that play in high school?"

Her eyes widened. "Yes, exactly like that."

"What did this person say?"

"The only thing I really understood was when he said to mind my own business or TJ would be hurt. Then when I couldn't find TJ . . ."

Ben tapped the notepad. "Was anything specific mentioned? Like the flash drive?"

Her jaw dropped. "You think this is because someone's still looking for that stupid drive?"

"Leigh, I don't know. I'm just trying to make sense of everything that's happened since Tony's death."

"Maybe it's that father that I turned in for suspected child abuse. That would fit with what the caller said about minding my own business . . . except for . . ."

"What?"

"He—I'm assuming it's a he—said I had something that belonged to him." She looked at him with troubled eyes. "How did he get my cell number?"

"How many people have your number?"

One corner of her mouth turned up. "Half the hospital staff. Getting my number probably wouldn't be that hard."

"Well, just keep TJ close, and I'll beef up patrols around here."

"Keeping him close won't be hard. After what he did today, he's grounded for life."

"Don't . . ." He swallowed a grin. "Don't be too hard on the boy. He's had a lot going on lately."

"Maybe so, but that's no excuse for running off today. Thanks for bringing him home." Leigh hesitated. "And I want to apologize for getting upset Friday night."

The words ran together as they rushed out of her mouth, and he took a second to decipher them. He tried to ignore the heat creeping up his neck. "I should never—"

"If you're going to apologize for kissing me again, then I'll take back *my* apology." She'd fisted her hands on her hips.

"It's not that I didn't want to kiss you . . . but after the report from the fire marshal, and now this . . ." He swallowed. "Until this person is caught, I can't afford to have feelings for you."

He shouldn't have said that, either. He couldn't afford to have feelings for her. Period.

Her shoulders softened. "Oh. Then that makes me feel even worse."

The scent of her perfume drifted from the swing. Like a camera lens, his mind captured the image of her sitting so close, her green eyes the color of jade, the few freckles across her nose, her chestnut hair curving delicately toward her cheek. He almost reached and brushed it back.

Ben had to get out of there before he said or did something stupid. He stood and edged toward the steps. "I'll call you if I learn anything more from the fire marshal."

At his truck, he stopped, almost tempted to go back. To try and erase the hurt from her eyes.

15

Armero went over the shipping list for Maxwell's Fine China. The shipment of raw materials was still on the schedule for a delivery to Mexico next Wednesday. He checked and made sure Gordon Roberts was still scheduled to make the run. Next, he clicked on the manifest and added the Blue Dog Company for an offload of kaolin. No one had ever questioned a delivery to the dummy corporation.

Two hundred AR-15 rifles with no serial numbers sat boxed in a corner of the ceramics warehouse with a hold order on them. Tuesday evening after the lines closed down and everyone left, he would load the boxes on the truck. This was the most dangerous part of the operation. If anyone questioned him, he had a ready answer—a rush order came in and he couldn't find anyone else to load it. But there was always the chance something could go wrong at any stage.

Just thinking about the guns sitting in plain view sent a surge of blood racing through his body. Just like it had when he was a teenager and walked through the doors of a department store with no intention of paying for what he walked out with. It hadn't been about needing a watch or any other item. It had been about getting away with it, and not once had he been caught.

Until Tony. That had been a piece of bad luck. On a day that his own computer had been down, Armero used Tony's to access his Switzerland account and thought he'd erased all traces of activity. His heart almost stopped when Tony showed him the web address that popped up on his screen and asked who'd been using his computer.

Even though Tony seemed to buy his answer, he had not gotten this far taking anything for granted. He downloaded the spyware onto Tony's smartphone and viewed the company security videos daily, which paid off when he saw Tony download data from his computer onto a flash drive. When he froze the screen and zoomed in on the computer monitor, the Switzerland website was up. Then the phone calls to Ben Logan. Armero had known he had to get that flash drive. Even if it took killing Tony to get it.

Except Tony didn't have it on him at the hotel, and three weeks later he still didn't know where the drive was. Hopefully burned to a crisp in the house fire. But he couldn't count on that. If the drive still existed, it was probably in Leigh Somerall's possession. She could have it and not even realize it. He needed insurance. He needed to put enough fear in her so that if she found it, she'd be afraid to take it to the sheriff.

It was time to give her another call and mention the flash drive this time.

■ ■ ■

By Wednesday morning Ben was no closer to solving the mystery of who'd been setting the fires or who set the snakes loose in the park. He tapped his pen on the desk. Six crimes in a month, and only one definitely solved with Billy Wayne's death and the discovery of the Sub-2000 in his saddlebags. Not good results. He dialed Livy. "I don't suppose you've gotten a ballistics report back on the bullet you found or the .38 Smith and Wesson?"

"Nada. The crime lab has a backlog of cases, but I'll call and see if I can rush them."

He disconnected as his dispatcher stuck her head in his office. "What is it, Maggie?"

"Ruby Gresham is at the front desk, asking to see you."

"Did she say what she wanted?"

"No. Do you want to see her?"

Not really. Every time he saw the poor woman, he thought of the boy who drowned. "Yes."

A minute later Tommy Ray's mother stood in front of his desk. Today she was dressed in what he thought was probably her Sunday best. White shirt and black pants. She wasted no time in getting to the point of her visit.

"I've been hearing how my boy shot that Jackson fellow." She pressed her lips in a thin line and leveled her gaze at Ben, steel glinting in her blue eyes.

Ben put down his pen and closed the report. "Won't you sit down, Mrs. Gresham?"

"Ain't staying that long. Everybody says Jackson got kilt around eight o'clock." She pulled an envelope from her purse and threw it on Ben's desk. "Iffen he was in Memphis killing that man, then how did he get a ticket here in Logan Point at the same time?"

Ben leaned forward and picked up the envelope. Inside was an Automated Red Light Enforcement ticket, complete with a photo of a motorcyclist running the red light at the intersection of Highway 72 and Reynolds Road. The time stamped on the ticket was 20:10:05. Ten after eight. The same night and about the same time Ben had entered the Peabody and ridden the elevator to the fifth floor. It was a forty-minute drive from the hotel to that intersection, ruling out any possibility that Billy Wayne could have been Tony's shooter . . . if he was the cyclist.

The ticket indicated the green Kawasaki belonged to Billy Wayne, and it certainly looked like the same one that he'd wrapped around a tree on Highway 310, but the tinted shield on the silver and black helmet made it impossible to identify the rider. "How can you be sure this is Billy Wayne? The racing suit, the helmet, it's hard to tell who's on the bike."

"That there ticket says it was his. And I know my boy. I would recognize him anywhere. 'Sides, that bike was new, and nobody rode it but him. He didn't shoot that Jackson man, but somebody wants you to think he did." Her eyes narrowed. "I want you to find out who's trying to make my boy out to be worse than he was, Sheriff. You owe me that."

Her words stung. He squared his shoulders. "I will, Mrs. Gresham. I will."

■ ■ ■

Two hours later, Ben leaned back in his chair. Wade sat across from him. Ben ran his thumb back and forth along his jaw as Taylor Martin turned from the whiteboard where she'd been writing. This afternoon, the willowy brunette had opted again for casual with blue jean capris and her hair in a ponytail. On the board, she'd listed the crimes—Tony's murder, the ransacking of his house, and the shooting the next morning, the torching of the house, the snakes on the ball field, and finally, the criminal justice center fire.

"Six crimes, one of them solved, possibly more, when Billy Wayne overshot the curve on Highway 310." Taylor drew a bracket around the first three crimes. "Before you called this morning with the information about the traffic ticket, I already had problems with these three being committed by the same person. Let's start with Tony's murder. How did the shooter know where Tony would be the night he was killed?"

She nodded at Ben. "According to your notes, Tony thought someone might be after him, and he was paranoid about calling you on a phone that could be bugged, so it stands to reason, he'd make sure no one followed him to the Peabody. In all likelihood, whoever shot him arrived at the hotel before Tony did. Did he call you and give you the room number?"

Ben nodded. "I was tied up in a traffic jam when he called with the room number."

Wade leaned forward. "I bet whoever killed him downloaded the same kind of spyware on his phone that's on mine."

Taylor nodded. "Which means the person knew Tony was meeting with Ben that night at the Peabody."

"And even the room number," Ben said. "Who could get access to his phone?"

Wade said, "From what I know of Tony, he didn't trust anyone, and I sure don't see him leaving his cell lying around."

A strand of hair had worked its way out of Taylor's ponytail, and she hooked it behind her ear. "For someone who knows what they're doing, spyware only takes a couple of minutes to install. All Tony would have to do is leave his phone on his desk or a table while he went to the men's room or to get a cup of coffee. If a spy program was used, the program will be on the host phone as well. Did you recover a cell phone on Gresham?"

"Not in one piece."

"Too bad."

"Can the program be erased from the host phone?"

Taylor shrugged. "Forensics could probably find it, but I feel certain if someone downloaded the spyware on Tony's phone, they would have gotten rid of their phone. I only asked about Gresham because he might not have had time to get rid of his. Did Tony have a girlfriend?"

Wade chuckled. "According to gossip, more than I can count until about a month or so ago when he started attending church with his nephew." He looked at Ben. "I think you talked with one of them—Tiffany, the receptionist at Maxwell Industries."

Taylor picked up a folder and glanced through it. "I don't see a mention of a cell phone in his personal effects."

"He didn't have one on him, just like he didn't have the flash drive he talked about when he called." Ben massaged the knotted muscles in his neck. "I think I need to take another drive out to Maxwell Industries. Do you think Billy Wayne was capable of putting spyware on Tony's phone? They'd spent time together, and Billy had lost a couple of grand to Tony in poker."

"Judging from his computer skills, yes." She pointed to the ticket on Ben's desk. "But he couldn't be in Memphis and Logan Point at the same time."

"If that's Billy Wayne. There's no way to prove this is or isn't him, other than his mother's assertion. Could it be his brother?"

"Junior?" Wade asked. "He's much bigger."

"I think I'll go talk to him anyway. See if his brother had any friends who might have been on the cycle. If he did, then Billy Wayne could've been at the hotel."

"I'll be surprised if it's Billy Wayne," said Taylor.

Ben looked at her. "Why?"

She picked up the file she'd brought in with her. "I studied his websites and Facebook page. If he had assumed the persona of the assassins he created, why didn't he kill either you or Leigh that morning? I took the crime scene photos and drove by Leigh's house. He had a clear shot. There was no reason for him to miss unless he only intended to scare or threaten you or he was a bad shot."

"He's a Gresham," Wade said. "He grew up with a rifle in his hands."

"Maybe a human target made a difference," Ben said.

Taylor shook her head. "Then he probably didn't kill Tony, because if he had, another murder wouldn't have bothered him."

"So you don't think Tony's death is related to the other things on the board up there?"

"Only the ransacking of the house. I believe his killer was looking for something he expected Tony to have on him at the hotel. When it wasn't, he searched the house."

"Do you have a profile of what type person I should be looking for?"

"Someone educated and a professional, well-respected in the community, likable, social even, midthirties to late forties, and a male, of course."

"About 10 percent of Bradford County's male population." Ben scratched his jaw. "Could it be someone he gambled with?"

"Perhaps."

"No possibility of it being a redneck ne'er-do-well?" he asked, thinking of some of the men he'd seen Thursday night at the dog-fight.

"If they have highly developed reasoning skills, it'd be possible, but I'd be looking elsewhere."

"How about the other crimes? Same person?"

"It's my opinion you are looking at two different perpetrators. I think you're right that someone is trying to make you look incompetent."

If Ben were a betting man, he'd put his money on Jonas Gresham. But he didn't have a single piece of evidence against him.

Wade's cell phone vibrated, and he picked it up. "It's Cummings." The deputy leaned back in his chair as he answered. "How's it going, Lester, my man?"

Silence followed for less than ten seconds. "Today? I thought we'd agreed on tomorrow. Oh, I see. Well, sure, I'll just tell Ben I'm going on patrol. See you in an hour." Wade hung up and grinned. "Looks like I'm going to see a man about a dog."

"Then let's check to make sure I can connect to your phone." Ben took out his cell phone and dialed the number to activate the listening device on Wade's phone. Then he turned on the speaker on his phone.

Wade stared at his phone. "It's not doing anything."

The words echoed in the room.

"Well, I'll be," his chief deputy said. "You better never activate that when I'm with Ruth."

Ben disconnected. "How do you know I haven't already?"

Wade glared at him.

"Now turn on the pen."

Wade clicked it on.

"Testing, one, two, three." Ben's cell phone rang. "Okay, it seems to be working. Don't turn it off."

"I'm private, not stupid," Wade retorted. "Everything will be fine. Stop being such a worrywart."

Even with the surveillance tools, Ben didn't like this. He didn't like it at all.

■ ■ ■

Wednesday was only a half day at the Helping Hands clinic, and Leigh wasn't altogether sorry. Monday and Tuesday had been a whirlwind of activity, and she could use a breather. She turned as Emily called her name.

"Is that your last patient?" her boss asked.

"Yes. Strep throat. Probably see the rest of the family by Friday," she replied with a grimace.

Emily tilted her head. "So, how do you like working here so far?"

"I love it. I'm looking forward to getting to know my patients and treating the whole family. You really don't want that to happen in the ER."

Emily laughed. "You're doing great. Everyone who's been in here has commented when they checked out that they hoped you stayed on."

Guilt pinged her conscience. She hadn't mentioned Johns Hopkins to her boss, and evidently neither had Ben. "I, ah, we might need to talk. Last week I received an offer to work at one of Johns Hopkins's free clinics, and I accepted. I wanted you to know up front."

"Johns Hopkins? I can understand. We—"

Leigh's cell phone rang.

"Go ahead and take that," Emily said. "We can finish talking later."

Leigh glanced at the caller ID. Ian. She hadn't seen him since Friday although he'd called almost every day, usually with a dinner offer. "Hello," she said.

"Dr. Somerall, I have this problem, and I really need to see a doctor." Ian's rich voice teased.

"And what seems to be your ailment?" she asked.

He sighed. "I have pains around my heart from lack of seeing a certain doctor. Do you think you can help me? I know the clinic isn't open on Wednesday afternoon, but I thought perhaps you could prescribe a luncheon date to cure me?"

She stared down the hallway. He never gave up. And it wasn't like her dance card was filled with admiring beaus. She hadn't even heard from a certain sheriff, not even to escort her to and from the clinic. He'd sent Andre or Wade. She looked out the front window. Andre's cruiser waited in the parking lot.

But why this campaign of Ian's to court her? Did he view her as another notch on his belt? Was that his motivation for letting her have the house?

"Are you still there?"

"I'm here, and I'll go on one condition."

"And that is?"

"That you won't try to push our relationship beyond that of friendship."

"Friendship is a good beginning."

"Ian." She drew his name out.

"Okay," he grumbled. "Strictly friendship, nothing more."

"Then, yes, I'll go with you, but let me go home and change and check on TJ."

"Wear something casual." He sounded mysterious.

At home, Leigh found a note from Sarah saying she had taken TJ to the pool. Her stomach twisted. She needed to spend more time with her son. Quickly she scribbled a note telling TJ they would watch a movie later, then she hurried upstairs to change.

The front doorbell rang just as she pulled a white V-neck T-shirt over her head, and she quickly pulled on a pair of blue jean capris. When she opened the door, she gaped at Ian. "I don't believe I've ever seen you in shorts."

"First jeans, now shorts." He grinned at her. "You must be a good influence on me."

He escorted her to his black Escalade and opened the passenger door. Ian Maxwell knew how to make a girl feel special. As she slid into the seat, she noticed a picnic basket in the backseat. "We're going on a picnic?"

"You've never seen my cabin at the lake. I thought I'd give you the grand tour. Of course, if I'd planned ahead, we could have boated across the lake instead of driving the long way around."

Ninety minutes later, Leigh felt like Cinderella when she stepped into the ballroom. Her grandmother's house that had burned would have taken up no more space than the living room of Ian's cabin. She'd only ever read about spreads like this. Rooms that could be in *House & Garden*. Or *Architectural Digest*. So this was how 10 percent of the world lived. She moistened her lips. "Did you do the decorating?"

He laughed. "Hardly. No, a decorator out of Memphis pulled all of this together."

She'd hate to even try to put a figure on how much he'd spent.

"Could you imagine yourself here? In this house?"

She laughed. "You're joking, right?"

"Depends on what your answer is."

"Have you already forgotten the condition of this lunch?"

"Well, you can't fault me for trying. Just remember, more than one couple started out as friends."

She'd have to give him credit for not giving up, and in spite of her resolve, the question of what life would be like with Ian Maxwell darted through her mind. Never worry about money. Jetting to Paris . . .

Reality cooled her face. She didn't love Ian, not the way a wife should love a husband, and she'd been there, done that before with the man everyone thought was TJ's father. Not that she hadn't been grateful to Matthew or that she hadn't loved him in her own way. She shook off the dark thoughts. "I thought you brought me here for a picnic."

He tilted his head and said nothing, his blue eyes holding hers. Finally he sighed. "So I did. Follow me."

Ian led her out of the house to a stone walkway that wound around the grounds to a gazebo that overlooked Logan Lake. He flipped a switch, and a bamboo fan whirred softly, sending a soft breeze against her cheek. She took the rattan chair Ian offered and sat back as he spread an enormous amount of food on the table.

The throbbing hum of cicadas competed with the fan. Cicadas always made her think of hot summer days. To her left was the lake, and she knew there had to be several other cabins around, but she didn't see a one. "What's that?" she asked, pointing to a granite building that matched the house. It was too large to be a garage.

"It's where I keep my Beechcraft. There's a grass runway on the other side of the trees." He used a pair of silver tongs to transfer ice from a bucket to their goblets, and then he filled their glasses with tea.

"You have an airplane here?"

He nodded. "See what you're giving up," he said, his lips curving into a teasing smile. "I'm not quitting, you know. In fact, I'd like to do something special for you. Like fly you to Baltimore for a weekend. Doesn't your son like baseball? We'll stay at the Hilton and watch an Orioles game from your balcony."

Just when she didn't think Ian could surprise her again, he did. A trip to Baltimore . . . an opportunity to talk face-to-face with Dr. Meriwether and see where she'd be working. And if TJ could see a professional baseball game, it might change his mind about moving. It was an opportunity too good to pass up. "I . . . I don't know what to say."

"Yes will do. How about this weekend?"

Ian was moving too fast for her. "Are you a pilot?"

He bowed slightly. "Yes, ma'am, as is Danny and our new chief accountant, Geoffrey Franks."

Tony's replacement. For a second she faltered then caught herself. A company like Maxwell Industries couldn't leave the job hanging.

"He will never take Tony's place," Ian said softly.

"I know." His tenderness touched her heart.

"So, can we fly to Baltimore this weekend?" he asked.

"Not this one. TJ reminds me every day at least ten times that he has a play-off game with his team. If they win, they'll go to State. Maybe the next weekend?"

"It's a date. I'll make all the arrangements." He offered her a white-chocolate-chip cookie.

Leigh took the cookie and nibbled around the edges. She was too excited to eat. Baltimore.

He refilled her goblet with tea. "I didn't see your bodyguard when I picked you up."

She frowned. "Oh, you mean Ben? He's too busy . . . he just sends one of his deputies to escort me back and forth to the clinic."

"How's that going?"

"Busy. Wonderful. I love engaging in an actual relationship with my patients."

"Imagine how much better it'll be at Johns Hopkins."

Maybe so. She thought about the twenty-year-old college student who came in earlier in the day to get information on abortion but who left with a changed mind and a follow-up prenatal appointment. That was one case she'd like to be around for at delivery time. She'd miss some things about Logan Point. The thought startled her.

"Oh, by the way, what was the fire marshal's conclusion on the fire at Tony's house?"

Tony again. And the question reminded her of one of the reasons she wanted to leave Logan Point behind. "Arson."

"You're kidding. What led to this conclusion?"

"A steel-tipped arrowhead similar to the one found in the jail fire. And traces of kerosene."

"Does Ben have any leads?"

She shrugged. "If he does, he hasn't told me."

Ian offered her another cookie. "Did he ever discover who ransacked your house? Or found the missing flash drive?"

She stared out at the lake. A sailboat tacked into the wind, its white sails fluttering. "I'm not sure the drive ever existed. And I have yet to figure out why Tony was meeting with Ben. Why didn't my brother tell me what it was about?" She turned her gaze to Ian. "Do you have any idea why Tony wanted to talk to Ben?"

"No, although it did seem that he was bothered by something lately."

"I know. He wouldn't talk about it, but one night he had a nightmare. Woke me up yelling something about a dog."

Ian's pupils widened slightly. "A dog? Did he explain?"

"No. And a week later, he was dead."

Ian's expression softened. "This has been a sad chapter in your life."

Leigh's breath stilled, and she closed her eyes against the pain. Ian leaned forward and squeezed her hand. His kindness unleashed the tears she held back.

"I'm sorry. I didn't mean to make you cry."

"I rarely get to choose the time or place." She blinked back more tears that threatened.

"I know this isn't the time, but . . ." Ian sighed. "Leigh, I care very much for you."

She pulled back. "I . . . I—"

"I'm not asking for a declaration of love from you."

She pressed her fingertips to her lips."Oh, Ian. I don't know what to say. I enjoy being with you, but I'm not in love with you."

"That could change."

"I don't see how. I'm leaving soon. Can't we just be friends?"

He lifted his eyebrows. "I can settle for friendship right now, but be warned. I will wear you down."

"You're not used to hearing no, are you?" She was beginning to understand that was part of his attraction to her.

"My experience with no is that it usually ends up meaning not yet."

■ ■ ■

According to his phone and the GPS chip on Wade's key ring, Lester Cummings's old rattletrap was a good mile ahead of Ben. He'd put his cell phone on speaker so he could listen to the conversation between Wade and Lester, and so far, the old farmer didn't seem suspicious. But then, Wade had only been making small talk. It would've been much easier if Ben were the one riding with Lester instead of his chief deputy.

"Where is this dog?" Wade asked.

That's what Ben would like to know. According to the GPS, they were on Sloan Road, a narrow, twisting, and sometimes one-lane sand road at the edge of Bradford County. Much farther and they'd be in Tennessee.

"Almost there," said Cummings, his two-pack-a-day voice low.

"Why don't you just sell me one of your dogs?"

"Don't fight my dogs."

"Who said I wanted to fight this dog we're going to look at?"

A long silence followed, and Ben wished for the hundredth time he'd vetoed this idea.

"You telling me you don't?" When Wade didn't answer, the older man chuckled. "That's what I thought. We're almost there. The road's gonna be a little rough from here on out. And when we get there, leave that Glock in the truck unless you want your head blown off. This fellow tends to shoot first and ask questions later.

And he don't know who you are, just that you're a friend of mine, so don't make me regret bringing you out here."

"Don't worry, I won't, but I don't like leaving my gun behind."

"You're with me—he won't shoot you."

At least Wade still had his ankle gun. Ben backed into an old logging road. There was just no way to get any closer without being seen.

"This it?" Wade asked.

"Yep. Get out real slow and follow my lead."

Truck doors slammed, and the sound of walking rustled over the phone. Then dead silence. Had he lost contact? What if someone had been behind Ben's truck and made them?

"Where is he?"

Ben relaxed at Wade's question.

"Yonder."

Where was yonder? Sweat popped out on Ben's face. He uncapped a bottle of water and took a long draw.

"Smokey, this here is that friend I was telling you about. That the dog you got to sell?"

Ben could imagine Smokey sizing Wade up.

"If Lester says you're okay . . ." Ben's phone crackled, and his heart nearly jumped out of his chest as he lost contact again. He'd give it one minute, and then he was on his way in.

A minute passed, and he licked his dry lips and put his truck in gear.

"You got a handsome dog there, Smokey. You say his name is Bo?"

Wade's voice came across the airwaves, and Ben almost fell back against the seat. *Don't scare me like that, Wade.* He must've bent over to pet the dog and lost reception.

"What's your asking price?"

"Ain't got but one price." Smokey's voice was soft with a steel undercurrent. "Four."

Four thousand dollars. Wade didn't have that kind of money on him. The sheriff's office didn't have that kind of money. Period.

"Before I spend that much money, I want to see what he can do."

Now Wade was pushing it. Why didn't Smokey or Lester respond? There had to be a way to get a camera on Wade before the next meeting. He had to see what was going on. If there was another meeting.

"What do you think, Smokey?" Lester's gravelly voice asked the question.

Smokey didn't answer. *Don't push it, Wade.*

Lester spoke up again. "We got that big fight next week."

"I'll think on it. Let you know."

"I have the money," Wade said.

"Like I said, I'll think on it."

The sound of walking again. They must be leaving. Lester's old rattletrap fired up, confirming his hunch. A few minutes later, he heard Lester's voice.

"Too rich for your blood, Dep-u-ty?"

"I got the money. You didn't expect me to pay that much for a dog and not see what it can do, did you?"

"Naw, guess not. Maybe you'll get an invite next week."

"Where's it going to be?"

"Who knows. You get the invite, I'll take you."

Ben glanced at the GPS. He had to move. He pulled his truck onto the highway and sped toward town. He had to hand it to Wade. He'd carried the meeting off, and he might even get an invitation to what sounded like the annual biggie. Time to call another meeting in Memphis.

16

B en hung up after talking with U.S. Marshal Luke Donovan and turned to Wade. "They want to meet at eight. We'll go in separate vehicles this time—you might be under surveillance, so watch your back."

Wade adjusted the ball cap on his head. "You don't have to worry about that. I've heard what they do to people they catch infiltrating their rings."

"Well, for the record, I still don't like what you're doing."

"I ain't too happy about it either, but somebody has to stop these pigs. You can't do it—you're too straight up to make it believable." He grinned. "That's where my good-ole-boy reputation comes in handy. Lester and Smokey didn't have any trouble taking the bait."

"Just be careful." Ben stood. "I'm going to Maxwell Industries to talk to Billy Wayne's brother. Want to tag along?"

"I think I'll run by and check on my mom." Wade stopped at the door. "Oh, and tell Marisa thanks for taking her those tea cakes. She enjoyed the visit."

Ben nodded. "Mom said she enjoyed it too."

Fifteen minutes later, Ben scanned the parking lot at Maxwell, not seeing Ian's black SUV. But he did see Danny's. The Maxwell boys had different tastes, but either vehicle would probably cost more than Ben's yearly salary. Tiffany Davis was on the telephone when he walked into the reception area. He flashed a quick smile when she held up her finger.

"Yes, Ian will be back around three, I believe he said. I'll give him your message." She hung the phone up. "Sheriff, what can I do for you today?"

"I wondered if I could speak with Junior Gresham for a few minutes."

She made a few clicks on her computer. "Is he in trouble?"

"No. Just a few questions."

"Well, you're in luck. He's working the loading dock today. Do you know how to get there?"

"I'll show him." Danny Maxwell's voice came from behind Ben.

He turned around. It'd been awhile since he'd talked one-on-one with Danny. They just didn't run in the same circles. And there'd been that high school athletic rivalry that ended simply because they'd taken different directions for college. The most he'd seen of Danny was a couple of years ago when he came to church with Livy's cousin. Then she'd left for the mission field in Mexico, and Danny sort of disappeared. Maybe it was time to put the past behind them. He held out his hand. "Good to see you, Danny."

"You too, Ben."

Danny's grip was firm, the calluses on his palms surprising Ben. But then, judging from the circumference of Danny's biceps, he probably acquired his rough hands from lifting weights.

"Follow me. The loading dock is this way." Danny walked past Ben toward the back of the plant.

"Have you heard from Bailey?" Ben asked when he caught up with him.

"A letter every now and then." Danny's clipped words warned Ben away from the subject. He pushed open the door that led outside to the loading dock and looked around. "Anybody seen Junior?"

One of the workers pointed toward another building. "He's in the receiver building."

They turned and headed toward a white metal building. "How well did you know Billy Wayne?" asked Ben.

"Well enough. He couldn't be beat when it came to computers." Danny unlocked the door.

Ben followed him inside the building, and it locked shut behind them. Several tables with the dark gray lower receivers awaited stamping with serial numbers. "Where do you add the trigger?"

"During assembly in another building. This is our most secure building—wouldn't do for one of these receivers to get in the wrong hands before they were stamped with a serial number."

"Yeah. My dad had an email a few months ago from a sheriff in Texas about an assault rifle without serial numbers. It was found after a shoot-out with drug dealers."

Danny shook his head. "No serial number, no paper trail to a manufacturer or distributor."

"I know." Ben took a copy of the ticket from his back pocket and handed it to Danny. "Do you know if this is Billy Wayne?"

Danny stopped and examined the photo. "Hard to tell, but Junior should be able to tell you."

He nodded toward a stocky man in his midtwenties loading the receivers into boxes. "Junior, take a break. Sheriff here wants to talk to you."

Junior Gresham took his time getting to them. He stopped three feet from Ben and planted his feet as he slowly removed his heavy work gloves. "I already told your deputy everything I know about Billy Wayne."

Ben handed him the photo. "Is this your brother?"

"Which one? I got three. Sorry, make that two now."

Heat flushed through Ben. "Billy Wayne." Junior glanced at the paper and handed it back to Ben. "Maybe. Looks like his cycle, and I've seen him in that Spiderman suit." He took a round tin from his back pocket and opened it, then tucked a pinch of tobacco into the right side of his bottom lip. "Yep. Pretty sure it's him—he wouldn't let nobody touch that new Kawasaki of his."

Ben masked his disappointment. If this was indeed Billy Wayne on the photo ticket, then he didn't kill Tony—he couldn't be two places at the same time. He could have been the one who ransacked Tony's house, though. But why? None of this made sense.

"Thanks," he said. He turned to Danny. "You too. I'll find my way out."

"No problem. I'll walk back with you."

Silence walked with them, hanging heavy, like the humid air as they made their way back to the main plant. "Uh, do you ever hear from Bailey?" Danny asked.

"Through my sister. They're tight. I think she received a letter last week."

Danny nodded, his lips pressed in a thin line. "Did she say anything about coming home?"

Ben shrugged. "I don't know. I can ask."

"No, don't do that. I'm thinking about making a trip down to Mexico soon. I'll check on her then."

"I don't mind asking, just let me know." When they reached the parking lot, Ben glanced around for Ian's SUV, but it still hadn't returned. He wanted to ask him about Tony's replacement, Geoffrey Franks. "Do you know where I might find your cousin?"

Danny's mouth twitched. "I think I overheard him making arrangements with my father's cook for a picnic. Then he called Dr. Somerall."

Ian took Leigh on a picnic? "I thought Ian was engaged."

This time Danny laughed out loud. "Not as of a couple weeks ago, and I haven't seen the woman yet who will get him to the altar. Ian is all about the chase. And apparently he's after the doc now. That bother you?"

"No, why should it?" Danny still knew how to get under his skin.

"I don't know, maybe because you seem to have an interest in the doc as well? You probably don't have anything to worry about with Ian, though."

Ben snapped a curt nod. "Thanks for your help today."

"Anytime, Sheriff. And I'll let Ian know you were looking for him."

Halfway to his truck, Ben stopped and turned around. Danny hadn't moved. "You may be able to answer my question. This Geoffrey Franks that took Tony's place—what can you tell me about him?"

"Not much. He's worked here since he was seventeen. Ian can probably give you more information, since he deals with the employees. I do know he's Junior Gresham's first cousin—his mother is Jonas's sister. And he worked in the office with Tony ever since he got out of college, about four years ago. But if you're thinking he killed Tony, you're off base. Geoffrey would be too squeamish for that. He doesn't even hunt."

Ben nodded his thanks and walked to his truck. He needed a fresh brain to pick. Livy. Maybe they could get together tonight after the meeting with the FBI and U.S. Marshals. He sighed. He was pretty sure the gun they found at Gresham's would not match the bullet, and Detective Olivia Reynolds was not going to be happy about this latest development, either.

For that matter, neither was Ben.

17

Saturday morning Ben went through a mental list of deputies who could escort Leigh to TJ's late-afternoon ball game. Most were off duty and spending time with their families. Wade and Andre were coaching the team . . . maybe one of them. No. They both would be distracted. Maybe she didn't even need an escort. Nothing had happened in the past week. Maybe whoever was wreaking havoc on Logan Point had lost interest. Yeah, and maybe it would snow in August.

Face it. It was his responsibility. He didn't need to add additional work on his deputies. He dialed her number, his heart quickening when she answered.

"Thought I'd let you know what time I'd be there to escort you to the game."

"That's not necessary. Ian is taking me." Her cool, professional tone raked his nerves like squeaky chalk. First a picnic, now he was taking Leigh and TJ to the ball game? The muscle in his jaw twitched, and he eased the pressure on his molars. "He doesn't have the train—"

"He has plenty of training—I've seen his self-defense certificates, and he has a permit to carry a gun. Not that I think he'll need it."

"Well, I'll be around anyway."

"Ben, don't bother."

"I'll see you there."

■ ■ ■

The sun dipped below the horizon as Ben leaned against the bed of his truck. What little breeze there'd been died a long time ago, and sweat dripped down his face. From his position behind the center field fence, he could keep an eye on traffic in and out of the park as well as on Leigh.

He directed his gaze away from Ian and Leigh on the front row of the bleachers, past Sarah, who sat apart from them, to the mound as TJ shook his head at the catcher's signal. The home team trailed by one run. Only two more outs and Andre's team would take their last bat and try to score. He glanced toward the dugout where Martin cheered on his team. He'd recovered sufficiently from the snakebite to suit up, but not to play. Wade paced the sidelines, yelling encouragement while Andre motioned for one of the other boys to take a few warm-up pitches.

"Stee-rike!" The umpire clenched his right fist.

TJ had a good arm. Ben needed to caution Andre about letting him overuse it. TJ threw a change of pace, and the hitter popped the ball up. The runner on first stayed put as one of the twins got under the ball and caught it. Two outs, one to go. TJ wound up once more and let the ball fly again. *Crack.* Uh-oh. Ben recognized that sound. He held his breath as the ball sailed to the center field fence. Home run. His heart broke for TJ as Andre headed out to the mound.

They talked, and Ben knew TJ was asking his coach to leave him in the game. Finally Andre nodded and walked back to the dugout. TJ rolled his shoulders and kicked the mound, then turned to the next batter. Five pitches later, he struck him out, and the home team came up to bat three runs behind just as the night-lights flooded the field.

If he were coaching . . . Ben caught himself. He wasn't coaching. But maybe he could. How hard would it be? If they won this game, he could give them a few pointers, show the boys how to tighten up their double play . . . teach TJ how to throw a slider or how to tell if a runner was going—

No.

What if he had a panic attack in the middle of a practice? His mouth went dry just thinking about it, and he stepped toward the cab of the truck, half tempted to leave. But he couldn't as long as Leigh was here. Maybe he'd patrol the area. Check on the carnival that had set up at the edge of the park. Be useful.

With one last look at the ball field and a check to see if Leigh was okay, Ben strode toward the walking trail and picnic area. It gratified him to see families picnicking, enjoying time together. He trekked on to the carnival, just to let his presence be known, nodding at one or two of the carnies.

One of them threw up a hand. "Howdy, Sheriff. Reckon how much longer before the ball games end?"

A tattooed snake started at the man's wrist and wrapped around his arm, the tail ending at his shoulder. Ben could remember when the carnie would've been one of the sideshows.

"Probably in the next half hour," Ben said. Very few of the rides were engaged. "Then you ought to have plenty of customers."

Near the entrance, an ice cream truck pulled in and parked. Rich's Ice Cream. Rich had been in business when Ben was a kid. In fact, the van looked like the same one Rich drove all those years ago. A long-haired, pimply-face teenager stepped out of the side door. Rich was scraping the bottom of the barrel to hire this guy. As he raised the awning, Ben nodded to him. "Should be a big crowd in here soon."

The driver gave him a blank stare, and Ben noticed the ear buds. He waved and walked back toward the ball fields. The boys' game should be wrapping up soon. As he neared the field, yelling and cheers met him. Maybe the boys had scored, and he picked up his pace.

"Come on, TJ, you can do it!" Leigh's voice rose over the crowd.

Ben positioned himself where he could see. The bases were loaded, and TJ was up to bat. Ben glanced at the scoreboard. They were still three runs behind with two outs. The game rode on TJ's shoulders. Adrenaline surged through Ben's veins. He knew how the boy felt.

"Get the bat off your shoulder," he muttered.

Almost as if TJ heard him, he lifted the bat, waiting for the pitch.

"Stee-rike one!"

TJ stepped away from the batter's box and looked at his bat. Then he stepped back into the box and tapped the bat against home plate. Finally he lifted it and waited, poised to swing. The ball came in low and fast.

"Stee-rike two!"

Ben's heart faltered. *Come on, TJ. Keep your eye on the ball. Be ready for a change of pace.* Evidently TJ expected it as well, because he planted his feet wide. Sure enough, the ball sailed lazily toward the plate. At the right second, TJ swung, and the bat connected with the ball with a solid *thwack*.

Ben followed the arc of the ball over the fence. *Yes!* He pumped the air with his fist as pandemonium erupted on the field and in the stands. The boys whooped and pounded TJ. The team was going to the State playoffs in September. With a grin stretching his mouth, Ben turned to see Leigh's reaction, and his smile faded as she and Ian hugged each other.

This thing with Ian was starting to look serious, and regret tugged at his heart. But what had he expected? Well, he hadn't expected her to fall into Ian's arms so soon. *God, just one more chance with her . . .* He shook the thought off and trotted over to congratulate Andre and the team. Then he could leave Leigh in Andre's or Wade's care.

He grabbed his deputy's hand. "Great game, Andre."

His deputy's smile stretched almost from ear to ear. "They did good."

Behind Ben, a cell phone rang, and he turned around just as Ian answered it. Leigh had left his side and was talking to TJ at the dugout.

"I'll be right there," Ian said and slid the phone in his pocket then looked around for Leigh.

"She's probably not ready to leave," Ben said, pointing toward the dugout. When Ian frowned, Ben said, "I couldn't help but overhear. Feel free to go and take care of whatever the problem is. I'll make sure Leigh gets home all right."

A slow flush crept up Ian's neck. "You may be right, but I think I'll check and see."

Ben followed as Ian walked toward Leigh. After Ian spoke to her, her brows creased in a frown. He moved closer. "I can take you home, if you want to stay."

The frown deepened.

"Or one of my deputies, if you'd rather."

"I'm truly sorry, Leigh," Ian said. "But Uncle Phillip wants to see me *now*."

She patted his arm. "I understand. I think I will stay a little longer, celebrate with the boys. I can always ride home with Sarah," she said with a pointed glance at Ben.

"I'll check with you as soon as the meeting with my uncle is over. If you're still here, I'll swing by and pick you up."

Leigh nodded her agreement, and for a second, Ben thought that Ian was going to kiss her, but Leigh forestalled the action by stepping back. Maybe she wasn't as interested as Ian was. Hope beat in his heart.

"Mom!" TJ pulled at Leigh's hand. "Everybody is going to the carnival. Can I go? *Please?*"

Leigh looked from TJ to Josh and Jacob at his side, their eyes pleading with her to say yes. "Oh, okay. But don't get too far ahead of me."

Her words were lost as they took off running. Waving to Ian, she hurried to catch them, and Ben fell into step beside her.

"You don't have to stay," she said. "Andre's here, Wade too."

"I know. But Andre and Wade have their hands full with the rest of the team."

Leigh looked around. "No, they don't. Most of the boys' parents are here. Look, there's Emily." She waved, and his sister waved back.

"Well, I'll feel better if I stay."

She shot him an odd look and shrugged. "Suit yourself."

TJ returned, asking for money to buy tickets for the rides just as Sarah joined them.

"Twenty dollars," Leigh said. "Choose wisely because that's all you get."

"Here's ten more." Sarah pulled a bill from her purse.

Leigh shook her head. "You're spoiling him."

"I know." Sarah looked pleased with herself.

Ben laughed as TJ ran off again to find the twins. "How about you two? Care to ride something?"

Leigh looked at him as though he'd lost his mind. "Hardly."

"What? Are you scared?"

"No. I just don't want to ride anything."

"Oh, go ahead," Sarah said. "Ride the Ferris wheel."

Leigh glanced toward the towering wheel, and for a second her eyes lit up before a mask slid in place. "No."

"Chicken." He took her hand. "Come on. You too," he said to Sarah.

Sarah waved him off. "No, sir. I'll leave that to you young people. I'll watch TJ."

Leigh held back as he pulled her toward the Ferris wheel.

TJ appeared beside them. "Are you going to ride, Mom?"

"Yeah, Doc! Are you?" One of the twins echoed TJ's question.

"No!"

"Yes," Ben said, overriding her. He tamped down the whisper in his heart that this wasn't a good idea.

"Come on, Mom, you can do it!" TJ grabbed her other hand and helped Ben pull her toward the line.

With a red face, Leigh gave up. "Okay. Okay."

■ ■ ■

As the attendant snapped the bar in place, Leigh decided she'd lost her mind, agreeing to go on this ride. Next to her Ben sat entirely too close. The seat jerked as the wheel moved, and they were lifted a few feet off the ground. It stopped for more riders, moving them higher, until finally all the seats were full. Her stomach tickled as they made the rise to the top. One of her favorite memories was rocking at the top of the world with her father beside her. At least it seemed like the top of the world in her six-year-old mind. At the bottom, she waved to Sarah, who was talking to the attendant.

"Now aren't you glad you agreed?" Ben said.

She gave him a smile for an answer. The wheel made several revolutions then stopped at the top, rocking them back and forth in the seat. They were above the lights, and stars twinkled in the black sky. She could ride this contraption all night.

"My daddy used to take me to the fairgrounds in Memphis, and we'd ride that big old Ferris wheel as long as I wanted to."

"I don't remember your dad."

"You never met him. When he died, we moved to Logan Point to live with my grandparents." His death was her fault, at least according to her mother.

"Did he have a heart attack?"

"Car accident coming to pick me up at school. He'd forgotten me and was in a hurry." Forgotten. The story of her life. She picked out a star and focused on it. "The janitor found me outside, waiting in

248

the dark. He called the principal, the principal called my dad, and in his haste, my dad ran a stop sign, and someone T-boned him." The star seemed to dim. "My mom never forgave me."

"Surely you're mistaken. It wasn't your fault."

"You didn't know my mom. She never wanted me, anyway."

"Leigh, every kid thinks that at one time or another. I'm sure your parents loved you very much."

"You don't understand. I heard my mom tell my dad that having me was a mistake. She only wanted one child. Actually, as far as I could see, she never had but one child, and even Tony couldn't keep her from committing suicide."

A breeze chilled her skin, and she shivered. Why wasn't the wheel moving? They'd been stuck at the top for what seemed like forever. Ben put his arm around her, and his touch sent shivers through her heart.

"I'm so sorry. I didn't know."

"You couldn't have." Other than Sarah, she'd never shared this part of her life with anyone. "I don't want TJ to ever think he's a mistake."

"Leigh, you are not a mistake. You are an incredible, beautiful, caring woman. A woman that I . . ." Ben groaned. "God help me, Leigh, but I love you."

When she realized what he'd said, she waited a second for him to take it back. Instead he lifted her face until she stared into his warm brown eyes.

He loved her.

"Are you sure?" she whispered.

For an answer, he lowered his head and pressed his lips to hers, gently at first, then as she closed her eyes and leaned into the kiss, he groaned and pulled her close. He kissed her again.

The seat lurched as the Ferris wheel moved. She blinked her eyes open, and Ben laughed. "I wonder who paid the attendant to keep us at the top."

She quirked a corner of her mouth. "Sarah, I'm sure."

When the attendant unhooked their bar, he winked at Leigh. "Enjoy your ride?"

She felt heat rising in her face. "Did someone pay you to stop us at the top?"

He held his hands up. "I know *nothing*."

Ben took her hand as they walked in search of Sarah and the boys. "I'd like to do that again sometime soon."

She glanced up at him. "What? Kiss me?"

Now it was his turn to blush. "That too."

"Leigh!"

The panic in Sarah's voice turned Leigh around. She searched the crowd for her friend and spied her hurrying toward them as fast as her seventy-three-year-old legs would go. Leigh met her halfway. "What's wrong? Where's TJ?"

"I can't find him . . . or the twins." Sarah wrung her hands.

Leigh jerked her head around, searching for the boys in the crowd that filled the park. What if someone had kidnapped him? She never should have left him.

"Where did you see them last?" Ben stilled Sarah's hands.

"They were right here." Tears rimmed the older woman's eyes. "They asked if they could get some of those frozen beads from the ice cream truck. I told them to come right back. When they didn't, I went looking, but I couldn't find any ice cream truck."

"It was near the entrance earlier. Maybe they're with Emily." Ben took out his cell phone and dialed his sister. Leigh held her breath as Ben spoke to her. "TJ and the twins are missing. Are they with you?" His face lost some of its color. "Maybe they're with Wade. I'll let you know."

Leigh tensed as Ben called his deputy and repeated the same question. Her throat tightened when he turned even paler.

Ben spoke into his phone again. "Meet me at the entrance to the park. Sarah said they went to get ice cream, and that's where

I last saw Rich's truck." He turned to Leigh. "Stay here in case they come back."

"No. I want to go with you."

"They've only wandered away, that's all," Ben said. "You need to be here in case they return to the Ferris wheel."

"What if someone has them?"

"Don't borrow trouble. I'll call you as soon as I find them."

Leigh nodded, swallowing her fear. "Hurry."

Two minutes after Ben left, her cell phone rang, and she yanked it out of her pocket. Maybe it was TJ.

"If you don't want your son hurt, cooperate with me." Slow and deep, the warbly voice screeched from her phone.

Leigh's breath left her. No, not again. "Where's my son!"

"I want Tony's flash drive."

"You're crazy. I don't have it, and I don't know where it is."

"Find it. Until then, your son isn't safe. I can find him, no matter where he is."

"What did you do with him? With the twins?" She gripped the phone when he didn't answer right away. "Don't hang up. Tell me where they are."

"Do what I say." The words stretched out and ended in strangled laughter.

Sarah grabbed her. "Who is it? What are they saying?"

Leigh pressed her hand across her mouth. Where could the flash drive be? She didn't know, but she had to find it. And when she did, they could have it. Anything to keep TJ safe.

18

Ben jogged toward the entrance. He should've expected something. This week had been too quiet. When he reached the place he'd seen the ice cream truck, the spot was empty. The pimply-faced teenager hardly seemed the type to kidnap three boys. He scrubbed his jaw. He had to call Emily.

His stomach roiled as he made the call. "Keep looking and call if you find them."

He disconnected and called dispatch for backup and issued a Be On the Lookout for the ice cream truck.

"Ben, what's going on?" Wade yelled, jogging toward him.

"I don't know. Josh, Jacob, and TJ are missing. Sarah said they came after ice cream, but the truck is gone. I've issued a BOLO for it." He raked his hand across the top of his head. How had he lost three boys? "Fan out. Wade, you take the left, and Andre, you take the right. As soon as more deputies arrive to secure the entrances, I'll comb the center." Sirens sounded as he spoke.

"Ben, have you found TJ and the twins?" Leigh's ashen face sent his heart spiraling.

"Not yet. We're spreading out, checking all the vendors. I told you to stay—"

"I received another call. Just like the one before, but this time the caller mentioned the flash drive, said if I didn't hand it over,

TJ would die. Ben, I don't have it." She gripped his arm. "What if he doesn't believe me?"

Ben would've liked to tell her not to worry, but he couldn't. "We'll find them, Leigh. I promise. Could the voice have been that of a teenager?"

"I don't know." She paused. "No, too old sounding even through the synthesizer. Why?"

"The ice cream truck is missing. It'd be a good way to get three boys out of the park."

"No. You're looking in the wrong place. TJ would never get in some ice cream truck willingly. He knows better."

Leigh was right. Josh and Jacob would never go anywhere with someone they didn't know either—he'd told them enough horror stories to ensure that. "I still want to know where that truck is," he said as police cars converged onto the park and deputies spilled out of their cruisers.

"Can I stay with you until you find them?" Desperation cracked her voice.

"As long as you stay out of the way." He turned away from her as a deputy slapped a radio and microphone in his hand. "Get a set of these to Wade and Andre," he said.

Half an hour later, there was still no sign of the boys or the ice cream truck. Ben spoke into his mic. "Anyone check the restrooms?"

Andre responded. "I'm near them now. I'll check." A minute later, he was back on the radio. "I've found the driver, and he doesn't look good. Is Dr. Somerall with you?"

Ben called for an ambulance even as Leigh took off running toward the restrooms. Andre met them outside the men's facility. "He's in here."

"You stay here," Ben said to Leigh, then entered the men's room. The driver he'd seen earlier lay unconscious on the concrete floor with his hands bound in front and duct tape around his mouth. Overhead, the fluorescent light flickered, casting the room in an eerie light.

He knelt and removed the gray tape then took his pulse. Steady. Just like his breathing. He started to untie his hands and noticed a wire from the plastic zip tie around the boy's hands to a lump under his uniform shirt. Slowly, he unbuttoned the shirt, his fingers freezing at the second button. The wire led to two sticks of dynamite strapped to his chest.

Sweat popped out on Ben's face. Bradford County's bomb squad was nonexistent. As it was, Ben was the only one in the department who'd even had any training in defusing a bomb. He spoke into his mic. "Evacuate the park. We have a bomb."

He took out his cell phone and speed-dialed his dispatcher. "Call MPD in Memphis. Get their bomb squad here. *Now.*"

Leigh tried to push past Andre, and Ben held up his hand. "Don't come in here. The guy has explosives strapped to his chest."

"I need to check him out."

"No, you don't. What you need to do is get out of here so I can assess this situation." One wrong move, and they all could die. She glanced at him, uncertainty in her eyes. "Please, Leigh. You can't help him. His pulse seems fine, breathing too. He's probably been drugged. So please leave."

A no formed in her face. "Think of TJ," he said. "When we find him, he'll need you."

She nodded slowly and backed out of the men's room. Ben turned back to the driver. A patchy beard barely covered the acne scars on his face. The kid couldn't be over twenty. Skinny too. Probably wasn't much of a match for his attacker.

His dispatcher's voice sounded in his ear. "The MPD bomb squad is mobilizing. ETA is thirty minutes. I'm patching them through to your radio signal."

Immediately another voice sounded in his ear. "What do you have there, Logan?"

Sweat stung Ben's eyes. "Unconscious victim, his hands bound with a plastic zip tie that connects to two sticks of dynamite."

"Do you see a timer?"

"Not yet. I'll have to unbutton his shirt to expose the complete bomb." Ben examined the shirt and saw no evidence of wires attached to the front of it. He took a deep breath and unbuttoned the shirt halfway, fully exposing the dynamite. "No timer. And no detonator that I can see."

"Where do the wires lead?"

Ben chewed the inside of his lip as he followed the wires that were attached to the blasting cap in the sticks. He pinched his brow together as the wires disappeared under the shirt where it was still buttoned. The boy groaned as Ben gently tugged the buttons loose. "Don't move," he said as the teen's eyes fluttered open. "You have a bomb on your chest."

The teenager's eyes widened.

"It's going to be okay. Just be still," Ben said. He unfastened the last button, exposing the end of the wire where it was taped to a card on the kid's stomach.

BOOM!

His muscles slackened even as the boldly written letters taunted him. He sucked in a shaky breath. "I think it's a hoax," Ben muttered into the mic and relayed what was on the card. At least he hoped the bomb wasn't real.

"Ben!" Andre's voice overrode Ben's. "They've found the ice cream truck. It's parked outside the jail."

"Are the boys in it?"

"Randy is checking now. And I'm on my way. Leigh is going with me."

He prayed to God that this nightmare would not get worse.

"Am I going to die?" The words rasped from the boy's throat.

Ben jerked his attention back to the boy. "Not today," he said. "But be still until the Memphis bomb squad gets here. Can you tell me what happened?"

"I ain't got a clue. I came in here to go to the bathroom, and next thing I know you're telling me there's a bomb strapped to my chest."

His radio crackled again, this time with Randy's voice. "They're here. Trussed up like calves at a branding. But Ben, they're unconscious."

"All three of them?" he asked and held his breath.

"Yeah, all three of them."

If the boys were harmed in any way . . . He clenched his jaw. "Dr. Somerall will be there soon to check them out, but go ahead and untie them. I'll be there as soon as I can."

"Uh, Ben, there's a note pinned to TJ's chest."

"Read it, but put latex gloves on first."

"I can read it without touching it. It's a nursery rhyme. 'Three blind mice, three blind mice. See how they run, see how they run. They all ran after the ice cream man who could've killed them with a carving knife. Did you ever see such a thing in your life as three dead mice?'"

"Are you sure they're breathing?"

"They're definitely breathing." Randy paused. "Who would've done something like this, Ben?"

He didn't have an answer to his deputy's question.

■ ■ ■

The ambulance arrived with its lights flashing at the same time that Ben pulled into the county jail parking lot. The blue and white ice cream van had been parked on the side lot where it could easily be seen. Randy had the boys on the ground while another deputy rigged lights for the area, and Leigh knelt beside TJ. Ben pulled on latex gloves and took the card Randy handed him while Leigh accepted the stethoscope a paramedic handed her and listened to TJ's chest then moved to the twins.

"How are they?" he asked.

"All pulses and respirations are fine." She handed the stethoscope back to the medic. "Take their blood pressure and notify ER we're bringing them in," she said, then turned to Ben. "How's the driver?"

That was one of the things he admired about Leigh. Her calmness and care for another person even though her emotions had to be on a roller coaster. "Scared, but okay. The bomb was a dud."

Her shoulders visibly relaxed. "Thank goodness." She nodded toward the card he held in his hand. "What's that?"

"Uh . . ." He wished he could shield her from the message. He held it where she could read it. "It's a note from their kidnapper."

Leigh's face paled. "Why?" She whispered the word.

"I wish I could tell you." He examined the note. Same type paper that was taped to the teenager's chest, and the nursery rhyme had the same bold strokes. He sniffed it and blinked at the pungent odor. Just like the other note. He identified the scent—blue permanent marker.

The paramedic approached, and they both turned toward him. "We're ready to transport. One of the twins is rousing from whatever they were given."

"How are their vitals?" Leigh asked.

"Near normal. Are you riding with us?"

"Go with them," Ben said. "I'll call Emily and send her to the hospital."

As Leigh followed the medic to the ambulance, he turned to his deputy. "What do you have so far?"

"Just the boys and the note," Randy said. "No one saw the driver, so we don't have a description. I found them on the floor."

Ben surveyed the area. Whoever kidnapped the boys probably entered from the side street, an alley really. And he parked where the truck would be seen sooner than later, so he didn't want the boys to die of heat stroke. The boys weren't the target. He was. The whole setup was to make Ben look incompetent.

And only one person in Bradford County would risk going to jail to do that. Jonas Gresham. Another thought niggled Ben's brain.

Or someone who wanted his job. That was an angle he hadn't pursued. He shrugged off the thought, hating the suspicion that accompanied it, and followed Randy to the back of the ice cream van. The double doors stood wide open, exposing the stainless steel interior. "Go over it with a fine-tooth comb. Dust everything. If there's a fingerprint that doesn't match the driver, I want to know who it belongs to."

He took his cell phone out and dialed Taylor Martin. "How soon can you meet with me?"

■ ■ ■

"I cannot believe you boys climbed in that ice cream truck." Leigh slid the stethoscope in her pocket. The three boys had been put in a room with three beds and seemed no worse for wear from the Versed found in their bloodstream. Whoever had administered the short-acting drug used for sedation had known what they were doing. "TJ, what have I always told you about talking to strangers?"

"Yeah, Twins." Emily crossed her arms across her chest. "I'd like an explanation as well."

Ben stepped closer to the beds. "Did you forget those stories *I* told you?"

The boys hung their heads.

"We won't do it again," Josh whimpered. At least Leigh thought it was Josh.

"But the man was so nice," TJ said. "He gave us a free cup of Dots."

Leigh exchanged looks with Ben and nodded to the question on his face. Since she hadn't found an injection site, she'd already surmised the boys had received oral Versed. Now she knew how—in the small BB-sized ice cream pellets TJ loved so much.

"Can you describe this man?" Ben asked.

TJ and the twins shared a look, then TJ shrugged while the twins shook their head.

"Do you remember anything about him? Was he old or young? Tall?"

The boys flinched at his sharp words.

"Biting their heads off won't get any answers," Leigh said. She took TJ's hand. "Think about it. Was he as tall as me?"

He thought a minute then nodded. "Not as tall as Ben, though."

"Good. What color hair did he have?"

"He had on a cap!" one of the twins cried. "You know, like you wear in the winter."

"Yeah, we thought he was cold," the other twin said. "And he didn't smell good."

"And he had a big nose," TJ added. "And a mustache. A brown one."

"I don't think his nose was real."

"Why do you say that, Josh?" Emily asked.

"'Cause he kept trying to fix it, you know, like it was trying to come off, and he'd push it back."

"I didn't see him doing that," TJ said.

"That's 'cause you were trying to get all the Dots."

Ben cleared his throat. "If one of my deputies took you down to the station, do you think you could help Miss Maggie draw a picture of him?"

"Yeah!" the boys cried in unison.

"I'm coming with TJ," Leigh said. He wasn't going anywhere without her. Not today and not tomorrow . . . not ever if this madman wasn't caught.

■ ■ ■

Ben's headlights cut through the darkness as he turned onto the red gravel road that led to Jonas Gresham's house. He had zero evidence that Gresham had kidnapped the boys, but his gut feeling drew him to the white plank house around the curve.

"You think he's home?" Andre asked.

"Don't know. If he isn't, maybe Mrs. Gresham will tell us how long he's been gone."

He pulled into the drive, his lights flashing on Gresham's old Chevy parked under the giant oak beside the house. He parked in front of the dimly lit house and stepped out of the truck, and the oppressive heat and humidity of August enveloped him. The air was breeding a storm.

With Andre pointing the way with a Maglite, Ben walked to the porch and rapped on the door. The smell of fried chicken wafted through the open door. Someone was cooking late. He rapped again, and a backlit figure moved toward the door.

"Sheriff?" Mrs. Gresham cocked her head. "You're not here to tell me another one of my boys is dead, are you?"

Ben's throat tightened, and he shook his head. "Looking for your husband. Is he around?"

She turned slightly and yelled over her shoulder. "Jonas! Sheriff Logan's here to see you."

Before she could leave, Ben said, "Mrs. Gresham, how long has your husband been home?"

She stared at him with dull eyes. "Why?"

"Don't you be talking to the sheriff, woman. Ain't none of his business what I been doing."

A nerve twitched in Ben's jaw. "Mrs. Gresham?"

"Sheriff, that truck set under that tree all day. Now if you'll excuse me, I don't want my supper to burn."

"Satisfy you, Logan?" Gresham's lip curled into a snide grin as he stared through the screen door.

"Are you saying you haven't left your place?"

"That's right, and the missus will verify it. Now, if you ain't got no more questions . . ." He turned his gaze toward Andre. "I'd 'preciate it if you and your deputy would get off my porch."

Ben rested a hand on his sidearm. "You're not even curious why I'm here?"

Gresham lifted his shoulder in a shrug. "Figure somebody done somethin' that shows you ain't fit to be sheriff. Right?"

Gresham had kidnapped the boys. There was no doubt in Ben's mind. He leveled his gaze at the old man. "You're going to make a mistake. And I'll be there when you do."

"Why, Sheriff, I ain't got no idea what you're talking about. Good night to ya." Gresham turned and sauntered away from the door. Before he disappeared into another room, a snigger reached Ben's ears.

19

Sunday morning the smell of fresh coffee drew Leigh from sleep. Sarah must be up. She threw on a robe and hurried down the stairs to the kitchen.

"Good morning," said Sarah.

"Morning." Her glance slid to TJ, and she treasured in her heart the sight of him sitting at the table in his pajamas. If anything had happened to him . . .

"Mom! Hurry. We don't want to be late!"

"You better be worrying about getting yourself dressed, young man." After yesterday, she would never complain about his high-powered sentences. She glanced at the clock. Only seven. Ben had said he'd be here at eight-thirty. *Ben.* Was the Ferris wheel ride a dream? She let the memory linger as she walked to the coffeepot. "We have plenty of time. Can I have a hug this morning?"

TJ rolled his eyes, but he left his plate of bacon and eggs and came over to hug her.

"Thank you, young man." She pressed her lips together and swallowed the lump in her throat and noticed that Sarah's eyes were awfully bright and wet-looking.

Sarah half-coughed and half-cleared her throat. "Would you like some breakfast?"

"Just coffee right now." She poured herself a cup and stirred in a splash of creamer. "Remember what you promised me last night, TJ?"

"Mo-om."

"Terrible things could've happened yesterday, son," Leigh said.

Sarah ruffled his hair as she picked up his empty plate. "And not just to you. When you didn't come back, I about had a heart attack."

He dropped his head. "I won't ever talk to strangers again."

Leigh didn't want him afraid of people. "It's not about *talking*, TJ. It's about going off with them. Or getting in the back of a truck or in a car. I hope you learned a valuable lesson yesterday."

His eyes grew round. "I did. I promise."

"Okay, go get your bath."

"And your clothes are on the chair by your bed," Sarah added.

Leigh took her coffee to the table, listening for the sound of running water. Once she was certain TJ couldn't overhear, she said, "I'm afraid the kidnapping didn't make a big impression."

"I noticed that." Sarah joined her at the table.

"Why should it? They slept through the whole thing, and when they woke, everyone treated them like royalty."

Sarah raised her hand. "I for one am guilty. But I was so happy they were okay."

Leigh leaned and put her arm around her friend. "I want to thank you for being here. I don't know what I'd do without you."

"Pshaw. Go on with you. You're like family." Sarah blinked rapidly as tears rimmed her eyes. "If you weren't going off to Baltimore, I'd sell my house and move up here. Get my own place, of course."

Baltimore. It was what she wanted. Wasn't it? "It's been my dream for so long," she said.

"But you're needed here at Emily's clinic."

Leigh thought of the petite, eighty-five-year-old grandmother who came to the clinic Friday with an elevated pulse. Leigh had run a simple blood test and discovered her potassium level was dangerously low. But anyone could've found the problem. "Dr. Hazelit will be here."

"I heard Emily say he was retiring." Sarah poured each of them more coffee. "And how about Ben? I see the way he looks at you. The man is in love with you."

Leigh's heart warmed. But a future couldn't be built on lies.

"And I already know how you feel. When are you going to tell him about—"

Leigh jerked her head toward the upstairs. "TJ might hear you."

Sarah leaned forward with her arms on the table. "Right is right and wrong is wrong, and this is all wrong. The man deserves to know the truth. Your son deserves it as well."

"It's not that easy." Leigh's taste for coffee disappeared, and she grabbed her cup and walked to the sink. The battle between truth and protecting the lie warred in her heart. Sarah might be right, but didn't she realize how telling the truth would upend Leigh's life? And not just her life, but Ben's and TJ's. She poured the coffee down the drain. No. She couldn't do it. Not yet.

Thunder rumbled overhead, and she peered out the kitchen window at the dark clouds churning against the sky. A storm was almost on them.

"Remind me to tell TJ to wear his everyday shoes to church," she said. "And to take his raincoat."

"You're evading the subject, Leigh." Sarah's words were gentle but firm. "Put it in God's hands. He'll open the door, but you have to trust him and go through it. He's big enough to handle the aftermath."

Leigh heaved a sigh. "I have to get ready for church."

■ ■ ■

Sitting beside TJ in church, Leigh wanted to nudge him and tell him to be still as he shifted first one way then another. Rain pelted the windows as thunder punctuated the minister's sermon, yet again on forgiveness. She searched her heart. Was there anyone she needed to forgive?

The name came instantly. Tom Logan.

No. He didn't deserve forgiveness.

Bitterness soured her mouth. She clenched her hands. If it hadn't been for Tom, TJ would have his dad, and she wouldn't be wrestling with telling them the truth. But it had been her choice. She flinched as thunder shook the windows of the little church.

Tom should never have made such an offer. *He thought he was protecting his son.* Maybe she needed to forgive herself as well.

"Forgiveness isn't about the person who wronged you." The pastor's gentle voice carried over the storm. "It's for you. Forgiveness releases you from the chains of anger and bitterness."

"I wish Tom could tell you how sorry he is." Marisa's words that first night in their home pricked Leigh's heart. *Let it go.* Could she? She closed her eyes and willed her mind to say the words silently. *I forgive him.* She didn't feel any different. Except her hands had relaxed. She sighed. Forgiving Tom wasn't her biggest problem, anyway. She smoothed the wrinkles from her cotton pants. If only she could be certain of the outcome of telling Ben the truth . . . *Turn it over to God.* Sarah's words just this morning echoed in her heart. If only she could.

After the service, Leigh found herself agreeing to have lunch at the Logans'. She simply couldn't say no to the pleading in TJ's eyes. All through the meal, conversation and laughter flowed around the table. She looked up more than once to find Tom's eyes following her, and for some reason, they didn't seem as cold. His coordination was much improved, and he was able to feed himself without making a mess.

Marisa passed her a plate of homemade rolls. "I'm so glad you joined us," she said. "And after dessert, I have a surprise for TJ. Actually, a surprise for everyone."

Leigh shot Ben a questioning glance, and he shrugged, then he winked at her. So, he was in on the surprise.

Sarah took a roll and bit into it. "Mmm, Marisa, these are so good. I must have the recipe."

"Oh, dear." Marisa laughed. "I'm afraid you'll just have to watch me make them and write down what I mix together. It's a cup of this and a pinch of that." She passed a bowl of potato salad to Leigh. "Emily said you went into TJ's Sunday school class today."

"I thought Emily could use my help. I'd forgotten Ben helped her." After yesterday, she couldn't bear to turn TJ loose, even in church.

"I, for one, was sure glad to see you. The class was a handful today." Emily grinned at her.

Indeed they were, wanting to talk about the kidnapping, plying TJ and the twins with all kinds of questions. Leigh glanced around the table. Happy, smiling faces, even Tom's today. TJ's family. Laughter floated around the room again. Sunday dinners at her grandmother's had never been like this growing up. Her mother rarely made the effort to get out of bed, and her grandfather could be counted on to start an argument with someone. She tried to remember what it'd been like before her dad died, and no pleasant memories surfaced. Marisa tapped her glass, bringing Leigh back to the present.

"Now for the surprise," she said. "Tom has something he wants to say."

All eyes, including Leigh's, turned to him, but his gaze was fixed on TJ. Unease crawled down Leigh's spine. Tom looked . . . different. More alert. For the first time, she noticed he sat in a regular chair, not his wheelchair.

He licked his lips. "I . . . w-w-want . . ."

A sharp pain twisted her gut. *He can speak?*

"I . . ." He tried to form words, but they wouldn't come.

Marisa nodded, encouraging her husband. When he tried and

failed again, she said, "Why don't you show them how you can use the iPad instead."

Frustration pinched his lips together, then he nodded, and Marisa handed him the tablet. Very slowly he typed a few words, and she held it up. *TJ. Thank you.*

A grin spread across TJ's face. "You can do it! Mom! Pops can communicate!"

Tom turned to Leigh and typed again. *Thank you.*

The room swirled. If he typed one more word, she would scream.

"He does very well as long as he doesn't get excited," Marisa said. "And all the praise goes to TJ for showing him how to use that iPad. Tom finally made the connection and started working with his therapist. I believe he'll be talking soon."

Leigh connected with Tom's eyes. They held warmth she'd never noticed before. Maybe he wasn't going to spill the beans.

At least not yet.

But, if she read the look in his eye correctly, he would if she didn't.

■■■

Armero folded the Sunday newspaper and slammed it on his desk. What was Gresham thinking? Kidnapping the three boys. The only good thing about it was the timing—stroke of luck it happened about the time he made his call. Now if the flash drive surfaced, he figured the doctor would give it up. Maybe one more call to make sure she knew what to do if she found it. He jumped as his door swung open, and Jonas Gresham strolled in. "What are you doing here?"

Gresham hooked his thumb in his overall straps. Under his arms, half-moon circles of sweat stained his long-sleeved shirt, and Armero wrinkled his nose.

"Seeing my boy. He's on the loading dock today. I saw your car in the parking lot and thought we ought to have a little chat."

"You shouldn't be in my office. What if someone sees you?"

"Who? Nobody's here on Sunday but the loading crew. Chill out."

"What do you want?"

"I want to make sure you ain't planning on this being your last shipment of rifles."

How did Gresham know? "You're not giving me a lot of choice."

"What are you talking about?"

"This war on Ben Logan. It's bringing too much attention to Bradford County. You need to back off your little games."

"My little games, as you call them, are keeping Logan off balance. Otherwise, he might've figured out you killed Tony."

Armero jutted his chin. "You don't know what you're talking about."

"Don't I? It doesn't take a rocket scientist to figure out you killed Tony. Been meaning to ask you why, but I figure I already know the answer. Tony discovered you were stealing the unmarked receivers."

Armero pressed his lips together. The fast-food sausage and biscuit he'd eaten on the way to the office churned in his stomach.

"I keep hearing something about a flash drive."

Armero's blood drained from his face and his stomach went into free fall.

A sly smile crossed Gresham's lips. "That's what I thought. And you don't have the drive."

Armero regained his equilibrium. "I don't even know if it's still in existence, thanks to you and your stupid fire at his house." He spit the words out. "And if I want to quit selling rifles to Mexico, there's nothing you can do about it."

Gresham shrugged. "Be a shame if a little bird whispered in Logan's ear that receivers were disappearing before the serial numbers were stamped on them."

"You wouldn't dare. If I go down, you'll go down."

"Why do you think I always insist on cash? You ain't got nothing tying me to your gunrunning operation. Nothing." He spit the word out. "If Logan knew where to look, he might find a lot of interesting information about a certain Blue Dog company."

Whatever happened to honor among thieves? And how did Gresham know about the company? "What do you want?"

"A bigger cut. Fifty percent."

"Fifty percent? No way."

"Seventy-five, then."

"What? You're crazy."

"That's a possibility. I'm tired of doing all the dirty work, and you getting the biggest part of the money."

Gresham leaned over the desk, and stale sweat assaulted Armero's sensibilities. Did the man never take a bath? The old man pointed his finger in his face.

"You're going to let me into that offshore account, and I want half of the money you collect. Starting with this shipment. And there'll be no quitting. At least until *I* say we quit."

Armero narrowed his eyes at Gresham. His mind raced, trying to find a hole. He wasn't giving Gresham half. He'd die first.

Or maybe Gresham would die.

20

Forgiveness. Since church this morning, Ben hadn't been able to get the word off his mind. Even the chatter and laughter around the table hadn't been enough. It wasn't that he didn't want to forgive himself for Tommy Ray's death. He couldn't.

Forgiveness was way more complicated than the pastor indicated.

Ben pushed away from the table that Sarah and Leigh were already clearing. The boys had disappeared, probably into the living room to play one of their video games. He glanced out the dining room window. The skies had cleared.

Leigh reached over his shoulder for his plate. "Finished?"

Her voice soothed the jitters in his stomach. "Yeah. Would you like to walk down to the lake with me?"

He'd give anything to recapture what they'd had last night at the top of the Ferris wheel—if it had actually existed. But it was like everything that had happened before the boys' kidnapping didn't exist. Did he imagine that she was receptive to his kiss? And where did he want to take his feelings for her? After all, she was leaving in six weeks.

She glanced down at her clothes. "How wet is it outside?"

Emily passed by. "I have something that should fit you upstairs. A pair of sneakers too, if you wear a size 8."

"Thank you." Leigh held up her index finger. "Be right back."

"I think I'll change into something old too. Meet you outside."

The white pea gravel crunched under their feet as they walked in silence. Leigh seemed preoccupied. Maybe this wasn't such a good idea.

"Do you have any leads on who kidnapped TJ and the twins?" she asked.

"I'm afraid not. The only fingerprints inside the van belonged to the driver. The boys did remember the man wore rubber gloves, but they didn't think anything about it."

"Was TJ the target?"

"I think I was the target," Ben said.

"But the phone call . . ."

"He's trying to hurt me by targeting the people I'm sworn to protect." He heaved a sigh. "But whoever is responsible will make a mistake. He'll get too cocky."

"I hope you catch him soon, but until then, I'm keeping TJ close. Emily said I could bring him to the clinic. I think she's bringing the twins with her when she's there."

Frustration boxed him in like iron bars. He needed a break in this case, evidence against Jonas Gresham—if he was the one. Maybe now that Dad was getting better, he could talk to him. Ben dismissed that thought immediately. His father wasn't that much better. Ben hadn't even brought up the shooting yet, for fear thinking about it might cause his dad to have another stroke.

"Hey!" Leigh stood in front of him and waved her hand in his face. "We came out here to relax. Let's try to do that before we have to face reality again. Why don't we take the paddleboat out?"

"Nah." The sun glinted off the white fiberglass craft tethered to the pier. He hadn't been out on the lake since Tommy Ray. "There's a shady place around the bend. Let's walk."

Fifteen minutes later, Leigh panted beside him. She wiped her face with the tail of her shirt. "Are we there yet?"

"Five more minutes," he answered with his standard reply to the twins. "Just around this next bend."

Sure enough, five minutes later, they reached the shady spot he'd promised and flopped down on a patch of grass under a water oak.

Leigh fanned herself. "The breeze feels good."

"I didn't remember it being so far over here." Ben plucked a blade of grass and chewed on it, savoring the green taste. "I'm glad you came for lunch."

She breathed deeply, not answering.

"Were you surprised that Dad was so much improved?"

"Oh yeah. I had no idea he'd come that far. Did you see the look on TJ's face?"

"Yeah. Wish I'd had a camera."

She fell silent again.

"Thanks for helping out in Sunday school this morning. In fact, you can take my place until Jeremy comes back, if you'd like."

"What? You don't like helping?"

"Sometimes it's hard."

"How hard can teaching nine- and ten-year-olds . . . oh." The laughter died in her voice. "They remind you of Tommy Ray. But I thought he was older, fifteen."

He nodded, not sure if he could trust his voice not to break. It'd been three years. He should be able to put it behind him. He grabbed a breath of air. "I'm not comfortable around kids of any age, but if they were fifteen, I don't think I could do it at all."

She put her hand on his arm. "Look at me a minute."

He turned his head. Her emerald green eyes had darkened.

"Did you not hear anything the pastor said this morning?"

"I don't need to forgive anyone."

"Ben! You're beating yourself up for something that wasn't even your fault. I wish Sarah was here. She's so much better at this than I am." She licked her lips. "Do you believe God has forgiven you for what happened that day?"

How could God forgive him? A boy had died. A family suffered.

"Wait, before you answer that—exactly what do you believe needs to be forgiven?"

That was an easy question. "I was responsible for those boys. I should have known he wasn't horsing around. And when I did realize it, I should've gone in the water right away."

"Did you do what you were supposed to do?"

Go into the water only as a last resort. The words had been drilled into Ben's head from his first lesson as a lifeguard when he was a teenager. So what if he followed protocol. It didn't ease his guilt. Ben closed his eyes, reliving the horror. "We were so close to making it. I tried to capture his arms. I couldn't breathe."

He sucked in a deep breath, then another. "He let go of me, and I knew if I didn't get air, I'd die. I shot out of the water and grabbed some air and went back down to find him, but he was gone."

He balled his hands so tight his knuckles hurt. "I keep replaying what happened, looking for a different answer. One where I wasn't a coward."

Leigh took his hands and gently pried his fingers open. "The instinct to survive is the strongest instinct we have. You are not a coward. Look at how you raced into our smoldering house to get TJ. That's not the act of a coward."

He *had* saved TJ. Hadn't thought twice about what to do, either.

"You can second-guess yourself for the rest of your life, and it won't change anything. I don't think there's anything God needs to forgive you for, but if there is, he did it a long time ago. Now it's simply a matter of you receiving his grace."

Forgiveness seemed so close, almost like he could reach out and touch it. *"You killed my boy. Let him drown."* Jonas Gresham's bitter words echoed in his mind. "Not everyone feels that way."

"Ben, you're the most caring, courageous man I know."

Leigh's passionate words branded his heart. He could almost believe her. He could certainly believe he might be falling in love

273

with her. But what if she took off again? There was no what-if—she was taking off, to Baltimore. "Are you still leaving in September?"

She bent her head, studying something in the grass. When she looked up, uncertainty clouded her eyes. "Sarah wants me to stay here. She says I don't have to go to Baltimore to make a difference."

"She's right, Leigh."

"TJ doesn't want to go, either. But I'm not sure it's an opportunity I can turn down." She picked up a stick and drew a stick figure in a bare patch of ground. With a shake of her head, she pierced him with her gaze. "Let's talk about something else."

Even if she changed her mind, Ben wasn't sure he could trust her. She'd left him before with little explanation. She might do it again. "What happened ten years ago? I never understood why you wouldn't take my calls."

The color drained from her face. "W-what?"

"Why did we break up? I never knew why. Oh, I know what you said, that you were going to med school and couldn't afford the distraction of a relationship, but I never thought that was the whole story. We could have made it work."

She pressed her lips together. "That's water under the bridge."

"But I need to know what happened or it might happen again. It really hurt when you left."

Leigh shot a skeptical glance his way. "It doesn't seem like you were hurt to me. When I came back for my grandmother's funeral, you were engaged."

Gabby Jordan. His heart winced. What a mistake that'd been. "Rebound. Then she lied to me about something insignificant, and we broke up. I can't deal with lies." He looked into her green eyes, and it was like gazing into her soul. "You were always truthful with me."

Leigh fanned herself furiously with her hand. "It's hot. I think it's time to go back."

"So you're not going to tell me what happened to us?"

She stilled her hand. "We were in different places in our lives. I still had a lot of years of school. You needed a wife who would be an asset in your life, not someone who had been hauled into the county jail with a bunch of strippers. How would that look on an election poster?"

"Leigh, that was when you were seventeen and look at you now. You're a doctor. And totally an asset."

She turned her gaze toward the lake. "It was a summer romance."

"I didn't think of it that way. I wanted to marry you."

"But you never told me that."

"Then I'm telling you now. I wanted to marry you then . . . and . . . and I want to marry you now. Or at least explore the idea, see if what we had is still there."

Her mouth dropped open. She clamped it shut. "Everything is different now. I have a child, and you don't want the responsibility of children."

A band constricted his heart. Tommy Ray's face flashed in his memory. Could he take that responsibility? Suddenly, TJ's sooty face overrode the memory of the drowned boy, and the band loosened. "I know you and TJ come as a package deal."

"Well, don't get too excited about it."

"You know I like being around TJ." He gazed into her green eyes. Just being around Leigh calmed him.

"Ben, I don't think—"

"I care about you, Leigh. I'll care about your son." He took her hand and ran his thumb over her palm, not expecting the tremor that raced through his heart.

Her pupils widened, and a look he couldn't discern flashed across her face.

Leigh bit her bottom lip. "There are some things we need to talk about first."

She looked so kissable. He was done with talking. "Mmm-hmm." He leaned toward her, and her lips parted as he cupped her face in his hands and drew her to him. He kissed her gently, and electricity charged through him. "I need you in my life," he murmured.

"Oh, Ben . . ."

She closed her eyes, and he kissed them as well. When he trailed his finger down her neck, she opened her eyes, and he lost himself in a sea of green. With a groan, he wrapped her in his arms and pulled her close, capturing her lips once again. Leigh's arms slid around his neck, and she pressed against him, returning his kiss with a passion that surprised him.

When they parted, he brushed a strand of chestnut hair from her cheek. She stared at the top button on his shirt, and he lifted her chin. "You look mighty serious."

A soft sigh escaped her lips. "There are still things I need to tell you, but not today."

Lightning zigzagged across the lake followed by a clap of thunder, and he stood and grabbed her by the hand, pulling her up. "Good. We have to get out of here," he said, pointing toward the building thunderheads. They would be lucky if they made it back to the house without getting drenched.

The frown faded, replaced by wide eyes. "Oh, my!"

Hand in hand, they raced for the house. Whatever she wanted to tell him would never change the way he felt about her.

■ ■ ■

Two hours later at the house on Webster, Leigh tossed the wet clothes Emily had loaned her into the washer and turned it on. Part of her wished she'd gotten it over with and told Ben the truth. If Tom knew, it was just a matter of time before he would be able to speak well enough to tell the whole family what he suspected. Ben needed to hear it from her first.

Wait . . . maybe she could talk to Tom, convince him to keep quiet. Or maybe she was imagining he knew. Besides, Ben wasn't ready to be a father. That was evident. He wanted her, but he'd been less than enthusiastic about a relationship with TJ.

Hadn't he said he couldn't deal with lies? His actual words echoed in her heart. Once he discovered she'd lied to him all these years, he would reject her. Which meant he would reject TJ as well. That was not happening. No one was rejecting her son.

And how about TJ? Didn't her son deserve to know the truth? Pain gripped her stomach, and she doubled over and sank to the floor. Tell him or don't tell him? The decision went back and forth.

She pulled herself up from the floor. Why did truth have to be so hard? And what good would it do to tell the truth? Why stir up trouble when in six weeks she and TJ would be out of Logan Point? They could start over, but not if she told the truth and they had to take all that baggage with them.

No. This truth would only hurt those she loved. She squared her shoulders. She would not tell Ben *or* TJ. And maybe, someday, there would be a man in her life who could love her and her son. Actually, Ian already seemed to enjoy TJ, and that was at least a start.

She padded into the kitchen to search for the Earl Grey she'd bought and almost bumped into Sarah putting on the teakettle. The box of tea bags sat on the counter.

"You need a cup of Earl too?" Leigh asked.

Sarah nodded, then handed her several pieces of mail. "These came to the Logans this past week."

Leigh had requested the post office forward any mail sent to the house that burned to the Logans'. She sorted through the letters as Sarah set a plate of cookies on the counter. "I found the neatest bakery in town. Thought we'd try their homemade biscotti."

"That sounds good." Leigh's hand stilled at a notice from the post office. Seems Tony's box payment was due. She didn't even know he had a PO box. She'd bet it was full to overflowing. She'd check on it in the morning. No, she had to be at the clinic by seven-thirty. "Would you mind taking care of this?" she asked, handing Sarah the card.

"Be happy to. But how about TJ? Do you want me to call Ben so he can send a deputy over to stay with him while I go out?"

"He'll be with me."

Sarah jerked her head up. "What?"

"He's going to the clinic with me this week. I don't think I could concentrate on treating patients if I'm worrying about where TJ is."

"That's going to be awful boring for him."

"The twins will be there when Emily comes. And I'll let him use my netbook to play games on."

"Why not let him stay with Marisa? That place is a virtual fortress."

"No." She softened her tone. "He'll be fine at the clinic. And maybe by the time school starts next week, Ben will have caught that madman."

Her friend started to say something more, but Leigh's cell phone rang. Ian. He'd had to go out of town after the meeting with his uncle, although he'd called as soon as he heard about the kidnapping. "I probably need to take this," she said and walked to the lanai just outside the back door. "Hello. Are you back in town?"

"No. I have to stay over until tomorrow afternoon. Just wanted to check on you and TJ."

"We're fine." Leigh suppressed a sigh. If only she had the same feelings toward Ian that she had for Ben, life would be so much simpler.

"I miss you. Can we have dinner tomorrow night?"

She really needed to tell Ian that if he wanted something other than friendship, he was wasting his time with her. "Tomorrow night would be nice." She would tell him then.

21

Thanks for taking time to do this before you leave," Ben said as Taylor Martin handed him a folder. She had an early Tuesday morning flight to Seattle, and he imagined she could have used her Monday afternoon getting ready instead of briefing him and Wade.

Taylor handed Wade a file as well. "I want to help get this guy, and after Saturday's kidnapping, I didn't figure we had any time to waste."

Ben scanned the folder. "So you still agree these attacks are directed at me?"

"My gut says Tony's death and the ransacking of his house are separate crimes. That said, profiling is not an exact science, and anything is possible. The rest, definitely directed at you."

Ben doodled on the pad in front of him. "You don't think the guy Leigh reported to Child Services committed any of them?"

She shook her head. "He's a heavy drinker, and his profile doesn't indicate the level of intelligence it would take to pull off these crimes. I keep coming back to one person. Jonas Gresham. I think it's twofold with him. He believes you're responsible for two of his sons' deaths, and he's attacking you where it will hurt the most—your competency and the people you care about."

Wade closed the file. "There may be another reason Gresham is pulling these stunts," he said. "The dogfighting ring. He probably figures if we're busy investigating all these other crimes, you won't notice new traffic in and out of the county."

"There's one thing I don't understand—why would Gresham call Leigh and demand the flash drive?" Ben didn't believe Leigh had told him the entire conversation. He'd asked about it again this morning after he escorted her and TJ to the clinic, and even though they'd been out of TJ's hearing, she clammed up, claimed she'd told him everything. She was so frightened for TJ, he was afraid that if she found the flash drive, she might think she could trade it for his safety.

"What if Tony was Gresham's partner?" Wade asked.

Ben didn't want to believe Tony would be involved in dogfighting. But what if he was? He nodded. "If they were partners, Tony could have created a file with the names of all the people involved and put it on a flash drive. That could explain how Gresham knew about the drive, and give us only one perpetrator for all the crimes." Which was a whole lot easier to deal with than two. "But he wouldn't try to frame his own son for Tony's death. Family is too important to him."

"Ben, we're talking about Jonas Gresham—you know, the guy who hates your guts." Wade leaned forward. "But would he torch Tony's house with no way of knowing for sure the flash drive was in there?"

Ben wanted to throw up his hands. This was like being in a maze.

"Let's look at each of these crimes and see how many of them we can link to Gresham." Taylor walked to the whiteboard. She wrote Gresham's name in the middle and drew a circle around it then drew lines and wrote Tony's name, the house ransacking and shooting the following morning. In parentheses she wrote *Billy Wayne*. Then, one by one, she listed the other crimes—Leigh's fire, the snakes, the fire at the jail, kidnapping, phone calls. By those crimes, she wrote *circumstantial*. Last of all she listed dogfighting.

She turned to Ben. "A steel-tipped arrowhead was found at the scenes of both fires? Is Gresham proficient with a bow?"

Ben riffled through the papers on his desk until he found the report from the game warden. "In this county, only fifty-three people applied for a permit to hunt with a bow and arrow this year. Jonas Gresham and two of his sons' names are on here."

Taylor wrote *means* by the fires. She put a question mark by the phone calls. "I wish we could get his cell phone records," she said.

Ben shook his head. "I looked at Leigh's cell phone. The number was blocked. Besides, whoever made the calls probably used a disposable phone."

"How about Tony's? Do you have his?"

Wade leaned forward. "His phone records came in last week. Nothing important . . . business calls, calls to Leigh and Ben."

As Ben stared at the board, the puzzle pieces began to click in place. Taylor was right. Every crime on the board pointed to him personally. But unless he caught Gresham in the act of committing another crime or found the disguise he used when he kidnapped the boys, Jonas Gresham would get away with his crimes. "Gresham has an alibi for Saturday night."

Taylor turned to him. "Really?"

"I'm not sure how solid it is. Andre and I drove out to the Gresham house, and his wife more or less alibied him. I figure she was afraid not to." He turned to Wade. "Why don't you follow up? Maybe Mrs. Gresham will tell you something she won't tell me."

"You might want to put Andre on this. I don't think it's a good idea for me to nose into Jonas's business this close to the big dogfight. Figure it'll be one night this week, maybe even tonight."

The dogfight. Another thing Ben didn't feel good about. "I don't like it."

"I don't like letting him get away with what he's doing, either. And don't tell me you wouldn't jump at the chance to take my place if you could," Wade said then pointed to the whiteboard.

"We can't prove he did anything up there but dogfighting, and we saw that with our own eyes. It's a felony in Mississippi, and when he crossed over into Tennessee it became a federal crime. I heard he has at least four dogs in the fights, and that would put him away a few years. If we can find out when the next fight is, we can catch him in the act."

"Wade has a point," Taylor said. "Think back to the 1930s and Al Capone. The feds couldn't get anything on him for murder, drug dealing, or prostitution, but they finally put him away for tax evasion, and he died in prison."

Ben sighed. Sometimes you had to take what you could get. He glanced at his watch. Almost five. The clinic closed soon and he didn't want to delegate someone else to be there. "It's time to escort Leigh and TJ home," he said and stood.

"You could let Andre go." Wade grinned as he took out his cell phone and checked his messages.

He narrowed his eyes at his chief deputy. "I'll do it."

"I saw you two at church Sunday," Taylor said. She raised her eyebrows expectantly.

He ducked his head, grinning.

"Ben and Leigh, sittin' in a tree, k-i-s-s-i—"

"Shut up, Wade." But he couldn't stop the heat rising to his face. "We're friends."

"I wish I had—" Wade's phone rang.

"It's Cummings." Wade answered the call. "Hatcher." A few seconds later he said, "Of course I am." When he hung up, the chief deputy took a deep breath and let it out. "The fight is tonight."

"What time?" Ben was already dialing the U.S. Marshal.

"He didn't actually say it was tonight, just told me to be ready for a call."

"Oh." Ben's thumb hovered over the disconnect button. No, he better put their backup on alert. When Luke answered, Ben filled him in.

"I'll notify the FBI, and you can call the different sheriffs who wanted to be in on this," said the marshal.

"Good deal." After he hung up, he turned to Wade. "Start calling the Tennessee sheriffs and advise them to be on alert. I'll notify the Mississippi Highway Patrol and TBI when I return."

A grin stretched across Wade's face. "Yes, sir!"

Ben groaned. "You do have your key ring with the GPS in it? And the microphone pen?"

His chief deputy showed him both.

"Be careful, you hear?"

"Ben, this is going like clockwork. I feel it in my bones."

Ben's bones told a different story.

■ ■ ■

"Breathe deeply for me," Leigh said and repositioned the stethoscope on the veined chest of her last patient for the day, a seventy-five-year-old grandmother. She didn't like the crackling she heard. She lifted the chest piece. "How long have you had trouble breathing?"

The woman's daughter answered for her. "She's been like this for a week now. Wouldn't let me bring her in until today."

"Is that right, Mrs. Smith?" Leigh ducked her head so she could look the older woman in the eye.

"Don't like taking medicine." Mrs. Smith's voice quivered.

"So what made you decide to come?"

"I couldn't breathe. Figure I have pneumonia again."

"You would've made a good doctor," Leigh said with a smile. "I'm going to take a couple of X-rays, and then I'll decide if you need to go to the hospital."

"I ain't goin' to no hospital. Doc Hazelit always treated me here, and you can too."

"Oh, Mama, if you need to be in the hospital, you're going."

Leigh kept a straight face until she was out of the room. Her older patients were most determined to stay out of the hospital. The sight of Ben and TJ talking in the waiting room startled her as she turned to the X-ray tech. She didn't know Ben had arrived. "Beth, I know it's after hours, but Mrs. Smith needs a chest X-ray—PA and lateral. If you need to leave, I can take care of it."

Beth's eyes widened. "Emily would have my hide if I left a patient. I have it covered, Dr. Somerall, but thank you for offering."

It was such a joy to work with people who went the extra mile. Leigh thanked her then stopped by the waiting room. "I won't be much longer," she said. She looked closer at what TJ held in his hands. "Is that a Rubik's Cube?"

TJ looked up and grinned while Ben's face turned red. "I'm showing Ben how to do it."

"Good luck."

"Thanks, I'll need it," Ben replied.

Leigh laughed. "I was talking to TJ."

Twenty minutes later, Leigh handed Mrs. Smith a prescription. Even though her X-ray was inconclusive, everything else pointed to pneumonia. "With the shot today, this antibiotic should clear up your infection. I want to see you again Friday." She turned to the daughter. "If her symptoms worsen, take her to the ER and call me."

Leigh finished her notes then shrugged out of her white coat and slipped the netbook she'd brought for TJ into her purse. TJ was probably getting antsy. But he'd handled being at the clinic better than she'd expected. Of course, it helped that the twins were here most of the day.

Dark shadows filled the empty waiting room. Maybe they'd gone outside. Her heart in overdrive, she hurried out the back door. Even though he was with Ben, she didn't like TJ not being where she thought he was. She calmed down when she spied them near the monkey bars. The clinic had been a daycare at one time with swings and other playground articles.

They didn't see her, and she watched them for a minute. She'd never seen Ben as relaxed around TJ as he was now. He actually seemed to be enjoying her son. Was it possible . . . She sighed. In a perfect world, she would tell Ben and TJ the truth, and everyone would live happily ever after. The sun dipped behind a cloud, plunging the playground in dismal gray hues.

Unfortunately, this wasn't a perfect world.

TJ spied her and came running. "Mom! Can I have your keys? I want to start the car, let it cool off some."

She handed TJ her keys.

"I'm gonna see if it'll start from here." He turned and aimed the key fob at the Avenger. Nothing happened.

"You'll probably have to get a little closer." She turned to Ben. Out of the corner of her eye, she saw TJ move a few feet closer to her car. "Any news about the identity of the kidnapper?"

"Not—"

The explosion drowned out Ben's words.

22

In slow motion, pieces of the car blew in different directions. TJ sailed into the air, and she grabbed for him even as the impact knocked her to the ground. With her ears ringing, Leigh struggled to get up. *TJ!* She had to get to him. She scrambled to where his limp body lay on the ground. But it was his leg that she couldn't tear her eyes from. A jagged bone protruded through the skin, and blood spurted from the wound with every beat of her son's heart.

Ben knelt beside her. "An ambulance is on the way. What can I do?"

She read his lips more than heard what he said. "He's bleeding out. I need something to press against his leg." She looked around frantically. "And something to elevate his leg with."

Ben shrugged out of his sports shirt then stripped off his white T-shirt and handed it to her. Leigh pressed the soft material above the break, being careful not to touch the open wound.

"Will this do to elevate his leg?" Ben held up her oversized purse.

Leigh hesitated. Did she want to risk moving him? The distant sound of a siren made the decision for her. "We'll wait. But put it in your truck. I'll need it at the hospital."

TJ's eyes fluttered open. "Mom?"

"Be really still, son." She continued to apply pressure as the shirt turned bright red. "Take his pulse," she said to Ben.

"So cold," TJ murmured and closed his eyes again.

Ben looked at her. "His heart is beating really fast."

His skin was clammy as well. He was going into shock. "TJ, can you hear me?"

He opened his eyes. "I'm sleepy."

"I need you to keep talking to me. To stay awake. Okay?"

"My leg . . . it hurts," he moaned.

Her stomach twisted. *Hurry, ambulance. Hurry.*

Minutes later, the ambulance pulled into the parking lot, and paramedics spilled out. One of them knelt beside her and quickly yelled over his shoulder, "We need a pressure gauze here."

"See if you can get his blood pressure," Leigh said. She glanced at the paramedic's name badge. Tim Watkins. "His pulse is very rapid."

"Dr. Somerall, I didn't recognize you." Tim wrapped a small cuff around TJ's arm. "Do you want me to take over applying pressure?"

"No!" She knew it was irrational, but she didn't trust anyone else to apply the right amount of pressure. "The bleeding has slowed. Let's get him transported STAT. Notify the hospital to have at least three units of O negative ready."

The paramedic sucked in a breath.

"What?" Leigh and Ben asked the question at the same time.

"It's August. The hospital blood supply is down, especially on the rarer types."

TJ had lost so much blood and would lose even more during the surgery to set his leg. Without a transfusion, he could die, and he could only be transfused with O negative. "Would you please check it out?"

She pressed her lips together, waiting for an answer. After a minute, Tim shook his head. "One unit. That's all they have. How about you, Doc? Are you O negative?"

"No. He inherited it from his father's side."

"It runs in families . . . any other relatives around?"

She struggled to breathe. *Tell him.*

"I'm O negative," Ben said. "I'll donate."

Leigh's heart stilled in her chest. She looked up, choking down the knot in her throat. "Thanks. Go on to the hospital while we get an IV going. And Tim, call the hospital so they'll be ready for Ben."

"TJ," Ben said, and her son fluttered his eyes open. "Hang in there, son. Everything is going to be all right."

The next few minutes were a flurry of activity as they readied TJ for transport. When they were finished, she looked at the three paramedics prepared to lift TJ on the gurney and then into the ambulance bay. "On the count of three."

Once they had him loaded, she added a fresh pad to the blood-soaked one. He should have stopped bleeding by now.

"Why don't you let me apply the pressure," Tim said. "I'm sure you're tired, and I have a little more hands-on experience."

Leigh hesitated. Her arms ached, but giving up control—

"Come on, Doc. If it were anyone else, what would you advise?" The paramedic's words struck a nerve.

She took a deep breath and nodded. "On the count of three, again."

They switched positions seamlessly. Leigh knelt beside TJ and laid her hand on his forehead.

He blinked his eyes open. "Don't tell . . . twins," he whispered. "But I'm scared."

"I won't tell them." She smoothed his hair back. "We all get scared sometimes. But you're going to be fine. You'll have a nice cast all the kids can sign."

"I like Ben . . ."

TJ's eyes closed again, and Leigh activated the blood pressure cuff. Much too low. "Tell the driver to hurry."

A team met them at the ER entrance and rushed him inside. Leigh followed to the examining room, nodding to the surgeon in charge. Dr. Gordon was a good surgeon. "I think when the bone fractured, it nicked the femoral artery."

"I'll take him from here. Do you want to scrub and observe?"

"Thank you, yes!" Dr. Gordon didn't have to extend the courtesy, and she was certain he didn't really want a patient's mother looking over his shoulder. She hurried to the OR suites before he could change his mind, grabbing a pair of scrubs from the supply room. After she changed, she noted on the scheduling board that TJ was in Suite 4.

Once she'd scrubbed, she dried her arms and hands before slipping into a surgical gown one of the scrub nurses held. As she shoved her hands into gloves, another nurse informed her that two units of O negative blood were being sent from the blood bank in Memphis. With Ben's blood, maybe that would be enough. She couldn't think about him connecting the dots right now. The nurse stepped behind her and fastened the tabs to the surgical gown. "Thank you."

Once she had everything in place, she walked toward the operating table, where a unit of blood dripped into TJ's veins. She faltered at TJ's still form on the table, where Dr. Gordon worked to repair the damage from the bomb blast.

Icy fingers gripped her throat, and cold spread to her face, making her head spin. Her legs threatened to buckle.

Dr. Gordon spoke without looking up. "I stitched the femoral artery and have set the bone. Next I'll insert an intramedullary nail into the canal from the hip."

She nodded, not trusting her voice.

He glanced up, frowning. "If you even suspect you might become ill, leave the operating room immediately."

Stiffening, Leigh managed a nod. And she would. She didn't want to endanger TJ by contaminating the sterile field. Pulling on her reserves, she moved closer to observe the surgery. Her gaze focused on Dr. Gordon's hands as he worked on TJ.

An hour into the surgery, he asked for another unit of blood. That would be Ben's. As the nurse hooked up the unit of blood, Leigh's mouth felt as though it'd been swabbed with cotton. Her heartbeat pummeled in her ears. Black dots swam before her eyes as the walls closed in. Leigh backed away from the table.

She could not faint.

"Tell Dr. Gordon I have to have some air," she mumbled.

Leigh stumbled from the operating room.

23

As Ben strode down the hall toward the operating room, he pressed his cell phone to his ear to better hear his chief deputy. "Take over the investigation until I can get there."

After Wade assured him that he had everything under control, Ben hung up and hooked the phone on his belt. He itched to get to the crime scene, but not before finding out how Leigh and TJ were. A question scratched at his mind, one he couldn't even put words to. It was like he had something he was trying to remember on the tip of his tongue.

He sidestepped a door opening, and Leigh stumbled out. She looked as though she didn't have an ounce of blood in her body. "What's going on? Is TJ all right?"

Her eyes widened when she saw him, then suddenly she pitched forward.

Ben swept her into his arms and strode to the ER. "She needs a bed and a doctor to check her over," he said to the first nurse he encountered.

Cathy, from church, glanced up from behind the nurses' desk. "Bring her this way."

As he followed the RN toward a room, an orderly stepped toward him. "Let me have Dr. Somerall."

The strapping orderly took Leigh from Ben's arms. And not

a minute too soon as the adrenaline rush died, leaving him with trembling arms and insides that felt as though they'd been wrung out. Maybe he needed more than the orange juice and donut he'd been given.

"Didn't you just give blood? You shouldn't have lifted her," Cathy scolded as she led the way to an empty exam room.

"Thanks for the tip," he shot back, and her face reddened.

"Sorry."

At the door, she turned to him. "I think I saw some brownies in the nurses' lounge. That might help."

"But I want—"

"Get some OJ while you're at it. I'll call you back when the doctor is finished."

He backed away from the door. "Of . . . course."

In the lounge, he drank a large glass of juice and tackled the brownies. The door opened, and a nurse he didn't recognize entered. "Can you tell me how Dr. Somerall is? And her son, TJ?"

She hesitated.

"I'm Sheriff Logan. They were with me when the car blew up."

Understanding lit her eyes. "Oh. I didn't recognize you. Dr. Somerall is alert now, but I'm not certain about her son."

Ben's cell phone buzzed in his pocket, and he slipped it out. Sarah. That reminded him that he needed to call Emily and his mother.

"Ben, I heard about the explosion. Leigh doesn't answer her phone." Sarah's panicky voice crackled over the line. "No one will tell me if they're all right."

"Leigh's okay and TJ is in surgery. Where are you?"

"In the ER waiting room."

"I'll be right there."

When he passed the desk, Cathy flagged him down. "Dr. Somerall is fine. Just got woozy in the OR. We're going to roll her down to the surgical ICU waiting room."

Patricia Bradley

He nodded. "Inform her that her friend Sarah is here, and we'll meet her there."

He turned to leave.

"Oh, wait, Sheriff. Dr. Somerall said you had her identification."

"Yes, it's in my truck. I'll get it."

When he strode through the ER double doors, he spied Sarah at the desk.

She hurried toward him, worry clouding her eyes. In her hand she gripped a canvas tote bag. "What happened?" she asked.

He guided her toward the hallway that led to the ICU. "I don't know yet. Leigh's car blew up, but she's all right. TJ is in surgery. His leg is broken, and he lost a lot of blood."

"Where's Leigh? Is she in surgery with him?"

"No. She was, but she almost fainted. She should be in the surgical ICU waiting room by now."

A few minutes later, they rounded the half wall that divided the waiting room from the hallway just as Leigh arrived from a different direction. Sarah bent over and hugged her. "How's TJ?" she asked as soon as Leigh was settled in a corner chair.

"He was stable when I . . . became faint and had to leave."

She glanced at Ben, and he handed her the purse. "What's in this thing to make it so heavy?"

"My netbook. Thanks."

Ben nodded. "What happened that made you faint?"

She rolled her lips in and took a deep breath. "They were hanging a unit of blood, and everything seemed to come unglued." She blinked away the wetness that appeared in her eyes. "It was the blood you gave. Thank you. With the shortage, I don't know what—"

"Don't. I'm just glad we're a match."

A soft gasp came from Sarah's lips, and he glanced sharply at her. "Is something wrong? You're not going to faint on me, are you?"

With her gaze on Leigh, the older woman shook her head. "I

. . . didn't know there was a shortage. Maybe I can donate? I'm O positive."

Leigh placed her hand on Sarah's. "Wrong type, but thanks. The blood bank in Memphis is sending two units of O negative."

Sarah shook Leigh's hand off. "You—"

"Ben, do you think you can find coffee around here? I think we all could use some. And when you come back, I'd like to talk about who blew up my car. Do you have any leads?"

He didn't need a lead. His gut shouted Jonas Gresham. "Wade's working on it, and I'll be joining them as soon as TJ's operation is over. Be right back with your coffee."

Leigh held up her hand. "If you need to leave, go. I'll get our coffee."

The relief in her voice puzzled him, just like the vibes between the two women. "Sit tight," he said. "You just fainted a little bit ago, and five minutes won't make any difference."

With one last glance at the two women, Ben rounded the corner. He knew a station with real coffee, not the instant in the waiting room refreshment center. Something was going on between the two women, something more than the stress of what had happened, and when he returned, he intended to find out what it was.

Before he'd walked far, his cell phone beeped a text, and he stopped in the hallway beside the waiting room. It was from Wade. *How's TJ?* As he started to reply, Sarah's voice lifted over the open wall that separated the waiting room from the traffic coming into the hospital.

"He deserves to know he's TJ's father, Leigh."

Leigh's response was lost as the question that had been trying to surface in his brain exploded. Of all the people in Logan Point, what were the odds of him and TJ sharing the same rare O negative blood? Sarah's words gave him his answer.

TJ was his son.

Everything fell into place.

Leigh's reluctance for TJ to be around his family, that quirky smile he'd seen in his own mirror.

She'd lied to him. For ten years, she'd lied to him.

He wheeled and rounded the corner, pinning his gaze on Leigh. Her hand flew to her mouth, her eyes wide.

"Why?" He gritted his teeth. "Why didn't you tell me?"

"I can't do this now, Ben."

"You owe me an explanation."

She closed her eyes. "Ask your dad," she whispered as tears rimmed her eyes.

Dad?

His father knew all these years, and he didn't tell him either? And now he couldn't? *Wait.* If Dad knew, then so did Mom. If Leigh wouldn't tell him the truth, maybe his mother would. He turned to Sarah. "Call me if there's any change in TJ."

■ ■ ■

Leigh paced the floor in the waiting room. She'd heard nothing from Ben since he'd left an hour ago. TJ's surgery should be over soon. Every time she looked at Sarah, her friend teared up and tried to apologize again. The mess she was in wasn't Sarah's fault. Leigh should have told Ben years ago. At the very least, this last week.

"Oh, Leigh, I almost forgot." Sarah picked up a canvas tote bag from beside her chair. "I picked up Tony's mail."

Leigh stopped pacing to take the bag. *Tony's mail?* Leigh rubbed her temple then remembered she'd asked Sarah to empty his PO box. The black phone in the waiting room trilled. The volunteers who manned the phones had long since gone home, so Leigh grabbed it, thinking it might be the OR nurse. The voice on the other end asked for the Duncan family, and Leigh's shoulders slumped.

"They were moved to a room," she said, her voice flat. When would they be in a room? TJ would stay in ICU overnight at the very least. She pulled letters from the bag.

"No, I don't know what room," she said, flipping through the mail. Her hand stilled at Tony's familiar handwriting. She hung up and turned to Sarah. "Why would Tony mail himself a letter?"

"Open it and see."

Before she could open the letter, footsteps sounded in the hallway. She stared at the corner, half hoping, half fearful, that it would be Ben. *Ian.* Danny and someone she didn't recognize trailed behind him. She slid the envelope into a pocket in her scrubs and stood.

"I'm so sorry," Ian said, wrapping her in a hug. "How is TJ? And how are you holding up?"

She leaned into his hug. "He has a broken leg. The nurse called earlier and said the surgery was in the final phase. Probably another thirty minutes before they'll be finished and I can see him. How did you know?"

"The receptionist at the plant called while we were driving home from the Memphis airport. I can't believe it. Are you sure you aren't hurt?"

"I'm woozy, but nothing serious." Her glance slid past Ian to Danny to the stranger.

"I'm sorry," Ian said. "This is Geoffrey Franks."

The one who took over Tony's job.

Franks bobbed his head. "I'm so sorry for everything that's happened."

"Thank you." Where her brother had never looked much like an executive, Franks did. The dark eyes that stared from his angular face seemed to be permanently serious. She fingered the envelope in her pocket. "Would you excuse me a minute. I need to . . ." She glanced toward the restroom.

Ian's face colored. "Of course."

Inside the restroom, she ripped into the envelope and pulled out a white business-sized envelope with Ben's name on it. A small flash drive fell on the floor.

Leigh picked it up. The missing flash drive. It had to be. She closed her fingers over it. What was on it that could be worth a child's life? *Get it to Ben.* She quickly dialed his number, and it went to voice mail.

Leigh slid the drive in her pocket where it would be safe until she could get it to him. Someone knocked at the restroom door, and she stuffed the letter back in the envelope and slid it in the same pocket with the flash drive.

She stared at her swollen eyes in the mirror and splashed water on her face then wet a paper towel and pressed it to her eyelids. The cool dampness eased the throbbing. Then, she straightened her scrubs, pulling the shirt past the pocket, and returned to the waiting room. "Sorry to take so long," she said to the woman standing at the door.

"Sarah was saying she emptied Tony's box at the post office," Ian said as she sat down. "I imagine it was quite full."

"Not so much." The thick letter she'd stuffed in her pocket pressed stiffly against her thigh. With a casual movement she pulled it from the pocket and placed it in the canvas bag beside her chair. She froze as her gaze shifted to a spot on the carpet. The flash drive lay between the chair and the bag. It must have been caught in the envelope and dropped out.

Her heart thumped as she leaned over and scooped it up and returned it to her pocket. She didn't understand the urgency that pushed her to keep the drive secret until she could hand it over to Ben. Tony had died because of it, and that was reason enough.

Leigh jumped as the doors to ICU opened, and Dr. Gordon strode through them. She hurried to meet him halfway with Sarah trailing right behind her. "How is he?"

"Doing well, and the surgery went perfectly. Your son should have no residual effects from his injuries other than a cast for a couple of months." He patted her shoulder. "We brought him straight to ICU rather than take him to recovery. Give us a few minutes, and you can go to his room."

"Thank you so much, Dr. Gordon."

He disappeared back through the stainless steel doors, and she wrapped her arms around Sarah. "Did you hear him? TJ's going to be okay."

"Praise God," Sarah said softly.

"Yes, praise God." Joy bubbled from her chest. Another arm went around her shoulders as Ian joined them. She turned to him with wet eyes. "TJ's going to be okay."

"I heard."

"Thank you so much for coming. It means so much to me."

The skin around his blue eyes crinkled as he smiled. "I had to make sure you were okay." He nodded at the other two men. "After I drop Danny and Geoffrey at the plant, can I bring you something to eat?"

She hadn't even thought of food and glanced at the clock on the wall. It couldn't be eight-thirty. "The grill is still open. Sarah can go down and get us something before it closes."

"Are you sure?"

"Yes, and thank you for coming."

The men stood, and Leigh walked with them to the hallway. Ian turned to her. "Will you call me if you need anything?"

"Yes."

He kissed her lightly on the cheek, and tears stung her eyes once again. She turned as the nurse called her name.

"Go," he said.

■ ■ ■

Leigh and Sarah paused just outside TJ's room. Sarah squeezed her hand, and then together they entered the room. TJ's leg was splinted and elevated, but at least he had a little color in his cheeks. She glanced at the overhead monitor, relieved that his blood pressure was normal for a nine-year-old boy. Heart rate was still a little fast, but that was to be expected. *Ben.* If only he were standing here with her.

Leigh smiled as Sarah brushed TJ's hair back. She'd been with them since the very beginning, and there was no way Leigh could be angry because Ben had overheard her words. Words spoken in truth and love. And now she had to tell her son the truth. Leigh just hoped TJ would be more forgiving than Ben.

■ ■ ■

"Ben, you're white as a sheet," his mother said as she set a glass on the kitchen counter. "Sarah called me. Is TJ all right?"

"He's in surgery."

"Did you know TJ was my son?" His voice broke. His son. And he hadn't even known. But his mother had. It showed on her face. "Why didn't you tell me?"

"Leigh told you?"

"No. I had to overhear it. When did you know? Does Dad know?"

"You mean, did she tell me? No. I've suspected for a few weeks now, but I didn't know for sure. And your dad? I don't know. It's hard to tell what he knows."

"I asked Leigh why she didn't tell me. She said to ask Dad. Why would she say that?"

"Ben!" His father's voice came from the den, and his mother hurried past him. A minute later she wheeled him into the kitchen.

"Rrhay mrie goah."

Garbled words, words Ben couldn't understand, and his father pounded his wheelchair.

"S-s-sor-ree."

That he understood. He turned to his mother. "Why is he sorry?"

She wiped her hands with a towel. "Sit down. It's a long story."

"You know?"

"Just sit down."

He pulled a chair out from the kitchen table and straddled it. His father rolled to the end of the table. Outside the window, darkness closed out the day. Ben crossed his arms over the back of the chair and waited.

"First," his mother began, "I didn't know about this when it happened—it was only later I found out, and your father made me promise not to tell you. By then, so many years had passed, and I didn't think it would help, so I honored my promise."

Ben started to say something, but his mother cut him off.

"This isn't easy, so bear with me." She glanced at Tom, and when he nodded, she continued. "When your father discovered you were getting serious about Leigh, he wasn't happy. He—"

"I don't understand. What did he have against her?"

"She and her brother both had questionable reputations. Neither ran with the best people. It hadn't been that long since your dad brought her in with the strippers at the local—"

"She was a hostess, that was all."

"I know that, but there was Tony. He was involved with drugs."

"Tony? I don't remember—"

"Think back, Ben. That summer when you and Leigh were dating, Tony was sitting in a cell at the jail for possession of marijuana."

A vague recollection of Tony in jail floated through his memory. But what did that have to do with his relationship with Leigh?

"I don't see what Leigh's past has to do with this."

"It has everything. You know your father always had aspirations of you following in his footsteps, being elected sheriff. He wanted you to marry someone who would help you attain that dream."

Ben rubbed his forehead. This was all about him becoming sheriff? Suddenly the memory of Tony became stronger. He'd heard that the drugs had been planted on Tony and questioned his dad about dropping the charges against Leigh's brother, and when Tony was released, he'd thought that was the reason why. He stared at his dad. "He offered Leigh a deal," he said softly.

His mother nodded. "Quit seeing you, and Tony would be released and Tom would get a judge to expunge his previous records."

Leigh loved her brother, and it'd been an offer she couldn't refuse. But why hadn't she told him after she discovered she was pregnant?

Because he was engaged when she returned for her grandmother's funeral. A funeral he hadn't bothered to attend. Leigh had thought he'd moved on.

"Your father realized he made a mistake when he saw how miserable you were that fall, but then Leigh married so quickly, he convinced himself he'd done the right thing. It wasn't until she returned to Logan Point that we both realized what a terrible mistake he'd made."

Ben stood. He had to go to Leigh. They had to talk this out.

As he passed the wheelchair, his dad grabbed his arm with his left hand. "Rerrreo."

Ben flinched. He swallowed his anger and knelt beside the wheelchair. Tom slid his hand to Ben's holstered gun. What was it about the gun that agitated his father so?

His dad worked his mouth, producing babble. Ben looked around the kitchen. "Where's the iPad?"

"In the den." His mom hurried to get it.

She handed it to him, and he powered it on. Once again Ben knelt beside the wheelchair. "Can you show me?"

Tom pressed his lips together and lifted his left hand. With a shaky finger, he touched the alphabet app then very slowly touched letters. *M-a-x-w*—

"Maxwell?" Ben asked and received a short nod. His dad's finger touched the *g*. "Guns?"

Again a short nod.

"They make guns."

"Naa! E-ma . . . ma." Tom's face twisted. His breath came short. He focused on the iPad. *M-e-x*—

Ben's cell rang one short note. He took his eyes off the iPad long enough to see who'd called. Wade? He stood. "I need to take care of this. Keep working with Dad."

Stepping away from the table, Ben speed-dialed his chief deputy. It went to voice mail. Odd. Too odd. He activated the microphone on Wade's phone and heard Wade speaking.

"But I might need my phone."

"No cell phones tonight. Not if you're going with me." Ben was certain that was Lester Cummings's voice.

"I'm going. Can I drop my truck off at the jail?"

"Ain't nobody gonna bother that piece of junk. If you're going, let's go."

A door slammed, and then silence. Ben's heart dropped into his stomach. He'd known this sting would go bad. He should've stopped it before it went this far. He punched in the FBI agent's number. Eric answered on the first ring.

"The dogfight is tonight." Ben flexed his hand into a fist and released it. "And Wade is with Cummings without his cell."

"How about the GPS? See if he's moving?"

Ben pulled up his screen and clicked on the GPS app. After what seemed like hours, it started beeping. *It's moving!* "Yes, it's on."

"Yeah, I see it on my end. Luke is here with me and everyone else is sitting on ready, so I'll send out the word to move. Let me know if you recognize the location they're headed to, and we'll close in. When we get close enough, the pen should let us listen to the conversation around him."

"If he has the pen."

24

Armero eased the forklift under the second crate of rifles. Adrenaline pumped through his body. Carefully turning the forklift, he lumbered toward the truck heading to Mexico tonight. Once he slid the crate into the truck, he slapped a Blue Dog sticker on the end.

Done.

Now for the other task at hand. He walked to his office, his mind whirling with solutions to the problem that had cropped up at the hospital. He checked his phone. One solution hadn't returned his call.

Leigh Somerall had Tony's flash drive. The one she'd dropped looked just like the one in the company surveillance video. He ought to know. He'd stared at it in the video enough. Small, squarish, and blue.

He needed one more incentive for Leigh to give him the drive. And Gresham was it. He redialed Gresham's number. One, two, three rings . . .

"Hello!" Gresham's gravelly voice echoed in his ear.

Dogs barked in the background. "Why didn't you answer earlier?" Armero slipped a small recorder from his pocket and put the phone on speaker. He needed to record only one part of the conversation—if he could get Gresham to say what he wanted.

"I'm busy," Gresham snapped. "What do you want?"

"I need your help tonight."

"Sorry, I'm busy taking care of me a chief deputy."

"What are you talking about?"

"Wade Hatcher thinks I'm a fool. Like I don't know he's trying to infiltrate my inner circle so he can arrest me."

"Leave the deputy alone. You're going to get us both caught with your stupid schemes." Armero hovered his finger over the record button. "How did you get near enough to the doctor's car to blow it up, anyway?" He pressed record and waited.

Gresham was quiet, then he laughed. "Nobody pays any attention to those cars behind the clinic. Just slid underneath the one nearest the road and worked my way to her Avenger. And didn't take ten minutes to hook the bomb up."

Armero paused the recording. "You must've used plastic explosive, as big as the explosion was." He hit record again.

"Nah. I would've had to buy that, and too easy to trace back to me. The box of dynamite I have can't be traced to me since I never bought it, and this time I used a real blasting cap."

Perfect. And Gresham's voice held exactly the right tone of pride he'd hoped for.

"Just didn't figure on a remote start button. Otherwise the doc and boy would be history. I won't miss the next time."

Even better. He paused the recorder. "Blowing up her car and hurting her son was the stupidest thing you've done so far. Do you know how much attention that's going to bring to Logan Point? Don't do anything else stupid, you got it?"

Dead silence answered him. Gresham had hung up. But he'd gotten what he needed. Something the doctor would trade that flash drive for.

■ ■ ■

"It was nice of Ian to stop by," Sarah said.

"Yes, he's thoughtful that way." Leigh assessed TJ's vitals as the heart monitor beat a steady rhythm. Everything looked good. The 99.1 temperature concerned her only slightly. Close enough to normal, but bore watching. Which she was certain Dr. Gordon would do. She adjusted TJ's pillow, and his eyes fluttered open. "Hey there," she whispered.

"My leg hurts." His eyes closed then fluttered open. "I'm thirsty."

"How about ice chips?"

"Hmm," he murmured.

"I'll get them," Sarah said as she rose. Using a plastic spoon, she scooped up a few chips and put them against TJ's lips. With his eyes closed, he ran his tongue over his lips before dozing off.

"He'll probably sleep most of the night," Leigh said as she sank into one of the two chairs in the room. At least if he was sleeping, he wasn't hurting. That would come tomorrow. Her jaw tightened. If she could get her hands on the man who did this to her son . . . well, she might not kill him, but she wanted justice.

"Why don't you try and get some shut-eye? If he wakes up, I'll take care of anything he needs," Sarah said.

"I have something I need to do." Leigh slipped her phone from her pocket. She wasn't thinking straight. She should have called Ben again.

Her cell phone rang, and caller ID registered "unknown caller." Probably the caller from Saturday night. She stood and walked outside TJ's room before she stabbed the answer button. "I don't know who you are," she said, keeping her voice low. "But I will see to it you pay for what you've done."

"Whoa . . ." Again the voice sounded like something out of a horror movie. "I didn't have anything to do with that bomb. But I'll trade you his identity for Tony's flash drive."

She frowned as she concentrated on the caller's slurred voice. "You want the flash drive?"

"Yes."

Her stomach clenched, and heat flamed her cheeks. "You'll never get it. I'm giving it to the sheriff. You will rot in jail." She jerked her hand over her mouth. She just admitted she had the USB drive.

"Then you don't value your son's life. Your sheriff hasn't protected you yet. Your house burned down, your car blew up."

"What proof can you give me that you have this information?"

"I have it recorded. Listen."

Suddenly a cackle came through the line then a clear voice. *"Dynamite, with a real blasting cap this time. Just didn't figure on a remote start button. Or the doc and boy would be history. I won't miss the next time."*

Ice water pumped through her veins. She didn't recognize the voice, but Ben might. "How do I know you'll give it to me? Or that you won't kill me?"

"Because I keep my word."

Hearing the person on the other line talk about honor in that horrible voice scared her almost as much as anything.

"And I don't hurt women and children."

"Let's say I agree. How would we make the exchange?"

"At Friar's Point on the lake. There's a box where campers leave the keys to the cabins. Put it in there. Once I see you do that, I'll call you and tell you where the recorder is."

"No. I get it first."

Silence.

"This is what we're going to do," Leigh said. "You put the recorder in the box. I'll listen to it to make sure it has the evidence on it. Then, and only then, will I drop the flash drive into the box."

"Be at Friar's Point in thirty minutes. And I'll be watching you . . . the hospital parking lot, the lights behind you . . . you won't know where I am. Don't bring anyone else into this."

She glanced over her shoulder. Could he be here? "Thirty minutes? Did you forget my car was blown up? I have to find transportation."

"Then you better get on it. And, Dr. Somerall, if you copy the information on that flash drive, my aversion to harming women and children will change. There will be no place you can hide. That's a promise."

Leigh shivered as his eerie words hit their mark. Whoever this person was, he would do exactly what he promised. She licked her dry lips. She had to have a car. Sarah. Somehow she had to convince her friend to hand over the keys to her car without asking any questions.

Don't do this alone. Call Ben.

The voice spoke softly in her head. She flexed her fingers on her left hand and stared at her phone. She scrolled to her contacts, and her finger hovered over his number. With a quick breath, she punched it and waited.

It went straight to voice mail.

What did she expect? She quickly dialed Wade's number, but it went to voice mail as well. It was up to her. She summoned a reassuring smile and stepped back into TJ's room. "Can I borrow your car to run an errand?" she asked Sarah.

"What?" Sarah's jaw dropped open. "You're going to leave TJ?"

"I won't be gone long. An hour max."

"The only way you get my keys is to tell me what's going on."

Leigh rubbed her forehead. "Please, Sarah. It's a matter of life and death that I run this errand."

"Then you better start explaining."

Her heart pounded, and she swallowed down the bile that rose in her throat. She took a deep breath to steady herself. "I had another call from—I don't know who it is, but he said he had evidence on who bombed the car. I heard the man's voice myself. He'll give me the recording if I give him Tony's files. The flash drive was in Tony's mail, and I'm taking it to Friar's Point to trade. Satisfied? Now give me your keys. Please."

Reluctantly, Sarah fished her keys from her purse and handed them to Leigh. "I don't like this. I don't like it one bit."

"Neither do I, but I don't see that I have much choice. He threatened to kill TJ if I didn't."

"Call Ben first."

"I did, but it went to his voice mail. Wade's too." She remembered the letter with Ben's name on it and fished it out of her pocket. "Give this to Ben if he comes by here." She hugged her friend and grabbed her purse. "Hopefully, I'll be back in an hour and a half. If I'm not, you call Ben. Maybe he'll take your call. And Sarah, if anything happens to me . . ." She squared her shoulders. "If I don't come back, help Ben raise TJ."

In the car, she tried Ben's number once more, but he still didn't answer. She slipped the flash drive from her pocket. Her netbook was in her purse. She could download the contents of the flash drive and email it to Ben. *But he said he would be watching and he'd kill TJ.* Ben had not protected them so far. It was just as well she couldn't reach him because he certainly would not allow her to do what she was about to do.

Maybe she could download the drive as she drove. She jerked the netbook from her purse that TJ had been using all day as she scanned the parking lot. Even if he was here, it was too dark for him to see what she was doing. As long as she kept moving. She eased the car from the parking space as the computer booted up. *Yes!* She was still in range of the hospital Wi-Fi. With one hand, she inserted the drive in the netbook, but just as the download started, the screen went dark. No! Her heart crashed to her stomach. The battery was dead.

25

B en turned onto County Road 213 and called the FBI agent back. "It looks like Wade is at the old Edwards farm. I'm traveling east on County Road 213 headed that way. Five of my deputies are on the way."

"Gotcha, Ben. I've located the logging road on Google Maps and we should be there in minutes. Tennessee is putting up roadblocks and checkpoints on their side of the land," said Eric.

Ten minutes later, Ben turned onto the logging road. Eric's dark SUV was parked on the side of the road, and the FBI agent leaned against it with a map spread across the hood, talking to Luke Donovan, the U.S. Marshal.

Ben pulled on a tactical vest and hooked his radio to his belt as he stepped out of the truck and shook hands with the two men. The area was crawling with all kinds of law enforcement personnel—sheriffs, game wardens, Ben even recognized a Mississippi Department of Transportation agent. Everyone really was sitting on ready.

"Been trying to connect to the receiver in that pen," Ben said, "but so far all I get is static."

"Same here," Eric said. "Let's don't waste any time."

Headlights flashed as four additional cars pulled into the field. "I'll ride with you, but first let me instruct my deputies."

Quickly, Ben stationed two of his men at the entrance, and instructed Andre and the others to follow the FBI agent's SUV.

Once under way, they rode in silence, listening for any change in the static. Ben winced as the vehicle hit a rut. Suddenly Wade's voice came over Ben's phone.

"I just want to buy a dog."

Wade was cornered. Ben heard it in his voice.

"You're lying."

Jonas Gresham's voice. The dull thud of fist hitting flesh made Ben's skin crawl. "Hurry," he said as he patched in to his dispatcher. "Send an ambulance to the logging road on the Edwards farm. A couple of deputies will be stationed there."

"I'm not lying."

"You think you're so smart. Let's see if this pipe loosens your tongue—"

"Hit the siren," Ben yelled. "He's going to kill him."

Eric activated the siren and floored the gas pedal, sending the SUV bouncing over the rough road. They rounded a curve, and their headlights flashed on Gresham standing in a small clearing with a pipe against Wade's throat. The five or six men gathered around Wade and Gresham scattered into the nearby bushes.

With his gun in his hand, Ben jumped out of the SUV with the two agents. His deputies spilled out of their cruisers and took off after the men.

"Let him go, Gresham," Ben ordered. "Kill him and you're facing the death penalty."

Gresham blinked against the bright lights. "We're just havin' a little fun, Sheriff. Ain't we, Wade?"

Suddenly Gresham shoved Wade forward and pulled a gun from his waistband as he dove for the bushes.

Gresham's first bullet hit the ground in front of Ben, the second a little closer. Ben fired and hit the dirt, rolling behind the SUV as the other two men took cover.

"I think you hit him," Luke said.

Cautiously Ben peered around the car. "Gresham, give it up," he yelled.

"You'll . . ." He coughed. "Have to come get me."

"Throw your gun out."

"Think I'll hang on to it a while." Gresham coughed again.

"Sounds like he's been hit," said Luke.

"You need medical attention." Gresham couldn't die—it'd be too easy an out for him. Ben wanted to see him serve time for what he'd done.

"Figure it's too late for that. Got a question, Sheriff. You checked on that pretty little doctor lately?"

Ben froze. Was he threatening Leigh? He wouldn't play Gresham's game. "You're able to talk, so it's not too late. Just throw your gun out and then come out with your hands high." Gresham didn't answer. "Jonas, if you hurt Leigh, you'll wish you'd died."

"Ain't me after her now. What's in it for me if I talk?"

Nothing would drag Leigh away from the hospital and TJ. Ben wasn't negotiating. "You have two choices, Jonas. Lay there and bleed to death or give yourself up."

Minutes later, a black object sailed out of the bushes, hitting the ground ten yards from Ben. "Don't shoot. I'm coming out."

Ben kept his finger on the trigger as the older man staggered out of the bushes, holding his stomach. He took a few steps and crumpled to the ground. *No!* Ben raced to where he fell and knelt beside him. "Why did you blow up her car?"

"So you'd know what it's like when somebody you love dies," Gresham whispered.

"I never meant for your boys to die. Tommy Ray's death was an accident."

"It hurt all the same."

"Why Tony? I never really knew him. Why did you kill him?" Where was that ambulance?

"Didn't kill Tony." Gresham coughed. "Too bad about the doc . . ."

"You are not dying, old man. Tell me who's after Leigh!"

"Don't know what you're talk . . ." He closed his eyes.

Ben lowered him to the ground and felt for his pulse. Thready, but there. Then he turned to check on Wade. Eric and Luke were helping the chief deputy to his feet. "Are you all right?"

"Yeah. Guess you figured out there wasn't a dogfight tonight."

"Something like that. If I'd had to tell your mother . . ." Ben let the sentence dangle as he looked around. His deputies had returned with four of the men in custody. He wasn't needed here any longer. "Do you know why Gresham mentioned Leigh?"

Wade shook his head.

He took out his cell phone. No reception.

"Go check on her, Ben," Wade said. "I can take care of this."

"Don't let Gresham die," Ben said.

Wade waved him on. "Don't worry. He's too ornery to die."

"I'll take you back to your truck," Eric said.

There was one bar of reception when Ben reached his truck, and he dialed Leigh's number again. She didn't answer; she was probably with TJ. His son. He still couldn't believe it.

"Do you want me to come with you?" Eric asked.

"No. I'm just going to the hospital, but thanks."

As he pulled out of the logging road, he called Sarah's number. Maybe she could tell him where Leigh was.

"Oh, Ben, thank goodness!" Sarah said when she answered.

"What's wrong?"

"She's gone to someplace called Friar's Point to deliver Tony's flash drive. Whoever wants it said they'd kill TJ if she didn't give it to him."

"How long has she been gone?" His phone buzzed, and he glanced at the ID. His mother.

"Maybe ten minutes."

"Do you know exactly where at Friar's Point?"

312

"No," she wailed.

"Okay, I'm heading out to the landing now."

Ben switched over to his mother's call. "What is it, Mom?"

"Your dad is beside himself. He keeps trying to tell me something about guns and Mexico and some email. He keeps typing Max so I'm assuming he's talking about Maxwell Industries."

Pieces clicked together. The email in the papers that had been on his dad's desk the day he was shot. He wished he'd looked at the photo better.

"Mom, ask Dad if the gun in the email he received was a Maxwell AR-15." He waited for the answer.

"Yessss!" His dad's voice rang loud and clear over the phone.

The Maxwell AR-15-type rifle. Mexico. Tony. What if someone was stealing rifles and shipping them to Mexico? And Tony discovered it and downloaded the information on a flash drive? And now Leigh was meeting that someone to hand over the information. "Mom, I'll call you back."

Ben called Andre on his radio. "Where are you?"

"Still at the crime scene," his deputy replied.

"I need backup at Friar's Point, but come in without sirens or lights. Leigh may be in danger. Is the U.S. Marshal still with you?"

"Eric and I both are still here," Luke said over the radio.

"Good. I have a wild hunch." Ben explained his theory. "Can you find out if Maxwell Industries has any outgoing trucks tonight? And if there is, can you stop the truck without a search warrant?"

"I can't, but your MDOT agent here can."

Ben should have thought about the Mississippi Department of Transportation agent that had joined the raid. "Get him on it. I'm almost to Friar's Point, and I'm going in on foot."

"You need to wait on backup—"

Ben cut the radio off.

26

With the quarter moon providing faint light, Armero cut the power to the blue and white MasterCraft and drifted to the end of the dock, noting two jet skis moored to the bank. He hadn't counted on company. Laughter floated from somewhere to his right. Teenagers, from the sound of it. He hoped they stayed put, at least until he finished his business.

Armero loosely tied the boat to the dock in case he had to make a quick getaway then grabbed a nylon cord and stuck it in his pocket. One never knew. He scanned the parking lot, not that he expected Leigh here yet. He'd made the call to her from the lake house, and the trip across the lake hadn't taken twenty minutes.

He climbed the hill to the vacant office and found the key drop box. Someone had jimmied the lock long ago. *What if she doesn't show?* She would. She was scared for her kid.

He took the recorder from his pocket, and a shriek almost jarred it from his hands. Sweat popped out on his face. The teenagers. He heaved a breath and steadied his heart before placing the recorder in the box. Now to wait.

Fifteen minutes later, he thought he saw lights, then nothing. Maybe she missed the turn. He took out the synthesizer and disposable cell phone and dialed her number.

"What do you want?" she asked.

"Where are you?"

"I'm lost."

She sounded near tears. Good.

"I just passed County Road 920."

She was five minutes away. "Turn around and come back a couple of miles. You'll see an old sign, an arrow pointing left. The drop box is in front of the office." He paused then whispered, "I'll be waiting."

■ ■ ■

Friar's Point. Ben navigated the s-curves on the back roads to the old campground and boat ramp. The place had been popular at one time, but that was before budget cuts killed renovation of the cabins and boat ramp. Now it was used mostly by fishermen or teenagers looking for a place to drink and smoke pot.

His headlights caught a weathered sign pointing right. Friar's Point. He killed his lights as he eased the truck into the road. At the first side road, he parked, estimating he was about half a mile from the boat dock.

He unsnapped his holster as he stepped out of the truck and silently eased the door shut. A quarter moon hung in the sky, giving off just enough light for Ben to see where he was going. Too bad he didn't have the full moon from a couple of weeks ago.

From deep within the woods, a shriek sent him reaching for his gun until he realized it was probably teenagers. Looked like he needed to send his deputies by here a little more often. Headlights swung onto the road, and he slipped into the trees. Sarah's white Honda with Leigh driving sped by the spot where he hid.

■ ■ ■

Just like Armero expected, five minutes after the doc's call, headlights appeared on the road. He barely breathed as the car pulled up next to the office. From his vantage point beside the toolshed, he had a clear line of vision to the box ten yards away. He willed her to move faster, but she took her time as she stepped out of the car and surveyed the area.

She couldn't see him behind the shrub, but that didn't keep him from ducking. Abruptly, she stood straighter and marched to the box. He held his breath as she removed the recorder and played the message and Gresham's disembodied voice broke the silence.

Dynamite, with a real blasting cap this time. Just didn't figure on a remote start button. Or the doc and boy would be history. I won't miss the next time.

His nightmare was almost over. Once he had the drive, he would have nothing to worry about.

Suddenly she wheeled and ran to her car.

■ ■ ■

After Leigh passed, Ben stepped back on the road and jogged after the car. If he could only catch her before she did something stupid. Her lights disappeared around a curve, and he stopped and bent over, bracing his hands against his knees as he panted in the humid night air. He shed the tactical vest and wished he'd parked closer. Leigh was probably already parked and getting out. He rounded the curve. *Almost there.* Leigh was running to her car.

"No!"

The cry rent the night like the howl of a wounded animal. Ben fell into an all-out run.

"Let me go!"

Leigh stood with her back to him talking to a man in the shadows. He crept to the back of her car as the man stepped toward her.

Geoffrey Franks.

He held a gun on Leigh.

"You just had to mess it up," Franks snarled. "You couldn't do what I said. Give me the flash drive."

Ben willed Leigh to give up the flash drive. If he could just get to her.

316

"You killed my brother. You're going to jail."

"No, you're giving me the drive or I'll kill you and your son."

"You want it so bad. There." Leigh tossed something as Ben sprang toward her.

A gunshot rang out.

27

Leigh stared at Ben's still body. His head was so bloody. Her heart thudded against her ribs as time slowed. He'd taken the bullet meant for her. This couldn't be happening. If she'd just given Franks the drive. But thinking Tony's murderer would get away blinded her to reason, and now the man she loved . . . She couldn't say the words. "Why did you shoot him?"

"Shut up."

Pain shot up her leadened arm as Franks grabbed it and twisted it behind her back. "Now reach the other one back."

She couldn't, her body wouldn't respond, and he twisted her arm until she forced it to move. When he had her secure, he nudged Ben with his foot. Her heart sank when he didn't move. He'd died trying to protect her. She squeezed her eyes together to keep tears from escaping. And now Franks was going to kill her.

She had to get away.

Franks dragged her to where she'd thrown the flash drive.

She taunted him. "You'll never find it."

"I said shut up." He swept his hand over the ground.

She heard a commotion, and then someone yelled from the woods. "Who's shooting over there?"

Hope soared.

Franks stood and cupped his hand to his mouth. "Just shooting some snakes."

318

"They'll come to see," she said.

With the gun on her, he bent down once more, fumbling on the ground. "I got it." He stood and jerked her toward the pier. "Move."

"No. You'll have to kill me here."

"No problem."

"Those kids will hear you, and they'll be here before you can get—"

Pain rocked her head as he brought the gun down on her skull.

■ ■ ■

Leigh's voice penetrated the fog in Ben's head. Franks was going to kill her. He cracked his eyelids just as Leigh slumped against Franks. Ben tried to move, but nothing cooperated. Powerless, he could do nothing as Franks hoisted Leigh on his shoulder and carried her toward the dock. For the first time, he saw the boat.

Ben couldn't let Franks take her on the lake. He staggered to his feet and stumbled back to his knees. Blood streamed into his eyes. He touched his head, his fingers finding a gash. Franks . . . the gunshot. The bullet must have grazed him. He wiped the blood from his eyes.

Get up!

His gun. He needed his gun, and he felt for it, finding only sticks and rocks. The motorboat roared to life, freezing his heart. He stumbled toward the dock. "No!"

Franks raised his gun, firing.

Bullets dug into the wooden pier, and then the boat shot forward.

He searched frantically for a way to stop Franks. His gaze landed on two jet skis moored near the ramp, and he sprinted toward them. Icy shivers chased down his spine.

Water. Deep water.

Ben pushed the thought away. He had to save Leigh.

He leaped on the nearest jet ski and stared at the controls. He'd never driven one, but it couldn't be harder than a motorcycle, and he had driven those. He felt for the ignition and pressed the button.

319

The motor rumbled and caught. He looped the plastic coil that hung from the kill switch around his hand. He'd seen enough safety films to know if he went in the water he didn't want the boat to run over him. He pressed the throttle, and the jet ski almost shot out from under him.

Four teens raced toward him on the pier. "Hey! Where are you going with my jet ski?"

"Sheriff!" he yelled over his shoulder. "Don't follow me!"

Dizziness threatened to send him over the side of the jet ski, but he held on. Ignoring the pain that shot through his brain, he pressed the throttle again, and the nose of the jet ski shot out of the water as it raced forward. As he roared across the lake, wind whipped his face. Franks's boat had a good lead on him, but the jet ski responded to more pressure on the throttle, bouncing against the boat's wake. Ben steered to the right of the wake and gained on the boat.

Suddenly the boat seemed to stall. Ben drew closer, close enough to see Franks's silhouette on the back of the boat as he stood with Leigh in his arms.

Leigh's scream stopped his heart as Franks threw her overboard then jumped back in the seat and roared off.

Ben killed the motor, and the jet ski coasted to the circle of waves where Leigh had disappeared. He looked up at the roar of another jet ski. The teenage boys had followed him.

He tried to swallow but couldn't get past the ball of fear in his throat. His breath came short, shallow.

Tommy Ray's face reflected off the moonlight in the water.

An image flashed in his mind. Leigh just before she went into the water with her hands tied. She couldn't save herself.

■ ■ ■

The water wrapped around Leigh, cold and dark as death. She held her breath, struggling against the rope, but there was no give to the nylon. She kicked, trying to slow her descent, but still she sank.

320

TJ. What will he do? Ian's plane. No! Franks will get away . . .

Her lungs hurt, demanding air. Pain rocked her head. Darkness encroached the edges of her mind. Slowly she relaxed, giving in to the water.

An arm grasped her waist, jerking her upward. Franks had come after her. She fought, kicking and bucking until she broke the surface of the water.

"Leigh! It's me, Ben. Stop fighting me."

She gasped for air. "Ben?"

He'd come into the water after her? She gulped more air as he pulled her toward some sort of boat. Strong arms lifted her from the water.

"Thanks, guys." Ben's voice sounded far away. "Get her to shore."

"Wait!" She fought the fatigue that threatened to shut her down. "He can fly . . ." She caught her breath. "Pilot. Ian's plane."

It was the best she could do.

28

Leigh shivered under the blanket one of the teens had offered her. Someone, probably one of Ben's deputies, had built a fire, but the heat didn't touch the cold inside her. Her wrists burned where she'd struggled against the cord, even though one of the paramedics had put lidocaine on them. Randy Jenkins held out her purse that she'd asked him to get from her car.

"Th-thank you," she said against her chattering teeth. With trembling fingers, she dialed Sarah and asked about TJ.

"Still sleeping. There's a deputy outside the door. What's going on? Where are you?"

A deputy. Bless Ben's heart. Leigh informed Sarah that she was all right and with Ben and would explain later. After she hung up, she looked around for Ben. She hadn't talked to him since he saved her life. He was probably hopping mad at her. She buried her head in her hands. He'd probably never forgive her, and she didn't blame him. She'd made such a mess of things. How different it could have been if she'd told the truth long ago and trusted God with the outcome.

"Hey." Ben's voice was as soft as his touch. "You okay?"

She raised her head. A bandage covered his head. His eyes glinted in the light from the fire, and she threw her arms around him. "Oh, Ben! I'm so sorry."

He wrapped her in an embrace and held her while tears rolled down her cheeks. "It's going to be okay," he murmured against her wet hair. "How is TJ?"

"Sarah said he's sleeping still." She licked her lips. "I'm so sorry I lied to you all these years. And to TJ. I—"

"Shh." He pressed his finger against her lips. "We'll talk about this later. I know what my dad did, and I need time to process everything. Then we'll decide together how to tell TJ."

She caught her breath. "What if Franks tries to get to him?"

"He won't." Ben lifted a wet strand of hair from her cheek. "I never would have thought to look in the air. Thanks to you, we're tracking him. It looks like he's headed to Mexico. He'll have to come down to refuel, and based on Ian's projection of how much fuel the plane had when Franks stole it, we have a good idea of where he'll land."

The band around her heart loosened. "Are you hurt bad?"

"I'll have a headache for a few days, but the bullet just grazed me and knocked me out for a bit. Why didn't you call me?"

"I tried." Her voice cracked. "It went to voice mail. Wade's too. I was scared he'd follow through on his threat if I didn't give him the flash drive. And I was trading it for a recording. I . . . I heard the man who blew up our car admit it." She felt in her pockets and pulled the recorder out. "It's probably ruined."

"Jonas Gresham blew up your car," Ben said. "He's on his way to the hospital. If he lives, he'll spend a long time in jail."

"You . . . caught the man?"

He nodded. "Not that he's talking. And one of the Maxwell Industries' trucks was pulled over tonight, and authorities found two cases of AR-15 rifles without serial numbers on them. And those cases? They were labeled with a Blue Dog sticker. That's what Tony was trying to tell me. Your brother is a hero. Just wished we had that flash drive, but even if we can't pin Tony's murder on him, Franks will spend a long time in jail for attempted murder."

Leigh leaned into him, and he wrapped her in his arms. She wished he'd hold her forever. But that was a wish that would probably never come true. He never said that he'd forgiven her.

Probably because he hadn't.

29

Leigh closed the door behind Ben and took a deep breath. She wasn't ready for this, and she didn't understand why he insisted on being here. It was almost like he didn't trust her to tell TJ.

"How does he feel today?" Ben asked.

"Good." It amazed her how TJ had bounced back from the bomb blast and surgery. Better than she had. Every time she thought about it, her mouth became so dry she could barely swallow. If any of them had been ten steps closer . . . the thought turned her stomach. "You don't have to be here. I'm perfectly capable of telling him by myself."

"Don't fight me on this, Leigh. It's time for TJ to know I'm his dad."

"I don't know if he's ready."

"You said he was doing better."

She closed her eyes briefly. "I'd rather not have an audience."

"I'm hardly an audience."

She turned as her son called her name. "Be right there, TJ."

"Is that Ben?" Excitement rang in his voice.

Ben looked at her. "Ready?"

"He's in the den." She led the way, dread dogging every step.

TJ looked up from the game he was playing on the iPad. "Is something wrong, Mom?"

She pasted a smile on her lips as Ben sat in the chair nearest the couch. "No, nothing is wrong, but we do need to talk. There's something I need to tell you."

"We need to tell you," Ben corrected.

She took in another breath and let it out. It was time. "You've always believed your dad died before you were born, but that's not true . . ."

■ ■ ■

Leigh zipped the suitcase closed. A lot had happened in the two weeks since she and Ben had told TJ the truth. He'd been ecstatic Ben was his dad. Which made him even more resistant to the move.

This weekend away from him would be good for them both. Ian was flying her to Baltimore to finalize the paperwork at Johns Hopkins. TJ wasn't happy about that. Neither was Ben, for that matter.

She sighed, counting her blessings. She had her life, and TJ was no longer in danger. She should be grateful for that, and she was. Just like Ben promised, Franks had been caught when he landed to refuel, and now he sat in a jail cell, awaiting trial along with Jonas Gresham, who was now claiming an insanity plea. And after Gresham's fingerprints were found on one of the rifles, he was awaiting a federal indictment along with Franks. At least they had turned on each other, and the whole story was coming out.

She paused, thinking about her brother. It was no wonder he'd had nightmares. The letter he'd sent to Ben was an apology for not coming forward after Tom Logan was shot. Seems one night he'd been playing cards with Gresham and the old man was drunk, bragging to Tony how he'd shot the sheriff. Once Tony became a Christian, he couldn't live with himself and not tell Ben. And because of the letter, Ben was checking Gresham's rifles to see if any of them fired the bullet that hit his dad.

The doorbell rang, and she went to answer it. With TJ staying at the Logans' this weekend, Sarah had returned home to Jackson for a few days. Leigh had asked her to consider moving to Baltimore with them, but so far Sarah had not given her an answer.

"Ian, you're early," she said when she opened the door.

"I thought you might want to get a head start. The plane is fueled up and ready."

She smiled at him. No matter how many times she told him there was no future for them, he ignored her, saying her friendship was enough. "Then, I'm ready."

Two days later, Leigh sat in Dr. Meriwether's office. Two days of whirlwind tours at Johns Hopkins and evenings out on the town with Ian. Both had been amazing.

She raised the pen to sign the contract. She couldn't believe it was about to happen. Johns Hopkins. Dad's dream come true.

30

ey, do you want to go fishing?" Ben asked. The twins had kept TJ company most of the day, but now it was just the two of them. They both were still exploring this new relationship. The amazing thing for Ben was that the panic attacks had almost disappeared. Occasionally anxiety would grab his heart, but one look from TJ's admiring eyes, and Ben could let it go.

TJ tore his gaze away from the retreating taillights of Emily's car to stare at him. "How about my cast?"

"No problem. I'll take lawn chairs, and we'll fish from the pier. Just you and me."

TJ tilted his head then nodded.

Ben gathered the chairs and fishing tackle and loaded everything in his truck before he lifted TJ up into the seat. The boy had lost weight since he'd broken his leg, something Ben's mom had tried to remedy this weekend.

When they pulled up to the pier, he breathed a prayer of thanks for the shade covering the end of the dock. After he had TJ settled, Ben took out a wrapped box, his heart swelling as he handed it to the boy. His first gift to his son.

"For me?" TJ's eyes lit with excitement. "Cool paper."

Ben smiled. He'd scrounged around in his mom's recycled paper until he found last week's comic pages. "It's a fishing rod just like the one my dad gave me when I was ten," he said, unable to wait.

The boy's fingers stilled on the wrapping string. "Why didn't you want me before now?"

Ben couldn't speak for fear his voice would crack. He swallowed hard. "I didn't know about you. Remember, your mom told you that."

"I know," he said. "But why didn't she tell you?"

"It's complicated, TJ."

He seemed to consider what Ben had said. TJ looked sideways at him. "Are you going to marry her?"

Ben swallowed hard. "Uh, we, uh . . . I don't know."

"Are you still mad at her?"

"No."

"Then you can marry her, and we can stay in Logan Point."

"TJ, it's not that simple. Sometimes people make mistakes that can't be undone."

The boy's shoulders sagged.

Great. Now he'd made it sound like it was all Leigh's fault. "It wasn't just your mom who made a mistake. She did the best she knew how, and sometimes we just have to forgive people and put it behind us."

TJ lifted his face, his eyes locking on Ben's. "Do you forgive her?"

Ben searched his heart. Did he? What he'd said was true. Another thought niggled in his brain. Why hadn't he gone after Leigh ten years ago? Because he was too wrapped up in himself, and if he admitted it, her rejection had made him angry. If he'd known about TJ, would he have done the right thing? Been the father the boy needed?

Shame for his hard heart pierced Ben. He'd made as many mistakes as Leigh.

"Do you . . . Dad?"

Dad. The shell encasing his heart crumbled, and he swallowed the lump that almost choked him.

"Yeah, TJ. I do." The words rasped from his lips.

"Good."

Ben ruffled TJ's hair. "I'm glad we have that settled. Now open your present so we can get to some serious fishing."

For the next half hour, Ben showed his son how to use the rod and reel. For a short time his heart was lighter, then a weight wrapped around it again. Forgiveness was a choice. But so was receiving it. What if Leigh refused his forgiveness?

Ben scanned the water beyond their little cove. The water he'd feared for so long. What if Leigh believed she didn't deserve forgiveness? Like he believed he didn't deserve it for what happened to Tommy Ray? He had to make her understand that she did deserve it. That like he'd told TJ, it wasn't all her fault. That people make mistakes, mistakes that had to be put behind them.

Isn't that what God wanted to do for him?

If Ben could forgive Leigh . . . then why was it such a stretch to believe God could forgive his mistake?

"Dad! I caught a fish. Look!"

"Hey, that's a catfish! You're a natural-born fisherman." When TJ reeled the fish in close enough, Ben scooped it up with a net. He glanced toward the lake once more. "You know, TJ, after you get that cast off, how about we do some lake fishing?"

"Really? I've never been on the lake!"

TJ's shoulders slumped. "Oh, but I won't be here. We're moving to Baltimore."

Ben had almost forgotten that. He pressed his lips together. He hadn't found his son only to lose him. Or Leigh, either. "I hear there's pretty good fishing up in that area. Maybe we can even fish on the ocean."

■ ■ ■

Leigh unlocked her door and took the suitcase from Ian. "Thanks so much for everything."

"Doing things for you is easy. Want me to come in and wait with you until TJ gets home?"

She shook her head. She'd called Ben on the drive from Ian's private airstrip to let him know she was back. "I need a little time by myself. This weekend was a big step."

"You made the right choice, Leigh."

She sighed. "I know."

He kissed her on the cheek, and she waited until he drove away before going inside. Maybe she could get unpacked before TJ got home. A car door slammed before she reached the foot of the stairs, and she set her bag down. Ben and TJ were early. She smoothed her blouse as the door opened, and he swung through on his crutches with Ben behind him.

"Mom! I caught a fish!"

She took a step forward as he hopped toward her. TJ sounded different. She knelt in front of him. Laughter was in his eyes. "Really? So you had a good time this weekend with your dad?"

"Yeah, and we're going fishing in a boat as soon as I get this cast off. Dad said he'd come to Baltimore. He said he would move there!"

She lifted her gaze. Ben's dark chocolate eyes were unreadable. Ben was willing to give up his dream of being sheriff? For them?

"Mom, why are you crying? That's a good thing."

She wiped her eyes with the back of her hands. "I know. But he'd be up there by himself."

"What?" Ben and TJ stared at her.

She looked into Ben's eyes. "I'm not taking the job at Johns Hopkins. I'm staying in Logan Point."

Ben took her hands and pulled her up. "But I thought . . . I thought it was your dream."

"So did I. But when I picked up the pen to sign the contract, I couldn't. It was my dad's dream. Logan Point is where I belong. Where TJ belongs."

She didn't have to practice at Johns Hopkins to prove her worthiness. Ben's strong arms drew her close, and she laid her head on his chest, feeling the pounding of his heart. Or was it hers?

"Eww! You two are mushy. I'm going to my room to play a video game."

She lifted her head. "Only fifteen minutes," she called after him.

Ben cupped her face, and she shivered as his fingers traced her jawline.

"Are you sure?"

"Maybe he can play the game twenty minutes." She gave him a teasing smile. "Yes, I'm sure."

He bent toward her, and she raised her face to meet his lips.

She'd never been more sure of anything in her life.

Patricia Bradley is a published short story writer and is cofounder of Aiming for Healthy Families, Inc. Her manuscript for *Shadows of the Past* was a finalist for the 2012 Genesis Award, winner of a 2012 Daphne du Maurier Award (1st place, Inspirational), and winner of a 2012 Touched by Love Award (1st place, Contemporary). When she's not writing or speaking, she can be found making beautiful clay pots and jewelry. She is a member of American Christian Fiction Writers and Romance Writers of America and makes her home in Corinth, Mississippi.

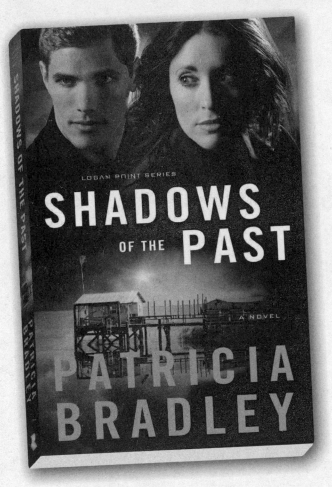